—KNIGHTS OF—
MACRAGGE

More Ultramarines from Black Library

DAMNOS
A Space Marine Battles novel featuring Cato Sicarius
Nick Kyme

VEIL OF DARKNESS
An audio drama featuring Cato Sicarius
Nick Kyme

• DARK IMPERIUM •
Guy Haley

Book 1: Dark Imperium
Book 2: Plague War

BLOOD OF IAX
A Primaris Space Marines novel
Robbie MacNiven

OF HONOUR AND IRON
A Space Marine Conquests novel
Ian St. Martin

SPEAR OF THE EMPEROR
An Emperor's Spears novel
Aaron Dembski-Bowden

BLADES OF DAMOCLES
A Space Marine Battles novel
Phil Kelly

THE PLAGUES OF ORATH
A Space Marine Battles novel
Steve Lyons, Cavan Scott & Graeme Lyon

ULTRAMARINES
A Legends of the Dark Millennium anthology
Various authors

• THE CHRONICLES OF URIEL VENTRIS •
A six-volume series of novels
Graham McNeill

Nightbringer
Warriors of Ultramar
Dead Sky, Black Sun
The Killing Ground
Courage and Honour
The Chapter's Due

—KNIGHTS OF—
MACRAGGE

NICK KYME

BLACK LIBRARY

A BLACK LIBRARY PUBLICATION

First published in 2019.
This edition published in Great Britain in 2020 by
Black Library,
Games Workshop Ltd.,
Willow Road,
Nottingham, NG7 2WS, UK.

10 9 8 7 6 5 4 3 2 1

Produced by Games Workshop in Nottingham.
Cover illustration by Mauro Belfiore.

See Black Library on the internet at

blacklibrary.com

Find out more about Games Workshop
and the world of Warhammer 40,000 at

games-workshop.com

Printed and bound by CPI Group (UK) Ltd, Croydon, CR0 4YY

For our dearly departed house rabbit, Shakespeare.
Sleep tight, little man.

It is the 41st millennium. For more than a hundred
centuries the Emperor has sat immobile on the Golden
Throne of Earth. He is the Master of Mankind by the
will of the gods, and master of a million worlds by
the might of His inexhaustible armies. He is a rotting
carcass writhing invisibly with power from the Dark Age
of Technology. He is the Carrion Lord of the Imperium
for whom a thousand souls are sacrificed every day,
so that He may never truly die.

Yet even in His deathless state, the Emperor continues
His eternal vigilance. Mighty battlefleets cross the
daemon-infested miasma of the warp, the only route
between distant stars, their way lit by the Astronomican,
the psychic manifestation of the Emperor's will. Vast
armies give battle in His name on uncounted worlds.
Greatest amongst His soldiers are the Adeptus
Astartes, the Space Marines, bioengineered super-
warriors. Their comrades in arms are legion: the Astra
Militarum and countless planetary defence forces, the
ever-vigilant Inquisition and the tech-priests of the
Adeptus Mechanicus to name only a few. But for all their
multitudes, they are barely enough to hold off the ever-
present threat from aliens, heretics, mutants – and worse.

To be a man in such times is to be one amongst untold
billions. It is to live in the cruellest and most bloody
regime imaginable. These are the tales of those times.
Forget the power of technology and science, for so much
has been forgotten, never to be re-learned. Forget the
promise of progress and understanding, for in the grim
dark future there is only war. There is no peace amongst
the stars, only an eternity of carnage and slaughter, and
the laughter of thirsting gods.

'We stand at the edge. Ahead of us lies the darkness of the void and the great undertaking we have sworn oaths to accomplish. Make no mistake. Mankind faces extinction. We have existed on the brink for ten thousand years, but know that if we do not succeed, if the Indomitus Crusade fails, then all is lost. We live in exceptional times. Though we long thought him gone, poised on the threshold between life and death, and beyond our reach, our father has returned to us. Guilliman has risen. The primarch is reborn. And he is not alone.

'Primaris Space Marines stand shoulder to shoulder with us, the first defenders of mankind. Have no concern about these warriors, for they are your brothers just as I, Cato Sicarius, am your brother. We must learn to alloy our strengths quickly, for the galaxy is benighted and only we, the Ultramarines, can lift this shadow. Have heart, cleave to your oaths. Fleet Avenger stands ready for us and the brave souls of the Imperial Navy will see us to our battlefields. Never has there been a darker moment in all of Imperial history. We are the driven spear. We are the redoubtable shield wall. Courage and honour, brothers. We are Macragge!'

– Captain Cato Sicarius, Second Company Ultramarines, on the eve of deployment, Indomitus Crusade

PROLOGUE

'They have breached the hull, they are here.'
– Final transmission of the strike cruiser *Emperor's Will*

Praxor Manorian had been amongst the first to die. When the attack came, it had come fast. Far faster than anyone on board the *Emperor's Will* had been prepared for. The strike cruiser was assailed the moment His light had died. The Geller field flickered. A momentary, infinitesimal lapse. In the wake of the half-second of its failure, neverborn creatures infiltrated the ship.

They were not alone.

Renegade warbands, prisoners of the warp, fell upon the stricken ship like carrion crows. Their vessels were not large, nor were they powerful, but they were numerous. A foetid swarm of every foul creed, spawned by Chaos.

Sicarius had rallied the defence at once. Strongpoints were established, outer decks sealed off and their silent borders reinforced. Overwatch zones threaded the ship, poised to unleash devastating enfilades the moment the enemy dared to breach their cordon.

And they dared.

First came the horned, red-skinned foot-soldiers. They ran on bent-back legs, hoof beats rattling the deck plates, their long swords trailing sparks and hellfire. A defence line met them, Praxor Manorian at their head.

He had two squads of Ultramarines, his own and that of Sergeant Tirian. A brutal fusillade started up the moment the neverborn horde was sighted. They materialised, rather than making a breach, emerging from smoke and shadow, presaged by the tang of hot metal on the tongue and the coppery scent of blood.

Manorian uttered no order. He didn't need to. His men knew what was at stake. Instead, he levelled his sword and gave an incoherent shout of defiance. This was the old enemy, the one that few had fought but that deep down all knew existed.

Daemon.

Muzzle flare lit up the dingy corridor, a light so bright it blazed like a white sun. The red-skinned daemons drove into it. They wove through the bullet storm, deflecting missiles with the flats of their blades and scurrying up the walls and across the ceiling with perverse, arachnoid grace. It confounded the shooters for a few seconds, and this was enough to gain the barricade that had been erected to impede them.

The first daemon over the auto-barrier leapt for Manorian. The sergeant was ready. He had been fashioned to be ready, a perfect exemplar of genetic science, every cell of his body manipulated to make him a better warrior. Yet, in spite of that, the thing he fought was not of reality; it came from the realm of the supernatural. And it fought with supernatural speed and prowess.

Manorian countered its first blow, acutely aware of the others barrelling over the wall, his battle-brothers engaging them. The second blow scored his shoulder guard, a deep cut that left a greasy pall behind it that stank of offal and decay. A thrust of Manorian's sword found its mark in the creature's midriff but, far from debilitate, the wound only seemed to embolden it. It laughed, or at least gave an approximation of doing so, a long forked tongue unfurling from its mouth and shivering with every mirthful paroxysm.

With a grunt of effort, Manorian pushed the creature back. He rammed it into another of its kind, impaling them both as the potent disruptor field in his blade went to work burning their unnatural flesh. The first creature bared its fangs, still defiant. Manorian filled its mouth with the barrel of his ivory-chased bolt pistol and blew off its head. The detonation tore a chunk from the shoulder of the second creature, which was still squirming, pressed against the corridor wall, and both abominations dissipated in a slurry of viscous, foul-smelling material.

Manorian staggered, a wound he hadn't realised he'd suffered oozing down his thigh. He clutched at it with the hand holding his sidearm and took a backward step. The corridor was thronged with the enemy. Seconds had lapsed, but the onslaught was total. A hatch had blown off, ringed with the telltale glow of melta-burn, and renegade soldiers were pouring in. A heap of bodies lay around the breach, a slowly accumulating barricade of wasted human flesh. They wore Militarum uniforms, but ragged, patchwork and besmirched with the sigils of traitors and defectors. How many worlds had turned during this long fight? he wondered. How many more would fall with the advent of the Great Rift?

His light had failed, that's what they were saying. The

Astronomican had ceased to exist and it had cast the galaxy into abject darkness. The Emperor was dead, that's what the warriors chanted, rejoicing as they were slain.

A salvo from Tirian's squad boomed loudly behind Manorian. The explosion tore the heart from the advancing renegades, the frag missile unerring and catastrophic in the densely packed corridor. Heavy bolters ratcheted up, the slow churn of thrice-blessed loading mechanisms rising to a tinnitus whine as the belt feeds reached optimum speed. Bodies evaporated beyond the barricade, ripped apart in a cascade of violent detonations. Manorian saw limbs ripped from torsos, and torsos blown to pieces. Nothing survived. Not even the daemons, whose vanguard had been largely obliterated or simply faded as the exertions of reality proved too much for their otherworldly bodies. It didn't really matter; they had accomplished what they'd set out to. The barricade was in tatters, its defenders reduced to two-thirds of their original strength. Whatever bulwark remained, it would not last long, for through the cloak of smoky weapons discharge and blood mist came a third wave.

'Heretic Astartes!' roared Manorian, a renewed call to arms as much as it was a warning.

Dregs of the human cult soldiery had survived, and carried on fighting with the reckless abandon of zealots. The warriors in baroque powered plate who succeeded them simply mowed through the chaff. Their heads were enclosed in red-lensed battle helms and they clutched bolt weapons of archaic provenance. They advanced down the corridor in metronomic fashion, weapons lit. No thought was given to who or what was in their path, only that it stood in their way.

Manorian fired back, a slow awareness creeping over him that the defensive salvo had lessened dramatically in its intensity.

A throat shot killed Sergeant Tirian. He had been issuing orders to what remained of his Devastator cadre, stooping to retrieve the fallen heavy bolter of Brother Arcadius. His voice across the tactical feed, which had become a tangled profusion of alerts and desperate imperatives, silenced with a wet gurgle and the snap of bone. He fell back and was lost to Manorian's sight.

'Hold the line!' Manorian bellowed. 'We are the shield bearers! We are the vanguard! We are–'

He felt the bolt shell breach his abdomen, tearing wider the wound he had taken from the red-skinned daemon. It entered him and detonated. The impact threw him off his feet, turning him sharply through ninety degrees. A sense of dislocation and outer-body paralysis stole upon him, and he was momentarily confused as he saw his own brethren and not the enemy in front of him. His world sank then, and pain crashed over him like a tide of hot knives. It threatened to drown him as he struck the deck, confounded by the fact he was now looking at his dismembered left leg. Critical damage alerts scrolled rapidly across the vision of his retinal lens, too fast to see, their finality obvious in the sudden cold sweeping through him.

He tried to reach for his sword. The bloody hilt was just too far for his spasming fingers to grasp. He'd lost his bolt pistol too.

The vox crackled in his ear, the comm-feed resolving into the desperate sounds of another battle. A voice he recognised was repeating his name.

'Scipio...' rasped Manorian, gasping between spits of blood.

'*Brother...*' Scipio sounded afraid, but that wasn't possible. Fear had been bled out of them, another facet of their miraculous genetic rebirth. '*Brother, we are coming.*'

'They're everywhere, Scipio...'

'*We are coming, Praxor.*' He sounded urgent now, and Manorian realised that the fear he heard was for him. It was grief, and a note of vengeance waiting in the wings behind it.

'They're dead, Scipio,' was all Manorian could think of to say.

'*Hold on, Praxor. We are almost to you. Sicarius has driven them back. The Master of the Watch has rallied the field.*'

'Tirian is dead,' he said, continuing as if he hadn't been interrupted. 'They were Guilliman's Hammer. They fought at Arcona City.'

'*Praxor...*'

The barricade collapsed and the handful of Ultramarines defending it were taken down with deadly efficiency.

Manorian looked up through a bloodshot eye as heavy boot steps resonated close to where he had fallen. The horned effigy of the Adeptus Astartes' darker reflection gazed down at him. It didn't speak, it showed no emotion of any kind. It merely drew its sword, a serrated thing that carried an age-old stamp of manufacture. Manorian didn't recognise it, but he could guess it was from the old Legions.

'We are all still fighting the long war...' he breathed, though he could not say whether he meant those words for Scipio or his enemy as he watched the blade fall.

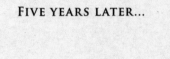

FIVE YEARS LATER...

PART ONE

LOST IN THE WARP

PART ONE

CHAPTER ONE

THE ARENA

Silence had fallen across the arena. A crowd gathered at the edges: two groups, very alike and yet also very different, each keenly eyeing their champion.

Pillium felt their eyes upon him and ignored them. He wasn't here to entertain. He was here to prove his superiority. He hefted a blunted spear – an uncommon weapon for a Space Marine, but he liked the feel and the balance of it. The charging unit in its flat, circular ferrule had been disengaged to accord with training etiquette where lethality was generally frowned upon. He had shed his power armour too. This was also unconventional, especially given the extended period of high alert conditions currently in force, but it had been quiet for weeks. Maddeningly so. Even the Emperor's angels needed an outlet. They were made for battle, and to deny them that was to deny a man oxygen or a fish water. Pillium had another reason for his lack of armour. He desired to hone his skill at arms and his martial instincts without a technological crutch. In the training cages, he considered such things an encumbrance. War, of course, was a different matter. Well-refined skill and instinct allied to the finest trappings of the Martian priesthood would render him formidable and the equal of *any* opponent. Thus was Pillium's creed. It spoke to decades, even centuries of war-making, but in fact Pillium had only served in a handful of campaigns, and had seen but a few major engagements.

'Are you sure you want to do this again, Daceus?' said Pillium, languidly rolling the spear around his shoulders, one hand to the other and then back again to tuck into the crook of his right arm.

He moved barefoot around the ten foot by ten foot cage, the light from the overhead sodium lamps describing the immaculately chiselled cut of his finely muscled body. He had no upper armour, though a light training cuirass had been offered and refused, and he wore a pair of dark blue fatigues.

His opponent, a gruff and squat-looking pugilist with a shaved head and a flattened nose, had taken the chest armour and wore soft boots. He carried a blunted gladius and a small, de-energised buckler. Cuts and bruises to Daceus' face and exposed flesh told the story of the previous bouts. The patch over his left eye, a simple thing of brown leather, covered a much older injury. The fact he also surrendered almost a foot and a half in height, and a significant amount of breadth across the shoulders and his overall frame, made it clear by any level of observation that the two Ultramarines came from differing provenance.

The two groups of supporters who had gathered to watch the contest were each relative to the size and stature of one of the fighters. Old versus young. Experience against vigour, with obsolescence in the balance.

'Just getting warmed up,' said Daceus, spitting out a red gobbet and wiping away the residue on the back of his craggy hand.

'I think you might have left more blood on the floor of this arena than you have left in your body, old man.'

'Is that right…?' said Daceus, moving into an en garde position.

'Take him!' said one of the onlookers loudly, eager for some retribution.

'In good time, Gaius,' Daceus replied, though his eyes never left his opponent. 'I'm going to wear him down.'

'Of course you are,' muttered Pillium, unconvinced.

Daceus flicked the tip of his gladius in a gesture for them to commence.

Both sides began to chant, anticipating the fight. An as yet unproven point was about to be declared and settled one way or the other.

Pillium smiled. 'Willing to oblige, sergeant…'

He didn't hesitate. A quick thrust drew a parry from Daceus' buckler, and the older warrior followed up with a savage riposte from the blunted gladius that sent fiery needles down Pillium's arm as it grazed his bicep.

A braggadocio cheer erupted from Daceus' supporters.

'Yes, brother!' bellowed Gaius, who slammed his combat shield against the bars three times to signal his appreciation. 'We roar!'

Had Pillium not reacted as fast as he did, blood would already be flowing.

He grimaced but swept low with his spear, forcing Daceus to leap back or be tripped. A second swing kept Daceus on the defensive, the blow pranging loudly against the combined defence of blade and buckler.

'Do not get complacent.' This from Secutius, on Pillium's side of the cage.

More cheering broke out, this time from both sides.

Pillium leaned in until his weapons locked with his opponent's, both hands on the haft of the spear, and braced. He pushed, feeling Daceus yield to his superior strength. Daceus was a fighter, one of the veterans who called themselves 'Lions' and believed strength and determination could carry any fight if meted out in the proper quantity. But he was wily, too. He dropped his left shoulder, intending to use Pillium's own momentum against him and overbalance him. Pillium read the move and instead lunged with one knee, bringing the spear from horizontal to vertical, sweeping the ferrule up to connect hard with Daceus' chin.

Stunned silence fell.

Momentarily dazed, Daceus staggered, blood gushing from a bit lip. He swept his gladius diagonally, left to right, a warding cut to buy time, but Pillium saw that too. He stepped around Daceus and struck so swiftly that the sergeant barely registered he had been disarmed and that the ringing in his ears was the chime of his gladius hitting the arena floor.

A rapid blow to the solar plexus finished it, driving the air from Daceus' lungs and putting him on his back.

Gaius swore loudly, prompting a bellow of vicarious triumph from the other side of the cage.

Pillium revelled in this petty glory, despite what his better self told him about not wanting a spectacle, and made sure he met the other warrior's gaze. There was anger there in Gaius' eyes, hidden behind fraternal discipline but as hot as any forge. He raged – they all did, those of the old kind, when faced with the new. Pillium knew what he represented. It was extinction.

He caught Secutius' gaze, who slowly nodded before turn-ing his back on it all.

Pillium ignored him and remained in stance for a few seconds, looking down on his opponent with the neutral satisfaction of a predicted victory.

Staying down, Daceus explored the crack in his breastplate with his fingers.

'That might leave a scar,' he murmured.

'Another for the tapestry,' Pillium replied.

'They taught you poetry as well, did they?'

'And weapon mastery, hand-to-hand tactics, unarmed combat. We are experts at war.'

'But not humility,' said Daceus, groaning a little as he began to rise.

Pillium frowned, letting the spear drop into a one-handed grip and reaching down to help Daceus with the other. 'I'm not sure I understand, sergeant.'

Daceus had regained his feet and was about to reply when a high-pitched whine shredded across the ship's vox.

CHAPTER TWO

ᚢ

WE ARE MACRAGGE

The alarms were sounding again. From prow to stern, deck to deck, men and women scrambled into sudden and urgent activity, driven by duty and an all-too-human instinct to survive.

To live. To go on. That was it. All they had left. Previously held illusions of glory or honour or even retribution had long since given way to the overwhelming likelihood of extinction.

An atonal whine went through the *Emperor's Will* like a rusty bandsaw. It drew Arna Reda's face into a sharp grimace that pulled at her scars and set her perfect teeth on edge.

'Get your gear...' she growled, her skin alternating from tan to red to tan as the warning lumens flashed across her face. 'Up, up!'

The ship's armsmen rose with bone-tired urgency from their bunks. Sleep routine had been scheduled for forty-five minutes. They had taken barely ten. Momentum grew as the inertia of fatigue faded, ready hands grabbing the stocks of autostubbers and lascarbines. The lights were off, barring the red strobes. The ring of booted feet thundered through the corridor adjacent to the barrack room.

'Armour on, flakweave and carapace. Heavy assault conditions. Move!' shouted Reda, her own armour strapped and locked. Reports came thick through her personal vox, describing encounters with the enemy across different parts of the ship. Frantically, the *Emperor's Will* strove to respond, its defenders coalescing the way white blood cells gather to fight an infection of the body. This ship was their body; lose it to that infection and they were all dead or worse.

Men and women filed out into the corridor clad in begrimed grey fatigues and scarred blue carapace. Reda followed them into the darkness, their numbers adding to the cacophony.

'Who are we?' she bellowed, her voice barely audible over the clamour.

But her charges all replied as one.

'We are Macragge!'

'Who are we?' she asked again, ratcheting a grenade into the underslung launcher attached to her shotgun.

'We are Macragge!'

'Damn right we are,' said Reda, ducking under an overhead branch of piping, and clapped the armsman in front of her hard on the shoulders to make him pick up the pace. 'Now, let's kick these bastards off our ship.'

She clamped on her helmet, hooking up the chin strap one-handed.

It had happened fast. Nothing, weeks of empty patrols and raw-nerved uneventfulness and then suddenly peril. Ships had materialised. With so few interceptors left and a dearth of still-functional anti-aircraft guns, the enemy boarders had been virtually unimpeded. But even without some of her guns, as weary as she was, the *Emperor's Will* still had teeth.

Inside the ship everything was red-flushed darkness as gaudy as a neon abattoir. As the walls of the minor transit-way pressed in, the air swilled with the stink of sweat and unwashed bodies. No time to think, no time to fear. Just fight. This was Ultramar. They were born to this, and she would not be found wanting in *their* eyes.

Through the press and the ruddy gloom, a small fissure of brighter light persisted ahead. The corridor's edge. From there, the ship opened out into one of its main arterials, a larger hall. An honour hall. Reda carried on into the ruck, closer and closer to the light. Like a dawning sun it began to fill her claustrophobic world, migraine bright and hot as a forge.

The hall was burning.

'That isn't the lumens,' she murmured as the armsmen flooded out in search of cover.

It was fire.

'Into position!' Fallad was shouting orders, as cerulean las-fire spat either side of his gesturing form. 'By squad, by squ–'

He stopped short when his throat was shot out. Blood exploded in slow motion, painting his armour plate and spinning Fallad so he fell face down in front of the advancing troopers. Others died too. Head shots, through gaps in their armour, some caught in the throat like their sergeant.

'Down, down!' shouted Reda, barely able to make out the enemy amidst the cascade of heat and light and smoke. 'Into cover,' she roared. 'Rebreathers on.'

She dragged on her own mask and the sound of her rapid, adrenaline-fuelled breathing resonated loudly in her skull. It failed to block the high-pitched whine of lascarbines and the thud of solid shot. Metal-on-metal ricochets lit the edge of the maintenance alcove in sparks like dying fireflies. Hunkered down, she gave a burst of retaliatory fire and a smoke-hazed silhouette sank from view ahead.

Reda estimated around seventy per cent of her force had survived deployment into the arterial. She had around twelve troopers with her in the alcove, and several groups of a similar size stood farther up the corridor or crouched directly across from her, exchanging blind snap-fire with their foes.

Cultists, she realised. No enviro-suits, no rebreathers, though they did wear masks. Leather, but not animal hide. Reda thought she recognised part of a human ear on one of them, dried out and beaten flat. Cheap armour, scavenged gear. They were inferior in every way to the Ultramarians, but they had a manic fervour, an utter disregard for their lives or the lives of their comrades that went beyond suicidal. Through drifts of smoke, Reda saw a cultist crouched over one of the injured. A crude bone mask hid gender and identity but revealed a balding skull, wretched with rad-scars and tufts of wiry, white hair. Clad in black leather and rough brown hessian, the cultist looked more like a butcher than a soldier and went to work on the injured armsman with a serrated knife about the length of a human forearm. The armsman screamed, already in agony, but now having to deal with the torture of his flesh too.

Reda fired two shots, and the boom of the shotgun's report barely registered in the madness of it all. The first shot almost cut the cultist in half and blasted it into the darkness to lie with the rest of the dead. The second killed the tortured armsman, and Reda said to herself this was mercy.

A heavy rate of fire was coming from the armsmen now, their

better training and equipment tipping the scales. The cultists had thinned, still trading shots, still seizing like hungry arachnids on the wounded.

Reda had seen enough.

'Push up, push up!' she roared, letting the vox-emitter strapped to her breastplate carry the order.

The armsmen moved as one, suppressing fire staving off the worst of the cultists' reply. It was all over in a few more minutes, the last of the cultists slashing its own throat and hollering some dark promise to its gods before it bled out all over the deck.

Recyc-fans had kicked in, draining off the worst of the smoke, and only then did Reda see the enemy's entry point. A crude breacher shell had cored through the hull, the melta-burns from its cutting array still glowing hot around the savaged metal, such was the rapidity of the engagement. Banners, parchment rolls of honour, had once stood in this hall. They were soot and charred remains now, despite the best efforts of the armsmen to save them. And now they realised where the fires had been started.

Pulling down the rebreather mask, Reda regarded the ragged horde her troops had just annihilated. Cannon fodder. Light enough fires, cause enough disruption and the true target of an attack is much harder to discern.

Reports of further engagements tripped over the vox-feed as if to confirm this fact.

'Lieutenant…' A bloodied trooper, Gerrant, approached Reda to ask an unspoken question.

The sounds of battle echoed from deeper in the ship, north of their position. The enemy amassing its disparate forces, trying to attain coherency. The armsmen had to meet them and make sure that did not happen.

'Anything from Colonel Kraef?'

Gerrant shook his head.

'Then we move up,' said Reda, and then louder so that all the survivors could hear. 'You three,' she said, her gaze quickly taking in three armsmen, 'get the wounded to the medicae. The rest,' she said, indulging in an emphatic reload of the shotgun, 'forwards on my lead.'

CHAPTER THREE

REPEL ALL BOARDERS

Pillium thundered through the ship, his battle-brothers from the arena right behind him. They had stopped only to arm, making swift observances to the machine-spirits of their bolt rifles and strapping on combat blades before hurrying on. They were still unarmoured, the complex rituals required in the donning of Tacticus war-plate an indulgence they could not afford.

'*This* is what we were bred for,' said Secutius as he racked the loading slide of his weapon.

'You find the cage is not to your liking, brother?' Pillium asked, to which his fellow Primaris Marine gave a snort of derision.

He heard Daceus, Gaius and the other veterans following in their wake. Pillium had set a ruthless pace and would not let up until they reached the enemy. He had absorbed enough vox chatter in the brief observance before the machine shrine to assert that a sizeable enemy force was moving on the warp engines.

'Poet...'

Pillium heard Daceus shout out, and turned sharply. The sergeant loitered at a junction point that Pillium had bypassed.

'This way is faster.'

Pillium frowned, hesitating.

'The warp engines, yes?' said Daceus. 'This way is faster,' he repeated, and disappeared from sight as he took the branching corridor. 'I know this ship, Poet...' His voice echoed loudly, though it was fading by the second, '...like my *tapestry* of scars.'

'You heard him, brother,' said Secutius.

Pillium scowled, then nodded to the others. They went after Daceus.

Smoke laced the stale air, a thin veneer of grey muddying Reda's vision and turning the ship hazy. She knew this vessel. She had served on it for years and seen active duty many times, but as the sounds of fighting and dying reached her through the fog, it felt like a foreign country. As if she had the map but had forgotten how to read it.

The armsmen moved through one of the ship's cargo holds. All available intelligence, and this was fragmentary and unconfirmed, suggested an attack on the warp engines. Reda did not want to imagine the consequences if that attack proved successful. She kept her ear to the vox and managed to piece together that the defenders stationed in that part of the ship had started to come under heavy assault. Calls for reinforcements issued regularly across the feed. Other voices broke in, too, from time to time, voices Reda knew but had chosen to ignore. The voices of the dead.

And there were shadows, familiar silhouettes in an unfamiliar setting. Reda found these harder to push away, every sudden jerk of her combat shotgun betraying her unease.

'Lieutenant?' Gerrant had seen her react and had a wild-eyed look of his own.

Prolonged warp transit took a toll. Young, but getting older by the minute, Gerrant had a dark wash of stubble over the lower half of his face and pressed a standard-issue auto-carbine close to his body. A winged skull tattoo was inked beneath his left eye with the name 'Edon' underneath. Edon Gerrant had served in the Imperial Guard. Vanko Gerrant had barely known his father, but the need to venerate in such a violent galaxy was strong.

'It's nothing, Vanko,' Reda reassured him. She kept her voice low so as not to break the eerie quietude that had fallen upon the ship, like a mourner at a funeral. 'Keep moving.'

She wanted to get out of the cargo hold and away from the shadows.

Give me something I can fight and kill.

'Where are the rest of these bastards?' asked Helder, keeping close to Reda's left shoulder. She smelled the man's fear-sweat through the dark patches in his fatigues. His breath was bad eggs and tooth rot. Nerves played havoc with his halitosis. Thin-faced and narrow-eyed, Helder had never been the picture of health but the last few years had been wearing on him. He looked like a ghoul and carried the aroma of one too.

Reda grimaced. She'd smelled worse, but Helder was breathing hard, and through his mouth.

'Just keep moving,' she repeated, gratefully turning away.

He had a point though. Since the skirmish, they had heard the enemy but not yet encountered them. Reda thought the ship must be carrying the sound and amplifying it.

Either that or the warp was playing tricks.

'Perhaps the ones we engaged earlier had ended up off

course, and hit the wrong part of the ship?' suggested Gerrant, overhearing the conversation. He had moved ahead of Reda and was acting as scout with three others.

'It doesn't matter,' Reda assured him. 'Our only job is to reach the warp engines and get them off this ship.'

'I can hear them,' said another of the scouts, Tebb. 'Seems to be getting louder.'

'It's always louder,' said another, Merln, 'but still nothing.'

'Maybe it's a trap,' offered Helder, unable to stop his fear from bubbling up to the surface of his thoughts and escaping through his pungent mouth.

A slight hesitation seized the front of the group, and Reda could have struck Helder for his weakness.

'Then we'll be ready for it,' she said. 'This is our ship. This is where we live, by Hera. It's our duty to protect it. This is Ultramar. This is your entire damn world. We make for the warp engines and eliminate anything unfriendly we meet on the way.'

A determined silence settled after that, fear subsumed by the desire to inflict violence against the enemy, just as Reda had hoped. The atmosphere grew hotter. Sweat gathered in the nooks of her body, stippling her back and forearms, clothing her neck in a scarf of perspiration. The air felt charged and had an actinic aftertaste. She heard the rising groan of the ship's enginarium beneath them and smelled the shanty-town aroma of toil, grime and effluvia. The warp engines were close.

Then they caught their second sight of the enemy.

Reda saw the las-sights too late, shouting a warning just as Tebb and Merln spun, their bodies riddled with las-burns. Darkness swept in again a moment later, the red emergency lumens doing little to lift it.

'I can't see them,' hissed Helder, pressed so hard against the wall that Reda half-expected him to push through it.

'Wait!' snapped Reda as Leff edged forwards. He got a further two feet, turning to wave his comrades on, when his neck snapped back, a las-burn coring his forehead. 'Hold, hold,' hissed Reda.

'We can't wait here,' said Gerrant.

The vox reports grew more urgent, louder now they had stopped moving. Reda shut it off.

'There could be dozens out there,' said Helder.

Reda gave him a scathing look. 'Or it could be two snipers.'

The cargo hold was large, with a vaulted ceiling, and ringed with gantries. Drums and crates were piled up like hab-stacks. Plenty of places to hide.

'We can't wait,' Gerrant said again and sprinted towards a bulkhead, diving behind it as las-fire stabbed at him.

'Gerrant?' said Reda when she couldn't detect movement. He was partly hidden by the shadows. 'Gerrant?' she repeated, more urgently.

He moved and she gave a relieved sigh. Edging into the light, he put up all four fingers on his right hand.

'Not even one dozen,' said Reda, scowling at Helder, who had the good sense to look sheepish.

Her gaze took in him and the five other armsmen gathered around him. 'I'll draw them out,' she said, 'then you take them.'

She ran, not waiting for confirmation. One side of the corridor to the other, las-blasts chasing her all the way, until she careened into the bulkhead where Gerrant hauled her up against the hard metal barrier. His eyes looked even wilder, with a hint of reproach that Reda ignored.

The shriek-flash and solid-shot boom of the armsmen's

weapons was still fading as Reda poked her head from around the cover to see four dead traitors crumpled in the corridor, scythed to pieces.

Helder gave her a thumbs up, and she nodded.

The dead had rigid dark armour plate over ragged flak vests. They wore spiked helmets, and crude rebreather pipes stretched like rubber tentacles from beneath ugly red ceramic masks.

'Different markings to the ones we fought earlier,' said Gerrant, standing over them to perform a cursory inspection. He'd already checked on Tebb and Merln, shaking his head as soon as he saw the state of both bodies.

'Could be shock troops,' suggested Helder as he emerged from cover. 'Armour and equipment looks better quality.'

Reda shook her head. 'They're a different warband. Markings, kit, tactics. Everything. Everyone wants a damn piece of us.' She glanced at the troopers she had left, trying to ignore the figure at the back in dated Militarum fatigues, his face always in shadow despite the direction and exposure of the light. 'They know we're coming,' she said, averting her gaze. 'And if they're setting up sentries, that means they have territory to protect. They must have a foothold close to the warp engines.'

They pushed on, straight across the hold and into a second arterial. Reda tasted acid on her tongue, a clenched fist of nausea rising in her gut. Helder vomited down his fatigues, but kept moving. A large blast door loomed ahead. It was sealed, and several feet of thick metal stood between the armsmen and the chamber beyond, but the noise of a heavy engagement could still be made out.

'Shields,' Reda called over her shoulder. 'Let's move.'

Twenty troopers, each carrying a hefty boarding shield,

moved up from the rear ranks. Each shield was a rectangular slab of reinforced ceramite, pitted and scored, acid-burned, scorched and dented.

'Line up, then we breach,' she said. The shields locked together with a sound like a bell toll. Reda tried not to think of it as a death knell as the echo faded. They braced, their comrades gathering behind them, several making use of the firing lips cut into the edges of the boarding shields. Once they were ready, Reda turned to Gerrant and Helder, who had taken up position either side of the door, each with their hands on a heavy manual release lever.

The lights flickered, letting in a few seconds of abject darkness, and making Reda hesitate. They had no idea what they would be facing on the other side of that door. Power returned in short order and she gave a curt nod.

'Now! Do it!'

CHAPTER FOUR

BREACH

Gerrant and Helder yanked hard on the levers with visible effort, prompting a loud hiss of released pressure. The door split, irising open along the carefully delineated sections of the metal. It opened by degrees, admitting light, noise and a scene of unfettered violence.

It was difficult to comprehend at first, and Reda experienced a measure of resistance as the armsmen lingered upon the threshold as if the air had thickened to the consistency of oil.

Light warred against dark, as sporadic gun flashes and the flare of powered weapons lit up the vast and gloomy chamber. Skirmishes were being fought over every inch of the place, small seas of bodies washing up against each other, clashing then parting before swelling together and charging again. Sparks flew from chainswords hitting hard armour or striking other blades. Tight groups exchanged close-arms fire over scraps of cover. Mobs overwhelmed individuals, dragging them down through sheer weight of numbers. Champions sought each other out and duelled, hell-bent on a heroic end.

It was madness. Reda noted at least half a dozen different traitor warbands. They battled for spoils against giants in blue power armour. They battled each other for the right to kill and claim those spoils. Near-naked savages, the frosty rime of the void still melting off their steaming bodies; flesh-masked cannibals wielding butcher knives and blood-matted cudgels; black-armoured soldiery with blank-eyed rebreathers and Munitorum-issue lasrifles; metal-clad hulks wearing visored war-helms, heaving spiked boarding shields. Too many to count, too many to kill.

And amongst the hordes moved the warriors of the old war, the Heretic Astartes. Of these dark legends, Reda mercifully saw little. She had witnessed Space Marines at war before. It was a brutal, terrifying affair, but to see them clash against each other... She realised they had no business being in this fight. But they were here and the notion of retreat had been excised from her psyche long ago.

She caught a fleeting glimpse of Colonel Kraef amidst drifting smoke, grey patrol cap, chainsword aloft as he led a large group in heavy carapace and carrying point-mounted guns. At his order, a rapier hummed to activation and jabs of hot, red light scythed the darkness.

'Move! Get in there!' she roared, and it felt like they had been standing still for minutes. Time had slowed, anchored by the inertia of fear, but as those words left Reda's lips, it sprang forwards again, alarming, dizzying and raucous. She lost sight of Kraef almost immediately.

A spit of angry promethium doused a clutch of ragged-looking traitors, turning them into candle flames. They collapsed, burning, writhing, their throats too scorched to scream even in their death throes. The warrior bearing the flamer that had killed them stomped through their brittle bones and ash, the red warning lumens catching his armour and turning the blue to violet. A moment later he was borne down by the horde, his fuel reserve igniting in a beautiful, angry sunrise that stripped bone and left a blackened, fire-licked void in his wake.

'Throne of Terra...' gasped Helder, as white as the dead, crouched behind his comrades' barricade.

Even Gerrant had grit his teeth, his autocarbine gripped so tight he was about to crack the stock.

They had to fight. If they just kept moving they would die.

'Engage them! For Macragge!' roared Reda, discharging her shotgun at the nearest traitor. A cannibal in black-brown daub turned hard as his shoulder blew out, scattering gore and bone. The rest of his tribe took heed. Whooping and hollering, they sprang towards the armsmen, as agile as felids, brandishing knives and baring needle-toothed smiles.

They hit the shields hard, blades scraping against ceramite. Solid-shot and las-fire took a toll against them, but the cannibals had the numbers and soon they got to stabbing and rending.

'Break the line and let them in,' shouted Reda, and the shield wall bowed and parted, letting through the daubed warriors who staggered on, drunk on slaughter, savage-eyed and wild. Shotgun blasts and auto-fire scythed through them. The cannibals notched up a few more kills but as the shield wall wrapped around them, herding them, crushing them, they lost their numerical advantage. Sensing the end, they barrelled into each other, a maddened herd lost to fear. Some were trampled or impaled on their own knives. Others were crushed against the shields, now locked and braced and turned into a deadly unbroken circle.

It was over quickly, and as Reda took stock she realised they were well past the threshold now and deeper into the chamber. She felt giddy, light-headed and worried she might pass out, believing at first that the sheer intensity of the battle had overwhelmed her, until she saw a large section of the upper wall had cracked and was slowly leaking atmosphere. She ordered rebreathers on immediately, partly distracted by the cohort of pallid-fleshed servitors and robed tech-priests trying to seal the breach. Clutches of traitors harassed them, and she saw several servitors dragged away to be dismembered in the hungry shadows.

She hurried on as the armsmen broke apart into smaller squads, seeking cover and engaging the smaller groups of enemy fighters. Her squad, which included Gerrant, Helder and seven others, briefly brushed shoulders with a battle-scarred group of Ultramarines in old-style war-plate. Their sergeant, who wore no helmet and had a craggy, weathered countenance with close-shorn white hair, nodded once to her before hurling orders as he and his men were gone again, lost to the melee.

'What the hell are we doing here, lieutenant?' asked Gerrant. 'What's the plan, other than to survive?'

They were taking cover and a fleeting moment of respite before re-engaging again.

Reda caught her breath. Her armsmen were strung out across the chamber, caught up in skirmishes or with heads down plotting their next move. She still couldn't see Kraef but knew he was in here somewhere, fighting.

'We try and reach the colonel and consolidate our forces. Failing that...'

Ahead, up a broad metal stairway thronged with dead and dying Ultramarines, she caught sight of the warp engine. It was colossal, a massive metal orb around which spun three studded, gyroscopic rings at hypervelocity. The metal, which was psy-conductive and forged from no ordinary mineral, was meant to shroud the reality-bending effects of the engine, but gossamer strands of unnatural light eked through its seams and made the air around it appear to shudder and vibrate. A figure stood in the shadow of its light, occupying a void space and apparently oblivious to everything around him in the same way that everything else was oblivious to him. A man in uniform, his face covered by darkness.

Reda tore her gaze away, instead fixing it upon the robed and power-armoured figure standing in front. Ithro Arkaedron did not stand alone as the psy-lightning crackled from his armoured fingertips and force staff. Two honour guard stood with the Librarian, fending off any traitor who came within reach. Scores of the dead lay at their feet. Two amongst the many bodies wore the same winged helms and gilt-edged war-plate as the standing honour guard. Despite their obvious prowess, they were losing.

Arkaedron shouted something, his hands and staff seemingly in perpetual motion as he conjured and abjured with fire and will. Reda did not have the language to comprehend though she saw the effects easily enough, a jagged arc of light tearing from the eyes of the silver eagle perched at the top of the staff to engulf a baying host below.

It took seconds to reduce the traitors to little more than ash and blackened bone, but more were coming, and Reda's gaze was drawn to something else that came with them. At first she thought it was a vagabond, dressed in ragged attire, shuffling on dirt-black feet, naked from the waist up and emaciated to the point of starvation. But then she saw the chain shackled around his neck and the manacles around his ankles. He turned, as if sensing her regard, and she saw his eyes... as red as fire, and scorching their sockets black. Shadows coalesced around his body, slowly taking on form and consistency. He smiled too wide, like a sickle pulling at the edges of chapped and bloody lips...

'Reda...'

The man who was not a man began to turn, no longer shuffling but *gliding*, his thick and yellowed toenails scraping along the floor, the sound like the scratch of a discordant harp or the shriek of a blunt knife against a whetstone...

'Arna!'

Reda blinked and saw Gerrant. The vagabond was not looking towards her. He hadn't come closer. Only the echo of that scraping remained, fading into tinnitus. She went to answer but her teeth were clenched so hard that it took a few seconds to get her jaw moving. The taste of warm iron tanged her tongue.

'I'm here,' she said, surprised at the roughness in her voice.

Gerrant looked annoyed. 'I know you're here, lieutenant. I asked for orders.'

Reda thought fast, still trying to banish her lingering disquiet. She gestured.

'Hug the east wall, cover to cover, and move up,' she said. 'We need to find a position from which we can mount some kind of defence. Get a toehold, maybe some reinforcements. We're in this fight, we need to make a difference.'

Gerrant nodded, his eyes lingering on hers for the slightest of seconds before they moved out. Half the squad had shields and went out in front. They got a little over six feet, the others right up behind them with heads down, when a deafening blast tore them apart. Pieces of ceramite cascaded like lethal rain, and three soot-black and bloody bodies sprawled partially dismembered on the chamber floor.

Ears ringing, Reda realised she was down. Gerrant lay nearby, alive but barely moving. Then she heard Helder.

'My shitting leg! Blood of Hera, my leg!'

Helder rolled around on his back, clutching at where his left knee ended in a cauterised stump. Reda rubbed her eyes, trying to knead away the blurring, still in shock.

A traitor in red-stained fatigues with battered brass plates stitched onto her gear held a smoking launch tube and was prepping for another shot. She looked like ex-Guard. Very, *very* ex-Guard. She dropped a flange-headed missile down into the tube and was hefting the launcher onto her shoulder when a las-beam took her in the forehead and she fell back out of sight.

Gerrant had crawled up on his knees, a scavenged laspistol in his outstretched hand. He locked eyes with Reda. He didn't look so good, but managed to gesture with his chin. Reda followed it. Another squad had seen them through the smoke and was moving up in support. Sergeant Yenti with about fifteen troopers. Reda waved them over.

'We need to regroup,' she said to Gerrant, scrambling her shotgun back into her hands. One of the other survivors, Menkin, grabbed Helder, who was still screaming.

He was about to start dragging when both men burst into flames as if spontaneously combusting.

Chains scraping against the deck caught Reda's attention as she made a visor of her hand to ward off the heat. The fire died away quickly, leaving Menkin and Helder as burnt meat, still steaming as the chained figure emerged through smoke. Not the vagabond. This one was short and stocky.

Dirt caked the pits of his milk-white skin, a grubby rime that lapped reams of flab like a snapped girdle. He was naked and only the extent of his girth kept him decent, if such a word could be applied to whatever this bloated thing was.

The corpulent man was not alone. He had minders dressed in long rot-brown robes and padded hauberks of rusty chain-mesh. One turned his face towards the armsmen, half-hidden by a grey moth-eaten hood. Reda saw teeth, perfect white teeth fixed in a permanent grin.

The fire exchange began with Sergeant Yenti's men, who opened up with lascarbines and autorifles. A rank of dirty stubbers replied in kind. They'd been modified to fire metal barbs, and one of Yenti's men screamed as the wretched ammo tore up his flesh.

Reda fired too, followed swiftly by the remnants of her squad. A barb hit Jenka in the throat, her arterial spray painting the deck and one of her comrades as she fell. The grinners were dying too though, the crossfire from both armsmen squads punishing them. All the while, the pale and bloated man amidst their ranks giggled, as if amused at all the deaths.

Then he lifted a fat finger.

Unzel came apart, splitting into four equal quadrants as if cut by a surgical las. The pieces struck the deck with a thud – perfect, clean, horrific.

Yenti got off a good shot, scoring a grinner's cheek but hitting the corpulent man in the left temple. The fat thing scowled, hissing like a wounded felid. Then he smiled, turning his gaze to Yenti, who was lining up another shot when his arm tore from his body. No one touched him; it just came away as if pulled, dangling strings of red tendon and wire-thin sinew. He staggered, his mind lost to shock and sudden, catastrophic blood loss.

Two more of the grinners fell at the same time, stitched up by las-fire. A gap appeared in the throng of minders. Reda took her chance.

Half the corpulent man's head came off with a shotgun boom, skull fragments and grimy matter spattering a grinner. He jerked, the chains attached to his bulk whipping around like a thresher blade and segmenting the last three grinners into separate legs and torsos.

'Try laughing that off...'

Reda's sense of triumph was short-lived. Something else was coming for them.

Because of course it bloody is.

It was moving heavily and cutting through everything in its path. Spikes protruded from dark war-plate that appeared to shift and vibrate like oil on water, monstrous images coalescing and collapsing only to reform again a moment later.

An Ultramarine stepped into its way, brandishing a broken blade, and despite the condition of the warrior's armour and the obvious wounds he had suffered to reach this point, Reda dared to hope.

The Ultramarine bravely stood his ground. Clenching his sword in both hands, he declared, 'For Macragge!'

The fight was startlingly brief, and it left the proud warrior gutted on a saw-edged blade. His fingers still clenched and unclenched impotently, reaching for his fallen sword as the Traitor Marine walked on. It wasn't unarmed for long. It drew an axe from a sheath of human skin, barely breaking stride. Closer, Reda felt the brutal violence radiating off its body and heard the discordant hum of its generator. And the smell... it reeked of cold and decay, of dying things and primordial fear.

Reda knew they were all dead, but resolved to go down fighting.

'We have to kill it,' she cried, hoping to inspire some resistance.

Her shotgun blast exploded high on the Traitor Marine's chest but it barely registered. Just a momentary pause, and it was moving again. Implacable and wrought for slaughter. More shots rained in as a fighting desperation took hold, las and bullets from autocarbines, and when they were spent the armsmen drew close combat weapons. Reda almost laughed out loud at their chances of survival as she pulled out her power maul and energised the flanged head. Gerrant's autocarbine clacked empty, so he and Keltzer grabbed up a fallen breacher shield and charged, Reda tucked right in behind them. The other armsmen trailed after them, a few drawn off into other skirmishes. Some fled, back into the darkness of the ship.

Almost close enough to touch, Reda smelled the ozone bleeding off the Traitor Marine's armour, and heard the barely perceptible sibilance of strange voices in the air around it. She lashed out with the power maul, a tongue of crackling energy smearing off the mace head... A swipe of the Traitor Marine's axe and the armsmen were scattered, the breacher shield shorn, useless and discarded. It had saved their lives at least, though Reda considered as she lay on her back, unarmed and bleeding, skull throbbing like a madman's drum, that the Traitor Marine might have wanted to spare them a quick death.

Gerrant stirred nearby, but then collapsed. Keltzer was screaming, an ugly scorch mark running from crown to groin where the axe's power field had touched him. Staring up at the ancient warrior bearing down on her, the noise of the warzone appeared to ebb for Reda, its bright fury dimming and the life-or-death desperation of other small battles slowing to an incomprehensible crawl.

Surrounded by this tapestry of violence and madness, she

felt utterly alone, just her and it, face-to-face, hopelessly, laughably outmatched. Reda pulled her knife, wincing as her fractured ribs ground against each other. The blood running down her arm reached the haft and made it slick.

'I'm just wearing you down...' she snarled through clenched teeth.

The Traitor Marine reached up to its helm, not deigning to acknowledge her. The left eyepiece was cracked, nearly entirely shattered. With a slight jerk, the helm came loose, turning fractionally as it pulled away from the neck brace. The Traitor Marine lifted it off, the helm ringing loudly against the deck as he let it fall from his grasp. Because it was a *he*, not a creature nor a monster. A man, only one elevated or degenerated to the point of something *other*.

Reda had been expecting a horror, a denizen of the warp. Instead she saw scars, not ritualistic marks but battle scars, no different to any son of Guilliman on board the *Emperor's Will*. The Traitor Marine touched a gash above his left eye. Gauntleted fingers came away shiny in the light. Reda had no memory of hitting him. He almost looked impressed as he regarded her and raised his axe, framing an executioner's blow. Up-close, the haft was as long as Reda's body, the actual blade twice as broad. Gods and monsters died to weapons like that, mortal man would only sully it. And then he did something Reda did not expect.

'I'll make it quick,' he murmured in Gothic, his accent thick and the words unfamiliar.

Reda gave him nothing except defiance.

His neck quivered and for a moment Reda thought he had succumbed to a seizure or some dark blessing of his gods. His mouth fell open, just a little, and as he reached up to his neck, he collapsed to one knee.

A spear jutted through the Traitor Marine's neck, spitting it like a piece of rotten meat. The bladed tip crackled with noisome ozone, the blood cauterising and burning off in seconds. He fell to his other knee, trying to turn his head. His fingers stretched for the studded, leather-wound haft of his axe, but the blade was firmly embedded in the ground. Blood bubbling up from his throat gently spilled over his lip. It hissed where it touched his armour, slowly corroding the metal. Giving up on the axe, he unclipped a baroque-looking bolt pistol holstered at his hip. The muzzle had been fashioned into a serpent's fanged mouth. He was glaring at Reda but his anger was directed elsewhere. As he began to turn his body, something fast struck the Traitor Marine in the left temple. Reda caught a half-second of heat trajectory before the Traitor Marine's head violently exploded, showering her with red, gory matter.

CHAPTER FIVE

TWO STORMS

Pillium retrieved the spear, yanking it loose from what remained of the Hellreaper's head and neck. The charge in the bladed spear flickered and gave out. Grunting, he tossed it aside and took his bolt rifle in a two-handed grip.

'You're bleeding...' said a voice beneath him.

He looked down to see a grizzled woman in worn fatigues and battered armour, brandishing a serrated-edged combat knife in one bloody hand. She'd lost her helmet, and her short, dark hair stuck out in tufty clumps from being sandwiched beneath it.

'Flesh wounds,' he replied, about to move on.

'Don't leave us,' said the woman.

Pillium turned to shout an order for his battle-brothers to come together, then made a swift count of the other armsmen with the woman. Deeming their combat efficacy negligible, he carried on.

'Please!'

'Can you fight?' he asked, calling out as he moved away. The bolt rifle bucked in his hands as he took shots of opportunity. Somewhere ahead of him, Secutius and his squad were taking the fight to the enemy. He wanted to join them.

'Yes.'

'Then fight,' he said, making for the warp engine, where Ithro Arkaedron fought alone.

The honour guard lay dead at the Librarian's feet, having given their last to defend him and keep safe the warp engine.

'What are those things?' asked Secutius, letting rip with another short sharp burst of fire, trying to conserve ammunition.

The Space Marines in the arena had consolidated together, and forged a half-armoured wedge of monstrously armed gladiators. They fought around a core of warriors, weapons facing out, constantly moving and engaging.

'Daemonhosts,' said Daceus. The old veteran had kept pace well, and fought with a tenacity Pillium had not seen in the arena. 'Our most effective tactic is to fight them up-close.' He brandished a revving chainsword. 'Blades only. In my experience they work the best. Bolt shells tend not to take.'

'I have no issue with that,' declared Pillium. 'I prefer to look my enemy in the eye as I vanquish it.'

'Then you had best get to vanquishing,' Daceus replied, and Pillium followed his gaze.

A host descended on Arkaedron and he looked hard-pressed to resist it. Arcs of lightning spat from his staff, raking the ragged cultists who were being joined by increasing numbers of Traitor Marines. A few carried the markings of the Hellreapers, others claimed allegiance to the War Dogs, the Exultant, Horde of Misery and half a dozen other warbands.

But it was the daemonhosts, the possessed, the ones in chains that posed the most severe threat.

A fresh whip-crack of lightning lashed through the traitors, scything limbs and rending bone, but their fervour was unbreakable. Fire uncoiled from Arkaedron's fingertips, a flame vortex hot enough to crack ceramite and turn power armour to ash. A rain of silver blades cascaded from on high, shredding flesh and piercing metal. The dead piled atop the dead. Sweat drenched Arkaedron's forehead, the hollows around his eyes deepening with every fresh conjuration. And yet the possessed endured.

Pillium waded into the fight, bent on reaching Arkaedron, and saw three such creatures slowly converging on the stricken Librarian and, ultimately, the warp engine. The first had the dishevelled disposition of an emaciated tramp; the second a woman with black, diaphanous hair, metal stakes rammed through her wrists and ankles; the last was an urchin boy, bald as pale marble, a crown of bony horns jutting from a malformed scalp.

Pillium had no way of knowing the true face of the horrors lurking beneath their distended and abused flesh, and he did not care to. All that mattered was ending them. Strafing his bolt rifle in a wide arc, he cleared a path then swapped his firearm for a gleaming combat blade. He saw Secutius had done the same.

'He is fast for his age, this one,' Secutius said. Daceus had already moved into the breach, urging others nearby to follow.

'Invictus!'

The other veterans were on his lead, fighting like they were born to it, like they had never known anything other. Pillium was determined not to be outdone by their example.

'Don't tell me this isn't about honour,' he said, though Secutius didn't argue. 'It's always about honour.'

He and Secutius drove their warriors on.

'For Guilliman and the crusade!' he roared, and a second spear wedge of unarmoured Ultramarines joined the first, eager to overtake it.

Reda rolled onto her knees and gagged, the stench of the Traitor Marine's blood forcing hot bile up her throat. The fight had moved on, following strength, cleaving to the worst of the violence. A few Ultramarines and the scattered remnants of armsmen who had managed to push up encroached at the edges of a thick horde of traitors. The disparate warbands had all but ceased fighting each other for the spoils, and their concerted effort was beginning to turn into a winning strategy.

Reda pushed up onto her feet, dragging those armsmen near her who were not dead up by their scruffs. Gerrant too.

'On your feet,' she said, vaguely aware she was slurring her words. She heard Kraef shouting nearby. He sounded angry. So was she. 'We're not done yet.'

The warrior who had killed the Traitor Marine and saved her life had cut a path into the horde, he and several others, all without their armour but no less imposing or brutal for that. To see them fight like that, sinews visibly straining, over-muscled bodies bulging with effort, it appalled her. By stripping away their armour, their mantle, they appeared even less human than when glaring from behind ceramite-sheathed retinal lenses.

The one standing on the warp engine's dais, he *radiated* power and as Reda felt the awe Ithro Arkaedron inspired, she made ready to sound the charge. It would likely be the armsmaster's last. Only now, at the end, did her fatigue threaten to finish her. She vowed to hold on for as long as she could.

'Who are we?' she bellowed, finding her voice and the last vestiges of her courage.

The reply never came. She had found her maul and raised it like a bannered lance, about to declare victory or death, when Arkaedron fell.

His fate was not obvious at first. The Librarian appeared to stumble as if reeling from a powerful blow, though no hand – at least not one that could be seen by mortal perception – struck him. Then he shook, and the lightning arcs spilling from his eyes and cascading from his staff grew wild and unfocused. Fire took hold of his robes and he began to burn. His conjured storm flared magnesium bright then dimmed and turned inwards. Arkaedron's skin glowed, a lantern's hot light beneath it, and tendrils of smoke uncoiled from his mouth and eyes.

Regaining a fighting stance, he cut apart the chained vagabond, bisecting him from shoulder to hip and violently shearing the two halves by the splaying of his left hand. His defiance was brief as two other chained creatures advanced upon him, a siren-like woman in dirty grey fatigues and an urchin boy with a swollen, malformed head.

As Arkaedron shrank back, the creatures seemed to grow, and they curved over the Librarian like shadows encroaching on the light, their claws extended, their grubby teeth bared. He grew rigid, jerking violently as if he were being impaled by a dozen invisible blades. The lightning died and in that moment so too did Ithro Arkaedron, the silver eagle staff falling from his nerveless fingers as he coughed up a spurt of rich transhuman blood. His limbs *folded*, snapping across the bone, armour tearing like parchment, legs and arms bent inwards by an unseen hand. His neck snapped back, his skull disappearing in a welter of bloody mist and bone fragments.

Reda screamed, a wail from the pit of her soul, from the deepest well of her despair. She lurched and fell as a discernible shudder of disbelief swept through the defenders.

A piece of crushed and bloody metal clanged to the deck. The remains of Ithro Arkaedron. The Librarian had been utterly destroyed, his armour, flesh and bone pulverised together as if by an industrial compressor.

Pillium fought on, harder than before, desperation lending him urgency and wrath. It was an unfamiliar sensation. The Indomitus Crusade had been baptismal, and the engagements he had fought in hard, but nothing like this. Not the bleeding edge, near-annihilation stakes they battled here in this hell-wracked chamber far from Terra's light.

'This is not glory...' Secutius said, echoing Pillium's troubled thoughts.

'It is death,' Daceus replied, the three fighting shoulder to shoulder as all the Ultramarines now were. 'It is Ultramar.'

Daceus cut down a War Dog, splitting the warrior's snarling face and letting the chainsword chew through the meat. Wrenching the blade free, the blood flecked across his face and for a brief moment Pillium saw the wildness of the ancient Macraggian Battle Kings in the veteran's eyes. 'We are Macragge,' snarled Daceus, clashing with another War Dog. 'We die on our feet or not at all.'

Pillium sheathed his combat blade in an Exalted's neck, a puff of cloying perfume spilling from the warrior's mouth making him gag. Scowling, he ripped off the dying warrior's helm and shattered his skull with a savage headbutt.

'I'm not dying here,' he declared, tearing his blade free and letting the Exalted fall. It felt good to rage, but like a fire eating up the last of its oxygen, it could not last.

The circle of defiance was shrinking, as one by one the Ultramarines and their allies fell to a traitor's blade.

'I'm not dying here!' he roared, but as the hordes briefly parted and he saw the way to the warp engines, he realised it would not be up to him.

The two daemonhosts had entered the unnatural aura of the machine and in the flickers of eldritch light, glimpses of their true forms were revealed. *Leathery wings, scabrous, bone claws and scaled red hides. A serpentine body, writhing with peristalsis, hoofed feet and gnarled...*

They would breach the warp engine's cowl and unmake the machine within.

'That engine fails and the Geller field fails too,' said Daceus, fighting against hopelessness. His gaze found Pillium and Secutius, the eyes of the three meeting in a brief moment of recognition. 'It has been an honour, brothers.'

Secutius gave a brief salute but Pillium could find no such charity within him. 'Defeat and annihilation are not honourable,' he said, and chafed bitterly against his fate. The cowl of the machine had been stripped away, a discarded metallic rind littering the deck.

'Who are we?' Daceus roared, the old fool defiant until the last.

A thunderous explosion answered, forcing Pillium to look up at the vaulted ceiling as it caught fire.

Reda had lost sight of the warp engine. The dais had become so crowded in the struggle for the machine that all she saw was an ever-tightening knot of Ultramarines, and the traitor hordes squabbling for the bloody honour of killing them.

'We are dead...' breathed Gerrant, slipping on one knee.

The pale and haggard faces of the other armsmen suggested they thought so too.

Reda did not deny it. She reached out and gripped Gerrant's hand. He turned and his eyes were pits of sorrow, of a life not lived. She wanted to say something, anything, but the words caught in her throat and the pain in her side she had denied for the last few minutes came into acute focus. The power maul fell from her fingers, shorting out with a few last sparks as it hit the ground. Reda followed it, her hand slipping from Gerrant's. His expression changed as he realised how badly she was injured.

The chamber dimmed, darkening at the edges, but the onset of shadow was swift. Pain kept Reda awake for a few more seconds. She barely felt the hard deck rush up to meet her, the jolt of metal against bone. She heard thunder and thought that must be impossible. With the dying of her sight, she saw fire as the dark metal sky crashed down, and a host of armour-clad angels soared from on high to deliver the defenders from death. She wept, holding on for a few more seconds just to catch a glimpse. The crested helm, the glittering sword, a regal cloak fluttering in the air. The courage and authority of his voice, the inspiration. Leading a golden charge...

We are Macragge!

Reda smiled as she faded into unconsciousness, tears welling in her eyes.

'Sicarius...'

CHAPTER SIX

Ʊ

BECALMED

Retius Daceus folded his arms across his chest, the scores and burns marring his armour still visible despite his best efforts to scrub them out. He was not a prideful man but a fastidious one, and when he stood in the presence of his captain, he at least wanted to look like he could do the job he had been given. He also didn't waste words.

'We have a serious problem.'

'From all accounts,' answered Sicarius, 'we have more than just one.' His cold, blue gaze took in the rest of the room and the audience he had summoned to his quarters. He had long abandoned the notion of having a private space, though there were times that he missed the luxury of isolation and the clarity of thought that came with it. Ever since the ship had been adrift, power had been failing and several decks had to be shut down and sealed as vital life support systems could no longer be sustained to an acceptable level of efficacy. It meant some of the briefing chambers had been repurposed as barracks, or living spaces for the non-combatant members of the crew. In turn, this had meant sacrificing privacy for pragmatism. A tacticarium hololith table had been moved in and most of the furnishings, including the slab cot where Sicarius had occasionally slept, moved out to make space for briefings and reports.

Even so, it was still crowded in the captain's quarters.

'Our failing power reserves are of significant concern,' said Haephestus, taking the opportunity to voice his findings first. The Techmarine was a towering presence, only surpassed by the indomitable figure of Argo Helicos who stood next to him. 'I have conducted numerous theoreticals based on the current depletion rates and have worked up a predictive algorithm to posit an energy half-life.' Haephestus tapped a panel on his left vambrace. Unlike the other Ultramarines in the room, it was red, like the rest of his armour, to denote his Martian training and allegiance. A series of complex computations and isometrical power forecasts flickered into being, rendered up as grainy graphical images that the Techmarine transferred to the hololithic table around which they were all gathered.

Sicarius looked on gravely and caught the gimlet stare of Haephestus' bionic eye looking back.

'I don't have your technical acumen, Haephestus,' he said, absently stroking the beard he had cultivated over the last few months, 'but even I can see these projections are grim.'

'A critical juncture will be reached in a matter of weeks,' Haephestus confirmed.

Sicarius leaned back in his chair, the fingers of his left hand drumming against the edge of the table. Unlike the fellow Adeptus Astartes currently in his presence, he wore light training fatigues, his bare arms displaying powerful muscles and his Chapter tattoos.

'It's draining then, our power.'

'The ship, our armour, everything,' said Haephestus.

'Can anything be done?'

'I will return to the lower decks, to the ship's main power core. I might be able to eke out more time, but it is not a long-term solution. We are haemorrhaging power.'

'But we shouldn't be, should we?'

Haephestus nodded. 'The *Emperor's Will* can maintain function for decades, and most of its critical systems are self-sustaining. Our armour generators also have years of operation. Until I have conducted further analysis, I can only assume a warp siphon.'

'You're saying while we linger here, becalmed in the empyrean sea, we are being bled dry?'

'A tad poetic but, yes, that is accurate.'

'And the severity of these outages?'

'I've received reports of power failures in the aft decks, eight through twelve, and am considering moving the crew in those sections to more stable areas,' offered a thin-looking woman wearing an amalgam of Militarum fatigues and Munitorum robes. Olvo Sharna blinked nervously at the captain behind a pair of wireframe glasses, a bleached bone servo-skull scribing every word to parchment with a neuro-quill. The reams of vellum gathered in a hefty stack beneath the floating machine, its tiny anti-gravitic impellers stirring the papery edges. 'And there is also the question of sustenance.'

Sicarius held her gaze for a moment.

'Food, captain,' she said.

'I know what sustenance means, quartermaster,' he said patiently. 'Would you care to provide a little more detail about the crisis?'

'Of course, captain,' she said quickly, shoving her wireframes a little further up her nose, 'of course. Put bluntly, we are reaching the end of our reserves and with the current power issues,' she gave a furtive glance at Haephestus before looking away again, 'we are unable to process the stocks that we do have. Our agri-stockpiles are already spoiling, far faster than we could have projected, and we do not possess the means to generate more. Rations have already been halved and I am stretching them out as far as they can go.'

'Then you'll have to stretch them further,' said Sicarius, firmly but not unkindly. 'The ship must still function.'

'And the crew have to eat,' Sharna replied, swallowing back her boldness. 'Starvation is imminent and there has been...' She paused, trying to wrap her tongue around the right word. '*Unrest.*'

Sicarius turned his attention to the man standing at the back of the room, behind the others and half-hidden by the shadows. Valesco Kraef looked grey and as tough as old leather. He had a wiry orange moustache, turning white at the edges. His patrol cap was folded under one arm, and his bald scalp shone in the light. He was a veteran like Daceus, only Kraef was not transhuman. He stepped forwards as soon as he realised he had the captain's attention.

'Civil disquiet amongst the ratings has increased,' he admitted. 'I am doubling patrols and cutting sleep rotations but we took a lot of casualties during the last assault. I'm stretched rather thin.'

'Aren't we all, colonel,' Sicarius conceded. 'What's the nature of the unrest, and can we just call it what it is? Five years lost in the warp, I think we've learned to be candid with each other by now, yes?'

That prompted a few nods and the odd muttered word of agreement.

'Rioting and murder, captain,' Kraef replied. 'Death tolls have gone up by at least eighty per cent. Some of it is warp madness. Deck thirteen remains under quarantine but we might need to do the same with other decks if this persists. The rest is sickness and fatigue. They want food, and they crave light and air. I cannot give any of that to them. Only the mailed fist and the promise of severe punishment if they transgress. They are locked in a steel box and the heat is rising.'

'I rely upon you to keep order amongst the crew, particularly the deckhands and ratings,' said Sicarius. 'You have the assistance of the over-seers – use it.'

'I do, sire, but frankly it is not enough. I have lost eight overseers in the last day alone. Five committed suicide by stepping into the plasma furnaces, while the other three were torn apart when a labour dispute turned ugly. *Literally* they tore the men apart, sire. Limb from limb.'

Sicarius regarded him pensively as he considered the problem. Kraef looked at the edge of endurance and Sicarius wondered when last he had actually slept. His eyes kept wandering as if he were struggling to maintain focus, and Sicarius was forced to consider whether the man was still fit for task. He decided he would have Venatio check in on him later. The Apothecary had a full slate but Sicarius needed his master-of-arms functional.

'Alright, colonel,' he said, and then looked at Daceus. 'Sergeant, task Squads Vorolanus and Fennion to assist in restoring order in the lower decks.'

'That will leave our defences threadbare, captain. If there's another attack–'

'It's either that or the ship eats itself from within. See it done,' he said.

Daceus nodded, and quietly relayed the order through his vox.

'As to the dearth of power...' Sicarius said, turning his attention to Haephestus, 'divert what you can to ration production and hydroponics. Conduct whatever further analysis is needed.'

The Techmarine's bionic eye noisily refocused as he made the mental computations.

'By your will, captain. But I must advise you that such measures will require taking most of the automated defences on the command, primary and secondary decks offline. Generator restoration cycles will also need to be expanded by a further twelve hours.'

'Duly noted. Master Zaadrin? Any contact, even a scrap, from the crusade fleet?'

A hooded figure in long violet robes turned his face towards the light. He had no eyes, but his features seemed to react to the meagre illumination as if perceiving by some other, less ordinary means.

'Whispers, but nothing more, captain,' he said, his reedy voice a match to his skeletal frame and hunched posture. He gripped a black obsidian staff adorned with a stylised silver eye – the symbol of the Adeptus Astra Telepathica, the astropaths – and leaned on it heavily. 'I cannot be certain it is our allies, either, and I dare not venture too far or for too long. The warp is ever close. I hear it scratching sometimes, just at the edges but it's getting louder.'

Kraef suppressed a shiver at the astropath's remarks, surreptitiously making the sign of the aquila when he thought no one was looking.

'Well, at least that's brief,' said Sicarius facetiously. 'Keep trying. If a message in a bottle is our best hope then we have to keep sending them out into the tides until one reaches shore. Is that everything?'

'Not quite everything,' said Daceus.

'Ah, the *serious* problem.'

'The matter of Ithro Arkaedron,' Daceus supplied.

The faces around the room, particularly those of the Adeptus Astartes, darkened at the mention of the Librarian's name.

'Without him, we have no Navigator,' Daceus added.

'Ithro's loss to us is a grave one. He served with courage and honour. But we have a Navigator, Daceus.'

'I meant a… ah… *functioning* Navigator.'

'You mean one who's sane.'

'That too.'

Sicarius' eyes narrowed and his face changed as if he had just tried a rare Iaxian vintage on his palate and decided the taste was not to his liking.

'We cannot remain becalmed, adrift on seas of fate. Sane or not, Barthus is needed. Venatio can make an assessment, but unless he's raving I want the Navigator back at his post. Inertia now will see this ship and everyone aboard dead within days, let alone weeks. We are prey in these blood-laced waters and the predators have our scent. Five years we've been gone and have managed to avoid the worst, but we have reached the bleeding edge. Colonel, can you spare a few of your men to retrieve Barthus from the sanctum?'

Kraef glanced at Daceus before giving his full attention to the captain. 'With the assistance of Adeptus Astartes reinforcements to help manage the decks, yes, I can assign some men for that duty. I will see it done personally, sire.'

Sicarius nodded. 'Very well. If that is all?' he asked the assembly.

They gave their murmured assent.

Sicarius nodded again. 'To your duties, then.'

CHAPTER SEVEN

TWO BROTHERHOODS

When the others left, Daceus and Helicos remained behind.

The Primaris lieutenant came to stand beside the sergeant. Even armoured as they both were, the mismatch was obvious.

Helicos held his Mk X war-helm in the crook of his left arm as if he were attending a ceremony. It had a thick white mark down the centre, which in turn was split in two by a thinner red stripe to denote his rank and status. His armour was pristine and glorious blue and gold. Purity seals cascaded from the breastplate, an indicator of the suit's fine forging and dependability.

By contrast, Daceus wore heavily scarred power armour, Mk VII, its appearance and design near ubiquitous amongst the Chapter before the arrival of the Primaris brethren. His helm was clamped to his weapons belt, the bright red an indicator of his sergeant's rank. He was a Lion of Macragge, one of Sicarius' honour guard – one of the four that still lived, the others having fallen defending the *Emperor's Will*.

Helicos led the demi-company of Primaris Marines that Lord Guilliman had sequestered to Sicarius' service at the beginning of the Indomitus Crusade. Four squads, including his own, sat under Helicos' immediate command, though Sicarius maintained overall authority of the combined Ultramarines force aboard the ship, including his own Second Company. He trusted Helicos, and valued him not only as a warrior and battle-leader but also a vital bridge between the Primaris brethren and those that some had begun to call 'first born', an appellation that felt overly reductive and colloquial for Sicarius' tastes.

'This is far from the glory and retribution we were promised,' said Sicarius, once they were alone. Helicos appeared a little stunned by the captain's candour but did well to keep it from his face. Where Daceus was grizzled and leathern, Helicos was handsome and marmoreal.

'I doubt even the primarch could have envisaged our fate,' said Daceus, having known Sicarius for decades and no longer surprised by his honesty and directness. 'After this long, and for our brothers in the crusade it could be even longer, I fully expect the *Emperor's Will* to be recorded lost with all hands.'

Sicarius gave a rueful laugh. 'Judging by the day's imminent calamities, we might yet be.' He got to his feet, turning to regard the armoury inset into the alcove behind him. His sword, the Tempest Blade, sat suspended in its scabbard behind a shimmering stasis field. An ornate plasma pistol named Luxos joined it, along with a pair of artificer lightning claws that Sicarius had not used in many years, and his relic armour, the Suzerain's Mantle.

'Another attack is inevitable. Regardless of whether we are becalmed or not, the traitor hosts will come.' With a fizz of displaced energy, the stasis field deactivated. Sicarius touched the faceplate of his war-helm, his warrior's mask and the defining image of his rank. The golden *ultima* in the middle of the red-and-white crest still gleamed.

'The last assault was severe,' he continued, his fingers moving to the hilt of the sword and drawing it reverently. 'We almost did not prevail. I ask then, are we of one mind and purpose, we sons of Guilliman?'

Sicarius let a moment of silence stand, taking a few seconds to admire the blade before returning it to its sheath and re-engaging the stasis field. He turned to face his officers.

'The finest blade is nothing without a skilled and focused hand to wield it.'

'You are referring to Pillium,' said Helicos.

'I am referring to every Ultramarine on board this ship, Argo,' Sicarius replied, his stern gaze falling on both Space Marines. 'Retius, do you speak on this matter?'

Daceus cleared his throat. 'The arena is an attempt at promoting unity through martial contest.'

'Is that all?' Sicarius looked to Helicos, but the Primaris lieutenant allowed the sergeant to answer.

'They need to blow off steam, Cato. That is the truth of it.'

Helicos stiffened at Daceus' use of the captain's given name, the familiarity of it evidently uncomfortable for him.

'The Primaris Marines are blooded but they are still raw,' admitted Helicos, adapting to the informality of the exchange. 'The crusade had barely begun when they, we, were cast into this limbo.'

'It's not limbo, Argo, it's hell. We know that now, we've seen it and all its daemons.'

'Hell or not, captain, Dac– Retius is right. Prolonged inactivity, kept in a heightened state of readiness… It is wearing even for an Astartes. An outlet was needed.' He paused, choosing his next words carefully. 'Division between us was not intended.'

'And Pillium?' asked Sicarius, watching for any reaction from Daceus, who stoically gave none.

'Will be spoken to.'

'With respect, captain,' Daceus cut in, 'I would prefer he wasn't.'

Helicos raised an eyebrow by way of interrogative.

'Pillium craves glory. He is arrogant and vain, but he is also skilled and a devoted Ultramarine. His hunger is useful. It will serve. *He* will serve. Respect will come, either in the cage or fighting for our lives aboard this ship. Let it happen in its proper course.'

'I believe redress is needed, captain,' Helicos argued, visibly dismayed by Daceus' suggestion.

'I agree, Argo, but I also trust Retius' judgement,' said Sicarius. 'It has never served me ill.' He regarded Daceus. 'Humble him, sergeant. You or Gaius, I know he has a point to prove also. And in so doing, return our two brotherhoods to one.'

'You have my word, Cato.'

'I appreciate your word, but I want your deed.'

'Of course, captain.'

'Argo, are you satisfied with this? Speak honestly, because I have no time for the diplomacy of hierarchy.'

'We'll do it Retius' way for now.' Helicos turned to Daceus. 'I have not known you as long as our captain, but I trust and respect you.'

'And I you, Argo,' said Daceus.

Sicarius smiled, nodding. 'Courage and honour,' he said, and heard his words repeated back to him. 'I need Retius for a moment longer,' he added, 'but you are released to your duties, Argo.'

Helicos nodded, saluted both men and then departed.

'I apologise about the arena,' offered Daceus after the door had closed again. 'I had thought it a way for our two halves to bond.'

'It's dealt with, or at least it will be, yes?'

Daceus nodded, reminded of his promise.

'Brotherhood suits him well, don't you think?'

'I do, captain. They are all Guilliman's sons.'

'As are we.'

'As are we.'

Sicarius left a pause to regard Daceus' lingering injuries.

'Did you let him beat you?'

Daceus gave a rueful look. 'Would you believe me if I said I did?'

Laughter echoed around the room.

'We are an outdated design, Retius. That's what I believe.'

'You do not look it, Cato.'

'Well, you do, old man.'

Daceus gave a raucous bellow. 'Ha! I expect I do.'

'I can feel it, though,' said Sicarius, serious again, 'time gnawing at the edges. This place, this ship. It doesn't help.'

'You *led* them, Cato, descended from on high like a glorious and vengeful angel. I saw their faces, Pillium's and the others. It was *awe*. The kind of belief and loyalty you inspire cannot be gene-wrought or created in any Mechanicus laboratorium. It's innate.'

'And yet we still lost Ithro.'

'A bitter cost, but it could have been much worse. If we had lost the bridge or the warp engine, it would have been all hands. Ithro gave his life for us. He gave you enough time to save us all.'

'Why then does it not feel like a victory, Retius?'

'Because by most measures it is not, certainly not what we are used to. For now, victory is survival.'

'I won't lie, it is a weight upon me, this… *stasis*.'

'You want to be out in the crusade, by Guilliman's side.'

'I want to be by his side, yes. But it's more than that… All the campaigns we've fought. The battles we have won.'

'Your honours are long and glorious, Cato. They will not end here.'

Sicarius' face darkened and he turned to look into the shadows. 'I'm not concerned about that. Some battles leave a mark, even those we think we have left behind.'

'You mean Damnos.'

He scowled, angry at the memory and not Daceus. 'Of course I mean bloody Damnos.'

'You came close to death. I thought you *were* dead that first time.'

'I thought I had lost my edge, Retius,' he said. 'After I fell to *him*. I threw myself into the business of war with such abandon. Seems foolish now. I do not want recklessness as my legacy.'

'You are hard on yourself, Cato. After what you endured… No Apothecary can heal a wound like that. Not truly. It sticks with you, like a brand under the skin, fused to the bone.' Daceus' eyes narrowed.

Sicarius caught the look and knew the sergeant had realised what he drove at.

'Several of the crew have reported seeing visions. Our brothers, too. Venatio and what remains of the mortal medicae is keeping a close watch.' Daceus tapped his one good eye. 'As am I. The warp… it has a way of *twisting* things, memories and half-truths.'

'It's important to remain vigilant,' said Sicarius, meeting the veteran's gaze again.

'I agree, Cato.'

'Thank you, Retius.'

'For what?'

'Your counsel and your brotherhood.'

'I could withhold neither even if I wished to,' Daceus replied. 'Do you need me for anything further, captain?'

'No, that's all. I appreciate the indulgent ear.'

Daceus made to leave. 'Just don't ask me for an eye. I have few to spare.'

Sicarius gave a rueful snort. 'Can Haephestus do nothing for it?'

'It is fine as it is. The occulobe compensates for the lack of depth perception.'

'I see. Well, just be sure to give fair warning when we're next in a firefight,' Sicarius replied with the suggestion of a smile. 'I don't want you shooting me by mistake.'

'That's low.'

'Your aim, you mean?'

'I shall take my leave now.'

Sicarius smiled. 'This crisis, Retius...'

'Yes, my captain?'

'I would have no other by my side during it.'

Daceus nodded. 'Cato...' he said, just as he was about to leave, 'you are not suffering, are you? Seeing visions of the past? You banished it. With a vortex grenade, no less.'

'I am fine, brother. Go to your duties and have no concern for me.'

Reassured, Daceus took his leave.

The lights dimmed as soon as he had gone and Sicarius strayed again to the darkness at the edges of his quarters and the silver-faced skeletal creature that waited there, its emerald eyes aglow.

'What are you looking at?'

CHAPTER EIGHT

THE RECLUSIAM

Sicarius left his former quarters a short while later. He had donned a gilt-edged red cloak and light carapace breastplate over his training fatigues. Due to the energy bleed, he had to conserve his use of his power armour, like many of his fellow Ultramarines. Its reactor was charging, part of the measures Haephestus had put in place to keep the warriors functioning.

The corridors of the ship were quiet, most of the crew on night cycle sleep rotations or attending to their duties elsewhere. Given the ship was becalmed, there was little value in him being on the bridge so he walked, keeping off the main arterials and finding a measure of solace in the less-travelled transitways. Those crew he did encounter saluted as they saw him, some even bowed or went to one knee. Sicarius acknowledged them all, from the patrolling battle-brother to the lowly maintenance serfs. He knew it was important they see him, their figurehead, the one they still looked to for salvation. He had revelled in this once, the renown, the adulation. He had once sought to turn honour and glory into advancement. Sicarius yearned for it, to pridefully hold aloft all the gilded laurels he could fix to his banner. But he had changed. The war had changed him. Damnos had been his crucible. Fighting against the necrons that first time. A machine race that fought without fear or restraint. Who never got tired or thirsty or hungry. Their metal bodies were as hard as ceramite and could self-repair, making them able to recover from the most grievous injury. Fighting an enemy like that... it had nearly killed him. He had survived, even triumphed, but it had taken something from him, something Sicarius had left behind in the ice.

And now he had this burden, a ship and its thousands-strong crew his responsibility. Daceus might not see it, or the years of their friendship might have made his eyes kinder than they should be, but Sicarius felt a wearing of the thread. He should rejoice. He did. The primarch had risen, a son of the Emperor, an actual *scion* ten thousand years old, and he had brought with him a stronger Ultramarine. Primaris Marines. Strength when the Imperium needed it the most. But, partly hollowed already by his worst experiences, Sicarius had seen what many of his kind had seen – replacement. Obsolescence.

He had spoken to his Lord Calgar of it, the old master of the Ultramarines, dwarfed now by the shadow of their long-forsaken father, returned from the edge of the grave.

Calgar had said little.

'It is the end and the beginning, Cato.'

Anger, defiance, a desperate scramble to cling to meaning. Sicarius could have understood any of that. But acceptance? It was as if they had been defeated by an enemy they didn't know they were fighting.

He needed to purge himself of these dark thoughts, and knew in part it was the warp trying to have its way. Like the metal overlord that haunted the edges of his sight, its cold eyes burning balefire green, it was a falsehood, a manifestation, but one rooted in some small piece of truth.

A voice intruded on his thoughts, but Sicarius had already heard its owner's soft approach and did not react.

'You should not walk these corridors on your own,' said Gaius Prabian gruffly.

'I hoped you'd leave me alone.'

'I am still company champion,' he said, coming in alongside Sicarius to walk in lockstep with his captain. 'It is my duty to watch your side, especially when you are unarmoured.'

'So are you,' Sicarius replied, frowning.

Prabian wore fatigues and light training armour like Sicarius, but he also had a small combat shield strapped to his left arm and wore a sheathed gladius at his left hip. A soft blue cloak with a silver trim swished in his wake.

'I am not unprotected,' he said. His dark eyes flashed as he faced forwards, as proud and regal as any of the Lions. They were a stark contrast to the scrub of white hair sticking up out of his scalp like a nest of spines. It was cut short, but was thick and hard like wire. A scar ran from the right side of his jaw, tracing a ragged fissure in his tough skin that stopped just short of his eye.

Sicarius parted the left side of his cloak, revealing the sheathed Tempest Blade he wore there.

'Neither am I, but what do you think I have to fear amongst these corridors, Gaius?'

'Nothing,' said Prabian. 'We know no fear, captain. Isn't that right? But there is still danger on board this ship.'

'It has been purged extensively.'

'Do you wonder,' said Gaius, 'how they managed to get so many aboard so quickly?'

'This is the warp, we are severely outnumbered. My only wonder is why there were not more.'

'Perhaps...' Prabian replied, his eyes on the middle distance, but Sicarius thought them farther away than that.

'I value this time alone, Gaius,' said Sicarius after a moment's silence.

'Pretend I am not here. I could drop back,' he said, giving his captain a furtive side glance, 'a few steps. It would be as if you were alone.'

'Not really the point, brother.'

'It is still my duty,' answered Prabian, resuming his forward-looking vigil.

Sicarius sighed, knowing it was pointless to argue. 'A few steps back then,' he conceded.

Prabian nodded. 'I shall be as silent as your shadow, captain,' he said, and fell back.

Only when they had reached where Sicarius was going did Prabian come to a halt.

'I'll await your return,' he said, straightening up into a guard stance, his back against the wall, his eyes on the gloomy corridor ahead.

Sicarius did not have the heart to argue. He nodded. The door to the chamber before him parted, expelling the aroma of incense and votive candles. A lambent, flickering aura beckoned and he followed it inside.

Sicarius might not have the solitude of his quarters to retreat to any more, but he still had the Reclusiam and she would still listen, as she listened to any who came to her adopted chambers.

'Is that you, Cato?' inquired a voice from the deeper darkness within.

'Madame Vedaeh…' he said, passing through a small entryway and into the modest chapel beyond.

There were books here amongst the religious iconography, and Vedaeh had brought in two large leather chairs and a stubby table with an arched sodium lamp to one side. A shrine occupied an antechamber at the back of the room, a stone rendering of the Imperial eagle with the symbol of the ultima in the middle, sat upon a circular dais. Votive candles were set around it, their long trails of wax like frozen yellow tears. The heat fluttered the edges of purity seals affixed to the shrine. A shallow basin in front of it held a black war-helm, an ornate mace laid before it and a talisman with its gold chain curled around it. These were the trappings of Trajan, the previous incumbent of the Reclusiam. One of the helm's eyepieces had a fierce crack down the middle and part of the crystalflex that made up the retinal lens was missing. This was the wound that had killed him.

'Blade or bullet,' said Sicarius, his gaze lingering on the helm as if it were a gravestone. He had barely realised he had crossed the room to stand before the shrine. 'We still do not know. Venatio has been unable to identity the provenance of the wound. He was simply gone.'

Vedaeh came alongside him. She was comically shorter than the captain, and ludicrously slighter across the shoulders and body. She walked with a cane, but was not particularly old by mortal standards. Her blonde hair was cropped short in the style of the schola progenium and parted down the middle to reveal the eagle tattoo inked upon her forehead. She favoured a little armour, a golden shoulder guard engraved with the icon of the Emperor upon His Throne and a ceremonial breastplate, underneath which she wore a loose-fitting surplice of green velvet.

'You tell me that story every time we meet here,' she said.

'Because it bothers me. For a warrior like Trajan to fall so ignominiously with no story to mark his passing.'

'And that is a warrior's greatest fear, isn't it?' said Vedaeh. 'To perish unremarked, to die an ordinary death. To be forgotten.'

Sicarius looked down at her, his face stern at first but then softening.

'Can we sit?' she asked, grimacing. 'I find I can't stand for long before the bloody thing starts aching.'

Sicarius regarded her leg, as if seeing it for the first time, and then apologised as he gently took Vedaeh's arm and led her to the chair. He took the one opposite and they stared at one another for a few moments before Vedaeh spoke.

'I am glad I can occupy this place,' she told him. 'That the Ultramarines have allowed me to. It's important to observe remembrance, to have a place to talk. Trajan offered that too, as well as his warrior's sword, did he not?'

'He did, though your methods are very different to his.'

'They have to be. I cannot seek to empathise with the fraternal experience of the Adeptus Astartes. I have no point of reference.'

She leaned over to light another candle and the surplice slipped enough to reveal the augmetic she had in place of her left arm.

'Ceramic casing,' she said, when she saw Sicarius looking.

'Sorry, I didn't mean to stare.'

'It's alright. I am fortunate,' she added, 'it's a thing of beauty.' It was bone white, and the servos built under the outer casing quiet enough that they were almost silent. Gold filigree caught the candlelight, describing lines of holy scripture and ornate detailing in reds and greens reminiscent of an illustrated manuscript.

'And strong too, I imagine,' said Sicarius.

Vedaeh flexed her bionic fingers for show. 'It helps when I'm reaching for books.'

His attention turned to the many volumes stacked around the main part of the room.

'Have you read them all?' Sicarius asked.

'Several times. Histories of ancient Terra, its cultures and nascent civilisations.' She ran her fingers down the leather spine of a book, her expression wistful. 'Do you know what they say about recorded history, Cato?'

Sicarius bid her go on.

'It's how we avoid repeating the mistakes of the past,' said Vedaeh. 'Do you think our ancient historians would believe their work wasted if they saw what had become of us now?'

Sicarius arched an eyebrow. 'You think mankind has repeated its mistakes?'

Vedaeh gave a sad smile. 'I think we survive any way we can. Our repeated mistakes are immaterial in the face of perpetuating our species. It has become so... complex.'

'You long for simpler times then?'

'Perhaps. More peaceful times, certainly.'

'It is simple for me.'

Vedaeh turned from her books then and the candlelight caught the edges of her features, her eyes glinting and abruptly serious.

'Is it, Cato? Do you truly think that?'

'I am a Space Marine, my purpose is gene-wrought into my very bones. I can no more deny it than oppose the fact that night follows day.'

'And is that all that you are?'

Sicarius frowned. 'I don't understand.'

'Why are you here, Cato?'

'For some peace. I find your company... calming. It soothes my mind. And there is the chronicle to consider.'

'And is it in turmoil then, your mind, when you step from this sanctuary and re-enter the ship and take up the mantle of captain?'

'It is... not as free,' he admitted, struggling to find the right words. 'There are burdens, matters I must consider. Many rely upon me to–'

'Save them,' Vedaeh finished for him. 'Is that what you were going to say?'

'Yes.'

'And a part of you worries that you cannot. That you have already failed in this.'

'Yes.'

'That you and your fellow warriors will die here, unremarked and unremembered, just like Brother-Chaplain Trajan.'

'I do, yes.'

'Do you have faith, Cato?'

'Not your kind of faith, but yes.'

Her eyes narrowed as if seeing more than her mortal perception could reveal. 'I believe you. Cato, you are the greatest warrior and leader aboard this ship. I have seen living saints command less devotion than you do. It's not a fear of failure that has you reliving the past, nor is it the fear that you won't be able to lead us out of the warp, it's that you will and you'll still be unremarked and unremembered. You think you have seen the end, and it wears a familiar face.'

'Damnos is in the past...'

Vedaeh scowled, the irritated teacher in her coming to the fore. 'I'm not talking about the soulless creatures you fought on that world, I mean your fellow sons of Guilliman.'

Sicarius opened his mouth to protest but found the words would not come. He closed it after a few seconds, turning his face from her, and adopted a brooding posture, smoothing his beard.

'Repeating the mistakes of the past,' he said at length. 'Is that what we're doing?'

'No,' said Vedaeh. 'We are surviving.'

Sicarius looked at her askance from across the table. 'Any way we can.'

Vedaeh nodded. 'Any way we can.'

She reached for a journal. It was leatherbound, and the same blue as Sicarius' power armour. As she leafed through the vellum, it fell open at a blank page and she asked, 'Shall we continue then?'

CHAPTER NINE

QUARANTINED

Olvo Sharna stood before the sealed door of deck thirteen. It was a colossal thing of dense grey metal and pistons, and she gazed up at it like a stranger at a fortress gate seeking refuge. Except, there was no refuge beyond the gate, and its purpose was to keep people in not out.

'How long have they been in there?' asked the armoured Ultramarine standing next to her.

He was a sergeant. Pillium, if she remembered rightly. Sharna had little to do with the Space Marines. As quartermaster, strictly speaking she was part of the Departmento Munitorum and responsible for the mortal crew aboard ship. That included equipment and weapons, and also rations, which were of chief concern during the current crisis. The Adeptus Astartes dealt with such matters internally. To be up-close to one was rare. She could count the instances of it on one hand, and that included the recent conference with Captain Sicarius. This one was different to most of the others she had met. More like Lord Helicos. A new breed, an evolution. Better at killing, she supposed. The Adeptus Astartes were conditioned to channel their emotions and keep them in check until they could be useful. This one, however, radiated irritation. She wondered if he considered this particular duty beneath him, or perhaps he considered it a form of punishment.

'Twenty-three weeks,' Sharna replied, her nose prickling at the heat stink of Pillium's armour and the heady aroma of the lacquers and lapping powder he must apply to each plate as well as his weapons. One thing she did know about Space Marines, they were fastidious when it came to their equipment.

'They are fed?' he asked.

'Of course,' she said, instantly regretting the tone of her voice, which suggested the question was not a sound one, and the answer to it therefore obvious. 'We also maintain regular contact,' she added quickly, hoping to cover her mistake. Even without the helmet, she found Pillium unreadable. He had a fierce appearance, shaven-headed with a dark growth of beard concealing the lower half of his face. He appeared youthful, which was unusual for one of his kind, who in her limited experience were usually crag-faced, scarred and grizzled, but he had hard eyes. He looked uncompromising, she decided, and seemed oblivious to the fact that she had probably just insulted his intelligence. The other one, the one who waited a little way back in the shadows, had the rough, resolute features she had come to expect, but he wasn't talking at present.

'Whom do you speak to?' asked Pillium. His eyes never left the door, as if all of his attention were focused on this one spot because it was the most likely place that danger would appear.

'Major Roan.'

'He is a punctual man, this Roan?'

'Every week, by the hour, by the minute. He's never missed a scheduled supply drop.'

'Until now,' said Pillium pointedly.

'Until now.'

'How many?'

'Almost a hundred men, a full platoon.'

'Any reported casualties?'

'Not that I am aware of.'

'And the reason for the quarantine order?'

'Self-imposed by the commanding officer. Spates of mania, catatonic behaviour, some psychosis, though to be honest it's not really my field. They were involved in the lower deck incursion a few weeks ago.'

Up until the most recent attack on the ship, the lower deck incursion had been the single worst and most penetrative assault the *Emperor's Will* had suffered. Hundreds had lost their lives and several important shipboard systems had been destroyed. Roan's men had fought in the engagement, albeit peripherally, and the trauma of it had inflicted psychological damage. Roan had simply done what any good officer would have done, made a hard choice and quarantined his platoon.

'Have any tried to get out?' asked Pillium.

'Not recently, though no one is getting through this door without industrial-grade plasma cutters and even then that's the work of hours, not minutes. We'd know if they had tried.'

'How so?' asked Pillium.

'I beg your pardon, my lord?'

'This deck has suffered power outages. Visual surveillance has been dark for weeks. How would you know if they had tried to escape or not?'

'I... well, I don't suppose...' Sharna was sweating, and nervously glancing up at the monstrous Astartes, who stared coolly. 'The door has not been tampered with, so I think we can assume–'

'Then you *assume* they have not tried to escape.'

Sharna swallowed loudly. 'Yes, of course. That's it. Confinement was for their own safety,' she added. 'There's no contagion here.'

'It's a disease of the mind, quartermaster. I expected not.'

'Ideas can be contagious...'

Pillium turned his hard gaze in Sharna's direction as if weighing the meaning of her words. She froze, imagining the ice creeping up her spine to be literal.

He turned away, allowing her to breathe again, and murmured something into his vox that Sharna didn't catch before declaring, 'Open the gate.'

His brethren took a step forwards at the same time and she could feel the tension ratchet up by several degrees. The fear instinct in her brain kicked in, that animal imperative that results in either fight or flight. Sharna doubted she was suited to either, and was glad of the small bodyguard of armsmen she had been afforded. It wasn't that she didn't trust the Ultramarines, she just didn't know or understand them. Certainly, ten armed and armoured Adeptus Astartes would prove a more effective deterrent than a hundred armsmen, but she felt comfort in the presence of her own kind, even if there were only five of them in carapace and flak-vests.

Sharna nodded and went to input the access codes that would unlock the gate. She caught the faintest whirr of movement, the micro-tremors of power-armoured servos tensing for immediate and explosive activation.

'Secutius,' she heard Pillium say into the vox, just loud

enough for Sharna to make out the name of the other sergeant.

The second five-man squad of Ultramarines in the background moved up to support the first. They occupied a slightly refused position as Pillium and his squad took point. She assumed Secutius' squad were there for her protection.

The gate took a few seconds to move, and even then the motion was slow. Pneumatic pressure hissed and ghosted in the air as it was expelled. The reek of stagnation and other less salubrious aromas came with it as the atmosphere of the sealed deck spilled out. Supplies had previously been delivered through maintenance hatches and via tracked servitor units. A recently revived pict screen that provided a view into the deck showed a grainy, black-and-white threshold and the supply crate unclaimed and untouched.

As the gate rolled aside, its pneumatic locks now fully disengaged, that self-same supply crate was revealed in full colour and clarity. Dingy lighting flickered over the scene, kept that way so as not to aggravate the warp sickness that had befallen the entirety of Major Roan's regiment, the 45th Mordian. Sepulchral as the vista and overall atmosphere appeared, Sharna felt an instant prickling of apprehension at the revealed stillness. A weird, crepuscular quality had settled over the deck, the air musty and softened by a sweaty fog.

Poised at the threshold, Pillium listened. Sharna could hear nothing beyond the usual settling of metal and the groaning shift of the deck itself. She assumed the Adeptus Astartes had greater aural acuity and that when Pillium ordered the advance that he had discerned nothing untoward.

As they walked slowly beyond the threshold, Sharna reflected on how the presence of the Ultramarines had quelled discontent in the lower decks almost immediately. Order had been restored, and with it proper function. It came as no surprise to her that this was accomplished through fear and the salient reminder that all must do their duty and make the appropriate sacrifice if anyone was to survive. How that situation could be maintained in the absence of the Space Marines she did not know, but she chose to focus on the present. Let such problems be consigned to the uncertain future.

'Seal the gate, quartermaster,' said Pillium once they were all inside.

'I beg your pardon, sire?'

'No one gets in or out without my sanction,' he said firmly, and Sharna had wit enough to obey without further question. Though the thought of being locked in here terrified her, even with all of her bodyguards.

She re-engaged the locks and watched as the heavy portal rolled back into position, sealing with a dolorous clang.

CHAPTER TEN

EYE

Sergeant Ludik hurried down the main arterial. He bypassed the barracks where the off-shift armsmen were taking advantage of a forty-five-minute sleep rotation and carried right on in the direction of the lieutenant's personal quarters.

A few feet from the turn where Reda's corridor was situated, Ludik saw another armsman coming his way. At first, in the low and sporadic light, he thought it was the lieutenant, securing her belt, adjusting her breastplate and helmet. He was about to call out when he recognised Trooper Gerrant. Ludik frowned as the two men met each other going in opposite directions.

'I thought you were on sleep rotation, trooper?' he asked.

'I am, sergeant,' Gerrant replied. 'Couldn't settle, warp insomnia, so I went for a walk.'

'Did it work?'

Gerrant yawned. 'I hope so.' He went on his way.

'Rotation is almost over,' called Ludik.

'I'd best sleep fast then.'

Confused, Ludik shrugged and carried on until he reached Reda's door. He knocked twice, hard with the side of his fist.

He heard a voice from the other side – nothing distinct, just assorted murmurings – and then Lieutenant Reda opened the door. 'Forget something…?'

Ludik swallowed hard. He had never heard the lieutenant speak in this way. She almost sounded *playful*. She also looked a little dishevelled, her hair slightly wild and her shirt and fatigues loose.

'Shit! Ludik, it's you. What the hell is it, sergeant?'

'I'm sorry, lieutenant. I did not wish to disturb you, I realise you are still healing and–'

'Throne! Out with it, sergeant. Why are you here?'

'There has been an incident.'

'What?' She scowled. 'What kind of incident?'

'The sanctum. Navigator Barthus. A squad went in to… ah, *retrieve* him. After what happened to Lord Arkaedron, he's needed.'

Reda's expression darkened, grew haunted. 'I know what happened to Arkaedron, I was bloody well there.'

'And so you understand then, lieutenant. The Navigator…'

'Yes, I understand,' she said, her irritation returning. 'What I don't understand is why you're standing at my door?'

'I have lost contact with the squad.'

'And what do you want me to do about it? Where's Kraef?'

Ludik paled a little. 'The colonel went in after Elam's squad. I haven't heard back from him either.'

Reda frowned, the gravity of what Ludik was saying starting to settle. 'Nothing?'

'Just vox static.'

'Could be interference? The sanctum is psy-warded.'

'I considered that, but no. The signal is live, there is simply no response. Either they won't answer or they can't.'

Reda paused, seemingly weighing up a decision.

'Shit,' she muttered under her breath, reaching for her gear.

'Should I alert the Adeptus Astartes?' Ludik offered.

'Absolutely not,' she answered from behind the door. When she reappeared, she had fully dressed and was pulling on her flakweave vest. She'd already clipped on her belt, the power maul deactivated on its tether. 'I don't want them thinking we can't handle our own business. We can deal with this,' Reda added, slinging her combat shotgun on its strap over her shoulder and grabbing up her helmet and carapace breast-plate. 'It's probably an equipment malfunction or power outage. Entire ship is susceptible.'

'Of course, lieutenant.'

'Good. Now,' said Reda, struggling with the breastplate. 'Help me get this damn thing on, and then I want you and four others with me.'

'I saw Trooper Gerrant just now in the corridor,' offered Ludik, tightening up Reda's armour straps as she adjusted the fit.

'Fine,' she said, not missing a beat, 'him and three others. Let's move.'

The part of the ship that housed the sanctum was all but deserted. A few lone servitors walked the decks, but other than that not a soul stirred in the gloomy, echoing depths. The ceiling lamps flickered constantly, an irritating insect buzz grating at the senses before a plink of deactivation and then cooling silence. A second later and the lights flared again, bright and angry.

The sharp report of the armsmen's footfalls resonated

loudly, the sound magnified by a stark sense of isolation. A wall-mounted vox-caster crackled out static. Occasionally the hiss and fizz of dead air coalesced into half-heard words and phrases. Just another gift of the warp and another reason, if they really needed one, to fetch Barthus and get him back to his station on the bridge.

After the repairs and the inevitable purges at the points where the ship had fallen under assault, the *Emperor's Will* had been becalmed for weeks. The crew had suffered. Violent outbreaks and paranoid episodes had worsened. Most of that time Reda had spent unconscious or recovering from her wounds, but she had heard stories. More scars had been stitched into her body. They itched like false flesh. The mental wounds went deeper still, her nightmares often taking the form of a hulking warrior encased in spiked armour, or a sickle-mouthed vagrant dragging the chains of his damnation behind him.

'Does it feel cold to you?' asked Reda. 'It feels cold.' She neglected to mention the figure in military dress she saw ahead, his face masked by the shadows. He never came with sleep. He only visited her during her waking hours, with the sort of frequency that Reda could not put down to fatigue or a trick of the light.

Ludik nodded, and blew out a plume of white vapour. He rubbed his hands together for warmth.

'It's usually hotter than this. The vents from the enginarium feed into this section.'

'Was it like this before?' Reda asked, exchanging a brief glance with Gerrant. He had three other troopers with him, Orrin, Pasco and Careda.

'Not like this,' Ludik replied. 'I thought it might be a power outage. Something related to the heat exchangers?'

'Those furnaces keep burning in the event of a power outage,' Reda countered. 'They don't just go out if there's a turbine malfunction. And on a ship this size? That amount of heat? You're talking years.'

'Sanctum up ahead,' Gerrant cut in, an autocarbine braced across his body.

'Is this a combat situation, lieutenant?' asked Pasco, an overly firm quality to her voice.

'I don't know what it is yet,' Reda confessed. 'The only weapons in the sanctum are whatever Kraef and his men took in with them. Even so, keep that flamer handy.'

'Are we planning on burning out the Navigator?' asked Gerrant.

'I hope not,' said Reda as they reached the sealed door to the sanctum, 'but I'm not rejecting anything at this point.'

The lights were out, so the armsmen turned on the lamp packs attached to their weapons. Six grainy beams of pale light stabbed into the darkness of the sanctum and hovered in mid-air.

'Keep it steady,' Reda said, quietly but firmly, when she noticed Orrin's lamp beam shaking erratically.

'Sorry, lieutenant,' he replied, 'it's freezing in here.'

Reda couldn't argue with that. She traced her gloved fingers down the wall and left four mushy streaks in the glittering frost. 'Could be a heating malfunction,' she murmured, examining the white powder on her fingertips.

'They could be anywhere in here,' said Gerrant.

'Sanctum's not that large,' Reda countered.

'Feels pretty large about now.'

'I didn't think you were scared of the dark, Gerrant.'

'I'm not. I'm scared of what's in it,' he said. 'I'm just saying, lieutenant, Kraef, Elam and the others came in here and they haven't come out, so where are they?'

Reda listened, thinking.

They had stalled about twenty feet beyond the threshold, loitering in a loose defensive formation, guns trained on the shadows. A corridor led into a vaulted atrium, which in turn led to the rest of the sanctum. This was the Navigator's domain, his expansive quarters aboard ship when he wasn't performing his duties.

'I heard he went insane,' whispered Orrin, as if to speak of it aloud was taboo or would turn the rumour into fact.

'He saw something he shouldn't have. It took a toll,' said Careda.

'You know or you heard?' asked Pasco.

'Shut up,' snapped Gerrant.

'But–' Pasco began to protest.

Ludik turned and glared at her.

'He said shut up, trooper. It's good advice. Take it.'

Reda agreed, silently impressed with Ludik's reading of the situation.

A slow, metronomic drip-drip could be made out farther into the sanctum. Reda considered it might be the condensing effect of the heat exchangers trying to kick in and melting some of the ice.

'Ludik, try the vox again.'

A sudden burst of static almost made her drop her shotgun and she glared knives at Ludik who raised a hand contritely.

'Just static,' he said, the hiss of the receiver proof of his words.

'The signal is getting through though?'

'Yes, lieutenant.'

'Then say something.'

Ludik did. He stated his name and rank, then requested confirmation of message received. His voice echoed from somewhere deeper in the cold darkness.

'Follow it,' said Reda, and Gerrant led them out. 'Pasco, take the flank and keep that burner lit. Ludik, repeat the message every ten seconds so we can pinpoint the source.'

They got moving again, treading carefully but with more confidence now they had a plan.

That confidence evaporated as soon as they found Colonel Kraef.

A lamp beam strafed across him slumped against the wall. He had come to rest in a large chamber, part of the outer sanctum, sat on his backside with his booted feet sticking out.

Orrin nearly tripped over them and swore.

'Get a light on him,' snapped Reda, slinging her shotgun over her shoulder and sinking down next to her commanding officer.

Careda's beam alighted on Kraef's face. He cursed as soon as he saw what had become of it.

'Throne...' hissed Pasco.

Kraef had taken his own eyes. A bloodstained combat knife lay within reach, his arms by his sides. He had taken off his patrol cap, which sat in his lap.

'Is he alive?' asked Pasco.

'His lips are moving,' noted Gerrant.

'What's he saying?' asked Pasco.

Reda leaned in, suddenly aware that her breathing and heart rate had increased. Ghostly white clouds were spilling from her mouth.

She got as close as she dared, feeling the gentle touch of Kraef's breath against her cheek as she listened.

She frowned. 'Eye...'

'What?' asked Gerrant.

'He's just saying "eye", over and over.' She leaned back, tried to look at Kraef's mutilated face. Ludik's fear breathing was sawing through the vox-unit attached to Kraef's breastplate. 'Shitting hell, Ludik,' Reda snapped, glancing over her shoulder.

Ludik turned off the receiver, muttering an apology.

Reda returned her attention to Kraef.

'Sir,' she began. 'Can you hear me, sir? It's Lieutenant Reda.' Kraef didn't respond.

'Sir, it's Arna. Colonel, what happened to you?'

Still nothing.

Pasco's flamer rumbled dulcetly but provided no comfort.

'He's catatonic,' she said. 'What could have made him like that?'

Reda got to her feet. 'Careda, Orrin, get the colonel out of here.'

'Lieutenant...' Orrin began.

'Just obey the order, trooper.'

'No, lieutenant. It's...' Orrin was facing the way they had come. 'It's Barthus.'

Orrin's lamp beam fell on a huddled figure in dirty green robes.

'Oh, shit...' hissed Pasco, bringing up her flamer.

Gerrant muttered something to her and she backed down.

'Navigator...' Reda ventured, lowering her weapon, her off-hand outstretched to show she meant him no harm. 'I need you to come with us.'

Barthus didn't move.

Reda had never before met him in person. Barthus was a solitary creature and kept to himself. She knew little of his kind, save that Navigators were mutants and incredibly highly valued by the Imperium. But this was him, she had no doubt. In the lumens she made out a hooded cloak, its edges threaded with gold and fashioned into the sigil of House Barthus. Ornate chains rattled around his neck. His back was arched awkwardly, the Navigator bent over and practically on all fours. Gold hung from his ears in thick hoops and a chain looped from left ear to nostril. Long fingers festooned with glittering gemstone rings ended in sharpened, golden nail caps that tapped against the ground in a manic tattoo.

'Why is he hunched over like that?' asked Orrin. 'Is he injured?'

'Barthus, do you know what happened to Colonel Kraef?' asked Reda, ignoring him.

The Navigator jerked abruptly. His sudden weeping put the fear of the warp in Reda, who realised she might have made a mistake in drawing his attention to the stricken officer. 'Back...' she whispered to Gerrant and the others.

'What's wrong with him?' said Pasco, her flamer back on high alert.

'Just back up,' hissed Reda. 'Give him some space.'

Barthus shuffled forwards, clicking fingers leading the way. His robes parted, revealing a pair of silver bionics glistening wetly in the light. His legs. Every step resulted in a sharp metallic *clink*. He appeared ungainly, as if walking on tiptoes, until Reda saw the bladed pinions he had in place of feet. Then something changed and his entire body began to unfold like a hinged bracket opening to its fullest extent. Long, reedy limbs hung down by his sides, gilded fingers loosely clicking together.

'You must see...' rasped the Navigator.

'Holy Throne,' said Ludik. He was already backing up, his

99

fear starting to override his sense of duty. 'Should we try
and stop him?'

Reda felt a tendril of unease worm into her gut as she
watched the whole transformation in slow motion. The lank
hair, the pale skin, the–

'Don't look at him!' She turned as she cried out, knowing it would already be too late. Pasco froze, petrified like
an old tree, a vein throbbing agitatedly in her forehead. She
slowly opened her mouth, like a screw had been turned loose
and the jaw allowed to fall slack, and then she died. Not in
blood or dismemberment, just died standing there, a look
of abject terror drawn horribly across her face.

Orrin convulsed, clawing at his eyes, raking out the squishy
sclera, his fingertips red as roses and wet and viscous as oil.
He sank to his knees, burbling something under his breath
and fell forwards. He started shaking, teeth smashing against
each other in his mouth as loud as clattering shields.

Careda was faster. He turned and was saved from madness but death touched him anyway, the plume of Pasco's
flamer igniting brightly in the darkness, triggered as she died,
a finger's rapid rigor mortis unleashing a tongue of fire that
bathed Careda utterly. He writhed, emitting a short-lived
scream before his lungs were overwhelmed by heat and his
mouth turned into a seared ruin. He collapsed like a body
suddenly without its skeleton and laid down, gently burning to death.

'Throne of shitting Terra!' Gerrant wailed, and the fact of
it terrified Reda more than any of the grim spectacles before
her. Gerrant had spine. It was forged of steel. It's why she
liked him. It's why they... To hear him so unmanned, it spoke
to a primordial fear she now unwittingly nurtured.

Eye, Kraef had said. The warp eye, that which Navigators

used to negotiate the empyrean sea. To look upon it was to court madness and death, or so the rumour held. As she grabbed Gerrant by the collar and ran, she knew the truth of that now and begged for ignorance. She ran and she heard Barthus running too, the bent-backed scuttling of an arachnid and not the natural gait of a man. Mercifully, the clacking refrain of his gold-and-silver claws receded.

She rounded a corner, making sure Gerrant got there too, put her back to the wall and breathed.

Careda was still burning. The crackle of fabric, the smell of hair and something like pig's fat in the air. She almost vomited.

'He killed them, Arna. He bloody well killed them all stone dead.'

Gerrant wasn't handling it well. Reda wondered privately if he'd caught a glimpse, a reflection of something perhaps? Did it work like that or was it more like the *medusae* of Terran mythic verse?

'We're alive,' she said. 'We're still alive.'

'Throne, Reda. He just turned that thing on them.' He took a long, shuddering breath and seemed to regain some lost composure.

'And then he fled,' she replied. 'I don't think he meant to kill them.'

'Three bloody corpses,' snapped Gerrant. 'I can still smell that poor bastard Careda and I don't honestly know which of them had the worst end.'

'They were bad deaths.'

'No shit.'

'Compose yourself, trooper.'

Gerrant scowled. 'Trooper?'

'You heard me. Get a damn grip.'

'If we stay here, he'll kill us.'

'He's lost his mind, Vanko,' said Reda. 'And we need him. The ship *needs* him. We have to–' She stopped suddenly as a thought occurred to her, and she looked out into the deeper darkness of the sanctum. 'Where the hell is Ludik?'

CHAPTER ELEVEN

REBELLION

The silos were burning and a thick, starchy smoke from their contents was starting to choke the air. It was furnace-hot down in the enginarium decks and the reek of all that slowly immolating protein grain only made the atmosphere more intolerable.

'How shall we handle this?' asked Iulus Fennion.

He had not drawn a weapon, but kept his left hand on the pommel of his chainsword in readiness. His right, a bionic along with the entire arm, twitched with the random firing of a servo. Haephestus had promised to look at it, but his slate was already full with figuring out the cause of the power bleed affecting the ship. Iulus had not complained, the occasional misfire of one of his metal digits an irritant and nothing more.

Standing beside him, Scipio Vorolanus trained his retinal lenses on the army in front of them.

'Delicately, brother.'

The emaciated labourers had stopped and gathered in a huge mob. Several work sections had broken with their designated tasks, the turbine grinders, the coolant haulers, the waste plasma gangs, and stood shoulder to shoulder, shouting at the thin shield wall of armsmen deployed to restore order.

The presence of the Ultramarines had immediately stalled whatever the mob had planned and a tense, unspoken ceasefire had settled upon both parties. On the one side, several hundred deckhands and on the other, approximately fifty armsmen and a few Adeptus Astartes.

'Well, at least they have stopped moving,' offered Iulus, earning a reproachful glance from his fellow sergeant.

A fragile no-man's-land of about fifty feet lay between the two groups, but it was patiently eroding like a cliff before a turbulent sea. Eventually the land would collapse and the water would swallow everything. Servitors stood amongst the horde or rested on their stalled track-beds, their bodies still quivering with vitality but otherwise unmoving and unblinking. Hulking stock-still effigies, their doctrina wafers had been removed, and with them their agency and work protocols. Akin to flesh and metal statues, they were rocks amidst a wasted human surf who had chosen the rationing yard to make their stand.

Scipio regarded the destruction. The caged defiles through which the labourers would be expected to line up to receive their protein grain or nutrient gruel had been torn down and the belt-conveyors that apportioned the food spiked and destroyed. Either side of a wide central aisle, plumes of thick mulch-smoke billowed up into the high ceiling to be captured by atmosphere vents. These were the silos, the immense grain stores used to feed an army. Smaller drums, roughly the same height as one of the servitors, sat on metal pallets waiting to refill the larger silos.

The Ultramarines had entered the ration yard from the upper decks. Discord had been minimal in those areas and now Scipio knew why. It was amassed here, almost in its entirety.

'How many do you think are in here?' he asked.

'North of eight hundred, I would estimate.'

Though the two sergeants had come together to discuss their plan, the rest of their men were spread out across this side of the chamber. Both Vorolanus and Fennion had left warriors behind in the decks above, either singularly or in pairs, to maintain order. Usually even one of the Adeptus Astartes was enough to remind men of their duty and dispel thoughts of discord. But here in the ration yard it was different.

'They are afraid of us,' said Scipio, noting the terrified faces that greeted the Ultramarines as soon as they had stepped into view. Recognition of the threat had spread like a bow wave through the masses, who physically and mentally took a backward step, clutching their improvised weapons a little tighter, huddling together a little closer. The herd had seen the predators at the edge of their domain and had decided to fight rather than be slaughtered.

'They were already afraid,' Iulus replied. 'We cannot raise our weapons against these people.'

'We may have no choice,' said Scipio, eyeing the slack-limbed bodies hanging from the gantries. Several of the dead were overseers, torn from their positions of strength and made to suffer. Others were workers, driven to madness and death. Or perhaps they had spoken out against rebellion and been strung up alongside the oppressors. Whether worker or overseer, they turned gently with the movement of the air, slowly putrefying in the heat.

'Prabian mentioned something that has me thinking,' said Iulus.

'A dangerous thing to do.'

Iulus gave a short bark of laughter. 'The cultists we fought,' he said. 'Their numbers. He thought they were excessive.'

'It felt excessive.'

Iulus snorted ruefully.

'You know what happens if we engage.'

'We are not negotiators, Scipio.'

'Nor are we butchers. You have fought closely with mortals before,' said Scipio, recalling the campaign on Damnos where Iulus had led the human conscripts he had dubbed the 'One Hundred'. 'How can we avoid bloodshed here?'

Iulus reached up to his neck and disengaged the brace connecting his helmet before removing it entirely. His nose wrinkled at the stench of the unwashed and the sudden prickling of heat. 'Let them see your face, brother,' he said, revealing granite-like features and a flat nose. He had pronounced scarring around his mouth and nose where he had once worn a rebreather. Believed to be a permanent addition to his face, Venatio's surgeries had freed him of the burden but left their mark all the same.

'I'll do better than that,' said Scipio, having weighed up the options and determining there were few that did not end in a massive death toll and a significant blow to the ship's ability to function. Warriors protected the ship, but without its labourers all they would be saving was a metal coffin.

He approached the sergeant of the armsmen, whose shield wall would be overwhelmed almost instantly if the rioters charged. The man saluted as soon as he saw the Ultramarine.

There was fear in his eyes, and that made him and the situation he was in dangerous.

'My lord,' he said with all due deference.

'What's your name, sergeant?'

'Bader, sire. Harpon Bader.'

Scipio gestured to the horde of labourers. 'Why are these serfs not at their stations?'

'I don't know, sire. A dispute with their overseers, all of whom are dead and so we cannot ask.'

'Have you asked them?'

Bader blinked once, incredulous. 'Whom, sire? The mob? That shield wall is the only thing preventing them rampaging through the rest of the ship. I dare not–'

'Noted,' said Scipio, choosing not to disabuse him of that falsehood. 'So you have no knowledge of their grievance?'

'Their grievance, sire? I don't understand. They are serfs...'

'They are afraid,' said Scipio, 'though not of you or I.'

'Sire?'

Bader looked like he wanted to break out the guns and have at the mob. It was a death sentence, he probably knew that, but the demeanour of the man implied he just wanted this to be over one way or the other. Dark circles around his eyes suggested a lack of proper rest, his slightly sunken cheeks a lack of decent nutrition, though what the armsmen were fed was of a higher standard than the nutrient gruel and protein grain supplied to the ship's labour gangs. A tremble in his voice, a slight breathlessness that was difficult to detect without Scipio's perceptive faculties, betrayed a mild warp sickness.

'Stand your men back,' he said.

'What? I mean, sire, if we–'

'Have them fall back ten feet. Do it now.'

NICK KYME

Bader was wise enough not to argue and gave the order. The shield wall parted, two men in the middle moving out and behind their comrades to allow a gap wide enough for a Space Marine.

Scipio could feel Iulus tense behind him. The other sergeant's voice came through his private vox.

'I'll wait here, shall I? I hope you know what you're doing, Scipio.'

'If this doesn't work then you're all that's between these serfs and the rest of the ship.'

'Then let's hope it works. I don't want the blood of Imperial citizens on my hands.'

'Nor I.'

Scipio stood his ground, reaching up to remove his battle helm as the wall of armsmen shrank away like the tide retreating from the shore. Iulus retreated with them. Scipio mag-clamped his helmet to his thigh. Curious eyes the colour of tanned leather looked out of a face younger than that of Iulus. Unlike his fellow sergeant, Scipio also still had a generous crop of dark brown hair, shaved back in the Ultramarian style. On account of his apparent youth, he suffered with good grace the gentle taunts of his veteran comrades, though he had fought in many campaigns and earned several battle honours. The bolt pistol he wore, which he now unholstered and laid reverently on the ground, was chased with gold filigree, its grip bound in red synth-leather. His other relic weapon was a power sword. It had been bequeathed to him by an old friend and the sight of it still brought grief to his heart. The edge was diamond-adamantium forged and it had a polished silver-plasteel casing embossed with the inverted horseshoe-shaped ultima. Scipio placed the power sword reverently next to his combat blade and alongside his sidearm, muttering a few words to their machine-spirits. Then he began to slowly walk forwards.

The baying of the mob grew louder with every step. A few brandished weapons, shaking them at the Ultramarine and jeering. Several others backed away like frightened cattle.

Ten feet away from the mob, Scipio stopped. His arms were by his sides, palms out to show they were empty. One man faced down a horde of hundreds. Scipio looked at them, undaunted. It was a small matter for one who had faced greenskin brutes and undying abominations.

'Who speaks for you?' he asked loudly.

CHAPTER TWELVE

THE HELL WE BRING WITH US

Ludik stopped running. He doubled over and was immediately sick. His heart thundered and he struggled to control his breathing. Plumes of white billowed from his mouth like steam from a ship's funnel. Hearing a sharp, metallic echo, Ludik brought up his gun. The stock trembled in the darkness. He smacked the lamp pack with the side of his hand, trying to coax it back into life, but realised it was smashed and no longer operable. He cursed, his voice reedy and tremulous, and took a few tentative steps. He had no idea where he was, though he knew the sanctum wasn't that big; in his panicked flight he had lost all bearings and dared not shout out for Reda or Gerrant for fear of rousing attention. Assuming they were still alive to hear him, of course.

Barthus had gone mad, that much was obvious. Exposure to the warp, isolation in his quarters, something had driven the poor bastard insane and now he was killing. Intellectually, Ludik abandoned the idea of trying to apprehend the Navigator.

That didn't matter now. Instead, he focused on trying to find the way out. He wanted to stay put, to wait for help, but help wasn't coming. He had to get himself out of this. They should have alerted the Adeptus Astartes, but it was too late for any of that now. Pragmatism was tamping down his fear, making it tolerable. Make a plan, focus on it, implement it. Ludik clung to this rope of sanity, suspended as he was above the abyss.

He went slowly, listening hard for any betrayal of movement. The echo he had heard a moment ago had ceased and he couldn't discern which direction it had come from. His teeth chattered so hard he tore a strip off his fatigues and jammed it between them to dampen the sound. It was so cold he had lost some feeling in his extremities, and had begun to worry about the lasting effects of exposure when he emerged into a large octagonal room.

Ludik froze upon the threshold. It was dark, but with what minuscule ambient light was available he could make out shapes. Harder and blacker outlines presented themselves. A sodium lamp flickered once. It was suspended above in the middle of the room and fixed to an ornate chandelier. In the half-second of light, Ludik determined the nature of the shapes. They all wore armsmen's uniforms.

'Elam...' he whispered, the rag keeping his teeth from chattering falling from his mouth.

'The eye will see...'

The voice, its sudden intrusion on the silence, made Ludik cry out. He shrank back, feeling the solidity of a wall behind him, and realised he had wandered into the chamber and no longer knew where the entrance was. He shuffled, side-stepping, one hand behind his back and guiding him along the wall, searching for a gap into which he could flee.

'The eye will see...' the voice said again, closer, stopping

Ludik dead as soon as he realised he was moving towards it. He began to shuffle in the opposite direction but started to hurry and got tangled up in something and fell hard. Hot spikes of pain drove into his knees and elbows. The lascarbine he had been clutching skittered away into a gulf of blackness. His fingers touched something curved and metallically cold but they were shaking so much that he couldn't grasp it, whatever it was, and it scraped away into nothing. Then he felt something else.

The lamp flickered, revealing frozen crystals of blood stuck to his gloves. Bodies ringed the perimeter, red tears streaming down their faces. The light died before he could find the way out. He crawled forwards on his hands and knees, desperate to distance himself from the dead as if their mortality were contagious.

'I have seen...' said the voice, and the sharp clicking of metal followed it as Barthus lowered himself down behind Ludik, who cowered on his knees, his hands contorted into claws and clutching at his fatigues.

'Please...' murmured Ludik, breath ghosting like thin wisps of smoke from a dying fire.

'You must see...'

Ludik felt the Navigator's breath on the back of his neck, and the undeniable sense of his arachnoid form arched over him.

He begged. 'I don't want to. Please...'

'It is coming. You must see...'

Ludik's eyes burned from the cold, from his partially frozen tears. He couldn't close them even if he wanted to.

'No...'

'From within...'

Ludik felt the bite of the Navigator's golden nails in his flesh. Barthus was strong, far stronger than him. He wanted to fight, but the terror had him, vice-like and unyielding.

'Please...'

'It is here,' hissed Barthus as the lamp flared brightly, revealing the ice panes surrounding the entire chamber, a many-faceted and mirrored labyrinth of frozen crystal.

Ludik saw his own horror reflected back at him. He saw the hunched Navigator looming over him. He saw thin lips parting to deliver their judgement.

'It is here...' Barthus repeated, 'the hell we bring with us.'

Ludik saw the eye... and screamed.

Reda stopped, eyes clamped shut but willing herself to go on.

'That was Ludik,' rasped Gerrant. He had his weapon up, casting its aim in every direction, searching for their terrifying quarry. The lamp pack was shaking.

'We can't kill him, Vanko.'

'Then how do you suggest we proceed? That was bloody Ludik. A death scream. You know it, I know it. The Navigator has murdered every poor bastard who's been sent in here to fetch him.'

Reda was thinking. Kraef might be as good as dead, but he was not a foolish man. He would have taken precautions, even if those measures had proven to not be enough.

'A visor,' she said, opening her eyes.

Gerrant frowned, still swinging his autocarbine around like a club.

'A blind, a shackle. For the eye. No chance that Kraef goes in here without one.'

'I didn't see anything like that when we found him,' said Gerrant.

Reda had searched him, cursorily but enough to know the colonel wasn't carrying any specialist equipment.

'So he must have dropped it.'

'Where?'

'Wherever that scream just came from.'

'Throne…' Gerrant was about to shake his head, but what other choice did they have? 'And if you're wrong?'

Reda didn't answer. She gave him a look, then reached out to gently touch his face. Gerrant's fear and anger abated, and he was about to touch her hand when the moment passed and she withdrew.

She turned her back on Gerrant to face the direction where she thought Ludik's scream had come from. 'When Barthus ran, he went to his refuge. That's where he is. That's where Ludik is. And the others.'

'And you want to walk in there?'

Reda tore a strip of cloth from her uniform, fashioning it into a blindfold.

'You're going to be my eyes, Vanko,' she said.

'He has claws too, you know,' she heard Gerrant say.

'I don't think he wants to kill us.'

'Really?' Gerrant sounded incredulous. 'And what gave you that idea?'

'He could have done it before when we found the colonel. Instead, he ran. He's afraid. I think he wants to show us something.'

'Yes, death from whatever warp terror drove him mad.'

'It's not that. He said, "you must see". See what? It's a warning. He's seen something, a portent from the warp.'

'How can you know that's true?'

Reda took off her helmet then tied the blindfold around her head like a bandana. Standing before her was a man in an old Militarum uniform, his face hidden by the darkness.

'It's just a feeling,' she said.

CHAPTER THIRTEEN

SPOILS

The mob gathered in the ration yard replied with fearful shouts and curses, though the volume lessened.

'I said, who speaks for you?' Scipio asked again, louder. His hands were still by his sides but he looked far from submissive.

The mob quietened, reduced to scattered murmurings. The noises of the ship became more prevalent. Footsteps could be heard, shuffling through the crowd.

Scipio waited.

A man emerged, a labour master judging by the metal rank stamp stapled into the flesh of his cheek. He had burn scarring on his face and blackened fingers from years working the plasma vents. Broad shoulders framed a short, stocky body. What little hair he still possessed was grey like ash, the stubble around his jaw a black gauze.

'I speak,' he declared in a strong, clear voice. His blue eyes were bright with intelligence, and Scipio wondered how such a man could have ended up in the bowels of a starship performing such a miserable task.

'You lead this rebellion?' asked Scipio as he and the man came face-to-face.

'I am not afraid to die, Space Marine,' he said. 'Slay me and another will just take my place. You can't kill all of us.'

Scipio touched the winged skull icon upon his chest. 'This sigil means I am a servant of mankind. I do not kill loyal Imperial citizens. My oaths given as an Ultramarine prevent it, as does my honour.'

The man made the sign of the aquila, though his hands trembled as he did so. Scipio knew he must be terrified. Whatever bravura he had managed to muster at first was already spent.

'Who are you?'

'S-sire?'

'Your name. I am Vorolanus.'

'Oben, sire.'

'And that is the name of your house, your tribe?'

'I have none. I am void-born, and have no house, no tribe.'

'You have Ultramar, you have Macragge. *That* is your tribe.' He tapped his chest. '*My* tribe. Do you see, Oben of Ultramar?'

The man nodded.

Scipio's eyes narrowed. He gestured to the hanging corpses. 'Did you kill these men?'

'Some, yes we did.'

'And the silos... you set them on fire?'

The labour master nodded.

'You burned your rations and you killed your masters. How am I to judge this, Oben?'

'We cannot eat it. We told them, but they would not listen. It is filth, sire.'

118

Someone stirred in the rear ranks of the mob, hidden by the shadows and the masses.

Scipio assumed it was more nervous shuffling. 'It is all the ship can provide. In this you serve the Emperor.'

A few muttered the words *Ave Imperator* at that remark.

'Aye,' Oben replied, 'and yet we will not eat it.'

'By Guilliman's mercy, why not?'

Iulus' voice came through the private vox. 'Scipio...'

Something was happening farther back in the crowd, a ripple of movement coming towards him.

'They would be fools to try anything,' he murmured back to Iulus.

'It is unfit,' declared Oben, seemingly unaware of the other conversation happening at the same time.

Scipio was only half-listening now, part of his attention on the mob.

'They are certainly desperate enough to be foolish,' Iulus replied.

The shouting returned, a few voices in isolation at first but growing as fear took a firmer hold.

'We cannot let this turn to bloodshed, brother,' said Scipio.

'Those who ate the rations grew sick and then the sickness spread,' Oben continued, finding his courage again. 'There was panic and the overseers thought to quell it with lash and cudgel. Some died, torn apart by those who had sickened. Others climbed to the rafters above and tied belts around their necks.'

The crowd parted to admit a metal ration drum, hauled by a pair of burly deckhands. It was upended, the contents poured in front of Scipio. It looked like grain. He didn't see anything untoward at first. Iulus was speaking into his ear.

'Something is wrong, brother. Movement in the crowd...'

Scipio saw the grain as if for the first time. It churned of its own volition, turning black before his eyes and suddenly alive with contagion. Plump maggots writhed in the mass. A dark spot blossomed on the head of one... then opened to reveal the sclera of a human eye. Scipio reached for an empty holster, his hatred for this thing white-hot and blazing. A slit ran down its obscenely ribbed body, splitting into an inhuman maw caged with newborn saliva. It squealed.

'Guilliman's blood...' uttered Scipio, and crushed the filth under his boot, where it died shrieking.

Oben recoiled, falling back into the other deckhands who had begun to turn at an unseen commotion behind them. Iulus shouted across the vox, and Scipio heard him vault the shield wall at the same time.

'Prabian was right. There were too many. The cultists, some of them came from within.'

The smoke had grown thick and the darkness heavy but Scipio saw the danger at last. Parts of the crowd had donned crude masks and daubed their ragged smocks in the sigils of Ruin. They had knives, sharp tools, and began killing. In the same moment, an explosion tore through the ration yard.

CHAPTER FOURTEEN

BLIND

They reached the octagonal room, and found Ludik kneeling in the centre. Reda couldn't see the sergeant's face because it was dark and he had his back to her. The gauzy light of the lamp pack picked out his hair, the bloody state of his uniform. It found the other armsmen too. She kept her gaze low and on the floor. There were no bullet casings, no burns from las-discharge. A squad of dead troopers lay in the octagonal room, but not a shot had been fired. She found no sign of Barthus either, and listened intently for the distinct clicking sound that signalled his presence, but all she could hear was her own breathing and that of Gerrant.

'Is he here?' Gerrant pressed his back against the wall, standing at the edge of the chamber. He looked down at Reda, who was crouching next to him in the open.

'Ludik, yes. Barthus…'

'I can't hear him.'

'Me neither.' Unhooking her power maul, she handed it grip first to Gerrant.

'That's the plan?'

'Keep the charge low,' she warned. 'Too much and you'll kill him.'

Gerrant shook his head. 'I can't let you do this, Arna. I'll bait him out.'

'You're barely holding it together, Vanko,' she hissed. 'You won't make it two feet beyond the door.' She held his gaze, daring him to argue. He didn't. 'Low charge,' she reiterated. Gerrant took the maul.

Reda pulled the bandana over her eyes and made a tight knot behind her head. Her last glimpse was of a metallic visor, a beam of light shining across it like a sickle moon. 'It's here,' she whispered. 'The visor. We get that thing on Barthus and only a damn tech-priest is getting it off.'

She stepped into the room. She'd left her shotgun behind. No sense in tempting fate. After her first few shuffling and uncertain steps, the vox gently hissed to life.

'*Edge left, half a step,*' came Gerrant's voice. '*I can't see.*'

Reda obeyed, hearing ice crunch underfoot. Effectively blinded, every other sense was heightened. The cold, the scent of blood particles merging with the frost. The rustle of fabric as she moved and the slow, deliberate breaths she took to remain calm and focused. She heard no rap of metal against metal, the telltale chime of Barthus' manic finger drumming.

'*That's better,*' whispered Gerrant, his breath sawing back and forth across the receiver. '*I have eyes on. Ten paces straight ahead.*'

'Keep that beam low and on the ground,' Reda warned as she started to advance, counting out the steps in her head.

'*Aye, lieu–*'

The sudden pause made Reda stop.

'I caught movement! Above…'

'Light on the ground, Vanko! Do not bloody well defy your ranking officer.'

'He's in there with you, Arna. Oh shit, he's really in there.'

Now she heard the clicking, faint at first and coming from overhead.

'How close, Vanko?' She moved slowly, but had lost count.

'Throne, Arna. He's right above you.'

'Gerrant.' She gritted her teeth, trying not to surrender to the fear, her mind on the mission. 'How close?'

'Six more, no… sorry, eight, eight more paces. He's following you, Arna.'

'I told you light down, trooper.'

'It's down, damn it. I can see his shadow.'

Reda counted the steps, trying to ignore the clicking overhead, and stopped when she touched something heavy with the tip of her boot. She was leaning down to grasp it when she heard the buzz of the overhead sodium lamp and guessed what had happened to Elam and the others.

'Shoot it!' she cried, sinking to her haunches and gathering up the visor as Barthus dropped down with arachnoid grace and enveloped her. 'Strafe the light!'

Light intruded against her blindfold, tingeing the black a muggy yellow.

She heard the discharge of Gerrant's autocarbine a second later, before being struck by pieces of falling glass. Barthus shielded her from the worst of it, and she heard the Navigator hiss in pain as the shards cut through his robes and into his flesh. Reda tried to raise the visor but her wrist was pinned, seized in a manacle of golden fingers.

'Navigator…' she gasped, the pain of his grip forcing her breath to catch.

'You must see...' said Barthus. 'The eye will see...'

Reda felt a hooked nail slip beneath her blindfold and recoiled. The ragged strip of cloth tore away and she clamped her eyes shut, but could feel the urge to open them and Barthus willing her to.

'You must see... All must see... It is coming.' He sounded more afraid than insane.

Reda lashed out with her free hand and felt her fist strike the Navigator's jaw. She roared, 'Gerrant. Now!'

The pressure on her wrist released, though she already felt the pain of an angry weal encircling it in a bracelet of red-raw skin. She heard hurried footsteps, and the sudden electric charge as the maul engaged.

She opened her eyes and saw Gerrant, his lamp pack swinging wildly as he ran, the cold glow of the maul as it cut through the air. Barthus had his back to her and was facing Gerrant, who stared into the abyss as he laid his blow.

'Vanko!'

Barthus fell back, his flailing, unconscious body blocking Reda's view. As the Navigator collapsed, Gerrant was revealed standing stock-still, the faintly crackling maul held loosely in his grip.

'Throne, Vanko...' Reda rasped, tears already blurring her eyes.

And then Gerrant blinked and aimed his lamp pack at the prone Navigator. He was breathing hard and dropped the maul, which plinked out as it hit the ground and quickly rolled to a stop.

'How?' asked Reda.

'I didn't see it,' was all Gerrant could say.

Reda looked down at Barthus and realised why. The Navigator's face had been badly cut. His eyes were shut, his hair plastered over his face with blood. Taking no chances, she pushed the visor onto Barthus' forehead, where it snapped shut like a trap.

Then she sank to her knees, and breathed again.

'What did he mean?' asked Gerrant.

Reda arched her head back and let out a long breath.

It is coming. The words echoed in her head. *It is coming.*

CHAPTER FIFTEEN

BLOOD AND BONE

Pillium regarded the human soldiers closing in around the Munitorum officer with disdain. Their tattered uniforms did them no service, nor did the way they held on to their rifles with such grim determination. Each of them, three men and a woman, carried a riot shield on their back and laboured with the weight of it. Pillium had studied hundreds of weapons. The stub-nosed autorifles would sit in the crooks of their shields as soon as they were planted, surrounding the quartermaster, with her the reptile hiding ineffectually behind their shell. They were brave enough souls, he supposed, but utterly superfluous in the current situation. He had considered this escort duty Helicos had assigned might be a punishment for humbling the veteran in the arena, but it scarcely chafed if it was. He had grown increasingly restive, knowing he was made for war and not knowing when he would next be able to fulfil his purpose.

He *burned* to prove his worth and demonstrate the superiority of the Primaris Marines. They had been gene-forged for the darker and more perilous galaxy in which mankind found itself. Pillium had expected glory aplenty from the primarch's crusade, yet instead he had been consigned to the fringes, lost in the warp and impotent to do anything about it. The distraction, then, of a missing platoon, quarantined on a sealed deck, was welcome if not particularly invigorating. It became more enticing when the resounding echo of the door shutting subsided and Pillium's heightened senses detected a different sound.

He had already advanced into the main entryway, bolt rifle in the crook of his armpit, steadied with one gauntleted hand on the grip and the other on the stock.

'Stay behind Secutius,' he said, gesturing to the other sergeant then nodding for the rest of his squad to move up. He spared no further thought for the quartermaster and her 'shield-bearers'. His attention focused on the faint cracking sound he could hear coming from further in. It could be stanchions settling, or even a drum-fire if the platoon had got cold in the abandoned halls. The deck section they had moved into was long and wide after the entryway, and he knew from the schematics he had studied that it ran far enough for sound to carry. As open and relatively uninhabited as it was, this would confuse matters where noise and distance were concerned.

As he reached the ration crate, which was larger than the shell of an armoured troop carrier, his men dispersed and took up sentry positions following his pre-prescribed orders. Secutius hung back, his squad's formation loose and almost at ease. They sensed no threat here and yet something niggled at Pillium's hindbrain as he tapped the massive ration crate with the barrel of his bolt rifle. It chimed dully but lighter than he had expected.

'Quartermaster…' His tone provided the order without him

even having to give it as Olvo Sharna shuffled towards him with her attendants. Secutius followed, but his interest lay elsewhere as he interrogated the half-dark behind red retinal lenses. He, too, carried a bolt rifle, but held it across his chest, over the skull-headed eagle that designated him an Angel of Death. The muzzle was pointed down and at a slight angle, and his gauntleted finger rested against the trigger guard.

'Can we hurry this up, brother?' he asked over the private vox.

'You're eager to return to patrol?' Pillium replied, looking askance at Secutius as he waited for Sharna. 'Or perhaps you want a rematch in the arena?' He raised an eyebrow. 'Because apparently your capacity for shame has greater depths.'

Secutius swore under his breath, and Pillium caught the tail end of an Iaxian curse. He nodded to his brother, acknowledging the request, to which Secutius returned the battle-sign for 'honour'.

Olvo Sharna stood before him, and Pillium looked down upon her as if she were an errant child about to be disciplined.

'Sire,' she said patiently.

Pillium rapped the crate with his knuckles, eliciting the same hollow resonance as before. 'Does that sound right to you?'

Sharna frowned, pressing her ear against the cold metal of the crate as the echo slowly died away into the distance. 'It does not,' she admitted, stepping back again.

'It's sealed,' said Pillium, gesturing to the hexagonal lock across the access hatch, where a red rune weakly flashed.

'Let me take a look,' she said, slightly hitching up her robes as she moved around to examine the hatch. A numeric keypad was attached to the lock. Sharna inputted the correct sequence and the light turned a pale green.

'Step back, quartermaster,' Pillium told her, 'and return to your escort.' He had one hand holding his bolt rifle up to the unsealed but still closed crate as the other reached for a hatch handle. Two other Primaris Marines had moved in behind him, one at either shoulder, weapons trained on the crate.

He shared a look with Secutius, who shifted his posture at this ready signal.

Then he thrust open the hatch.

It yielded noisily, old metal grinding against old metal and raising a cacophony of screeching. The armsmen jerked a little at the sound, and Pillium did his very best not to scowl.

'Nothing,' he said.

Sharna returned to shine a sodium lantern around the confines, but the crate was empty. She kneeled down, sweeping her hand across the floor. 'It's been utterly denuded,' she said.

'You sound surprised,' said Pillium. 'They ate the rations.'

'They *devoured* them. Everything. This is protein grain,' she said, evidently deciding an explanation was in order as Pillium's mind began to wander back to the sound he had heard earlier. 'It's akin to marsh-rice, only thicker and with a higher nutritional content.'

'What matter is the nature of the food you feed these men?' Pillium asked, though he was already gathering his forces for further exploration into the deck.

'It's small enough and numerous enough that pieces are missed or simply left once a unit has had its fill. I've never seen a crate this size so thoroughly stripped.'

'Perhaps they were hungrier than you thought,' said Pillium, waving Secutius forwards.

'But look at this...' Sharna pointed and Pillium followed. There were dark and grimy streaks in the metal.

'Drag marks from fingers,' she said, emulating the movement

in one particular place and having to splay her hand wide to encompass it.

Pillium's gaze hardened as he brought superior olfaction to bear.

'It's blood,' he said. 'Were they starving, these men?'

'No, they received regular batches of rations.'

Still the cracking sound persisted, irritating now that Pillium couldn't excise it from his head.

Not a fire. Not settling stanchions either.

'Secutius…' Pillium began, as he took hold of the helm mag-clamped to his armour.

'I hear it too, brother,' the other sergeant replied.

Pillium slammed on his war-helm and the seals connected with a faint hiss and a dull thud of metal against metal. When he spoke next to Sharna, it was through the rebreather grille of his armour.

'Keep your escort close and stay behind me at all times.'

Clearly afraid, Sharna nodded mutely. The armsmen did their best to look resolute. Pillium scarcely noticed them and moved up with his squad.

Pillium and Secutius advanced quickly, their squads in tow, clearing each chamber and corridor ahead. It was done with a well-practised synchronicity. No corner or blind spot was left unswept as the half-light gloom of deck thirteen beckoned them onwards.

They followed the cracking sound. It reminded Pillium of bone, crunched and ground under intense pressure. The sound a body makes when it is crushed under the tracks of a Land Raider. But there were no battle tanks on deck thirteen. As the door to the next section split and ground apart, it ushered in the thrum of languidly turning fan blades. An artificial breeze, it carried another scent over the salty tang of human sweat. It, too, was familiar to Pillium. Thick. Metallic. It was a battlefield smell, and though ships like the *Emperor's Will* had been fought over like any battlefield, it seemed utterly incongruous here.

'Vitae...' uttered Secutius, taking vanguard position at the threshold of the room. The targeter on his bolt rifle stabbed a red lance into the unwelcoming shadows ahead.

Pillium moved up to join him, resting his hand on the other sergeant's shoulder guard to alert him to his presence, and engaging his night-sight.

'I'll take the lead here, brother,' he said.

His vista turned a monochromatic green and he discerned a massive chamber, large metal columns flanking the entrance, lined up in ranks that disappeared past the limits of his retinal lenses.

It was a muster hall, a gathering place for armies. A ship the size of the *Emperor's Will* carried entire hosts to war. This is where they would array, where the officers would inspect the instruments of their will, where the Chaplains and priests would inspire them with the rhetoric of certain victory.

The lights had been doused and it was darker here than in any other area of the deck. The cracking sound had grown louder, no longer carried through pipes and vents but here, present, and the source of it in this immense room.

And then it ceased.

Pillium disengaged night-sight and gave the signal for 'forwards with caution', and the two squads entered. As soon as they were past the open archway, the Primaris Marines fanned out, engaging stab-lamps attached to their bolters and panning their beams across the room.

The columns reared again, dense and pitted pillars of metal. Some had scratch marks dug into them, the same as those found by the quartermaster in the base of the ration crate. Pillium spared a fleeting thought for Sharna, a quick glance across his shoulder reassuring him she was still keeping her distance but had followed the Primaris Marines with her escort troops.

He didn't understand why yet, but the air felt strange in the muster hall, as if it were too heavy. Inertia dragged against his body, though his power armour-augmented strength made it easy enough to overcome. The runes overlaying his retinal display blinked manically, suddenly manifesting threat alerts only to scatter, jerkily trying and failing to lock on to some invisible target. Their warning spectra went from low to high to extreme and back again with seemingly no rationale for each automated determination.

Baffled, Pillium stopped, halting the group at the same time, and removed his helmet. The smell hit him harder, blood scent and ammonia mixed with vinegar. At least his vision had cleared, and his eyes narrowed as his light beam struck a discarded boot.

He subvocalised a notification to Secutius, who then lit his own stab-lamp on the same target. The boot shone wetly. The curve of its toecap had a gelatinous film that could only be blood. It had been gnawed upon. Canine and molar teeth impressions distorted the leather.

From the boot, a crimson trail led deeper. Following it revealed further items. A belt. A torn epaulette. A shiny pink bone. Tendrils of skin stuck to it, threads of sinew stringing it to another piece of human skeleton.

A figure staggered out of the darkness then, staring at the stab-lamps as they fell upon him with the intensity of swords. He was naked from the waist up, his muscled body awash with red, his fingers dripping with it, barefoot and half-blinded by the light.

Sharna recognised him at once.

'Colonel Roan! Throne of Terra, what happened?'

Pillium felt her moving forwards and put out his arm.

'No further,' he warned, his fingers splayed in a gesture for her to stop.

'He's injured. And apparently catatonic. Take those beams off him,' she replied, moving again.

Pillium addressed one of her escort instead. 'Secure your charge,' he ordered. 'You are to come no closer.'

'What?' asked Sharna, suddenly nonplussed. 'That's an officer of this ship. He needs medical– Take your hands off me! Armsman, you will release–'

'Hold her,' Pillium cut in, his voice enough to shut Sharna up and quell any further commotion. His beam never wavered from Colonel Roan, who had yet to react to the presence of the Primaris Marine. 'Secutius…'

'I have him,' replied the other sergeant, still wearing his own helmet, his voice tinny through the vox-grille. 'Be careful. Something feels amiss…'

'He is but one man, Markus.'

'One man covered in blood, Justus.'

Pillium nodded. He trusted Secutius' instincts. They had fought together since the beginning and he was one of the few Primaris brethren he was on first-name terms with. He would rather have no other warrior to guard his shield arm. Pillium signalled to two of his men, Maxus and Eurates, who moved into flanking positions as he advanced on the horrific figure of Colonel Roan.

It wasn't only his skin; the officer's hair and clothes were both plastered with blood too, yet he showed no sign of injury. Pillium shone the stab-lamp into Roan's eyes but got no response. Not even pupil dilation. Roan was breathing, but showed no other signs of life.

'Find out whose blood this is,' he said to Secutius, who marshalled his own squad and delved deeper into the room.

A tense silence settled for several minutes, only occasionally punctuated by the mechanised growl of Mk X war-plate and the subvocalised clicks of Secutius' squad communing across the vox. During that time, Pillium kept his eyes on their sweeping stab-lamps slowly growing more distant. His gaze flicked back to Roan, who returned a glassy-eyed, slack expression.

'Please,' begged Sharna from behind a barricade of armsmen, 'let me at least see if he's hurt.'

Pillium was about to grant her request when Secutius' voice rasped over the vox.

'Guilliman's mercy…' He was scarcely audible at first. *'Pillium,'* he said, louder, *'there is something here. I do not… I cannot find the appropriate description, brother.'*

'You stay where you are,' he said to Sharna. Then he barked a raft of curt orders and the two flanking Primaris Marines converged on Roan, keeping him firmly in their sights. Of his other two men, Odyssian remained with Sharna and her escort whilst Tiberus went with the sergeant as he swiftly moved up in support of Secutius. A stretch of empty, riveted metal deck plates stood between him and the other sergeant. On the way, Pillium caught glimpses of pink bone shards and other visceral detritus. An errant lower jaw. Scattered teeth. A dismembered foot. Though disturbing, these ragged, bloody things had not provoked Secutius' reaction. As Pillium closed, passing the other Primaris Marines who stood in overwatch positions, he saw what had.

Flayed skin, snapped and chewed-on bone, the remnants of limbs, savaged ribcages, piled organs and hollow-eyed skulls… It all lay heaped in a disgusting mound of flesh and viscera. It stank of blood and cold, ruddy meat.

Roan's men were here. His entire platoon. Butchered. Gnawed upon.

CHAPTER SIXTEEN

METAMORPHOSIS

Pillium fought down his revulsion, even as his mind rebelled at the charnel sight of the butchered platoon.

'It must be burned,' uttered Secutius.

'We need answers for this horror first…' breathed Pillium, leaning into the vox-receiver in his gorget. 'Bind the colonel.'

Pillium heard the order acknowledged but then a moment later his men raised the alarm. Something had happened.

He turned.

Roan had collapsed and was on the floor shaking. Pillium was heading back to them when Secutius shouted a warning.

'Wait!'

Annoyed, Pillium looked back at the other sergeant, stranded in the no-man's-land between two decisions.

'It's moving,' said Secutius, and the Primaris Marines at the far end of the hall took aim.

Then Pillium saw it. The flesh undulated as tendrils of creation wormed through its mass, stitching and conjoining.

He barked into the vox. 'Maxus, Eurates, with me. Odyssian, do not let the colonel out of your sight.'

'What is this, Justus?' asked Secutius, his own men drawing in at his command.

'I don't know,' he rasped.

'Is it alive?' asked Secutius, and nodded to Helor for him to raise the alarm on the vox.

'If it is,' Pillium began, 'then we should kill it.'

Raucous bolter fire lit up the far end of the muster hall, tearing back the shadows with angry, flame-edged light. The shells thudded wetly into the flesh. A raft of small explosions rippled through it but did nothing to arrest its metamorphosis. A larger mass formed, a hulking and amalgamated body of sorts. Glistening limbs detached from it, strung with ropes of amniotic mucus. It waddled, this half-born thing, uncertain on its claw-toed feet and as large as a Dreadnought, staggering with fresh bolt-round impacts but not stopping. It grew, rapidly and exponentially, the red-rimmed caul sheathing its form stretching and splitting to reveal more horrors. A prehensile tail, a trunk-like neck attached to three human skulls. Its bulk expanded further, the entire charnel pyre revealed to be one concomitant organism.

It keened, an ululating and plaintive cry of agony. The sound came not from any of its hollow, skeletal mouths but from a slit that had unzipped across its colossal torso to reveal a dark red maw filled with ranks of uneven teeth.

'Target the limbs!' roared Pillium, shooting out one of its knees and tearing the leg from the body.

It slumped on one leg, wallowing and floundering.

Secutius destroyed the other one and the red-fleshed spawn collapsed, trilling in pain. With a wrenching of torn skin, eight distended arms speared from the body, the fingers of the hands meshed together into talons. They raised the thing up, tottering and insectile. The torso mouth widened, two large chitin pincers pushing through either cheek, experimentally snapping open and shut. Bolt-shells still ripping chunks from its bloated body, it charged Helor who stood his ground, weapon blazing.

The spawn barrelled through the firestorm, its grotesque visage lit by muzzle flare, and bore the Primaris Marine down. His brothers flocked to his aid, even as Helor drew his combat blade, the spawn's bulk crushing him, splitting ceramite and adamantium. A spray of blood splashed his faceplate and the scent of it drove the thing wild, pincers snapping feverishly, biting off pieces of Helor and hurriedly shovelling him into its maw.

Secutius let out a cry, part-rage, part-anguish. He threw himself at the spawn. They all did. Hacking and firing, levelling every inch of gene-forged strength towards ending this thing.

Pillium had Maxus, Tiberus and Eurates at his side. The four advanced in steady lockstep, bolt rifles at maximum discharge. During the fusillade, he caught a glimpse of Odyssian. He was edging towards the battle, discipline at war with the desire to protect his sergeant. Behind him, the figure of Colonel Roan arose on loose limbs like a puppet left slack on its strings...

Pillium fired, almost point-blank now. Blood spatter and stinking flesh flecked his face and armour. This thing, it would not die in any conventional way. They had to annihilate it. In his peripheral vision, Pillium saw Odyssian struggling with Colonel Roan clamped upon his back. The armsmen were backing off, two coming around with shields, Sharna screaming at the sight of it all.

He let his attention wander for a split second and one of the spawn's legs struck Pillium across the chest and he careened backwards. One took Maxus too, who went spiralling into the shadows. Eurates and Tiberus fell back, letting off short, sustained bursts. The thing shifted suddenly, putting its bulk between him and the other Primaris Marines, and Pillium lost sight of them.

Bony barbs jutted from the thing's forelimbs. They had raked Pillium's torso down to the mesh under-layer. One of the input ports for his armour was exposed. A cocktail of organic narcotics flooded Pillium's system to extinguish the pain. He was rising, bolt rifle swinging around, when he heard Sharna.

'Help us! Throne! Please!'

Blood thundered in Pillium's ears as he fought to reassert alignment. Odyssian lay face down, jerking in his death throes as Roan repeatedly stabbed him in the back with the bony spikes he now had instead of fingers. His shoulders had broadened too, his mouth distended and agape. Spiny teeth glistened, before his neck darted down with serpentine aggression and he bit right through the Ultramarine's gorget.

'Secutius...' Pillium slurred, only now realising how badly he had been injured. Some of the barbs had embedded in his flesh. He felt them pinch and then start to dig...

Secutius had emptied his bolt rifle and was hacking at the spawn two-handed. He drove his combat blade in right up to the hilt and then dragged it downwards. It was like opening up a balloon of bulging viscera, as rancid organs and malformed body parts spilled out in a gruesome flood. Acid hissed as it made contact with the sergeant's armour.

'Secutius... Markus!' Pillium said again, ripping out the last of the embedded barbs with his fingers and half running, half staggering to his feet as he made for Sharna and the armsmen. Two were already dead. Roan had left Odyssian's still-quivering corpse and had just ripped off the head of one of the quartermaster's escorts. Blood geysered from the femoral artery. Another lay nearby, riot shield bent almost in two, her ribcage open like a sprung hinge and steaming in the cold air. Her sightless gaze fell in Pillium's direction and he roared.

'Danger behind us!'

Eurates and Tiberus peeled off from the fight with the spawn. Pillium heard their urgent footfalls following on behind his own.

They reached Roan almost at the same time. The last armsman had been eviscerated and left to die in a pool of his own stinking innards.

Pillium put a bolt in the back of Roan's head, which had grown and distorted. Part of the skull blew out, releasing a plume of matter and broken bone.

Roan turned, except this wasn't Roan. A row of eyes had opened down one side of his chest, bloodshot, yellow and blinking feverishly at the advancing Primaris Marine. Two tentacular limbs unfolded from his flanks, a snapping beak in place of hands and fingers. Muscle mass exploded across his whole frame, uneven and burdensome. It gave him resilience, though. Several bolt-rounds struck him in the torso but failed to stop him.

Sharna had collapsed from sheer terror. She back-scuttled away from Roan, weeping and wailing every inch.

The Roan-thing barged into Eurates, who had the presence of mind to draw his blade, shove it into the neck and hold on.

Somewhere behind Pillium, a loud explosion went off.

Grenades. He heard Secutius shouting, something raw and indistinct, a primal reaction to the unnatural, a channelling of his fury. For his part, Pillium dropped his bolt rifle and picked up Odyssian's weapon.

'Stand clear!' he bellowed and racked a krak grenade in the bolt rifle's auxiliary launcher.

Slowly being crushed by Roan's tentacles, Eurates shouted, 'Do it!' and Pillium mashed the trigger. The explosion smashed him off his feet and tore Roan apart. Tiberus advanced on the gibbering mess, blasting at dismembered limbs and pieces of Roan's body until they were nothing more than red smears.

Getting to his feet, Pillium tossed two frag grenades into whatever was left, and shredded Roan – or the thing that he had become – out of existence. He looked back in time to see Secutius impaled on one of the spawn's barbed limbs. It speared him through the chest, instantly destroying both hearts. He shuddered with his final nerve tremors and fell still. His grip slackened, a blood-slick blade clattering as it hit the ground.

Pillium roared. 'Markus!'

CHAPTER SEVENTEEN

○

LET THE BLOOD FLOW

Dozens lay dead, killed by the explosion. The incendiary device deployed by the cultists was crude, but with the labourers so hemmed in it could not help but wreak havoc. At first, the survivors scattered. They ran in all directions, some genuinely unsure where the danger came from. Fear of secondary explosions rippled through the crowd like a shock wave. They stampeded. Some were crushed against the massive silos, others simply disappeared underfoot and did not reappear. Panic had seized the mob and turned them feral. It did not end there. The wounded were set upon, stabbed and bludgeoned, as shouts radiated through the ration yard.

Kharnath!

Kharnath!

It was a ritual, and these poor starving men and women were its sacrifice. Only to what, Scipio had no idea.

He pushed into the crowd, letting the terrified labourers rush past him as he made for the cultists moving through the throng. He was unarmed but there was no time to return for his weapons. *He* was the weapon, and that would have to be enough. Skirmishes had broken out, between the loyal and the traitorous, as some decided to fight to protect their ship. Scipio did not hesitate to join with them. He heard Harpon Bader across the vox.

'Hold steady,' he was saying, the catch in his voice giving away his fear. 'Shields together. Don't let them through.'

'Iulus,' said Scipio, 'they'll stampede that wall and Bader is too afraid to listen.'

He received a grunt of understanding and heard his fellow sergeant stomp back to the barrier to get ahead of the mob. A trickle became a flood, men and women hurrying for safety as they at last realised from where the danger was coming. Oben fought against the tide, he and those others who had decided to engage the traitors in their midst. They fought with wrenches and pipes and with their fists. The cultists were organised and fuelled by some insane doctrine. Beneath their masks they were crazed and utterly given over to a darker power. The warp had touched them, a small seed that had spread into a contagion of madness and blood. In the bowels of the ship, it would have been easy to conceal their deviancy, an allegiance born out of fear and desperation or a simple human desire to inflict pain on others and see your own weakness reflected in a victim's suffering.

Weakness of character, of resolve. It sickened Scipio. He would see it purged and the turncoats put to death along with their heretic creed. But first he needed to reach them.

An interrogative came over the vox. 'Should we engage, brother-sergeant?'

One of his men, eager to obey his genetic coding.

'No firearms,' Scipio replied, forging through the throng. If the Ultramarines spread out around the ration yard started shooting now it would be a bloodbath. The bolter was many things, but it was never subtle. 'Hand-to-hand. Hunt the bastards down.'

Scipio's weapons were gone, being kicked around or tripped over in the panic. He risked a backward glance. The shield wall had scattered, the armsmen ushering the scared labourers through. Iulus was slowly moving back up through the tide of bodies. It was the same across the ration yard. Scipio occupied the most advanced position. For now, he was on his own.

A ragged-looking man, missing his mask but daubed in the marks of heresy, flung himself at the Ultramarine. Scipio caught him by the neck, twisted it hard and moved on. A second he punched in the chest and felt rib bones yield. They flocked to him then, the traitors. He represented the Imperium that they had come to hate, the thing they had traded for the lies of Chaos. They leapt at him, and upon him, clawing and hacking with improvised weapons. Scipio used his elbows, his knees, his feet. He used the unarmed combat doctrines of his Chapter and saw the effort in the practice cages rewarded. It was bloody work, though the feel of splintered bone beneath his fists yielded a certain catharsis.

The cultists were waning, both in numbers and in purpose. The crowds had all but dispersed and the Ultramarines behind Scipio were making their superior strength and training count. The danger to the innocent dropped dramatically. The order to fire was given. And the riot ended moments later.

'What was the purpose of all this?' Scipio asked as Iulus rejoined him. He carried Scipio's weapons and returned them with due reverence. The blade was given back last, and done so with the utmost care.

'To sow carnage and terror,' Iulus replied. 'I can think of no other reason.'

Scipio regarded a body amongst the masses.

'Perhaps it is just insanity,' Iulus suggested when Scipio did not answer.

'Or something darker. It is a grim hope when that is the thing we must wish for, that there was reason to this and not just blind madness.' He kneeled down by the body, gently closing the dead man's eyes and carefully setting his hands upon his chest in imitation of the Imperial eagle.

'Who was he?' asked Iulus.

'Another loyal son of Macragge,' Scipio replied, and left Oben to his well-earned peace.

It was only later, when the vox crackled, that they learned why the massacre had taken place, and what it had brought forth.

CHAPTER EIGHTEEN

HELL SPAWNED

It had grown, the spawn-thing. A glossy carapace had spread across its hunched back. Wiry black hairs as thick as swords protruded from its eight gangling legs. It was still flesh, the gathered and partly dismembered leavings of Colonel Roan's former platoon, but had an overall arachnoid appearance.

'We have to kill it,' breathed Pillium.

Maxus lay unmoving, his twitching fingers caught in the flickering light of his stab-lamp. Eurates was blown half apart and Odyssian had been cut to pieces. It left Tiberus and whatever remained of Secutius' squad.

'Primaris Marines, fall back on my position,' Pillium snapped into the vox.

Aegidus, Cajus and Seppio laid down fire, retreating in good order.

The spawn appeared content to let them, suffering each blow with little reaction but trembling with further transformations. Its skin darkened, turning from pale pink to vibrant incarnadine. It hunched over, its limbs conjoining, entwining from eight to four. And they thickened, musculature growing at an insane rate, colonising its back, its chest. The spiny hairs fell out, replaced by patchy black growths that had the appearance of a shaggy hide. As the long neck retracted, the three skulls began to merge into a single head and face. The nubs of horns formed. Flesh blossomed like a sudden flourishing of lesions. The carapace that wrapped its body hardened and turned metallic, like armour.

'Sergeant…'

A whimpering voice, half-heard and on the edge of his attention, niggled at Pillium. The bolter storm had lessened on account of ammunition running low and the obvious fact it was having utterly no effect.

Pillium drew his sword. A scraping metal chorus sounded a moment later as the remaining Primaris Marines did the same.

'Sergeant…'

Louder now, the voice. He recognised it, though chose to ignore it. The bolters rang empty.

'Grenades?' asked Pillium. His warriors brandished what they had.

The thing had grown larger, its body more defined, even hunched over as it was, wracked in its unnatural birth spasms. It had legs and arms, an anthropomorphic pattern but with a distinctly canine aspect. Flaps of black skin spilled across its back like sail canvas and spread until they sagged to the ground. Bony scapularies tethering them to its body jerked and raised up the flaps, the skin unfurling into two draconic pinions. Ragged and gossamer thin, they had yet to form fully.

Olvo Sharna cried out. 'Sergeant! We cannot stay here.'

She was back on her feet, but barely holding on. Fear clung to her, threatening to drag her into an abyss out of which there was no escape. The mere *presence* of this thing... It was enough to do that. Pillium felt a measure of the terror it radiated. He did not recognise the emotion straight away, for it was a foreign concept, not fear exactly but a deep sense of unease.

'We can kill it,' Pillium replied, the need for revenge for Markus' death a cold flame in his gut.

'We have to seal it in here,' said Sharna. 'The beast or whatever it is cannot be allowed out of deck thirteen.'

Pillium hesitated. 'If we attack now, while it's changing...'

'Your weapons have been ineffective, sergeant. Please...' she begged him, 'I cannot endure this.'

'Tiberus.' Pillium turned to the Primaris Marine, who was about to escort Sharna away when she put both hands on his vambrace, clinging to it like a child hanging on to the arm of an adult.

'Neither can you.'

A second hesitation. Pillium let out a bellow of frustration.

'Grenades,' he said, 'everything we've got. Then fall back quickly. We make for the entrance.' He looked Sharna in the eye. 'Quartermaster, can you still seal the door once we're on the other side?'

She nodded mutely. Tiberus took her gently, leaving his grenades with Cajus and Seppio. Once they were out of the muster hall, he carried her and ran.

The Primaris Marines tossed their grenades, and the beast roared as a storm of shrapnel bloomed around it, shrouding it from sight.

'We move!' bellowed Pillium.

They ran. Hard.

And behind them the beast bellowed a savage affirmation.
'Kharnath!'

CHAPTER NINETEEN

POWER

Haephestus had descended into the bowels of the ship. A chemical atmosphere pervaded here, anathema to human life and necessitating both bodily protection and a rebreather. Crew still roamed these parts, equipped with the appropriate environmental trappings and a crude auspex to help with navigation, though sightings were rare. The lower decks, the *catacombs* as they were sometimes known, were as labyrinthine as they were deadly.

Stacked pipes ran in every direction, ferrying plasma, coolant, waste and other gases and fluids that all contributed to the running of the ship. They ran for miles, literally, snaking around colossal turbines, ranks of hydraulic pistons and mass compressors. There was power here, definable, tangible *power*. Haephestus had felt it ever since he had passed through the first bulkhead. He felt it now, sickly sizzling, as he walked through a pall of chemical fog.

A pair of heavy servitors, golem-alpha and golem-beta,

followed sullenly. Haephestus had modified them for adverse atmospheric conditions, and they wheezed like stimm addicts with every draw of their respirators. Adapted also for heavy lifting, each servitor had a pair of hydraulic fork arms and was swollen with rapidly grown muscle across the back and shoulders. Servos groaned in their trunk-like legs with every ponderous step.

Past the immense run-off tanks, it was here from where the fog exuded, and a huge gate stamped with the Icon Mechanicus stood. Even rust-rimed and colonised with clumps of biochemical algae, it looked indomitable. Forged of a ferro-ceramite alloy and placed here by the vessel's original shipwrights, it was the literal gateway to the beating heart of the *Emperor's Will*. The main power core churned behind it. Haephestus could feel it in his bones.

As a scion of both Mars and Macragge, he had a certain awareness of energy, its passage and purity, that his brothers did not. As a Techmarine he had been taught the ways of the Omnissiah and the machine-spirit. Even with the great gate sealed, Haephestus could feel an imbalance.

A warp siphon, that is what he had told the captain. It was an accurate, if imperfect, term for what was happening to the ship. As if perceiving his thoughts, the lumen arrays suspended in the ship's rafters above, the only source of light in this part of the catacombs, flickered and went out.

Haephestus engaged his armour's stab-lamps and two beams cut through the large chamber, alighting on the giant skull and cog of the Icon Mechanicus. Its hollow eye sockets glowed red like dying drum-fires.

'An ill omen, Omnissiah?' he queried, expecting no answer.

Techmarines did not usually put trust in superstition or signs. They believed in logic and the motive force behind all things, but Haephestus had seen enough on board the *Emperor's Will* these past five years to know that reason could not explain every existing phenomenon.

Flicking open an access panel on his vambrace revealed a small screen, data spooling across in crude green monochrome. He released a blurt of binharic, the complex machine language or *lingua technis* of the Martian priesthood. The device in his vambrace transferred the arrangement of ones and zeros into an unlock code.

He waited.

Nothing happened.

Behind the faceplate of his helmet, Haephestus frowned.

'Perplexing...' he said to the golems.

Neither replied, their slack-eyed gazes unmoving from the sealed gate.

Haephestus sent a second tranche of binharic, a breacher code known only to the master Techmarine aboard ship.

This time the gate reacted, the red fire changing to emerald green, and Haephestus took a step back.

A third binharic command saw alpha and beta move forwards and approach the gate, where two side panels had slid back left and right of the monolithic slab of alloy to reveal a large wheel recessed into the metal. Both golems locked their fork arms around each wheel like pincers. After a short expulsion of gas from their shoulder valves, they began to turn the wheels in perfect synchronicity. Inch by grinding inch, the gate opened. Heat and light bled out from the core furnace beyond, limning Haephestus' armour a wan orange. When the opening was wide enough, he started forwards and signalled for the golems to cease all activity. They slumped where they stood, unpowered.

What he saw past the gate quickened his pace across the

bridge that led to the core, a flow of chemical run-off bubbling beneath his feet.

The core was like a gigantic generator, only far more complex. There were signs of corrosion and chemical overspill at connection points. Parts of its metal casing had warped, twisting and bulging with corrupted expansions. Several of the wired conduits were scorched black and melted where they had burned out. The level of degrading Haephestus saw was the product of years of neglect and disuse. He had seen to the core's maintenance himself. Therefore, the corrosion was not of natural origin. The furnace burned timidly in the background, lethargic and close to extinguishment.

Some of the access ports were exposed, the inputs a match for his own mechadendrite interface. Black ichorous sludge dribbled from the cavities, having dried out in a crusted wound tract down the metal. It all led to an inevitable conclusion.

'Incursion.'

Though the warp had undoubtedly eroded the ship's ability to function, it had not done so without help. So when the threat markers lit up in Haephestus' retinal display, he was already engaging his defences. That split second of empirical premonition saved his life as a burst of weapons fire splashed against his hastily energised refractor field. Light flared with the shell collisions. It chased back the shadows and blinded his revealed assailant.

Part-cyborg, part-mutant, part-Astartes. It wore old power armour draped in ragged black robes, and recoiled against the actinic glare of the refractor field, shouting out in pain as its retinal lenses overloaded. In the same instant a volkite pistol sprang into Haephestus' hand, magnetised to his gauntlet, and he fired. The shot had been aimed at his assailant's faceplate but went slightly astray as they managed to turn.

Instead, it struck the coupling around the neck, instantly deflagrating the metal and splitting the hermetic seal. Air toxicity around the core was lethal, even for a Traitor Space Marine.

The Warpsmith's helm broke off, hitting the deck with a clang. A scarred, grey face looked at Haephestus with malice. The Traitor Marine fired back, a plume of burning promethium that lapped around the edges of Haephestus' refractor field. He was unscathed but momentarily blinded. It also fouled his targeting array, so his next shot went wild.

The Traitor Marine was moving, a swarm of serpentine mechadendrites uncoiling from its scabby robes and armour. It was also choking, though as the fire marring Haephestus' vision ebbed he saw a crusting membrane beginning to form over the Traitor Marine's exposed face as its mucranoid organ went to work. Skin was already flaking off though, dissolving like parchment in acid. Yellowed bone gleamed beneath. Haephestus fired off a rapid salvo, striking armour, eroding softsealed joints. The Traitor Marine stumbled, one of its serpentine arms whipping around some pipework to steady it as the others snapped out blades and churning saws.

Haephestus engaged further defences, stepping back as the abomination desperately hurtled at him. An array of las-cutters, plasma-torches and meltaguns attached to multi-jointed servo-arms snapped from their mountings on his back. The resulting fusillade cut the Traitor Marine apart, bisecting limbs and cleaving through armour as if it were nothing. The discombobulated pieces struck the deck in a noisy mess, mechadendrites sparking and flopping weakly with the dying dregs of abruptly severed power.

Only then did Haephestus feel the pain receptors in his body light up like mercury flares. He clutched his side where the shot had struck him. Blood and oil oozed from between armour plates. The wound was deep, and he staggered, holding on to the wall to steady himself before welding the armour shut and restoring its hermetic seal.

The weapons array retracted behind his back, and Haephestus was about to return to the core to determine exactly what had been done to it when alpha and beta charged at him through the gap in the gate. His termination protocols had no effect, some hostile code driving the cyborgs and overriding all other commands. It bled off them like an invisible fog, briefly fouling the Techmarine's visual returns and slowing his reactions.

Alpha struck him across the chest, the fork arm lethal and denting Haephestus' plastron.

Beta clamped his left forearm and squeezed.

Haephestus shunted away the agony to another part of his brain. The vambrace of his left arm had twisted, and the bone was being crushed. He used his right hand to unclamp a short-hafted axe from his belt. A thumb and forefinger twist of the grip saw the haft lengthen to a long polearm. Haephestus swung, the cog-toothed axe blade burring.

Oil and biological matter spattered his armour as he bisected alpha across the coronal plane. The resultant downswing clove beta's skull in two, the blow hard enough to split his rib bone and lodge the blade halfway down the servitor's chest. Organs and machine parts spewed out between the tear in beta's environment suit like an overstuffed sack finally bursting its stitches. The biological slop mixed with alpha's in a grimy, dark slurry.

Haephestus' armour systems registered severe damage. His primary and secondary heart showed massively elevated activity. The rapid influx of hyper-endorphins had made him groggy. He leaned heavily on the cog-axe, using its haft as a crutch. The left arm was useless and hung at his side. The plastron had held, but his rib plate beneath had suffered severe trauma, leaving every breath feeling like churned glass on his insides. Blinking rapidly and trying to prevent his body from going into extreme shock, Haephestus saw figures through the gap in the gate.

They were moving quickly, hunting through the shadows and the chemical fog. They wore masks. They were coming for him.

CHAPTER TWENTY

ALL HANDS

The vox had brought Sicarius to his feet. He strapped the scabbarded sword he had left by his side back onto his belt.

'Stay here,' he warned Vedaeh, who nodded mutely, knowing better than to challenge the captain after what she had just heard.

He was heading for the door to the Reclusiam and almost at the edge of the threshold when she said, 'Be careful, Cato. You are the heart of this ship and those aboard. All hands look to you.'

Sicarius paused to absorb that statement, opened the door and stepped out of the room.

Gaius Prabian was waiting for him on the other side.

'I assume you have heard, captain?'

'Roan's men were vetted by Venatio. No sign of taint, no moral corruption of any sort.'

'Darkness finds a way into men's hearts,' was the only explanation the company champion could give.

They started walking swiftly in the direction of deck thirteen, Sicarius only hesitating a moment to ensure the door to the Reclusiam was sealed behind him.

'I want protection for Vedaeh,' he said, cloak flapping behind him with the urgency of his steps.

'I have seen to it, my lord. A squad of armsmen are on the way.' Prabian paused, then added, 'There were no Astartes to spare.'

'We should have kept a closer eye on Roan. Isolated like that...'

'You think we could have stopped it?'

They had passed through the first corridor, Sicarius acknowledging the few crewmen they met along the way. The mood was feverish, on edge, although only the Ultramarines knew the nature of the thing that had manifested in deck thirteen. Its presence had been felt nonetheless, and spoke for the pervasive influence of the warp on ignorant and unready minds.

'I think the warp has depleted us, and I think we are currently ill-equipped for another crisis.'

Crossing a junction, they headed left. The next section ended in a chevron-marked barrier. Prabian dismissed the enginseer standing sentry outside with a curt slash of his hand. He then proceeded to lift the gate, hauling it up with raw strength and revealing the maintenance shaft beyond.

'I know there is no point in telling you to armour yourself before we commit ourselves to this encounter,' said Prabian.

Sicarius stepped onto the reinforced mesh platform and engaged the mechanism that set it churning down into the darkness below. Prabian jumped lightly aboard and pulled the security gate back down behind him. Flashing lumens lit the shadows in intermittent yellow light as they descended. They strafed Sicarius' face, picking out scars and old wounds.

Another face watched him from beyond the gate. It kept pace with the lift, a constant presence as the decks went past in blurry stencilled lettering. Its eyes glowed, burning dulcet and green, a malign intelligence contained in a mechanised body. Sicarius stared back. His hand, clenched around the haft of the Tempest Blade, tightened its grip.

'I have all the armour I need,' he replied and averted his gaze.

Musty air and the reek of machine oil drifted up to them on the noisy breeze of coolant fans. Heat came with it, drawn from the ship's engines. The maintenance shaft ran down the entirety of the lower decks. It moved steadily, but not quickly. It was made with dependability in mind, not speed, but it was direct and the quickest way to their destination.

'Then I ask only this...' said Prabian, drawing his sword. The gladius was forged of Talassarian steel. It had a blue tinge to the metal, a quirk of the folding process, and the words 'animo' and 'honoris' were etched in High Gothic on either side of the blade. The edge caught the light and flashed brilliantly like captured fire before returning to its original state. 'If you are planning on doing anything reckless then some warning would be appreciated. I would prefer you to at least afford me the opportunity to give my life for yours. Penitence for failure doesn't suit me, Cato.' Prabian gave a half-smile.

Sicarius laughed. 'I make no promises, Gaius. Stay on your toes.'

Prabian gave a short bow. 'It is my perpetual state of being.'

They faced forwards, the clunking refrain of the lifter the only sound between them until Sicarius drew the Tempest Blade. Lightning crackled down its perfect length, and it glowed with an inner fire that no darkness could quench. Its casting was perfect, a mirror-sheen blade of storm-wrack adamantium that appeared to churn with the wildness of oceans. Intricate filigree bedecked the hilt, the nobility of Sicarius' familial line captured in metal.

A metallic chime sounded as their two swords came together, both a signal to war and a mark of utmost respect between warriors. The weight of duty descended.

'We have to save them, Gaius.'

'On my honour, captain,' he replied, 'we will or I shall die trying.'

Pillium fell to his knees for the third time. He had one hand pressed against the red wound to his chest and his free arm draped around Sharna's shoulders. She could not bear his weight – the fact she even tried was almost laughable, but he had neither the strength nor the will to argue. She cried out as his armoured body pressed upon her, a small noise suggestive of stifled pain. It carried a note of desperation.

'Get up,' she urged, and Pillium heard the guttural retching and swallowing of the beast as it devoured the last morsels of Tiberus. 'Please...' More whimpering from the mortal. Her heart thundered and Pillium could tell her sanity hung by a tenuous thread.

'Get her out!'

A cry from deeper into the hall. Had deck thirteen really been this long? It had not felt far on the way in, but then he hadn't had to crawl on his hands and knees.

The words were Seppio's, one of Secutius' squad. Pillium turned, still down, and wanting to draw a weapon he no longer had in a hand that was unable to grasp it. The other Primaris Marine lived, then. The darkness hid him from sight. The lamps had shorted or the power drain had reached a critical mass. Either way, it was as black as the deep ocean and just as forbidding. Muzzle flare tore a hole in the dark, a savage rip doomed to reseal, that revealed a head, arms and torso but no legs. The beast had ripped them off.

It had caught them, half charging, half flying on its nascent wings, faster than they could outrun.

Aegidus had been the rearguard. He had engaged, bolt rifle spitting out the last of its rounds. He had died quickly, bludgeoned and crushed by a gnarled fist. Cajus had been less fortunate. His death was piecemeal and slow. Only Seppio and Tiberus dragging Pillium back from the torture had prevented him from selling his own life as cheaply.

It had bought them time, the beast's sudden fascination with Cajus' anatomy. It had obliterated Aegidus' skull, and smeared it across the deck, bone, blood and matter. Cajus' head it flensed whilst it was still attached to the body. His screams of agony rang for several haunting minutes.

They had got close to the entrance, where Sharna would roll back the gate and lock this thing in its prison until more warriors could be found to help kill it. Pillium could see the way out now, even as he remembered Secutius, caught up in the beast's claws and pulled apart like a piece of meat. And Tiberus, engulfed behind its wings as the beast pounced. Their ends were ignominious, inglorious.

Pillium hauled himself up, Sharna pushing ineffectually. In a part of his brain, the small part that was not otherwise occupied with thoughts of how he might survive to later kill this monstrosity, he supposed she needed to focus on something, some small act to keep the terror at bay just a little longer. Fear killed the mind and the death of the mind led to the death of the body, and that is why fear had been bred out of his kind. It had no purchase, but something had slipped in, regardless of his conditioning. In the presence of the beast, Pillium felt a primordial unease, a deep and abiding sense of wrongness that he could not shake.

Seppio's last act of defiance ended as his weapon fell silent.

Pillium ran, Sharna clinging on around his neck, though the agony was incandescent. His wounds knitted, the bones realigned. It hurt like a forge fire and retreat was anathema to him, but to stand his ground now was to meet death and condemn Sharna to the same fate. He would not have that on his conscience, even in death, *especially* in death where there was no hope of redemption.

'Hold on to me, quartermaster,' he said, and heard the roaring of the beast behind them.

'Kharnath!' it raged, in a voice dredged from some dark abyssal place.

They barrelled through the opening, pounding hoof-beats like a cavalry charge hounding their steps.

Pillium let Sharna down and turned to face the beast. It had slowed, perhaps to savour the kill. It was *huge,* a hulking shadow of red-meat skin and over-taut and bulked muscle. Hot, coal-black eyes regarded him with bestial malice. Wings at full stretch cast a bat-like shadow. Smoke, spilling from its hide, obscured the rest.

'Seal it,' said Pillium and unsheathed his gladius, determined to at least die with a weapon in his hands.

The emergency lumens at the edge of the entranceway flickered. Sharna failed her first attempt at the lock code, her shaking fingers making a mess of it.

'Do it now, quartermaster,' Pillium urged, getting into stance and readying himself for a fight he could not contest, let alone win.

Sharna tried again and this time the lock code was accepted. Gears grinding, the door began to move. It had reached halfway when the lumens winked out and all power failed. The door stopped moving. Sharna's anguish was a barely heard whisper.

'Oh, Throne...'

CHAPTER TWENTY-ONE

THE VITAL SPARK

They had been infiltrated. As Haephestus fought the cultists in the catacombs, he knew this was the only logical explanation. He also realised the goal here was not to kill him – even with one hand, he was destroying his enemies with ease – it was to delay him and sabotage the ship.

Power, it always came to this. Dominance, rulership, energy, everything that man and alien had fought over for millennia was for power. In the deep engine core it had a physical manifestation, the very force that drove the ship and gave it life. Sever that and the ship would die. But that had not been the sole aim of the Warpsmith he had fought and killed. The life blood of the ship had not just been cut off, it had been compromised. Tainted. Haephestus felt the data-corruption in the air. It had altered the golems' programming, turning alpha and beta against him. And it had crept into the entire vessel. The ship's data-feed fed through him. In nano-seconds he was able to parse vast screeds of binharic, deciphering the extent of the damage. Life support, motive function, everything had been compromised. A total and complete shutdown of all systems, barring one. The warp engine derived its power from a self-perpetuating source. Only it and the Geller field it generated remained operational.

Haephestus processed as he fought, multitasking with a Martian's cognitive assurance.

As he attempted to root out the data-corruption, a cultist came swinging at him with a chainaxe. It was an industrial model, designed for cutting pipes and metal plates. Even swung with a mortal's meagre strength, it would chew through softseal armour joints without difficulty. Haephestus took the blow on his shoulder, sparks spitting from the guard, chain teeth snapping at paint but little else. He swung his arm around, the volkite pistol back in his hand, and cored out the cultist's chest.

He shot two more at distance, deflagrating their crude environment suits and letting them die painful deaths from the atmosphere's toxicity. Stepping over the writhing bodies, he engaged the rest. The cog-axe was back mag-locked to his hip. His injuries had stabilised and he could walk and fight, but his left arm hung useless at his side. In the narrow spaces of the deep engine core, Haephestus had determined a pistol was the more efficient option. So it had proven.

Four more cultists lay dead. Haephestus took no satisfaction in it. To him, war and battle were equations, a balancing of effort versus efficiency. He counted twenty dead in total. All baseline human, all dressed in crude environment suits, all bearing the aquila, albeit the tattoo had been roughly scratched away. These men and women had once been crew. Now they were enemies. Privation and fear had driven them to madness. Haephestus had no logic to explain the influence of the warp but he knew the longer they were adrift in its capricious tides, the chances of their survival diminished.

He walked heavily back to the core. Principal amongst his concerns now was the reignition of the main furnace. The energy conversion rate of the core was less than suboptimal. Failure to boost output soon would result in permanent endothermic stasis. After that, no available measures would bring the power back online.

In the few minutes it had taken to reach the core, Haephestus had isolated and neutralised the hostile data-cyphers released by the Warpsmith. They had been rudimentary, scrapcode that even a low-level tech-priest could unravel. Its deployment, then, had not been to permanently disable the ship. The intent was temporary paralysis. He wondered what for.

The vox was still scrambled. The malicious code and his current depth in the ship conspired to make communication to above decks impossible. He was still scrubbing transmission bands when he re-interfaced with the core via mechadendrite implant. Engaged fully with the core's machine-spirit, Haephestus perceived the rapidly diminishing output and concluded there was a need for drastic action.

He disconnected from the core, quickly mounting an access gantry to where the furnace burned laboriously. An immense metal chamber contained the fiery heart of the ship, a molten promethium mixture like magma. Haephestus had to manually open up a small porthole in the coal-black vessel. It took considerable effort and the application of heavy-grade Mechanicus tools. A volatile sea churned within, its perfect actinic blue waves flickering with crests of white fire. Warning sigils instantly flared across the Techmarine's retinal lens display. He dismissed them. Even operating at a fraction of its potential, the heat spikes were significant. His armour bore the brunt, a convection wave that blistered paint and ate at ceramite.

Only a massive convective input would provoke the fusion reaction to reignite the core. It was a failing dwarf star, bleeding out radiation pressure and fighting a cascade of falling hydrogen layers. Heat death was imminent. Stepping back from the porthole, Haephestus' servo-armature unclamped the separate generator for his armour. At the moment of disconnection, he felt a sudden divorcement of flesh, cybernetics and suit. It immediately weighed much more heavily. The power plant's housing contained a small nuclear reactor. Its concomitant parts were hard-bonded, proofed against extreme kinetic stress and temperature shielded. He took a pair of krak grenades from his weapons belt and attached them to one side of the generator. Their combined incendiary reaction would magnify and split the housing, exposing it to the dying furnace.

It was crude and ill-considered.

If it worked, it would also very likely result in his death.

'Forgive me, Omnissiah,' uttered Haephestus as he dropped the generator into the furnace, praying for a vital spark.

CHAPTER TWENTY-TWO

I AM HIS SHIELD...

Pillium could barely stand. Though his body strived to repair his wounds, it could not restore him enough to face this monster and prevail.

'Run,' he told Sharna.

She was weeping, clinging to the arched door frame. 'I can't. You have to carry me...'

'I can't outrun it, quartermaster. I'm sorry. If we both run, it will follow.'

Since the flight from the muster hall, Pillium had begun to get some sense of the beast. The only reason it had not already borne him down was because he had turned to face it. He would die in this place, but at least his wounds would be to the front.

'Is anyone coming to help us?' Sharna whispered.

Pillium shook his head, his eyes on the darkness and the monstrous silhouette slowly stalking through it. His vox was dead, damaged when he had been struck. He had to hope reinforcements were on the way, not for his own sake but for the rest of the crew. This beast would devour them all.

'Close your eyes,' he told Sharna. Pillium was about to head back into the chamber and confront the beast when a voice stopped him.

'Stand aside.'

He turned. A warrior walked in front of him and stepped beyond the threshold of the stalled gate to deck thirteen. He was unarmoured, barring a simple leather cuirass, and a blue cloak swept behind him. At first Pillium thought he might be suffering from some form of delirium brought about by his injuries and exposure to the warp, for the warrior was a head and a half shorter than he and only seemed to be carrying a silver gladius and a buckler in his scarred hands.

But he was real, a white-haired warrior, a veteran of old wars.

'You can't...' Pillium growled. Pain knifed into him with every drawn breath. 'You can't face that thing alone.'

The beast had stopped, silently brooding amidst its own darkness, seemingly content to wait. Perhaps it had sensed the challenge, tasted the imminent violence on the air and welcomed it. Pillium did not know what appalled him more, the bestial and unfettered rage or the sudden rush of martial honour. Savage intellect glinted in its burning cinder eyes.

'Stay behind me,' said the warrior, his voice measured and calm. He glanced over his shoulder at the wounded Primaris Marine. 'And do not follow.'

Pillium recognised him then. This was Gaius Prabian, one of Sicarius' old Lions and martial Champion of the Second Company. An incongruous thought struck him in that moment of recognition, of how he had never sparred with the Champion, of how he had never seen him in the arena at all. But Prabian had a swordsman's gait, a light-footed tread and a loose readiness about his every movement. He considered then that he might have been fortunate not to have ever faced the Champion.

Pillium was about to go after Prabian when another voice stopped him.

'Do as he says.'

This one he knew instantly. Cato Sicarius was standing behind him, barely armoured, a red cloak across his shoulder and the unsheathed Tempest Blade in his hand.

'He'll die alone against it,' said Pillium.

Sicarius' reply was solemn. 'He isn't alone.'

The captain looked down at Sharna, who stared back with eyes wide.

'It won't close, sire,' she said. 'I can't get it to close.' She began to gibber, entering the lock codes over and over but without success.

'You've done all you can, Brother Pillium,' Sicarius told him. 'Get her to safety.'

'There will be no safety if that creature is not–'

'Do it now.'

Pillium thought about arguing further but this was Sicarius. Even if duty and discipline were insufficient to hold his tongue, the Knight of Talassar had a presence, an undeniable authority that went beyond Primaris Marine and first born.

'I vow to return, captain,' he said, gathering Sharna into his arms. His last sight as he hurried to get the quartermaster away was of the two Ultramarines, standing one in front of the other and facing down the beast.

Then the door began to move as power was restored throughout the ship, and Pillium stopped.

Sicarius cried out, 'Gaius!' but the way was swiftly closed

and too narrow for him to get through. The Champion did not react. Instead, he swept his cloak aside and it fell, rippling and as blue as an ocean. The beast bellowed, beating massive wings and signalling its intent to charge. The restored lumens defined its horror and monstrosity in sickly yellow light. Prabian brought the gladius up to his forehead, pressing the blade to his skin. A last salute. The Ultramarines sigil on his buckler glinted as his litany of battle began.

'I am His shield…'

Courage.

Honour.

The door shut, and a heavy toll resounded across the ship.

CHAPTER TWENTY-THREE

A GATHERING OF MIGHT

Argo Helicos had his sword drawn and Aequitas in a ready hand as he prepared to face what awaited him beyond the door. The auto-bolt rifle had been master-forged. It had a gilded stock and even its ammunition was machine-blessed with runes of accuracy. The sword's name was Vindicta, an honorific Helicos was determined it would earn this day.

He wore no helm, but the rest of his armour shimmered like a deep blue sky. He wanted them to see his face. He wanted *it* to see it, too.

Standing in the vanguard, the very tip of the spear, Helicos felt the regard of his men upon him. 'Beyond this door,' he said, his strident voice carrying, 'we face hell. It is why we exist. To fight the monsters in the darkness. It is our purpose. War and death are our creed. They call us angels, but we know better, don't we? We are not angelic. We are dread and we are blood, we are the red sword and the thrown spear. We are the final battle, the end, and we shall know no fear. This is what we are.'

A bellicose cry erupted from the ranks.

'Ah ugh! Ah ugh!'

They twice rapped weapons against their vambraces, curt and precise.

It was an affirmation and a call to arms.

'We are Macragge,' declared Helicos. 'We are Ultramar!'

At this signal, a host of Primaris Marines readied their weapons.

Thirty warriors in cobalt-blue armour stood at the lieutenant's command. On one side, a knot of tank-like Aggressors. Clad in bulky Gravis plate, they had the look of heavily armoured pugilists with their weapon gauntlets thrust forwards pugnaciously. Ammunition feeds ratcheted into position, a semicircle of bronze shell casings locking into every breech. Back-mounted grenade launchers angled into firing arcs. On the opposite side, the Hellblasters ignited plasma incinerators and a hot, azure glow lit up the energy coils of their weapons. Behind them, in the rear ranks, was every other Primaris Marine under Helicos still able to fight. Bolt rifles clacked to attention, each lethal barrel aimed at the sealed door to deck thirteen.

Not all were armoured. Some had come in light training plate as the warp siphon continued to wreak havoc and rob the Adeptus Astartes of one of their greatest assets. They went bare-armed, these Ultramarines, the interface ports rooted in their flesh visible and empty. Each of them had the tattoo of the ultima on his left shoulder, the inverted omega sigil of the Chapter inked in blue. Swords were drawn. Spears brandished. In their rudimentary armour, they had the look of much more ancient warriors so as to be almost anachronistic.

Silence descended. The hammering from behind the door had ceased. It had taken a battering. Huge fist-shaped indentations deformed the metal. The door was thick enough to deny a tank. Against the beast, it had barely held.

The light caught the bronze-coloured blade of Vindicta as Helicos raised it aloft.

'Open the gate,' he declared.

The lumens within the next chamber flickered frenziedly, animating a horrific scene.

Gaius Prabian hung for all to see. His grisly perch had been made from the ship's frame, struts ripped from its walls and bent with brute strength into the shape of an eight-pointed star. Prabian's arms were draped over two of its tines and nailed down with a jagged piece of metal. His legs dangled freely, blood slowly dripping from his feet and gathering in a shiny dark pool beneath. He had been eviscerated, his ribcage split and spread apart. His organs were scattered about like unwanted offal. A sword lay in front of him, half drowned in the blood pool. The blade side bearing the word 'animo' was face up. This was how Helicos identified him, for Prabian's head was missing and only a savaged stump of neck remained.

Helicos' expression hardened further when he saw what else was revealed in the lumen light. Grimly, he spoke into the vox.

'Brother Prabian is dead,' he uttered, 'and the beast is gone.'

Acid burns marked the sides of a massive pit. Tufts of wiry hair and thick, syrupy blood clung to its ragged edges. The beast had dug down into the ship, rending and burning its way through the metal and leaving a yawning, dark chasm in its wake. It had to be over a hundred feet straight down into a wretched mess of jagged, scything struts and rebar. There was no further sign, only the reek of blood, cinder and spoiled meat.

'You were right...' said Helicos, and felt his failure chafe. 'It's coming for you.'

Sicarius sent an acknowledgement and looked up into the vaulted ceiling. Not so long ago he had descended from that darkened place, wrapped in fire and bringing wrath. Now something else would follow in that wake, not an angel but a devil, bringing wrath all the same.

The warp engine roared behind Sicarius, its uncanny energies casting strange, flickering shadows upon the wall. They looked skeletal and loomed like destiny.

Daceus' voice broke their brief hold over him.

'Is he dead?'

Sicarius nodded, not meeting the veteran's gaze.

'He is, Retius. The Lions have lost another.'

'I shall mourn him,' said Daceus. 'After we have taken retribution.'

Sicarius could not argue with that. He donned his crested war-helm, the Suzerain's Mantle a reassuring presence clad upon his body.

'No quarter for this thing,' he said, his hand upon the pommel of his sword. 'No restraint.' He activated Luxos and heard the plasma coils build to a satisfying whine. He addressed the warriors stood with him, the last of the Second Company Ultramarines.

'We were once known as the War-Born and served a battle king of Macragge. These were elder days, remembered by a few,' he said, his powerful voice echoing around the warp engine chamber. 'Elianu Trajan remembered. Our dead Chaplain, he gifted me this truth. Of our proud heritage and the legacy of our forebears. We are not Ultramarines this day. We are not. For our realm is a civilised place that cleaves to the virtues of order and peace. This day we are the savage, we are the blood hungry, we are the slayers of monsters... It comes, this abyssal thing that has killed our brothers. It expects to find mere warriors. Instead it will find unfettered fury. It will find agony and bloody vengeance. Draw swords with me now, brothers,' he cried, letting the Tempest Blade slip free of its sheath, a cascade of lightning briefly crackling along its edge. 'Become wrath! Become terror! And let us kill this bloody thing!'

Fifty or more swords drew in concert, a feral shout of metal and defiance.

Above them, in the vaults of the chamber, the cacophony of the beast sounded, guttural and bellowing. The stench of dead things and fire and smoke choked the air in a filthy stranglehold. The ceiling caved with no further warning, and the beast came with it, dragging huge chunks of metal and stone. A deluge fell upon the Ultramarines, crushing bodies. Bolters sang their belligerent battle hymns in reply, sparking and ricocheting off the beast's impenetrable hide. It barely slowed down. A beat of its massive, leathery wings and it was amongst them, goring and hacking. It bit off heads and turned veteran warriors into shredded meat. It revelled in it, the blood and slaughter, seemingly empowered and emboldened.

Skulls rattled against its chest as it fought, strung around its neck with cords of human sinew. Sicarius knew that Gaius' head would be amongst them, his bleached-bone visage staring sightlessly, demanding revenge. He made his way through the throng, furious that the beast had put itself clear of his blade through sheer chance. Ultramarines were dying, cut apart as if they were nothing, but those who lived fought like bastards.

A flung spear embedded in the beast's flank and it roared, hissing pain through clenched teeth. A sword impaled its thigh, tainted meat run through on a silver spit. A blur of chain teeth snagged against its hip, chewing up tufts of greasy, black hair until a mechanism fouled. An axe nicked a piece of wing. The beast retaliated, tearing limbs and ripping off heads, war-helms and all. It threw the wretched trophies back at its aggressors, hailing them with the body parts of former comrades.

Sicarius ducked the grisly ammunition, bounding now as the ranks of his brothers thinned and the corpse piles grew. He leapt a falling warrior who had buckled over, hands clamped around his stomach to stop his innards spilling out, and fired Luxos. The bright blue beam seared the beast's right eye, bursting it and blinding it.

Such rage. Sicarius felt it buffet him, the unnatural heat blistering his armour.

'Here I am!' he shouted.

The beast turned, a warrior crushed in its fist. Casting the dead Ultramarine aside, it barrelled towards Sicarius.

Sicarius swept his sword as he lunged out of harm's way. He felt the storm-wrack adamantium connect and heard hot blood hiss against the blade. Then he was up, turning on his heel and moving, even as the beast moved with him. It ignored the other blades now, the spears sticking from its hide like mighty arrow shafts. It had found worthy prey, and though it still killed and maimed as it went, it only wanted Sicarius. The beast bore down upon him, sweeping its massive wings around Sicarius. He stabbed with the Tempest Blade, a thrust into its chest that drew an almighty bellow of pain. Wrenching the sword loose, he weaved aside as the beast threw out a claw. Sicarius hacked down, severing hand from wrist, and sent lightning coursing up its arm. Another roar. Ultramarines rushing to intervene were battered back and slain. Only Sicarius could stand his ground, as the dead began to amass around him. The war cry of bolters barely registered as he duelled the beast, cutting and slashing, determined to weaken it for the death blow and knowing any significant hit in return would see him ended, and another skull for its neck.

It *was* weakened. The sustained attack by his battle-brothers had begun to wear at it, as friction would fray a rope. The beast frayed too. It diminished, its dark skin paling to grey, its thick hide growing piebald. The heat of it dimmed, a smouldering flame. Its wings tore apart like gossamer, spittle-thin strands of sinew holding them together.

Whatever purchase it had on the ship was slowly being eroded.

'Hold your blades!' shouted Sicarius as he stood before the beast bowed and broken before him, now no larger than a man. It snarled its contempt, its eye upon the shimmering warp engine.

'I know what you are,' Sicarius told it. His sword dripped with hissing ichor as he held it to the beast's neck. 'Your *kind*. You chose poorly coming here. And you have met your end.'

The beast opened its dripping maw to speak, barely clinging to physical form at all.

'I am the end, I am Kha–'

It choked on the rest, Sicarius' sword thrust deep into its gullet and piercing the back of its head.

'*We* are the end,' he uttered softly, staring the beast down as it began to discorporate. 'We are Macragge.'

CHAPTER TWENTY-FOUR

DYING LIGHT

The warp had come. Not as an ephemeral, incorporeal thing. Not merely as conjured visions inflicted upon a weary mind, or creeping paranoia, or the glimpse of the uncanny in a poorly lit corridor, or a strange sickness or profound madness. It had reached out with an infernal hand.

And it had touched the ship, and everyone aboard.

Vedaeh had felt it, as all amongst the crew must have. It resonated in her bones, set her hackles up, her skin hot and perspirant. Dread. That's what had come upon her. That sense of something horrible and inevitable, but without form or tangible evidence of its presence. She had vomited, a violent and prolonged upheaval that had left her gasping and afraid on the cold floor of the Reclusiam. She knew now that this was the beast, the thing wrought from the stuff of the warp and made corporeal by death and slaughter. It had fallen in the end, despatched back to the ether by Sicarius' hand. Rumours persisted, even eight days later, when the facts should have been well established. That Sicarius had fought it alone with only his sword to protect him. That he had vanquished it with a single blow. That Guilliman or the Emperor Himself had invested him with power and the beast had quailed before it.

Vedaeh expected the truth to be uglier and yet somehow braver than all of that. She had not seen Sicarius since their last session, and as she knelt before the shrine to Elianu Trajan, she glanced up at the many volumes she had committed to his discourse. For five years, she had chronicled the journey of the *Emperor's Will*. She knew her history, even very, very ancient history, of the order known as 'remembrancers'. They too had been chroniclers, though during a time of great hope and aspiration that had turned to bleak and bitter darkness. She had only ever known darkness, for this was the galaxy they had made for themselves and now they had to live in it. Or survive it.

Olvo Sharna was dead. This much she had managed to learn. Her end was neither horrific nor worthy of note. She had simply faded, found in her bunk, eyes wide, pale of skin and bereft of life. She had seen it, the beast. She had felt its presence first-hand, and Vedaeh had no doubts, based on her own reaction, that this is what killed the quartermaster. It saddened her. She had liked Olvo, though she knew little of her life or desires. A quiet woman with a quiet sort of strength. To survive all that she had when even the Adeptus Astartes had perished almost to a man... it gave Vedaeh pause in considering the Emperor's benevolence.

'Are we all just children, crying at a golden sun for deliverance?' she asked of the shrine. 'Except the sun is dead and we simply don't realise yet because it is so far away...'

She bowed her head, chastising herself for such unworthy

thoughts, and wrinkling her nose at the scent of cinder still clinging to her nostrils. It was bitter, acrid, like old dying fires reluctant to grow cold. The nightmares persisted too. Of fire. Of blood. Of fell places and dark imaginings. She had slept in the Reclusiam these past few nights, finding no peace in her quarters, which stood empty and untouched like a tomb.

The ship was not much different. The dead were many. Olvo Sharna had not been the only casualty. Every day the overtaxed armsmen found more deckhands hanging by their necks or comrades with their skulls shot through and their brains spattered over the wall. Piece by piece, they were eroding, their collective voices quieter and quieter until the silence finally drowned them.

The sodium lamps flickered overhead, reminding Vedaeh of the other crisis. As if they needed another one. Haephestus had found a temporary solution to the 'siphoning', as it was being called by some of the crew, but the effect was like placing an ill-fitting bung in a split dam – the water still leaked out. It was almost drained. More decks had been shut off to preserve what little power remained. These places were now the province of the dead, left in void-frozen passageways and airless chambers to drift and to dream endless dreams...

Vedaeh shook herself, fighting down maudlin thoughts. She raised her eyes, meeting Trajan's shattered retinal lenses.

'You don't say much...' she said, then smiled sadly. 'Please forgive me, Lord Chaplain. I have a great need.'

She rose to her feet, grunting with the effort. The chain around her neck was heavy. It was heavier than she thought it would be. The lights flickered again, and went out for a few seconds. In the last eight days, they had lost power seventeen times. On one of those occasions the outage had lasted for six hours. Madness had seized the ship. Madness and fear. Not all of the interlopers and traitors had been caught. Or simply more had turned, desperate and afraid. Rabid. A purge had proven difficult, with resources so stretched – and the experience with the ration riots and the cultists who had been lurking in the open, men and women who had turned from the Emperor's light, suggested the problem was ingrained. With tens of thousands of crew, despite the losses, it made excision of this taint almost impossible. The warp would have its way, Vedaeh supposed. Only it seemed to coincide with the darkness. As the light came back on, she muttered, 'Ave Imperator.'

A gentle knock at her door saw her smoothing down her robes.

'Enter,' she said, when she had composed herself.

An armed escort bowed as they came in, a woman and a man. She was an older woman, her dark hair cut short and with a worn sort of appearance. By contrast, her companion looked young and slightly haunted about the eyes, but there was something about the two of them together that gave Vedaeh hope. She couldn't explain exactly why. Perhaps it was because they still looked human under all of the suffering, or that the woman favoured her with a genuine smile.

'At least we have light,' said Vedaeh.

'He's making his address on the hour, ma'am.'

'For posterity, is it?' asked Vedaeh, reaching for a leather-bound journal.

'I believe it must be, ma'am. That, or a course of action has been determined.'

'He always was impetuous. Saw things others could never see,' said Vedaeh, almost to herself. 'Liked to act on them, too. It garnered him an ill-deserved reputation.'

'I would not know, ma'am.'

Vedaeh snapped out of her reverie. 'I don't recognise you, I'm sorry.'

'Lieutenant Reda.' She gestured to her comrade. 'Corporal Gerrant.'

The man nodded to Vedaeh.

'What's your first name, lieutenant?' she asked. 'And you too, corporal.'

'Arna, ma'am. Arna Reda.'

'Vanko Gerrant, ma'am.'

'Arna... Vanko.' She looked at them both in turn. 'Please don't call me ma'am. That is an overly officious title. I am Vedaeh.'

'As you wish...' said Reda, though the awkwardness she felt was obvious, 'Vedaeh.'

'There are so few of us left, Arna. I think we should at least know each other's first names and take some comfort in that familiarity.'

Reda nodded, though it was unclear if she did so because she agreed with the sentiment or because she wanted to move things along.

Vedaeh didn't see the need to press.

They left the Reclusiam together, Vedaeh with her journal under one arm, as the young armsman led them out. The lumens were flickering again, the effect strobing and monochromatic.

'I'm not sure I will ever get used to that,' said Vedaeh, gesturing to the overhead strip lamp and tapping out a metronomic walking rhythm with her cane. 'I find it disconcerting. Do you find it disconcerting, Arna?'

'I do, ma'am.'

Vedaeh didn't correct her this time. Her gaze went to a knot of grubby deckhands coming the opposite way. The transit corridor was a relatively major thoroughfare of the ship, but recent events had left it almost always deserted. The appearance of the deckhands seemed incongruous then, but not unwelcome. At least it was evidence of life.

Again, the lights flickered, snapping out completely for a second or two, before juddering and fizzing back.

'Is it the main muster hall?' asked Vedaeh. 'Where Cato is making his speech?'

'I beg your pardon, ma'am?' Reda replied.

The deckhands were fairly close now, talking amongst themselves in low voices, their faces and fingers stained with enginarium grime. Loose smocks overlaid rugged uniforms beneath. Shaved heads showed old cuts and bruises from their heavy manual work.

'Apologies,' said Vedaeh, her eye lingering on the lead deckhand, who had not stopped looking at her for a few seconds. Perhaps she looked strange to him, a robed woman with a bone-white arm the texture of porcelain and inlaid with gold. 'It's a bad habit. Lord Sicarius, his speech is in–'

'The Ultima Hall,' Reda interjected to be helpful. 'That's correct, ma'am.'

Vedaeh mused to herself. 'Expansive for so few...'

Above, the whine of failing power conduits built to a scream. The deckhands, whom Vedaeh had not stopped watching, seemed to speed up just as a second group appeared to the rear. She was already moving, reaching for the pistol she kept beneath her robes, as Reda pulled her back, the lieutenant putting her body between Vedaeh and the threat.

The lumen strip popped and went out. In that same instance, the deckhands attacked.

CHAPTER TWENTY-FIVE

AT ANY COST

'Firing!' yelled Reda, and the explosive report of her shotgun rattled the corridor, hurting Vedaeh's ears. The forwardmost deckhand spun, smashed into the wall with half his torso missing. The shotgun's muzzle flare lit up the rest, who had donned makeshift scare masks painted with strange sigils.

From behind her, Vedaeh heard the younger armsman, Gerrant, shout out.

'Here too!'

The staccato blurt of an autocarbine sounded like an angry insect swarm as the two armsmen effectively swapped places and the corporal strafed the corridor. A muted cry, a grunt of pain. Another attacker went down.

Shots came back at them, stubber rounds that went wild or lodged in heavy carapace armour but couldn't penetrate. Vedaeh saw blades and cutters brandished in the noisy, fractured light of the fire exchange. She also counted five deckhands in front and a quick glance revealed three more behind.

Reda blasted another, before letting her shotgun fall loose on its strap and reaching for the power maul tethered at her belt as the fight swiftly moved to close quarters. At the back, Gerrant had already emptied his ammunition clip and switched to a combat knife.

Five remained, revealed in the energy dispersion field of Reda's maul. Three in front and two behind. Vedaeh shot one through the top of the skull, scalping and trepanning the deckhand who fell back in a smoking heap. She was about to turn, as Reda was engaging the other two, when she felt a massive weight bear her down. Flailing, Vedaeh lost her grip on the pistol, which went skittering off out of sight and out of reach. Her cane flew sideways as her bad leg buckled underneath her. Hot, stagnant breath washed over her face. A burly hand pressed her shoulder down with considerable strength. She half turned, as much as she was able with her attacker on top of her. Gerrant staggered, empty-handed, struggling to breathe with a length of chain wrapped around his neck, and a female deckhand on his back and pulling hard at the rusted links.

Vedaeh's attacker was bigger, much bigger. Almost certainly male, despite the ragged anonymity of his leather mask. He had a knife. Serrated. Made for filleting. As he stabbed down with it, Vedaeh realised the mask wasn't leather, and the meat he used that knife on was probably not animal either.

'Longpig...' he murmured, sweaty, eyes wide with cannibalistic hunger.

The blade didn't make the cut. It stopped short, instantly blunted as it struck Vedaeh's outstretched arm. A blood-shot, red-rimmed gaze regarded the augmetic arm and the knife dully. Vedaeh used the distraction to bring her knee up into her attacker's groin. He squeaked in pain, and she heard teeth clench. Then she punched a hole through his chest with her fist, and that was that.

She had managed to roll the burly cultist aside, his weight in death even more considerable, and was about to try to help Gerrant when a shot rang out and the female chain-wielder snapped back, her forehead cored through with a perfectly cauterised hole.

Breathing hard, Vedaeh looked up to see Reda, her concern for the younger man obvious as he retched on his hands and knees.

'This is yours, I believe, ma'am,' she said, handing the still-smoking lasgun back to its owner grip first. 'Damn fine weapon.'

'It is,' said Vedaeh, catching her breath at last and tamping down the sudden fear that came in the wake of spent adrenaline. 'You keep it. I'd say you earned it. If you could retrieve my cane, though, I'd appreciate it,' she added, picking up the journal she had dropped when she'd drawn the pistol.

Reda obliged, returning the cane as the lights fizzed on again.

'Is he alright?' Vedaeh asked of Gerrant, who had yet to regain his feet.

The corporal slowly nodded, getting up gingerly and rubbing his neck as he stooped to retrieve his autocarbine.

'He'll be fine,' Reda answered, though her gaze lingered on Gerrant and Vedaeh thought she saw concern in those hard eyes of hers. 'What about you?'

'I feel physically sick, but am otherwise unscathed.' She nodded her appreciation. 'Thanks to the two of you. I owe you my life.'

'Ours would not have been worth living if we'd let anything happen to you,' Reda replied.

Gerrant dragged the mask off the larger man who had tackled Vedaeh. 'This is a crew mark,' he said, 'lower deck, aft. He's not cult.'

Reda looked on with distaste. 'Well, he is now. Who can we trust any more?'

'I say, each other.' Vedaeh eyed the corridor ahead, lighter now but not without its shadows and alcoves. 'Is it safe to go on?'

'I have no idea, ma'am,' said Reda honestly. 'I thought this zone had been cleared.' She got on the vox, but cut the link when an Ultramarine appeared at the end of the corridor. He removed his helmet to reveal a youthful face with dark, inquisitive eyes.

'Apologies, Madame Vedaeh,' he said, raising his voice as he approached the group. 'I hope you are unhurt.'

'Were it not for Arna and Vanko here, I would not have been.'

'I'm to escort you the rest of the way. Sergeant Vorolanus.' He paid little attention to the armsmen.

'Did Sicarius send you?'

Vorolanus nodded.

'Do you have a first name?'

He paused for a second, momentarily wrong-footed. 'Scipio.'

Now it was Vedaeh's turn to nod. 'Very well, Scipio. You, I and Arna and Vanko are headed to the Ultima Hall together.'

Vorolanus briefly glanced at the armsmen. 'I assure you, I can see to your protection.'

'Nonetheless.'

Reda made to protest, 'There really is no need, ma'am. We can return to–'

'Trust, Arna. You saved my life.'

Vorolanus tried to hide a frown. 'As you wish, but stay close to me.'

'The ship remains unsafe?'

'It is still being determined,' he said, eyeing the armsmen with suspicion.

'As I said, Scipio,' said Vedaeh as she caught his look, 'I *trust* them.'

'Attacks have come from within,' he explained. 'Prolonged exposure to the warp can have a degrading effect upon the human mind, and we have been amongst the tides for a long time.'

'And you do not consider yourself human?'

'I did not mean...' Vorolanus gave a small sigh. 'Are you ready to depart?'

Vedaeh nodded. 'Please, lead on.'

The Ultima Hall echoed emptily, like a choir bereft of voices.

Banners hung from its vaulted ceiling, still and faded. It had a sepulchral quality. Even the air tasted old and dead. A statue of Guilliman stood proudly, though, a massive plinth raising it so high that you had to arch your neck to meet the primarch's gimlet eye. It had been wrought of Iaxian marble, Guilliman in the form of the warrior statesman, armoured but unarmed, a cloak hanging about his shoulders and a senator's wreath crowning his head. One foot rested upon some nondescript rock, a strange affectation of many an Imperial sculptor and ever the artistic fashion. It gave him a pioneering, redoubtable aura that Vedaeh found some comfort in.

The light was faint, and the low lumens cast lonely shadows upon the few that had mustered here.

Sicarius regarded them all, standing at the foot of the great statue, every inch the Ultramarian paragon that his father was. He had his Lions to his right hand – Daceus, his eyepatch giving him a roguish air; Venatio, clad in the white of the apothecarion and Vandius, ill at ease without the company banner in his hand. They were the only three left, now that Gaius Prabian had fallen. Vedaeh knew them by appearance, if not name. Sicarius spoke of them often, as a father might his sons, or a brother his closest siblings. To his left was a warrior Vedaeh did not recognise but knew must be Argo Helicos, commander of the Ultramarines Primaris contingent. He looked majestic in his fine armour, but could cast no shade on the Knight of Talassar. Here, even in this hall of heroes, Sicarius was peerless.

Sadly, his warrior vassals were few. Of the century and more Ultramarines who began this voyage aboard the *Emperor's Will*, barely half remained. Far from the proud and uniform force that had set out on the crusade, a piecemeal body of men now stood in that place.

Not all wore power armour, and even those that did had patched and battered war-plate. The hum of generators barely raised an utterance, as the warp siphon took its toll. Of the warriors standing in that hall, few were fully equipped, and a mixture of training cuirass and half-plate could be seen amongst the blue Aquila, Tacticus and Gravis armour.

Sicarius wore his Suzerain's Mantle, though the cloak had been torn from fighting the beast. It hung a little raggedly now, a flag at half-mast. He met Vedaeh's eye, giving the slightest nod of recognition. If he thought anything of the two mortal armsmen who attended her, he offered no sign of it.

'No more long speeches,' he said, his ice-blue gaze taking in the meagre crowd. 'We are badly bloodied and stand upon the brink. We can no longer remain in the warp and must break free of it.' He looked to the battered figure of his Techmarine, a bloody splash of red in the spattering of blue. Vedaeh noticed he shuffled uncomfortably as if carrying an injury. She also realised his armour's generator was missing, and could only imagine the heft of his unaugmented war-plate. 'Haephestus has bought us all the time he can. There is none left after this. So, we must leave.'

'My lord, how?' asked a sergeant in full plate. He had a hard face, as if carved from stone, with a flat nose and square-edged features. His right arm, Vedaeh noticed, was a bionic. 'Arkaedron is dead, may Hera have mercy, and our Navigator...'

'Has been returned to us, Fennion.' Now Sicarius glanced over at the armsmen, just a fleeting moment of regard, and Vedaeh realised these two must have been the ones responsible for retrieving Barthus from his sanctum. She had heard that had been a bad business, with many lives lost. Vedaeh regarded Reda and Gerrant with renewed respect. It took a strong will to keep your sanity after something like that. 'The Navigator will serve, and Apothecary Venatio has given assurance he is physically up to the strain.'

'Then our hopes rest on this creature,' said another warrior, much taller and wider than the one Sicarius had called Fennion. He was a Primaris Marine, and wore arrogance as casually as a cloak. No armour this one, barring a cuirass, and he clenched the haft of a spear with imperious disdain.

'Not a creature, Pillium, one of us. He is crew. Barthus will breach the confinement of the warp or we will all perish. It is a dangerous course, not taken lightly. We are few, but we must protect this ship, for have no doubt that when we attempt this feat – and we will attempt it – the hosts of hell will come for us.'

'And what of his mind?' asked Pillium. 'Is he fit for the mental rigours? Words have been spoken against it.'

'*My* words are all you need listen to, brother,' Sicarius

replied with a measure of steel in his voice. Pillium backed down at once, the change obvious even in his subtle body language. 'This *must* be done. There is simply no other choice. We shall protect this ship and this crew. It is all that matters now. We must survive. We must go on. And so we shall... at any cost. Measures will be taken. Defences readied. After that, we break warp and embrace our fate.'

The hall fell silent, all within determined to do their duty.

Vedaeh saw it in their eyes, in their postures. These men would die for him, and he for them. That was fortunate, then, for death was close. She felt it in her bones as she closed her book, leaving the last pages unfilled.

CHAPTER TWENTY-SIX

OUR LAST HOURS

Reda had fixed it on the chrono. Less than four hours until they attempted warp breach. She knew little of this arcane science, but enough to realise that trying to pull out of the warp whilst adrift and without certainty of safe harbour was akin to pushing one's self naked and blindfold through a maze of razor wire. And that not only the flesh but also the soul would be exposed to the barbs. Worse, without the light of the Emperor, navigating such volatile tides would be beyond dangerous and approaching suicidal. In all likelihood then, these would be their last hours, and so Reda decided they should at least be good ones.

'Are you alright?' She reached over to run her fingers down Gerrant's scarred back. He still had a mark around the neck and shoulders where the chain had bitten as he was slowly being strangled.

'Vanko?' she asked when he didn't answer straight away, rising slightly from her bunk and clasping the rough blankets to her chest.

Gerrant was sitting on the edge of the bed, naked and with his back to her. He stared into the darkness, unmoving but cold to the touch.

'I was just thinking about my father,' he said at length, his voice little more than a murmur. 'He was a soldier too. Not aboard a ship. He served in the Militarum.'

'I know, Vanko. You've told me this before.' Reda slipped behind him, gently wrapping her arms around his body and placing a soft kiss on the back of his neck. 'Come back to bed. We can just lie here.'

'I never knew how he died, you know,' Gerrant went on. 'A mortar shell, a bullet, trenchrot… was it something heroic, did he die fighting or was it a mundane end? Something pointless and unremarkable?'

'You shouldn't torture yourself.' She tried softly stroking his hair, but he was like stone. Unfeeling and unyielding.

'I do not think our deaths will be good deaths, Arna.' He turned to face her, eyes full of questions and regrets.

'No,' she said, her voice low, 'no, I don't think they will be either. We will probably die on this ship, and I am afraid of that, Vanko. I do not want to die here, in this way, torn apart, burned, suffocating in the void.' She tapped the chrono, and it flickered. 'But that's not now.' Reda gently caressed his stubbled chin and held it, the palm of her hand resting upon his face. 'We are just mortals amongst gods, so let us take what mortal pleasures we can, even if it is the simple comfort of companionship. If these are to be our final moments then I would have a little peace from them, wouldn't you?'

He smiled, but there was something missing in his eyes. He hadn't been the same since they had apprehended Barthus. Then she felt his hand upon her skin, warmer than his body, and her concerns melted away. They gently fell into each other's arms and back onto the bed as the chrono ticked on.

In the Reclusiam Vedaeh bowed her head before the shrine. The muttered words of a prayer passed her lips, asking the Emperor of Mankind to protect them from whatever darkness would come, to gird their souls against corruption, to light their way out of shadow.

She said these words and heard them echoed back. Her own voice, not the Emperor's.

And in that moment of revelation, surrounded by the cold stone of this place, and her hollow books and scraps of vellum, Vedaeh felt utterly, utterly alone.

The vambrace clanged loudly as it hit the armoury floor. Iulus scowled at the sudden clamour.

'How many times have you done this unassisted?' he asked, setting down his detached right shoulder guard and placing it with his helmet, gauntlet and arm greave. The bionic scraped and squealed as he flexed it, testing the automated joints.

Scipio unbuckled one side of his chestplate, venting a plume of pressure that had built up in his armour's systems. 'It's been a while,' he said.

'You never had to refit and repair your own armour on campaign?'

'I was always moving. Perils of a reconnaissance cadre, fast and light.'

'Not so light now...'

Scipio grunted as he removed his main arm greave, machining it loose with an auto-drill and carefully uncoupling the connection ports that linked it to the black mesh layer beneath, and to his actual body.

It was quiet in the armoury, a small dark chamber that smelled of oil, lapping powder and cooling metal.

'Your arm,' said Scipio, 'it's failing, isn't it?'

Iulus turned the mechanised rotator cuff. It jerked and stuck, emitting a low metallic groan before it managed to free itself. 'Like everything, brother. The power is bleeding away. I can feel the interface fraying. It's sluggish, heavy. Soon it'll be dead weight.'

'And then?'

'Then we'll either be ripped apart on the Sea of Souls or I'll have to get used to fighting one-handed.'

Scipio laughed. 'I expect so, but that's not what I meant. Sicarius is arming and armouring the brotherhood in preparation for what comes next. The power will last, hopefully just long enough for it to matter. All will fight... and die if needed. But after? I have seen our end, Iulus, and it wears the same armour and bears the same sigil as us.'

Iulus sighed, letting his bare hands fall onto his lap. He straightened his back, bending his neck to work out the kinks.

'After Black Reach, what then? Damnos... and then? The Damocles Gulf. And then, and then, and then. I trust Sicarius. He has led us for decades, Scipio. I grieve for our dead brothers. I grieve for Praxor most of all.'

Scipio nodded at that. The three of them had been friends, and had fought together since their early days in Second.

'They will not be the last.'

'What happens when the last Guardians of the Temple fall?' asked Scipio.

'Atavian may yet live.'

'Scant comfort. So few of us remain. It was a lucky chance that the Devastators ended up on another ship of the fleet.

He will likely be absorbed into another company, and with him the last of the old legacy.'

'You are uncharacteristically maudlin, brother. If we fall then others will take our place.'

'And you feel nothing for that? With every death here in the void, the reality of it comes closer.'

Iulus smiled sadly. 'Do not concern yourself with how our end will come. Ours has always been a violent, glorious life. Revel in that, and if it is our time to die, know that I salute you, brother, and it has been my honour to fight by your side all these many years.'

Scipio gripped Iulus' outstretched hand, and felt the strength and determination there. 'And mine, Iulus.'

The mesh of the cage crosshatched his skin with shadow scars. Pillium stood alone, drinking in the darkness and the quietude, his mind in turmoil.

He stood with a spear in his hands, leaning on its haft more than he wished he needed to. His wounds had healed, the skin and bone stitched with the miracle of his genetic enhancements, but they had left a mark. He felt... *weaker*, and that confession to himself felt as anathema as reneging on an oath to his Chapter.

A sword lay before him, a beautiful artisan's weapon that had no place in a training cage. It was Gaius Prabian's sword, the one that now had a crack running down the blade from where it had duelled the beast.

'I wish I could have fought him,' he said.

'Oh?' replied the warrior behind him. 'And do you think you would have bested him?'

'I do not know,' Pillium admitted, 'but I would like to have found out. Aside from Sicarius, he was their best.'

'*Their* best? Are we not also of the same creed, the same brotherhood, then, Pillium?'

Pillium knelt to retrieve the sword, wrapping his hand slowly around the hilt the way one might choose to pick up a venerable relic.

'We are as unalike to them as they to us, Argo. They believe we are their end, and it is true. Our strength, our endurance, every sinew, every fibre of muscle. It is superior. *We* are superior.'

'And what of experience, of courage and honour?' said Argo Helicos, stepping into Pillium's eyeline. He was not wearing his glorious war-plate but a suit of training armour, like the sergeant. 'Are they not worthy attributes?'

Pillium raised an eyebrow but made no other comment on the lieutenant's chosen attire.

'Of course,' he uttered instead, 'but it does not change the fact that they are the weaker iteration. Just because it has taken ten thousand years for evolution to catch up to them does not make it any less true.'

'Some deplore that arrogance, Pillium.'

'Such as you, brother-lieutenant.'

'I find it unbecoming.'

'But do not deny it, either.'

Argo's expression hardened then. He had also brought a blade into the arena, and its edge shone in the failing light.

'Choose,' he said.

Pillium looked from sword to spear.

'It is a relic, nothing more,' he said, putting down the sword. 'I would no more wield it than I would wield a tapestry. It did not serve Prabian in the end, so I doubt it would serve me either.'

'Spear it is then,' said Argo. 'In this, I am Argo and you Justus.'

Pillium nodded. 'I mourn them all,' he said, seconds before they were to begin. 'Prabian, Secutius… In the end, we all die the same, but we are still their betters. Let none say otherwise.'

'Let's see, shall we,' Argo replied, 'if your wounds are healed.'

'Is it a lesson you wish to impart then, lieutenant?' asked Pillium as he moved into a fighting stance, the spear held at half-haft and balanced over the outstretched forearm of his empty hand.

Argo gave a curt salute. 'A long overdue one,' he said, and attacked.

The armour felt like an anvil on his back, a tangible reminder of the weight he carried for his brothers. The warp siphon had bled them almost dry, and these last few hours were all that Haephestus could give, and no canticles to the Omnissiah would change that. They were almost spent. Soon, what little power remained would be gone. The mortal crew would die first, through the cold of the void, or the hunger in their bellies, or the slow asphyxia of oxygen deprivation, or from madness as the light failed and endless darkness fell, or a dozen other different ways. And then the Adeptus Astartes would follow, the heavy burden of failure and the ignominy of a bad death hanging about their necks like a gravestone, left to simply expire, to fade and not flare brightly in the conflagration of a last war.

In the solitude of the catacombs, Haephestus stood before the ship's dying power core and could do nothing more but watch its final embers burn down to ash.

'Captain…' he uttered, using the ship's vox, 'if we are to do this, it must be now.'

Sicarius stood upon the bridge, one hand resting on the Tempest Blade's pommel, the other loose by his side. He spent little time here, trusting in Shipmaster Mendace to perform his duties to the exceptional degree expected of a voidfarer with a Jovian heritage. For the last five years, there had been precious little to tax a man of his talents. Adrift in the warp, a ship's captain has no agency and must trust to those who know the arcane, who can see the Emperor's will made manifest, a guiding light in a sea of storms. But that light had become a spark, and now not even an ember. Darkness shrouded them, and rocks lay all about.

What little hope remained rested with Barthus, and the Navigator's recent history could best be described as patchy. Something had happened to him, a psychic spoor that he had detected during the corruption of the Mordian 45th and the subsequent manifestation of the beast. It had driven him to madness and murder. The remorse he felt at these events had been evident in his face as Venatio had declared him at least physically able for the feat ahead. It was a dire task, Sicarius knew that much.

Barthus had gone to his post on the bridge, a sealed antechamber in which he could look upon the warp without fear of condemning anyone else to insanity or death, with the determined look of a man prepared to meet his own death. It might yet come to that. Without him, should they even survive the ordeal of breaching out of the warp, there was no way they could traverse the empyrean tides again. Unguided, they would certainly perish, but that was a problem for another day. All that mattered now was survival.

Closing off the vox, Sicarius thanked Haephestus and regarded the ship.

A hololithic representation of the *Emperor's Will* floated in the air before him. Inhabited areas of the ship had been highlighted, white as opposed to the grey of sealed-off decks.

Strategic positions, those that must be defended in the event of an attack, glowed red. Even with so much of the ship now out of bounds and shut down, his warriors were still spread painfully thin. For decades, there were those who decried his tactical plans as reckless or vainglorious, and others who vaunted him for his strategic acumen. None of these commentators, regardless of their leaning, could dispute his results. The Second Company had more laurels and victories to their name than any other in the Chapter, but this was a challenge unlike any that Sicarius had faced. Survival itself was at stake, against an unknown enemy in uncertain territory with any and all tactical and technological advantages almost completely stripped away. It was, to put it mildly, unenviable. But the moment had come and there was no other choice but to seize it.

Let us at least drive our own destiny.

He turned to his Lions, all watching silently, their faces half-lit by the hololith's spectral radiance.

'The Rubicon is before us, brothers. Shall we cross it?'

'As you will it, my lord,' answered Venatio, a measure of starch in his tone as was the Apothecary's way.

Vandius raised his chin a little higher, his pride in his captain ever the shining beacon in his eyes and bearing.

Daceus had known Sicarius longer than the rest. A rugged equerry, in the manner of the old Legions, he merely nodded. 'Aye, Suzerain,' he said, using Sicarius' more archaic title. 'Let's see it done.'

Sicarius turned to the shipmaster.

'The honour is yours, Mister Mendace.'

Seated in his baroque command throne, Mendace gave a tight nod and saluted. The lights were dimmed as a ship-wide alert rang out.

'All hands,' he began, opening up the vox, 'this is your captain. Prepare for warp breach, and may the Emperor protect your souls.'

The final message he gave to Barthus, switching to the Navigator's private channel.

'All is in readiness, Barthus. We place our faith and hopes in you now. The Emperor protects.'

There was a momentary pause, the Navigator's response presaged by a little static and heard by only a few on the bridge.

'Let us pray He watches us all, captain. It has been my honour.'

The vox cut out and there was nothing left to do but brace.

CHAPTER TWENTY-SEVEN

STORM WRACKED

Hell came for the crew of the *Emperor's Will*, just as Sicarius had predicted it would. Across the entire ship, the denizens of the warp both mortal and unnatural descended in untold hordes. Whether they had been waiting for this moment, or whether the ship crashing out of the immaterium had forced their hand or offered opportunity, a brutal struggle unfolded.

The strain upon the Geller field could be felt throughout every deck, a cacophony of screeching and scratching as if something lurked on the other side of a closed door and was trying to get in. Lesser warp entities were able to make passage as the protective aegis thinned with the extreme rigours placed upon it, and all too soon the corridors and chambers rang to the sounds of desperate battle.

The breaches in the hull came swiftly and in such number they were impossible to effectively defend against. Hordes of slave warriors – mutants, witches and debased mortals alike – spilled into the ship with the virulence of a contagion.

Renegades came in their wake, archaic weapons chattering, their ages-tarnished armour cut with sigils of Ruin. They still fought the long war, once-proud warriors brought low by their many sufferings, only driven now by hatred and bitterness. Unlike the slave hordes, these warriors were not so easy to kill. Sections of the ship, bottlenecks and choke points were quickly overrun and taken.

The Ultramarines engaged in a fighting retreat, holding on to what they could for as long as they could before falling back to the next bulwark. And the next. And the next.

At the main enginarium, thousands of crew toiled in the shrieking darkness, feeding the heart fire that would keep the ship alive. It had been sealed off, a cohort of Space Marines at its aft and prow ends. The upper and lower decks that abutted it had been cut off and flooded with lethal toxins. A few breaching parties came this way, but found only death as armour seals corroded and flesh followed. But these were minor victories in a wash of defeats.

A warhost surrounded the warp engine, led by Argo Helicos himself. Here, the Primaris Marines stood shoulder to shoulder, glorious in royal-blue battleplate. Unlike many of the other defenders, Helicos' men had nowhere to retreat. They would hold or they would die. The hordes fell hard upon this part of the ship, and brought wretched engines and beasts into the fray. Helicos slew the first of these abominations, a grotesque arachnoid machine. His sword rang out like summer lightning, splitting the beast from crown to groin. Mounting its corpse in one swift leap, oil and blood still spitting from the egregious wound, Helicos cried out, 'Guilliman!'

In a roar, his brothers answered. In blood and in death.

Before the bridge stood Sicarius and his Lions, as well as

a handful of other Adeptus Astartes who could be spared. They fought in the corridors, from behind defensive embrasures and amidst the shuddering staccato of point defence guns whose ammunition ran dry long before the battle had reached its crescendo. After that, the Lions and their master went to their blades and, in the failing light, earned the ferocious reputation of their namesakes.

It had been Sicarius' plan to take all crew who could be moved from their quarters and to cloister them across only a few decks. It had made them easier to defend, but at greater risk of wholesale slaughter should their defenders be overcome. In upper deck aft-seven, hundreds were slain as a massive horde broke through the cordon of armsmen and Ultramarines pledged to protect them. The enemy attacked with base cunning, overwhelming and killing the Adeptus Astartes first before butchering the armsmen at their leisure. The rest, the deckhands too weak or afraid to fight back, were turned into unwilling cattle for their knives. Every soul aboard the *Emperor's Will* heard the massacre across the vox or echoing through the ship's pipes and conduits, or saw it horribly rendered on pict-casters or remote hololiths. Deck aft-seven was shut off before the end, Haephestus sealing its gargantuan blast doors and emptying the mile-long section of air and light, flooding it with lethal concentrations of hydrogen sulphide and methane. The enemy died in droves, with the exception of their renegade warlords, but it was bitter compensation.

As the deadly fighting ground on, it quickly became apparent that there would be no rout this time, no repelling of boarders. It was the pursuit of annihilation on either side, and nothing in between.

And as the killing continued unabated, the savage drag and

pull of the empyrean sea could be felt like a tentacled grasp, as if in trying to flee, the ship had awakened some leviathan of the deep unwilling to give up its prey. A relentless undertow had them, ripping at the ship's metal flesh, rending her iron bones and battering at her hull until the cacophony of screeching seemed to have no end, merging with the thousands of mortal voices raised in fear and anguish across her body into one agonised chorus.

She bucked and split, a spirited heart straining against a cruel leash. Talons raked her, tearing at her ancient body, pulling at her frame as a colossal sentience pitted its malice against her. But the *Emperor's Will* was a venerable ship, and she had seen many battles, ended many foes who thought themselves superior. She pushed hard against the warp, stretching the caul of unreality suffocating her, until her prow pierced its distended mass and broke through.

A shuddering lurch resonated throughout the ship at the sudden and painful translation back into the materium. Tendrils of corposant and the uncanny vestiges of warp matter clung to her frame like supernatural afterbirth. It faded, withering to motes and then to nothing at all, as reality took a firmer hold and the wound in the void resealed to the echoes of a deep, unearthly rage.

She crawled after that, her abused body left beaten and aflame by its violent escape. Cold void snapped at her. Gas and heat and bodies bled from the fissures in her armoured flanks. The ship was whole, but critically wounded.

Down in the catacombs, Haephestus kneeled as if by a holy altar. A trembling hand upon the dying power core, he wept.

'Praise the Omnissiah,' he whispered, his voice tight with emotion. 'Praise Her, oh maiden of the void.'

CHAPTER TWENTY-EIGHT

A FERAL WORLD

Bullet craters marked the walls, and the scorched metal of bulkheads betrayed the presence of fires recently doused. A few makeshift barriers had yet to be cleared, and the grim evidence of bloodstains showed here and there, thinned down to a dark residue but still not scrubbed clean. Maintenance servitors quietly toiled as the bridge tacticarium's other occupants surrounded their Techmarine, who directed proceedings at a hololithic projection table.

'A feral world,' said Haephestus, turning the flickering representation of a planet with mechadendrite fingers. It had several landmasses and even oceans. Mountainous regions jutted from its rural topography, creating vast canyons and defiles. The dense cloud patterns churning in its upper atmosphere suggested volatile storm fronts veiled the entire globe.

'Inhabited?' asked Daceus, the holo-light casting his features in sharp relief.

'There are man-made structures evidential of a crude culture. Yes.'

Daceus raised an eyebrow. 'Crude?'

'Rudimentary technology, abundant in untapped fossil fuel reserves. Medieval.'

'A primitive society then,' said Helicos, the Primaris lieutenant towering above the others even without his helm.

'As I said,' offered Haephestus, 'feral. But here is something potentially interesting...' He manipulated the image, which zoomed out as several data markers appeared in the negative space around it and were attached to the globe by straight lines. 'Energy output,' he explained, homing in on one of the markers, the largest. The area it connected to flared orange and red like a heat signature. The others were small and blue.

Helicos' eyes narrowed. 'What is that?'

'I don't know,' replied Haephestus, and everyone in the tacticarium looked at him in surprise. 'It is immense. A power output that massive, if I were able to harness it...'

Daceus answered for the Techmarine. 'It could reinvigorate the ship.'

'In theory... yes. Though it could also be an instrumentation fault.'

'And does it have a name, this world?' asked Helicos.

Haephestus shook his head. 'Not according to the ship's archives, though admittedly I have only been able to access a small percentage of those records.'

Helicos and Daceus exchanged a glance.

'So, we would be walking into the unknown, then, and with no guarantees of success,' said the Primaris Marine, and turned to one Ultramarine in the tacticarium who had not yet spoken. 'Is it worth the risk? We could send out scouts, see if there are nearby Imperial stations?'

Sicarius looked stern. None of this appealed to him, but with each hour that passed the options shrank. Barthus lived. Drained, shrunken even, but he lived. Through sheer will, or perhaps divine providence, he had a found a way through. From the immaterium, to the uncharted void. In truth, it had brought them no closer to salvation. They had simply exchanged the unnatural threats to their survival for ordinary ones. Haephestus had managed to restore some of the ship's power, enough to maintain critical systems and limited augur capacity, but they were still effectively becalmed. Without more power, much more, they would not survive. A skeleton crew, dwindling by the hour. Food and other rations were in catastrophically short supply and with negligible capacity to defend themselves from a distance, they needed aid. And soon.

Sicarius considered all of this – he had thought of little else – as he leaned in to the grainy grey image, as if looking for something in the light.

'Is it reachable?'

'Two days via atmospheric transport,' said Haephestus.

'Then we go,' said Sicarius. 'Daceus, prepare a gunship.'

CHAPTER TWENTY-NINE

HARD SKY

The gunship pitched against the heavy winds buffeting its shell. Vedaeh gripped her restraint harness like grim death, her eyes pinched shut and a prayer murmuring on her lips. She felt a hand on her shoulder, and unclamped her eyes. Turning her head was difficult. The hold was trembling so much, she was afraid she'd shatter her skull if she tried to move. Reda looked back at her, a reassuring smile on her face. Her helm sat comfortably on her head, far better than Vedaeh's, which felt like a bucket, and her mirrored goggles reflected the chronicler's face back at her.

She looked ill, ghastly pale and washed out in the yellow hold light.

'Is this normal…?' she roared, fighting the engine scream. She stole a glance at the Adeptus Astartes, meditating and muttering silent oaths over their weapons. Vandius had even disengaged his harness and crouched on one knee, the blade of his gladius held down and against the deck, the pommel pressed against his forehead. When Vedaeh looked back at Reda the armsman was tapping her right temple. Vedaeh frowned, and only understood when Reda then pointed to her mouth.

With fumbling fingers, reluctant to loosen her grip on the restraints, Vedaeh engaged the vox.

'I didn't think it would be this... violent,' she voxed.

Reda laughed, and to Vedaeh it seemed such an incongruous thing to do in the situation.

'We are in a metal box, ditching through a lightning storm,' said Reda. 'It's going to be a little bumpy.'

'That does not alleviate my concerns, Lieutenant Reda.'

'Lieutenant, is it? A little formal for you.'

'It feels warranted in the circumstances. How do you do it?' she asked, seizing the restraint strap as the gunship shuddered in a patch of sudden turbulence. The lamps turned briefly from yellow to red and then back to yellow again.

Vedaeh started to pray.

'Have no concern, chronicler,' boomed a deep voice from across the other side of the hold, carrying despite the storm's fury. It was one of the sergeants, Iulus Fennion, she thought. The friend of Scipio Vorolanus, who sat next to him, head back and eyes closed.

'Is he asleep?' Vedaeh exclaimed.

Iulus glanced at him then back to the chronicler. 'Preparing, as we all are. You are safe with us,' he said. 'I will allow no harm to come to you or the other mortals.' Iulus banged a gauntleted fist against the side of the hull. 'See? Strong iron from Konor.'

The ship lurched again, pushing Vedaeh up against her harness, and she had to clamp her mouth shut to prevent herself from vomiting.

'You don't expect me to believe that this vessel is forged of iron, do you?' she asked when she had recovered enough.

Iulus laughed. 'No, I suppose not, but I thought it sounded impressive and might make you feel better.'

'It hasn't.'

Iulus laughed again. Louder.

Vedaeh scowled. 'I'm glad you find it funny, sergeant.'

'It'll be over soon,' he said, warmly. 'It's a Thunderhawk, chronicler,' he added, 'she's made for the storm.'

Vedaeh rolled her eyes, and clung on. She felt another's gaze upon her and saw the Primaris Marine, Pillium, staring at her. He held his spear firmly and in an upright position, like a guard before a forbidden gate.

Reda's voice came across the feed. 'He doesn't want us here, that one.'

'He saved Olvo Sharna, didn't he?'

'I didn't say he wouldn't do his duty. I just know he would prefer it if that duty wasn't looking after us.'

'I'm still not entirely sure why I am here.'

'Apparently it's a primitive culture.'

'I heard the same thing. It still doesn't clear up why I'm sat in this deathtrap.'

'You know primitive cultures.'

'I've read a few books.'

'Perhaps they need an interpreter.'

'Perhaps. They speak the language of war well enough...' Vedaeh's gaze strayed back to Pillium. 'He certainly does.'

With the clamour of the storm even the enhanced hearing of a Primaris Marine would not be able to discern what they were saying but, under that unflinching gaze, Vedaeh whispered her next words.

'He scares me, Arna.'

There was a momentary pause before she replied.

'Me too.'

Pillium looked as if he were about to say something when the ship bucked hard, like an angry mule trying to dislodge an unwanted rider. A crackle of interference swept across the vox. Vandius was already back in his seat and locking down his harness as Haephestus' metallic voice radiated throughout the hold.

'*Brace yourselves…*'

The ship banked. Hard. Vedaeh felt her body slam against one side of her restraints. Even Reda clung on now, Gerrant next to her, the two exchanging a look that suggested whatever was happening was bad.

Red light flooded the hold as the engine noise cut out and was replaced by shrieking wind shear.

'What's happening?' asked Vedaeh, fear edging her voice.

'Engine's out,' said Iulus over the vox. He had donned his war-helm. All the Space Marines had, and a host of retinal lenses glowed a deeper red in the light-washed hold. They put Vedaeh in mind of blood splashes, and she prayed to the Emperor that the image was not prophetic.

Reda and Gerrant gritted their teeth as the hull started to shake uncontrollably.

'Are we…' Vedaeh said haltingly with each jerk of the ship, 'are we… falling?'

'Vedaeh…'

'We're falling… aren't we?'

'Vedaeh…'

She acknowledged her name the second time, trying to shut out the sound of plummeting metal whining through the hull. She looked over at Sicarius, his red gaze blazing like hot coals as the internal lumens shut off and cast the interior of the ship into darkness. She couldn't breathe. It was like a metal fist had wrapped around her lungs and was squeezing…

Sicarius gestured to his gorget. 'Your rebreather, Vedaeh… here,' he said, pointing again to his neck. 'Put it on.'

She did, clamping it to her mouth and nose, almost hyper-ventilating in the process.

'Calmly…' uttered Sicarius. 'Calmly…' he repeated slowly, and Vedaeh felt her breathing stabilise, although the gun-ship still shook and she felt something strike the hull with a loud clang. Blood thundered in her ears and set her heart beating in a frantic tattoo.

Sicarius said something to the others in Ultramarian battle-argot, the meaning lost on her. Then the ship jinked and turned. Light streamed in, shafts of dull grey slashing against the inside of the hold. It took a moment for Vedaeh to realise the side hatch had ripped off. Air rushed in, and tore Pillium away with it. Her last sight was of Daceus and Vandius reaching for him as Sicarius roared in desperation and despair.

'Brother!'

Then a blackness fell like a dark curtain suddenly drawn over her eyes, and Vedaeh knew no more.

PART TWO

AGUN

CHAPTER ONE

FLASHES

They had Pillium between them, dragging him bodily across the dark landscape. He looked dead, limp like an empty suit of armour only held together by its clasps.

A fire was burning nearby. Vedaeh heard it crackling and could smell smoke, harsh against her nose and throat. She coughed, then spluttered, struggling to breathe, and caught someone's attention.

'Up, mortal…' His voice was rough, curt. He sounded in pain. Her head turned and the eyepatch visage of Daceus glared back. There was blood on his face. And ash from the fire.

'B-burning…' she murmured, and felt him take her weight like an adult carrying a child.

'Haephestus is dealing with it. Here,' he said, and she felt rough cloth pressed into her trembling hands, 'put it on.'

Dazed, she wrapped the cloak around her shoulders, only now appreciating how cold it was as the shock began to wear off. Her head pressed against the coolness of his armour. No motor sounds emanated, or the growling of gears and servos. It was silent. Deadened.

'Hap-happened,' she rasped, struggling to articulate properly, 'w-what happened?'

'Crash landed.'

She felt the heavy trudge of Daceus' boots as he fought against the rugged terrain. His own cloak flapped in a shearing wind. He turned and she raised her head just enough to see the gunship. Or the wreckage of it. A large section of fuselage had ripped off, including the side hatch through which Pillium had been torn. Rents like claw marks deformed the hull. The nose cone had been dented inwards. Cracks distorted the glacis. A fire had overtaken the engines and a warrior in red armour was trying to douse it.

'Haephestus…' she said.

Daceus didn't acknowledge her but stopped moving to speak with someone else.

'Are you sure you want him to remain with the ship?'

'He says he can rig the beacon,' answered a second voice, one she also knew but was finding hard to place. The world went grey for a moment but she blinked and forced her eyes to open. She needed to be awake. She didn't know why, but she knew she had to try to stay conscious.

'Nothing is functioning,' Daceus replied. 'No vox.' He grunted with the effort of hefting a heavy weight. 'Not even our armour.'

'It's our only means of reaching the *Emperor's Will*,' said the second voice. 'Haephestus stays. Either he gets the beacon to work or he repairs the ship. We need one or the other, Retius.'

Daceus turned his head, looking at something.

'Pillium looks bad.'

'He's an Ultramarine, Retius. He'll live. He has to. Argo

won't thank me if, when we return to the *Emperor's Will*, I have to tell him I have lost one of his own.'

'Without Argo, without Venatio...' Daceus tailed off in silence.

'You think I erred in omitting them from the landing party?'

'I think we need more Ultramarines, both here and in the void.'

A gauntleted hand clapped Daceus on the shoulder and Vedaeh sensed him straighten a little, stand a little taller for it.

'We have always managed with less, brother.'

'Aye.'

The owner of the second voice stepped into her eyeline. A blurred face slowly resolved, its noble features, a dark beard and hair stirred by the wind. A cloak was clasped around the neck, snapping loudly with each gust.

'How is she?' asked Sicarius.

'I am...' she began, her voice still a croak but growing stronger, '...alive, Cato.'

He looked down at her, those eyes like ice chips laying bare all her secrets. For the briefest moment they softened with concern. 'My apologies for the heavy landing.'

'You call that... a landing,' she breathed, and fidgeted until Daceus put her back down.

'That's fair,' Sicarius conceded.

She scowled at Daceus. 'I don't need you to carry me, Retius.'

'Very much alive,' Daceus replied ruefully.

'What of Arna and Vanko? Are they–'

'Alive, like you, Vedaeh,' said Sicarius and gestured to where the other two mortals, wrapped in cloaks, huddled in the lee of a large rock.

As Vedaeh's senses and her strength began to return, she cast about to get the lie of the land. A marching party had begun to form. Vandius and Fennion had got Pillium back to his feet; he looked almost capable of walking, and Vedaeh was once more reminded of the incredible resilience of the Primaris Marines. Of Vorolanus, there was no sign and she assumed he had gone to scout ahead. To scout for what exactly, she did not know.

The ground was cold and sparse, like a patch of iron beaten into a landscape. It even felt hard, too hard for earth – but then she assumed it was partly frozen. Fog lay in thick carpets, drenching everything sepulchral white. But there was a narrow spire in the fog, many, many miles distant but looming like a colossus and beyond the ability of medieval man to craft. Vedaeh felt a strangeness to it, eerily familiar and yet with a deepening sense of incongruity. Above, darkening clouds had begun to gather, streaked with fine threads of lightning. It reminded her of veins, coursing electrical veins. They flashed, once, twice.

'What is this place?' she asked.

CHAPTER TWO

IN THE WILD LANDS

The rain slashed down in sheets, drenching their skin, hair and armour. It turned the ground into a bog underfoot and Daceus cursed loudly as the sodden earth clamped around his boot, holding him fast. Fennion went to his aid, hooking his arm under the veteran's leg and pulling hard. His foot came free with a slurp of wet earth, tendrils of the loamy matter clinging on like threads of spittle. Daceus gave a curt nod of gratitude, pulled his weathered cloak around his body and looked to the hills ahead.

The land here was as bleak as the ever-worsening weather, large patches of wild gorse separated by tranches of rocky escarpment and hard scrub. It looked rapidly grown; too wild and too thick. Sicarius stood alone on the summit of a stony promontory, looking out onto a sea of endless fog. Frail wintery light painted the sky an insipid yellow and did nothing to leaven the grey.

'We must find shelter,' Daceus called, his voice flat and

almost smothered by a biting wind. Ice slivers abraded his skin but failed to cut.

Sicarius stared a moment longer, as if seeing something in all of that gloom, or looking for and not finding it, before he turned and nodded to Daceus.

The mortals were suffering. The three of them stood shivering in their clothes and sodden cloaks, hoods held tight against the wind, their faces raw and bleeding. It had been a hard trek from the downed gunship.

'No,' shouted Vedaeh, several paces behind the veteran Ultramarine, 'we must carry on.' She leaned heavily on her cane and Reda's shoulder. She and the other armsman, Gerrant, did not look as determined to trudge through the wilds as the chronicler did. 'Besides,' Vedaeh added, shuffling up to Daceus' side, 'we are too far from the crash site to go back. I doubt I would make it.'

'And what makes you think our luck will improve if we press on?' asked Daceus, betraying a hint of irritation. He knew Sicarius placed stock in her presence and her judgement, but he found her an unnecessary burden and a distraction. She was also overfamiliar, especially for a mortal.

'It is the difference between certainty of expiration and the hope of salvation, Retius.'

Daceus gave her a sour look.

'The fog has closed in behind us,' offered Vandius, having taken the rearguard with Pillium, who limped badly, 'and without auspex or auto-senses,' he paused to look up into the sky, 'and no sun to speak of, I cannot guarantee we would even find the gunship again.'

'Well, we had best hope we do,' answered Sicarius, returning from the vantage point. 'I doubt Haephestus will thank us for leaving him behind in this bleak place.'

That the ship had crashed so suddenly and inexplicably bothered Daceus. He remembered the abrupt loss of power, as if they had passed through some unseen barrier that had knocked out their vox and engine. It reminded him of the warp siphon that had drained the *Emperor's Will*, but that could not have followed them here. Pillium had not been far away from the crash site, but was badly injured, his old wounds suffered at the hands of the beast reopening and redoubling his pain.

Daceus thought it miraculous he had lived, let alone that he could walk. After a fashion. His eye lingered on Pillium, ashen-faced, his sodden cloak held tight around his massive frame. He had never looked so weak, leaning like an old man upon the shaft of his spear.

Daceus drew in close to Sicarius, keeping his voice low so that only the Suzerain would hear.

'Cato, the mortals will perish if there is much more of this. And maybe Pillium too. Our Primaris brothers are not inviolable, despite their many gifts.' He gestured to the fog. 'How can we even find the power signature Haephestus spoke of in all this? We have no means of locating it.'

As well as nullifying the gunship, whatever barrier they had passed through had left their armour inert too. Each Ultramarine felt it like a heavy anchor upon their backs, the protection but also the mass of layered ceramite and adamantium. No power also meant no auspex.

'Then our eyes shall have to be enough,' said Sicarius, though he regarded Vedaeh and her two charges with concern, and looked as if he were about to say more when a cry from deep inside the fog arrested everyone's attention.

'That's Scipio,' uttered Fennion, running up the escarpment to the promontory.

Daceus drew his sword.

'He's shouting a warning,' said Sicarius, and everyone except the three mortals and the half-conscious Pillium drew swords.

'Vandius...' Sicarius began.

The warrior nodded, and went to usher Vedaeh and her companions away.

'We can fight,' said Reda, teeth chattering as she brandished her maul.

'I have no doubt,' said Sicarius. 'Nonetheless...'

Vandius urged them away and this time Reda relented, Vedaeh's gentle hand on her arm as they sought cover behind a heaped rockfall.

Belatedly, Pillium drew his gladius. 'Let them come, who-ever they are...' His words were slurred, as though heavy with drink.

Vorolanus appeared through the fog a moment later, run-ning hard in his heavy war-plate. He met Fennion on the steep rise and the two briefly clasped forearms.

'I have found the natives,' he said to Sicarius and the others. He then also drew his sword. 'And they are coming this way.'

'To the Suzerain's side,' shouted Daceus. 'Here, brothers. With me!'

They formed up, a strong wedge of blue war-plate, ragged cloaks snapping in the wind as the ice shards scythed down. All except for Pillium, who acted as if he hadn't heard the order or understood the tactics and stood alone. All eyes looked to the hills.

With a whicker, a heavily muscled destrier nosed its way through the fog, eyes shrouded by oval plates of thick armour, iron-shod hooves tearing at the earth. It was a beast, at least a hand taller than Daceus, and clad in a lamellar barding that was streaked charcoal and grey by the rain. Hot breath plumed spectrally from its flaring snout, and the warrior upon its back levelled a wickedly barbed spear at the Ultramarines.

'You fled from this warrior, Vorolanus?' asked Daceus, eyeing up the black armour plate, chain mesh and enclosed helm – fashioned into the likeness of a bird of prey – with some disdain. He also noted the broadsword sheathed at the warrior's belt, and the large kite shield currently strapped to his saddle. It looked well worn.

He stepped forwards, about to challenge the warrior when nine more, also riding destriers, came out of the fog. A small cohort of footmen in padded jerkins and round, cheek-plated helms joined them, the blades of their halberds angled aggressively at the strangers to their lands. Several also carried archaic-looking crossbows, quarrels primed to loose.

'I brought word of a hunting party,' Vorolanus countered.

Daceus had no doubt that if they wished he and his brothers could easily defeat these men. But something held him back.

'Who are you?' the lead horse-riding warrior asked, not lowering his spear. The beast shifted as he spoke, hooves grinding the rough lowlands, reflecting its master's obvious impatience and irritation.

Daceus hissed between his teeth, 'The battle would be a short one, captain.' When he felt Sicarius' hand upon his shoulder, he backed down.

'I am Sicarius.' He stepped forwards, lowering but not sheathing his sword.

'And who are you to come armed into the wild lands? This is Lord Athelnar's domain.'

'You are charged with watching his borders?' Sicarius asked.

'I am,' said the warrior, and trotted his beast forwards until the tip of his spear brushed the edge of Sicarius' armour. The

Suzerain did not move or turn his gaze from the horseman. 'But you've yet to answer my question. What are you doing here? Who is your lord?'

Now up-close, the warrior on horseback eyed Sicarius carefully, almost seeming to baulk at the Ultramarine's size and stature. As if a lantern had been lit, he suddenly realised the sheer size of *all* of these strange warriors, and felt the threat they radiated.

'Threatening us would be unwise...'

'That is to say,' a voice interrupted, Vedaeh's sudden appearance prompting a flurry of urgent and belligerent activity from the natives, 'we are strangers in these lands and are sorry for any unmeant offence or concern we may have caused.' She bowed, deeply, having to pull on her cane to right herself again.

'We cannot just kill them...' she whispered harshly to Daceus as she passed.

The warrior eyed the group carefully, as if deciding who the odds would actually favour if it led to a fight between them and his men.

'Please,' Vedaeh went on, 'we are allies.'

The warrior appeared to tilt his head. 'You met one of our messengers?'

Vedaeh gave a slow nod.

'I thought they had all perished.'

'He did not last long,' Vedaeh lied, trying to get a feel for what the warrior was asking.

One of the other horsemen leaned over to speak in the leader's ear. 'They must be from the south, like the vizier.'

'From the south, yes,' said Vedaeh quickly. 'We've travelled far and have lost many on the way.'

'And you answer our pleas for help,' said the warrior, 'to

fight for our cause.' The hope in his voice betrayed his desperation too.

Vedaeh gave Sicarius a furtive look, and he nodded in reply.

'Yes. To fight. But we need shelter.' She gestured to Pillium, who looked on the verge of collapse. 'And we have injured men. Do you have a healer?'

'Not with us, but at Farrodum, yes. A medicus.'

'Farrodum?' asked Daceus.

'Our city. We thought we were alone, but now you are here...'

The warrior on horseback visibly relaxed and now Daceus saw it. He saw it in the warrior's posture and that of his fellow riders, and in the shadowed faces of the footmen partly hidden by the rims of their helms.

They are a troop of old men and boys. He saw the same incredulous revelation reflected in Sicarius' face.

'We are knights,' said Sicarius, addressing the warrior on horseback, 'of a southern land called Macragge.'

The warrior stowed his spear in a loop attached to his steed's saddle and removed his helm, revealing the grizzled face of an old campaigner, his dark hair and beard riddled with more iron than coal. He had also lost part of an ear, the wound stitched and relatively recent. But his eyes shone with a keen awareness, the suggestion of old instincts still at their best even if his body was not.

'I am Scarfel, Castellan of Farrodum and retainer of my liege lord, Athelnar,' he said, tugging loose a heavy leather gauntlet and extending out a hand.

Sicarius took off his own gauntlet and the two men clasped forearms, though Scarfel could scarcely grip the Suzerain's and found his own arm practically engulfed by a large hand.

'You are welcome here in these lands, Sicarius of Macragge,' said Scarfel, seemingly relieved that his arm was still attached as they broke off. He looked to all of the Ultramarines and Vedaeh. 'As are you all.'

The tension eased considerably and the horsemen began to part, as did the surrounding footmen, all of whom lowered their halberds and crossbows.

'Please,' said Scarfel, 'Farrodum is close by. Allow me to escort you. The baron will be pleased you have come.'

Sicarius turned to Vedaeh, a savage glint in his eye that could have been amusement or annoyance.

'Milady?' he asked.

Daceus watched with some unworthy satisfaction as Vedaeh paled slightly.

'As you wish it, Captain Sicarius.'

He nodded and gave her the most surreptitious of winks, though Daceus saw it.

'Lead on, Scarfel,' said Sicarius.

CHAPTER THREE

Ω

RED EARTH

The 'knights of Macragge' marched in pairs, with Vandius at the rear making sure Pillium remained upright. He looked ashen, biting back a pain he strove to keep hidden from the others, but Sicarius saw it.

Of the natives, the footmen trudged wearily behind while Scarfel rode alongside his newfound allies, the other horsemen sent on ahead.

'It's not so far,' he offered, trotting his horse languidly through the mud. He looked well-practised in the saddle, his hand at ease on the pommel of his sword, his spear swaying gently with the steed's movements.

'What do you call this place, Scarfel?' asked Sicarius, gesturing to the lands around them.

'Agun.'

'*A-gun,*' Sicarius repeated, compartmentalising the pronunciation.

'Farrodum is its last known city.'

The region's or the world's? Sicarius wondered, but did not voice it.

Scarfel looked across at Sicarius, who stood almost to the man's eyeline despite the fact he was mounted. 'What is the name of your city, Sicarius? Do you hail from a city?'

'Civitas,' he said, without pause.

'I have never heard of this land, of Macragge.' Scarfel leaned over in the saddle, his a conspiratorial whisper behind his hand, 'and if you don't mind me saying, it breeds giants, not men.'

Sicarius laughed. He liked this man, simple though he was. 'We are men, Scarfel.' He looked over his shoulder at the young faces of the footmen, pale in the murky fog. A few took furtive glances out into the wild. More than once, armoured buckles and straps clacked noisily as a crossbow or pike was hurriedly brought to bear, but to no other end than causing momentary commotion. 'What happened to your army?'

Scarfel frowned. 'I don't understand.'

'Young, old,' said Sicarius, gesturing to the footmen. 'They are not typical soldiers.'

Now, the old campaigner's face darkened, and he looked out painfully into the fog. 'You're observant.'

'I lead warriors, I have to be. Your men are afraid. I can see that too. What is it out here that has them so afraid?'

'The bone-swine.'

Sicarius exchanged a quick glance with Daceus, who was listening to every word. The old veteran shrugged.

'Did they kill your men?'

Scarfel nodded sombrely. 'The ravagers came,' he said, face falling as he drifted back to a place of dark memories. 'At first, they raided our farms, isolated outposts and watchtowers. There was nothing the bone-swine would not eat, fight or burn. Nothing, no amount of violence could sate them. As the outer places fell, the people living there sought refuge in the city. And so the bone-swine became bolder. Our warriors clashed with them. Parties of hunters went out to cull them but met with less and less success each time they returned, until they did not come back at all. The bone-swine horde grew as our numbers diminished. Something had to be done. An army was raised, led by our general, Siegfried. I was his equerry and part of the muster. We set out on horse, six hundred cavalry men and twice that on foot.

'We knew the bone-swine laired in a wide gorge north of the city. The army rode with fury, killing every foul creature we met on the way, but these were stragglers and filled us with ill-earned confidence. A quarter of a mile from the entrance to the gorge, Siegfried gave the signal to charge. We began to move, certain of victory and eager for the fight. Almost at the entrance, my horse threw a shoe, and tossed me out of the saddle. I was left behind, slumped insensible in the dirt. By the time I came around, the rest of the army had gone. Almost six hundred horses went into the gorge.' He paused, wiping a glove across his nose and eyes. 'Less than twenty returned. I mounted a stray, bereft without its rider, and as the others fled for Farrodum I rode into the gorge. I mounted the high slopes, where the rocks would shield me from the bone-swine. I had to see it, do you understand?' said Scarfel, looking back at Sicarius, who held his gaze. 'I had to know what had befallen Siegfried and the army. I found red earth. It churned under my horse's hooves, damp and yielding. They were... *eating* them. I heard screams in the deep parts of the gorge. To my shame I did not venture further, but knew that some of the army must have been alive as they were devoured.

'Whether it was the scent of blood, or the presence of the bone-swine, or even my own fear... my horse kicked and panicked. I brought it to rein – had I not, I don't think I would be alive to tell this story – but one of the bone-swine turned, having noticed the scattered scree I had unwittingly disturbed. Looking into that gore-smeared face as it picked shreds of meat that had once been my comrades from its teeth, I became petrified. Something flashed out of the shadows at me and fire seared my face. I saw a stone spear lying on the ground, my blood on the sharpened flint tip.' He reached up to touch his mangled ear, fingers questing for the missing piece but finding it absent. 'I thought I would be chased down and overrun. Instead, it laughed. And I have never heard a more harrowing thing, like stone grinding, only deep and guttural. Then another turned and it laughed too, then another and another, until the horde raised up such a cacophony that I fled, their mockery chasing me into the night.'

Scarfel brought his horse to a halt as he tried to fight back his grief. 'You must think me weak,' he said, gathering himself again, 'to speak thusly.'

'You are not the first to lament the loss of fallen brothers-in-arms,' Sicarius told him. 'You lived and fight on still. There is nothing weak about that.'

Scarfel nodded, but the shame of that moment long ago had re-etched itself upon his face. He muttered something about riding on ahead, pulled up the hood of his cloak and spurred his horse.

'Bone-swine?' asked Daceus, when the old campaigner was out of earshot.

'An indigenous beast, most likely. How many monsters have we fought and killed?'

'Never enough,' replied the veteran grimly. 'And it seems we'll need to fight more before we can leave this place.'

Sicarius' gaze lingered on the now distant figure of the old campaigner on his horse.

'I pity him.'

'I pity this entire place,' said Daceus. 'It's defeated, cowed almost.'

'But not without its secrets, I suspect.' Sicarius gestured to the towering spire far away on the horizon. 'What do you make of that, brother?'

Daceus frowned. 'I do not think that's Farrodum,' was all he said.

'Nor do I,' Sicarius replied.

'Who are these people? How did they come to be this way?'

'A lost colony, perhaps? One that never emerged from Old Night.'

'That long, to be so... primitive.'

'It does stretch credulity, I'll admit. There are records of worlds whose populations have been cast back into a dark age by the onset of the Great Rift. In the Imperium Nihilus...' Sicarius postulated, 'there is much we do not know. Feral worlds are not so uncommon.'

Daceus considered that, the balancing of his captain's words evident in his face. He scratched at his eyepatch.

'Does that feel likely to you, Cato?'

Sicarius stared into the fog, seeing the skeletal silhouette of an old acquaintance, and ignoring the balefire glow that he knew no one but him could see.

'No, Retius,' he said at last, 'it does not.'

CHAPTER FOUR

FARRODUM

At first, Arna Reda had been glad to leave the *Emperor's Will*. The ship had become a tomb, wreathed with dark memories. She had almost died several times during her tenure as armsman, and though she did not entirely leave behind every ghost that prowled its echoing corridors, to see sky again, to feel air and rain – it had been a relief. And she had hoped it would leaven Vanko's spirits, too. His mood had grown ever darker since what had happened in the sanctum, and she worried that Barthus might have imparted something to him, intentionally or not.

The journey from the upper atmosphere had been... unpleasant, but she had undertaken combat drops before. Besides, they had survived and, though battered, the air – the sky that she craved – had unfolded before her. That relief was fleeting as the icy wind sawed through her clothes and storm cloak. It touched the bones, chilling them. Bleak was not a strong enough word, Reda decided, and she soon blamed Vedaeh, who had insisted on bringing her and Vanko as her aides or companions. She didn't know which.

'I'm sorry,' said Vedaeh, shivering against the cold and barely keeping pace as she clung to Reda's shoulder. 'Had I known...'

Reda instantly felt ashamed at her unworthy thoughts, realising they sprung from her concern for Vanko. He trudged a few steps ahead, bridging the gap between the Space Marines and the natives who walked sullenly behind them.

'He'll come around,' said Vedaeh, guessing Reda's thoughts.

'I've never seen him like this,' she confessed. 'He's different... *We're* different.'

'What we endured in the warp, the things we all saw, *felt.* No one emerged unscathed, Arna. The dreams do not go away, but they fade to the point where we can tolerate them.'

'I saw my father,' said Reda, apropos of nothing.

'On the ship?'

'Yes, he was there, his face always in shadow but I knew it was him. At first, I thought he was haunting me, a manifestation of the warp, my grief made real.'

'How did he die?'

'I have no idea. He left us when I was young, tithed to the Guard, our world's contribution to the engine of war.'

'You sound bitter.'

'Just tired. He was proud to serve. So am I, though I chose service defending a starship rather than fighting on a battlefield.'

'You seeing him, you think it was something other than the warp bleeding into your dreams?'

'Perhaps. I don't know, but it felt different, or started to, like he was warning me. Guiding me.' She glanced across and found Vedaeh looking at her. 'Is that possible?'

'If it's what you believe.'

Reda looked down. 'I don't know what I believe any more,' she admitted. She glanced ahead. Her partner trudged on, his cloak fluttering in the wind. 'I only know that Vanko is in pain and I can't help him, and that this damn world is colder than a Fenrisian's arsehole.'

Vedaeh laughed, louder than she'd intended, and drew a glance or two from the natives behind them.

Reda pulled her cloak tighter around her neck as the wind began to bite. Ahead there was fog and the slow reveal of the rugged landscape she had come to loathe. 'I'm bloody serious,' she said, though with a wry smile. 'Why did you insist on bringing Vanko and me with you?'

Vedaeh's expression grew serious. 'For company,' she smiled, brightening but only a little, 'and because I trust you.'

'You do not feel safe around the Adeptus Astartes?'

The six warriors marched ahead of them, alert and ready. They looked heavy in their armour, burdened by it, as they must surely be burdened by their losses in the warp.

'It's not a matter of whether I feel safe or not,' said Vedaeh. 'They are almost inhuman, Arna. I feel *alone* around them. They have no true concept of what it means to be mortal, though I do admire and respect them, especially Sicarius. But whatever part of them was once like us, that part has been excised. They have no mental or emotional architecture to relate to the human condition. The mission, martial brotherhood, the pursuit of an honourable death, these are the things that motivate them. Even Sicarius, though he is the best of them. I see him looking at me sometimes, a tactical problem he does not know how to solve. And I think that's why I'm here.'

'To confound him?'

Vedaeh gave an indulgent smile. 'I suppose I've done that on occasion. No, of course not. He needs someone who can act on his behalf when a sword or bolter proves ineffective.'

Reda knew they had little ammunition for the latter, hence the reason Sicarius and his men carried only their blades.

'An interpreter,' she ventured.

'Of a sort, yes, I suppose I am,' said Vedaeh.

'Or a negotiator.'

'It may yet come to that.' She lowered her voice. 'These are superstitious, primitive people, Arna. They have not sailed the void or braved the horrors of the warp. They do not know the Imperium or what lies beyond the vault of their own grey skies. I think if they did it would terrify them and the most human of primordial emotions would take hold.'

The lie about knights of Macragge, the cloaks, the swords and spears, now Reda understood.

'Fear,' she said. 'They would fear us.'

'They would fear *them*,' Vedaeh corrected. 'They would kill us.'

'A sobering thought,' Reda replied, briefly eyeing the dirty and miserable faces of the footmen behind them, slogging uphill through the wet earth.

'One to keep at the forefront of your mind,' said Vedaeh as they crested a rise. Beyond it, the fog began to lift at last and a city of iron walls and craggy towers emerged resembling a scorched black anvil. Banners hung from its dark battlements, stirring forlornly in the wind, and a stark gatehouse loomed up to meet them.

Farrodum.

And out of the corner of her eye, just at the very, very edge of the receding mist, Reda saw a figure, his face hidden in shadow.

CHAPTER FIVE

HORNS

'Are they men?' the baron asked, squinting at the armoured strangers passing through his city gates. 'They do not look like men. They are monstrous.'

He stood at the tower window, its lights doused, cleaving to the shadows. He lingered a few steps back from the south-facing sill, unwilling to be seen by the giants, though he could have sworn one of them looked right at him. The giant had an eyepatch, with a face like a weathered cliff. Privately he wondered if they were golems, with skin of stone instead of flesh.

'I believe they are men, my liege,' said the vizier, standing off to one side and just behind his lord.

'And this blue livery they wear,' the baron went on, seemingly ignoring the vizier's reply, 'have you seen its like before? I do not recognise the sigil. What is it supposed to be, a horseshoe?'

'Scarfel's riders reported they referred to themselves as knights, so that could be the case.'

'Then where are their horses, vizier?' He frowned, and stepped back a pace from the window. 'I do not like this. Not at all.'

'They claim to be our allies.'

'Well, we have sore need of those.'

'Indeed, my liege.'

The baron turned from the window, one hand on the pommel of a sword that he wore on his left hip. It was largely ceremonial, and he couldn't remember the last time he had needed to draw the weapon.

'Cloister them where they can do no harm,' he said. 'And have a guard placed.'

'Prudent thinking, my liege. I shall do so at once.'

The vizier bowed. He was a large man and his long robes pooled out across the floor.

'This Macragge,' said the baron, as he was leaving, 'have you ever heard of it?'

The vizier gazed through the window, though his eyes gave nothing away of his thoughts. 'I have not, my liege, but I am not so well travelled as some.'

Vedaeh slept fitfully, both too cold and too warm at the same time. A chill breeze had entered the hall through some cranny or crack and despite the furred blankets they had been given, she could not find a way to balance her temperature. Exhaustion had put her down in the end, as her body surrendered to the rigours of the past hours. She had not been the only one to succumb to fatigue and pain. Pillium had collapsed the moment they passed through the gates. He was taken without escort, despite Vandius' initial protests. She tossed and turned at the memory of trying to prevent any bloodshed as the Ultramarines looked to defend their own.

The medicus had stepped in, a young woman, slight but with a serious bearing. Vedaeh had liked her at once. Her presence helped diffuse a volatile situation, and after a few tense moments, the remaining Ultramarines stood down at Sicarius' unspoken order. They parted ways with Pillium, who was led away on the back of a mule cart, whilst the others were brought through narrow streets crammed with bent-backed hovels to a large gated hall away from the heart of the city. Here they were told to wait until the lord of Far-rodum was ready to grant audience.

Shuffling through the gate, Reda on one arm supporting her, Vedaeh had gratefully sunk down by a firepit towards the middle of the room, which was long, with a vaulted roof, though it appeared not to have seen use for some time. The firepit glowed, recently lit, but was already dwindling. Reda and Gerrant had found wood and stoked it until a decent flame rippled into being, and then crouched by it with Vedaeh to warm their weary bodies. They had been given a little food and she ate hungrily, as did her companions. She remembered little more after that, but other, older memories rose unbidden in her mind, of the horror she had felt aboard the *Emperor's Will*. She imagined a dark room, reminiscent of the Reclusiam. Her books were burning, and as the faces of the dead crowded in on her, the faces of other inhuman things joined them; turned into them. The last one had looked like Olvo Sharna, before her features distended, her skin thickening and reddening as a pair of ribbed horns uncoiled from her grotesquely misshapen skull and her eyes turned black. She lunged, now the beast and no longer Sharna, and a giant dark maw ringed with canine fangs reached out, ever hungry...

Vedaeh screamed, and awoke.

Damp with feverish sweat, she threw off the furred blanket, shivering instantly in the cold. The firepit had died to a few scattered embers. Her mortal companions were wrapped in each other's arms. Reda wore her nightmarish dreams openly in the frown on her face, but Gerrant looked inhumanly placid, like the sleeping dead. It worried Vedaeh. To be like that after what they had all endured, it was disturbing. She glanced to the Space Marines but found no reassurance there.

They did not sleep, they did not eat. They sat or stood, alert and nursing their thoughts in the quiet darkness. She turned away, reaching for the furred blanket again now she was cold.

No, she thought, her eyes growing heavy, *they never sleep*.

They hadn't really slept for over five years.

Iulus sat down on one of the stout benches arrayed around the hall, the wood creaking ominously as it took his weight.

'I have had warmer welcomes,' he said.

Scipio sat on the opposite bench and had just finished sharpening his gladius. 'They are afraid of us,' he said, sheathing the sword. Praxor's old blade, now deactivated, sat in a scabbard on his back.

'They are foolish if they think this place will hold us.'

'If it keeps them feeling safer and us from having to fight our way out of here...'

Iulus nodded. He gestured to the sleeping mortals, huddled close to one another. 'Much longer and they would have perished,' he said.

Scipio's gaze wandered to the metal sconce above, hanging by a rusted chain, its candleholders empty but tarnished by dusty old wax.

'Is this everything?' asked Iulus.

On a low table in front of them was a small cache of

grenades, all that the Space Marines had brought with them from the ship. It didn't amount to much and had needed to be carefully smuggled into the city, so as not to alarm the natives. Seven fragmentation grenades in all, and a small reel of det-cord. This last item had come from the gunship. It wasn't equipment ordinarily used by the Adeptus Astartes, but this mission had ceased being ordinary as soon as they made planetfall.

'No bolt weapons and certainly nothing more exotic. No chainblades either,' said Iulus.

Scipio brandished his recently sharpened blade. 'Only gladii, combat blades and non-active power swords, with the exception of Sicarius' artificer weapon, of course.'

The Tempest Blade had been forged by master artisans; it alone had resisted the effects of the warp siphon.

'Not much of an inventory,' Iulus observed.

'It will serve,' Scipio replied. 'How is your arm?'

The dimming firelight cast by the pit filled Iulus' face with deep shadows. He looked gaunt, weary.

'Barely functional.'

Scipio had noticed he kept the arm close to his body, as if it were wrapped in an invisible sling. His armoured greaves and shoulder pad hid the bionic well enough but the pain of it was evident in Iulus' haggard expression.

None of the Adeptus Astartes had slept for weeks. Even the rejuvenating effects of catalepsean meditation had been denied them. Fatigue was not something a Space Marine readily succumbed to, but nor were they immune to it. The warp siphon had bled more than the ship and their armoury, it seemed.

Scipio surveyed the room. Vandius stood by the only door, his blade drawn and stabbed tip down into the earth, both hands upon the pommel like one of the Emperor's Champions. The sentinel kept his head up, eyes straight, never wavering for a moment. Though Prabian had been an almost unrivalled swordsman in the Chapter, Vandius came a close second. He took all his duties immensely seriously, even for a calling as sober as the Adeptus Astartes. When the standard that had borne the Second Company's banner had been irrevocably shattered, he had bound the ancient cloth up and carried it on his person wherever he went, lest the need arise to unfurl it again. Quiet agitation seemed to be his default. He looked restive, even in his guard state.

Sicarius and Daceus stood off to one side, just at the edge of the firelight, and conversed in low voices. The old veteran appeared to be doing most of the talking, Sicarius clear-eyed and alert as he listened, nodded and occasionally spoke.

They had changed, all of them, since the warp. Not everyone wore full armour. Vandius had lost his left arm greave, damaged beyond repair as the ship broke warp and the denizens of hell descended. Scipio had only one shoulder guard, the right side split during that same battle. None wore their helms. This was at Vedaeh's insistence, the mortal chronicler apparently some kind of authority on ancient cultures. She believed that the people of these lands needed to see the Adeptus Astartes as human, or something close to it, or they would be shunned as enemies.

Scipio had no doubt that he and his brothers could overcome every warrior in Farrodum, but no Ultramarine would countenance such a slaughter, and it would not get them any closer to finding the power source Haephestus had revealed during the augur sweep.

'They have locked us in,' he said, his gaze straying to the gate.

Iulus laughed mirthlessly. 'I doubt that. Vandius could split that door apart with one blow.'

'Best that he does not.'

'Aye, we are to play as ambassadors from a foreign land for now.'

'It fits us poorly,' said Scipio.

Iulus could hardly disagree with that and nodded. He was about to say more when the gate was unlocked and opened.

The Ultramarines turned as one, and the warrior in dark padded armour who entered stopped short when faced with the indomitable figure of Vandius.

'Y-you are summoned,' stammered the warrior, a squire of some sort, and entirely too young for the blade he wore at his hip. A child carrying a man's sword. 'B-by the baron.' Through the narrow gap in the gate, Scipio could see several other foot-men, some with crossbows, others holding spears, and beyond them the brazier light of the city streets. Night had fallen quickly.

Daceus took a step forwards but the young squire held out a gloved hand.

'J-just him.' He pointed a shaking finger at Sicarius.

Daceus bristled. 'Absolutely not.'

Vandius took one hand off the pommel of his sword. Even Iulus began to rise from his bench until Scipio laid a hand upon his shoulder.

'Ambassadors, remember…' he said in a low voice.

Sicarius stood his Lions down. 'It's alright,' he said, look-ing the squire in the eye, though the man could barely meet his gaze. 'I am sure the baron means me no harm. Is that not right?'

The squire nodded vigorously. His face had begun to bead with sweat. 'The rest have to stay here,' he said, regaining some of his dwindling courage. 'Baron's order.'

Sicarius shared a look with Vedaeh, who had stood up from her place by the fire. She nodded, pale but visibly relieved.

'They will remain,' said Sicarius. He turned back to the squire. 'I assume you are to escort me?'

'Yes, milord.'

'Then to your duty.'

'Now we'll see,' Scipio said to Iulus, as Sicarius was about to leave.

'See what?'

'How well we can play the role.'

Sicarius would never be afforded the chance, as a long horn blast rang out before he had set one foot outside of the feast hall.

'What is that?' Sicarius asked.

'Never you mind,' said the squire, drawing his sword, suddenly more fearful of whatever was happening outside the hall than who was inside it. 'You must stay here while I find out what's going on,' he said, brandishing the blade at Sicarius.

Vandius looked poised to despatch the squire there and then.

'Are you going to use that, boy?' growled Daceus, fists clenched. He took a half-step closer.

Again, Sicarius stood the Lions down. 'He has no need to, Retius. For we will do as he asks.'

The horns skirled out again, a long, discordant note. Then another.

The squire backed out, the door shutting behind him, the locks and bars sliding into place.

'That's a call to arms,' said Vandius, as soon as the squire was gone, whipping his sword into an upright position.

'He's right,' Daceus agreed, gladius drawn.

Scipio got to his feet a few seconds before Iulus, and the five Adeptus Astartes converged around Sicarius.

'What's happening?' asked Vedaeh, joining them. Reda had fallen asleep on Gerrant's shoulder, but stirred with the sudden commotion, wide-eyed and alert.

'A fight, most likely,' said Sicarius.

'Between whom?'

'Farrodum and one of its enemies,' he replied. 'The bone-swine we heard talk of.'

'Are we fighting too?'

'It depends.'

'On what?'

'If whatever it is steps beyond this threshold.'

Iulus came forward. 'We cannot leave these people to die, captain.'

Vedaeh stepped in. 'You cannot defy the rule of law here.'

'I adhere to Imperial law and am sworn to defend mankind,' replied Iulus, turning on the chronicler.

'Please. If you leave now and draw swords, you might end up making it worse. You must wait.' She looked to Sicarius for support.

'I don't like this, Vedaeh,' he said.

'But you do agree with me, don't you?'

Scipio could see that Sicarius did, but felt the same frustration they all must be experiencing. 'What about Pillium?' he asked. 'He's alone and possibly still unconscious. We can't just leave him to fend for himself.'

'I don't disagree, but we have no idea where he was taken,' Daceus cut in. 'And even if we did...' He looked at Vedaeh, ever the counsellor for non-violence. 'None of us can step beyond these gates unseen.'

Sicarius scowled. 'We cannot leave him unprotected. I'm sorry, Vedaeh.'

Vedaeh was about to protest when Reda spoke up.

'Then let us do it.' She was standing by the fire, her arms by her side. 'Vanko and I,' she said. The other armsman stood too, his gaze cold and determined. 'We can slip through the streets unnoticed. It's narrow, tight and with plenty of places to hide. No different to a starship, sire.'

Sicarius took a moment to weigh up Reda's proposal. Then he nodded to Vandius, who swept out his sword. One blow north to south, straight down the narrow slit between the two halves of the gate. As he stepped back, the dull thud of the wooden bar and the clang of the bolt could be heard as they struck the ground.

The guards had already gone, the horn blasts summoning them to whatever crisis was unfolding across Farrodum.

Vandius edged one half of the door open with the tip of his sword and Sicarius nodded to an aperture small enough for Reda and Gerrant to slip through.

'Find him.'

CHAPTER SIX

ʊ

THE MEDICUS

He scarcely fit upon the medical slab. Cwen had never seen a man so massive, and as she struggled with the thick clasps of his armour, she wondered if he were a man at all.

'Help me with this,' she said to the guard who had been posted to watch the injured stranger. The young warrior did not respond, but for a slight shake of the head.

Cwen scowled. 'Fine, I'll do it myself.'

Part of the breastplate had been badly damaged and was almost hanging off, the odd nails and bolts used to secure it torn away or loose. Cwen got her lithe fingers around one of the bolts but couldn't turn it. She searched for and found a pair of iron tongs, like a blacksmith's tool, and used them instead. With considerable effort she loosened the strange bolt and it came out, thudding heavily to the stone floor.

The medicus swept her brow, sweating even in the winter chill of the infirmary, and threw a scathing look at the guard, who pretended not to notice. The room was small, and stacked with herbs and unguents, tonics and tinctures, all arrayed in deep wooden shelves off to one side of a medical bench. There were tools, knives and hooks and saws set up on a rack beneath a single small window that looked out onto a courtyard. The bench was made of stout wood and reinforced with metal braces, but it still bowed under the armoured weight of the stranger. He had been brought in without ceremony but with much commotion, no less than eight of the castellan's men labouring to carry him across the threshold. It took another six to help heave him onto the bench and there he remained, unconscious but breathing.

Cwen did not really know where to start. She thought it best to try to remove some of the armour but that was proving difficult, especially without help. She asked the guard again if he would assist her, and again the young warrior refused.

'Coward...' she hissed in the end, and hooked both hands around the exposed edge of the breastplate and tried to heave it off. She got it a few inches before the weight became too much and it slipped back. She leaned heavily on the stranger's chest, twisting her torso as she searched for something on her tool rack. 'Maybe I can find something to lever it off...'

A hand like a vice snaked around her wrist and she cried out.

The stranger's eyes were open, but barely. A snarl was forming on his lips and he glared over at the guard, who had only managed to half-draw his sword before being frozen in place by the stranger's hard eyes.

'Where am I?' he slurred, trying to get up but failing as the agony put him down again.

Cwen held out her other hand, bidding the guard to sheathe his sword. Her eyes were full of fear. Not of the stranger, exactly, but at what he might do when the guard tried and failed to harm him.

Paler than a winter storm, the guard took a step back and the sword slid into its scabbard under its own weight. He looked embarrassed at his state of disarray, trying to hide the wet patch staining his breeches, but dared moved no further.

'Please...' said Cwen, returning her attention to the stranger. She nodded to her wrist. 'You're hurting me.'

The stranger's grip relaxed at once. His face was ashen and flecked with sweat. He had an odd smell, thick and cloying, a mixture of oil and overly sweet spice. The scent of warm iron radiated from under his armour, but she knew what this was.

'You're bleeding,' Cwen told him. 'I need to fix that.'

'Who are you?' he asked, his eyes heavy-lidded and struggling to stay open. 'Where are my brothers?'

'I am Cwen, the medicus. I was asked to help you.'

'My brothers...' snapped the stranger, a sudden surge of anger forcing his shoulders up off the bench, but he quickly slumped down again.

'I don't know about them. I only know what I have to do for you. Please...' said Cwen.

The stranger let her go.

The guard stepped forwards again, desperate to find his courage, and was about to say something when Cwen beat him to it.

'Get out. Leave. Now.'

'You heard her,' rasped the stranger, attempting to rise again. The guard left at once, taking the smell of his urine with him. 'Are you a healer then?' the stranger asked.

Cwen nodded.

The stranger gave a curt laugh. 'I doubt you'll have tried to heal anyone like me before.'

'Are you in much pain?' Cwen asked, tentatively putting her hand on the stranger's forehead. 'You feel warm.'

'My kind have a tendency to run hot. It's my–' he grimaced, biting back the agony, 'my body's response to injury. It's working to heal me.'

Cwen shrank back a little, but was more intrigued than afraid. 'Incredible.'

'To you, yes, I suppose it is.' He leaned back and shut his eyes.

'Do you have a name?' asked Cwen, going to her medicine shelf to make up a tincture.

'I am Brother Pillium, one of–' he replied, stopping himself as he was about to say more.

'You are with the knights, from the south.'

The stranger raised a wry smile, and opened his eyes. 'Aye, that's us, from the south, from Macragge.'

'Drink…' invited Cwen, leaning over the stranger's chest and gently raising a cup to his lips.

The stranger frowned. 'What's in it?'

'A little turmeric, some henbane and hemlock.'

The stranger laughed again. It looked painful to do so. 'You're wasting your time, medicus.'

'Please,' said Cwen, proffering the cup again.

'As you wish.' The stranger drank every drop. 'There. Satisfied?'

'Is your pain leavened?'

'It is not,' the stranger answered flatly, 'but I have a piece of metal lodged in my side, deep enough that it's beginning to irritate.'

'Gods, where?'

'Underneath my armour.' He pointed.

'How have you endured it for so long?'

'I didn't know it was there until a few moments ago. My body, it tends to… shut down pain, so I can fight.'

'That sounds... awful,' said Cwen.

'It is my duty,' the stranger replied. 'My purpose.'

'Then I pity you, my lord. It sounds like a bleak existence.'

'It is necessary.' He winced in pain again.

'Your side?' asked Cwen.

The stranger nodded.

'Let me help you remove the metal.'

The stranger wrenched off his breastplate with one hand and it clattered noisily to the ground. A dark layer of mesh, like a finely woven smock that went beneath a suit of mail or a hauberk, shone beneath. Cwen had never seen the like and reached out with tentative fingers to touch it.

'This material, what is it? Some kind of chainmail?'

'Yes, *chainmail*. Finely wrought, by our master artisans.'

'Truly the south is a land of wonders...' Cwen breathed, running her hand along the tight-fitting mesh.

There were two bore holes in the mesh, both in the upper chest, and Cwen recoiled as she saw them.

'Are they wounds?' she asked, leaning in to take a closer look.

'Yes, wounds,' said the stranger. She didn't think he was telling her the entire truth but instead was tired of the conversation. 'Here,' he added, gesturing to his side.

Cwen walked around to the other side of the bench and saw a sharp piece of ragged metal sticking out of the stranger's flesh. It looked to be almost the length of a sword, only more jagged.

'You'll need to cut,' he told her. 'Into me. The shrapnel is barbed. If I just yank it out, it'll tear me open.'

'How are you even awake?' Cwen whispered, but reached for her sharpest blade. It had a saw edge, and she hoped it would be strong enough to cut through the strange mesh.

'I am from Macragge,' said the stranger, as if that answered everything. 'Now start cutting.'

Blood was leaking freely from the wound, pooling redly at Cwen's soft-shoed feet as she cut first into the mesh and then the skin. Both were tough, much tougher than she expected. The stranger bore it all, every one of her faltering, increasingly desperate attempts, not once crying out or expressing any discomfort beyond the occasional grunt.

It took almost half an hour, and by the end of it, Cwen's arms were trembling with exertion, but the mesh lay open like a partially peeled fruit and she had made a cut into the skin around the impalement in each of the four cardinal directions.

'Good,' rasped the stranger, 'now, guide my hand.'

Cwen did, taking his massive gauntleted fist in both hands and leading it until he had grasped the ragged metal.

'Step back...' advised the stranger.

Cwen took three steps and he yanked out the metal, letting out a sharp cry of pain as he did so. It landed heavily, a twisted blade easily the length and thickness of a broadsword. Blood spilled eagerly from the wound, and Cwen rushed to gather up cloth and bandages to staunch the bleed, but by the time she had returned to the stranger's side, the bleeding had almost stopped.

'Impossible...' she breathed.

'Thank you, medicus. I owe you a debt,' said the stranger, his voice thick with relief, and promptly passed out.

Cwen looked on at his body in awe, almost statuesque in its perfection. A sculptor's rendering in marble. To administer treatment to such a man... Cwen was glad he seemed so stout, but however enduring the stranger was, he could not reknit his own flesh. She would at least clean the wound and stitch it, she thought, and had taken up a bowl of clean water and a rag when the horns began to sound.

She went to the window, setting down the bowl, and looked out across the courtyard and to the city beyond. Warning fires had been lit for every tower. Shadows moved against the flickering light, hunched and bestial, and inside the city walls.

CHAPTER SEVEN

THE EYE DEMANDS

Reda ran through the streets of Farrodum. She kept her hood up, her cloak held close to hide her obscure attire. No one was really looking, though; they were too preoccupied with fleeing or shouting, and the ramshackle buildings cast plenty of shadows. In spite of all that, she kept low and moved quickly but not hurriedly, Gerrant staying close and just behind her. She still had no idea what was happening, but the horns blared and now a bell was ringing too, from a watchtower to the north side of the city. Smeared orange light coloured the clouds overhead and she realised some kind of signal fire had been lit.

A troop of footmen rushed past her and she ducked into the lee of an inn, though its lamps were doused and its shutters and door locked. It was the same across the entire street and the street beyond it: the people were barricading themselves inside as the soldiers ran to fend off whatever danger had infiltrated their walls.

She saw pikemen, a lad with a crossbow struggling to feed a quarrel into its breech, the string too taut for him to pull back. Some carried lanterns, either the very young or the old, just as with the hunting party they had met in the wild lands outside of the city.

'Inside! Inside!' a town cryer was calling, a small brass bell tolling in his hand to punctuate each repeated instruction. 'They are coming,' he bellowed. 'Inside!'

Reda stayed out of the lantern light, away from the running men with swords and spears and other archaic weapons, and tried to find anything that might represent an apothecarion. She reasoned it must be close, else why take a burden as heavy as Pillium at the gate? She turned, about to ask Gerrant if he had seen anything useful, but the other armsman had gone.

'Throne and shit, Vanko,' she hissed, 'where are you?'

She doubled back, worrying that she had somehow lost him somewhere in the labyrinthine streets. He had been quiet ever since they had made planetfall, muttering now and then but verging on the incoherent. She had hoped it was just exhaustion, a symptom of how arduous the journey had been, but deep down she knew it was something else, something worse.

The warp eye, she realised, though she prayed to the Emperor she was wrong. *He looked. He bloody well looked. Just a glimpse.*

But a glimpse would be more than enough. She dared not think what horrors might have been unveiled to Vanko in that briefest of moments, or what they might have done to him, might *still* be doing to him.

'Vanko!' Reda called out, a half-rasp, half-shout. This was dangerous, and could invite unwanted attention, but she had to find him. Vedaeh's words came back to her in that moment, and she cursed the old chronicler for ever saying them and herself for recalling them at arguably the shittiest time possible.

They would fear them. They would kill us.

She thought she caught sight of Vanko's cloak disappearing around a corner and gave chase.

'Get back here, corporal,' she hissed between clenched teeth, 'that's a damn order.'

Barrelling around the corner brought Reda face-to-face with a group of spearmen who were coming in the opposite direction.

'Hold!' said one, raising up a lantern and squinting at Reda through fear-edged eyes. They all looked afraid, all five of them. The leader had a sword and drew it as soon as he saw who Reda was.

'You're not from Farrodum,' he said accusingly, and the others started to move towards her, splitting into pairs and coming in from the left and right.

'She's an outsider,' said one of the spearmen, an elderly man with a white wispy beard and a tremor in his left hand that made the tip of the spear shake like a quill nib scratching out a frenzied letter.

'What's the punishment for breaking curfew in this town?' said Reda, taking a step back, but the spearmen didn't answer her and kept advancing. 'A few lashes?'

Kind of looks like it might be death, thought Reda, and realised she would have to fight them.

'Please,' she began, holding up her left hand as her right went to the maul at her belt, 'I got lost. I know I shouldn't be out here, but I am looking for someone.'

'Two of them...' she heard one of the other spearmen mutter to the leader. He was little older than a boy with bad scars across both cheeks.

Reda's fingers slowly wrapped around the well-worn leather grip.

'I have no quarrel with any of you,' she said, trying diplomacy one final time.

'You shouldn't be out here,' was all the leader would say, and she realised then just how desperately scared they all were and that they were running away from the distant sounds of the warning horn.

Deserters, then... Now she knew they would try to kill her.

She shucked the maul loose, glad to feel the heft of the weapon in her hand, and was about to engage when something rushed across her field of vision. It took the leader with it, lantern and all, into an adjacent alleyway out of sight, and the street was suddenly plunged into darkness.

A grunting sound followed, deep and porcine. Then tearing, as of rotted leather, then a horrible cracking and splintering, and finally a guttural slurping and chewing as the beast gorged itself.

Something wet had flecked her face. Reda's fingers glistened darkly as she brought them up to her eyes.

'Throne of Terra...'

She was already backing away as a second presence swept after the first. It grabbed one of the spearmen, the scarred boy, and he screamed in a high-pitched voice before he was silenced. The others ran. One dropped his spear. Something large and squat was scurrying over a rooftop; Reda saw its silhouette edged in the diffuse light of distant braziers before it slipped below the roof edge and was gone. She turned and fled, leaving the spearmen to their fate, her lungs and heart pumping despite her fatigue, and found another path up a different street. Skirmishes were breaking out everywhere, small knots of spear or pikemen bellowing and screaming as they fought against something that moved almost too quick to see. Whatever effort had been made to stymie the attack on the city had failed. The beasts were running amok. Reda caught the vaguest impression of dark green skin, so dark as to almost be black, and a muscular body loping on all fours. There was something simian about it, but she doubted these creatures were remotely descended from Terra's long extinct species of ape.

She wanted to cry out for Vanko, to find him and make sure he was safe, but she knew she would draw the creatures to her.

They came anyway.

Reda heard it, breathy and grunting as it lunged at her. It was so dark, she could barely make out its hulking shape and a pair of small red eyes regarding her with bestial hunger. She lashed out, maul still in her hand, and made a solid contact.

It recoiled, squealing as it shrank back. Fortune smiled on her as a troop of spears and crossbowmen came out of a side street and engaged it. Reda did not wait for them to realise she was a foreign element too, and hurried on. She tried to move away from the fighting, ranging the city outskirts but gradually edging into its heart.

She found the apothecary. Vanko had found it too, and was standing in a doorway, silently beckoning her. A faded caduceus, or some version of one, had been painted on a hanging sign above it.

Reda was livid. 'Emperor's mercy, Vanko, what happened to you? What the hell are you doing?'

He put his finger to his lips. 'It's here,' he whispered, and gestured to the door.

She paused at the threshold. 'Vanko, are you alright...' she began, but the words sounded ridiculous in her head, and she dared not voice them aloud. 'Vanko, I'm worried,' she settled for instead.

Inhuman howling from farther up the street interrupted any potential reply and pushed Reda into moving. They couldn't stay out here.

'Come on,' said Reda. She opened the door and plunged into the darkness beyond.

Cwen looked out of her small window, trying to catch a sense of what was happening outside. Her fingers clenched against the stone sill, knuckles turning white on account of how hard she was holding on.

She glanced back at the stranger, Pillium, but he was either asleep or unconscious. Perhaps he truly could heal himself, and this was part of that process. She longed to study him, his *physik*, but presently her mind was occupied with staying alive. She knew what the bestial howls meant and what the hunched figures loping through the darkness were.

Something heavy landed on the roof, sending a raft of dust motes cascading downwards. Cwen threw the shutter closed on the window, though she doubted it was large enough for one of the beasts to get through. She then grasped the biggest knife she had and hurried towards the door. She stopped short when confronted with the woman on the other side.

'Who are you?' she demanded, brandishing her knife.

'I mean you no harm,' the woman replied. She was a warrior, Cwen could tell by the way she carried herself. A long scar down one side of her face and the strange mace in her hand confirmed this assumption. An older woman, but with perfect teeth. She had dark hair cut short above broad shoulders. Judging by her cloak and attire, she was also one of the strangers who had come to Farrodum with her patient.

'Please...' the woman went on, slowly putting away her mace, 'we are with him.' She gestured to Pillium. A second figure stepped out from the half-darkness beyond the door. He was younger, unshaven, and had a strange tattoo under one eye. They had come up the steps that led from the infirmary's outer door on the street.

Cwen lowered her knife, but only a little.

'I am Reda,' said the woman, eyeing the blade as she gestured to her friend, 'and this is Gerrant. You have no reason to be afraid of us.'

'It's not you,' said Cwen as whatever had landed on her roof began to claw at it furiously. From below, there was a loud bang and then sharp grunting began to echo up the stairs. She turned wide-eyed to Reda. 'You didn't seal the gate?'

'It was already open.'

Cwen cursed the craven guard.

First he pisses on my floor and then he leaves the damn door open.

'We have to barricade this one,' she said, slamming the door shut and ramming a chair against it. Reda helped her drag a large chest over next. 'Here,' said Cwen, passing Reda an iron stake as something large and heavy barrelled up the stairs. 'Hammer them in,' she said, smacking one into the door frame to act as a jam. Reda nodded, doing the same as a massive weight smashed into the door, rocking it on its hinges.

Cwen fell back on her behind, grimacing with the impact, as Reda's stake came loose, clanging loudly on the floor.

'Damn it,' breathed Cwen, scrambling back to her feet. 'Hammer harder,' she snapped.

Reda obeyed, and made a better job of it this time. The beast came again, and a split ran down the wood, right in the middle of the door.

'What are these things?'

'Bone-swine. Killers.' Cwen's face darkened. 'They killed my husband.' Then she noticed the one called Gerrant. He had barely moved, beyond stepping into the room, and stood staring. 'Is he…?'

Then he drew an object from beneath his cloak. It was spherical with small ridges on the outside like a shelled fruit.

'I have to…' he said, his face contorted with sorrow. 'The eye demands…'

Cwen knew something was wrong before she felt Reda's firm grip on her arm taking her away from Gerrant and behind one side of the barricade.

'Down!' Reda cried, before everything was burning daylight and deafening thunder.

CHAPTER EIGHT

⊍

A BREACH ACROSS THE THRESHOLD

Daceus heard the explosion and turned to Sicarius.

'That was a grenade,' he said. 'I say we move.'

They had congregated around the gate with blades drawn, listening to the battle unfolding outside the feast hall, but had yet to engage.

Sicarius wanted to wait, to adhere to the wishes of the one who ruled here. They could not risk fear becoming hostility in the natives.

'Suzerain,' said Daceus when Sicarius gave no answer, his jaw tight as he fought every instinct not to act.

'We cannot,' he said. 'Our first deed in this city cannot be to defy its ruler.' He looked to Vedaeh, who lingered at the edge of the semicircle of Adeptus Astartes, an outsider to their brotherhood in every sense.

'Their ruler cowers in his citadel,' said Daceus. 'He has no thought for these people.'

Sicarius' face grew stern. 'I saw him too. But we are

foreigners here, not guests. Not yet. Our presence in the streets could lead to bloodshed.'

'It already has. Cato,' Daceus urged, his voice suddenly hoarse with emotion, 'they are dying.' He threw a one-eyed glare Vedaeh's way but she did not react, though the grief she felt for the suffering outside was etched on her face.

'We must not, Retius,' said Sicarius, firmly. 'Not until they cross this threshold, unless we are attacked and must defend ourselves...' He paused, frozen in anger and frustration when a different expression crept over his face. An idea. 'So, let's encourage them.' He nodded to Vandius who sheared the door in half across the diagonal in one blow.

The two sides parted and crashed noisily to the ground.

The city street outside was gloomy and echoed with the sound of distant battles.

Sicarius rapped the hilt of the Tempest Blade against his chestplate. Then the others did the same, the Ultramarines ringing out a challenge to the monsters in the darkness. It wasn't long before that challenge was met. A hunched thing, all dark skin and bunched muscle, came loping out of the night on all fours. It sniffed at the air, still covered in shadow but turning its head towards the light emanating from the feast hall, a moth lured to a lantern flame.

Three more joined it, snorting and grunting in porcine attempts at language. Then another four. And another four. Sicarius' enhanced olfaction detected the blood around their brutish mouths. He heard long claws scrape against the ground.

'Close enough,' he said, and the Ultramarines rushed them.

Sicarius impaled the first beast as it reared up on its hind-quarters to batter at him. The Tempest Blade was no ordinary sword. It had kept its edge and resisted the warp siphoning that had so enervated other power weapons. It slid through the beast's thick hide with ease then tore upwards, sweeping through bone and muscle and out through the beast's shoulder. Its two halves pulled apart as if hauled by an invisible thread in competing directions, spilling hot innards onto the street. He beheaded a second, a swift cut across the throat that severed the neck entire. A gout of dark blood plumed upwards as the arteries vented.

Daceus killed another, ramming his gladius into its eye all the way to the hilt and bearing the beast down as it collapsed.

Two precise cuts, one sagittal, the other axial, and Vandius claimed two more. His sharp thrust claimed a third.

Fennion and Vorolanus slew another two for no reply.

The Ultramarines were swift, methodical. Devastating. In less than thirty seconds they had killed or maimed every one of the beasts. The dead lay steaming, the injured mewling in agony until Vandius silenced them with a stab to the head.

Sicarius burned off the blood from his blade with a burst of its disruptor field and brought it up-close to one of the dead. The flickering false lightning coursing over the sword lit the beast's features and he saw it for what it truly was for the first time. They all did.

'This must be the bone-swine,' he said, his expression souring as he recognised an old enemy.

'Orks...' scowled Daceus and spat on one of the corpses.

'Ever do the greenskins harry our steps,' muttered Vorolanus.

Vandius was cleaning his sword on one of the bodies when he asked, 'What now?'

Sicarius flourished the Tempest Blade, loosening his arm after so long without using it and now wearing dense, unpowered ceramite. It felt good to kill the orks again.

He turned to Vorolanus, clapping his hand upon the

warrior's shoulder guard. 'Scipio. Find the mortals. Find Pillium. I should never have sent them off alone.'

Vorolanus nodded and hurried off ahead of the rest.

'Am I to remain here then, as you wage war, Cato?' asked Vedaeh.

'I doubt you would stay even if I asked you to. You stay by my side at all times. I cannot vouch for your safety otherwise.'

'And us?' asked Vandius.

Sicarius gestured to the shadows where the sounds of skirmishing warriors was loudest.

'We hunt.'

Dazed, Reda tried to blink back the flare of the explosion but all she got was blurred vision. She called out, first to Vanko and then to the healer or whatever she was. Her voice slurred, or it could have just been her hearing. A slowly fading tinnitus was impairing every sound.

Something was dead. She could smell the blood as she struggled onto her hands and knees, searching the rubble and the detritus of the door for her maul. A splinter dug into her flesh like a needle and she cursed loudly.

'Here...' a voice came through the fog. A firm hand took her arm and helped her up. 'It's dead,' said the voice, and Reda realised it was the medicus. Her vision crept back into focus. The woman was young, her red hair tossed all about as if frozen in the midst of a gale. Black streaks marked her pale skin and there were spots of blood on it.

'Are you injured?' asked Reda, still groggy and not quite able to stand unaided. The medicus shook her head. Reda searched the room for Vanko and found his boots jutting out from beneath some rubble. 'Holy Throne,' she gasped, edging the other woman aside. 'Please,' she said, hefting a piece of wreckage where part of the roof had come down on Vanko, 'help me.'

Together, they heaved a wooden beam off Vanko, throwing aside smaller pieces of wood and stone from the shattered door where an ork lay on its back, its chest torn open and ruddy bone jutting up through the gap like little arches of ivory.

It was definitely dead, but Reda's gaze lingered on the beast for a few seconds to make sure before she returned her attention to Vanko. Mercifully, he was alive, but in a bad way.

'We can't stay here,' said the medicus. 'They're attracted to loud noises.'

'Is there another way out?' Reda asked.

The medicus shook her head again.

Reda glanced at Pillium, lying on the bench, reasoning that if she could somehow draw the greenskins away, then he might be overlooked. When she heard the grunting from down the stairs, she realised that wasn't going to work.

'It doesn't matter,' she said. 'They've already found us.' She dragged Vanko to the back of the room and stepped between him and the door frame that led to the stairs.

'I'm sorry...' said Reda.

'I am Cwen,' said the medicus.

Reda nodded. 'I'm sorry, Cwen. I regret our acquaintance will only be brief.' And she whispered, 'I'm sorry, Vanko... for everything.'

The beast bellowed as it came through the shattered arch and into the light.

Reda roared back, 'We are Macragge!' and swept out with the maul as Cwen threw herself at the beast with her knife.

Their defiance, though brave, was short-lived. The greenskin, a hulking brute of a thing, laughed as Cwen's knife sank into its hide, backhanding her across the room and into a heap from which she did not rise. It easily caught the haft of the maul, Reda's blow imprecise and lacking in real strength. She found she could barely stand as the beast shoved her back and she went sprawling. Pain flared in her hip as she collided with a heavy bench. On her knees, doubled over, she spat up a wad of blood and looked to the medicus.

'Cwen...' she cried. The beast was taking its time as it sloped around the room. It reminded Reda of a dull-witted ape, its feral brain even less advanced than that of a common ork, as it picked up spilled jars and vials, lapping at spilled powders and serums but finding none to its liking. Just as Reda dared to believe that if the beast was distracted enough they might somehow slip away unnoticed, it turned on her and bared its teeth in an angry snarl. There was blood on its jutting mouth, small shreds of cloth and pale meat still snagged on its tusks. It wanted more.

Cwen stirred, groaning, glass crunching underneath her body as she tried to get up. The ork turned, flinging thick, ropey saliva. Hurling aside the meagre wreckage in its way, its tiny porcine eyes glinted as they fell upon Cwen, and Reda thought she would be sick. She could barely move, teeth gritted against the pain in her hip. She could scarcely shout. She reached for Vanko's hand, her fingers outstretched and touching his as the beast bore down on Cwen and after that surely Reda next.

The ork took a fistful of Cwen's hair and hauled her to her feet. She screamed, first in pain then disorientation. Finally, she screamed out of fear, forced to consciousness only to witness her own painful death as the ork ate her alive.

Except it didn't happen.

Instead, the beast jerked, turning sharply, a spar of ragged metal jutting from its chest. Pillium was on his feet, pale and breathing hard, but about as vengeful an apparition as Reda could have wished for.

He charged at the ork, smashing the bench aside with a roar as it dropped Cwen and rushed to meet him. As the beast flailed for his face and neck, Pillium ducked underneath and wrapped his massive arms around the ork's torso, lifting it up off its feet and smashing it against the wall. It squealed, a thick string of bloody snot spraying from its nose. Pillium batted back the ork's desperate swipe and, still pinning it against the wall, started pummelling with his fists. A tusk broke off, an eye swelled shut. Pillium hit the beast so hard that its nose caved and he punched his fist all the way through to the grimy matter underneath. When he wrenched his hand loose, it was slathered in blood and pieces of sticky bone. He leaned back, nearly staggering, and the ork slid down the wall, as limp as a scarecrow robbed of straw.

Pillium sagged, his face awash with blood as he first regarded the terrified medicus and then Reda.

'Can you fight?' he asked her, provoking a weary but warm smile.

The sound of splintering wood prompted them both to look up. A few seconds later, the ceiling came crashing in and a second greenskin with it.

They met Scarfel in the city square. He looked tired as he took off his helm to greet the Ultramarines, and his face had blood on it.

'Bone-swine are tough,' he said with a rueful grin.

'We call them orks in the south,' said Daceus, offering a respectful nod which Scarfel accepted and returned.

'Orks, bone-swine, they're a damnable plague all the same.'

'That we can agree on,' said Sicarius.

The square was scattered with bodies, mostly Farrodum's dead but also a decent amount of greenskins. They were big, this breed of ork, but without the meagre technologies of even feral tribes. They had regressed to a base state, something large and primordial. A primeval ork.

Scarfel had around fifty or sixty warriors with him, mostly young footmen and a handful of his ageing horsemen. He had dismounted to approach Sicarius and the others, leaving his snorting destrier with a squire.

'I thank you,' said the old campaigner, 'for fighting for us.'

'I hope your liege lord sees it the same way,' Sicarius replied. The Ultramarines had fought their way to the square with relative ease, despatching stragglers and small groups. They had met Farrodum's warriors only a handful of times and thankfully they had either fled or realised the knights of Macragge were allies and briefly thrown in with them. 'Tell me,' added Sicarius as he looked out deeper into the city, 'what's left for us to do?'

Scarfel had beckoned for his horse and was mounting up again as he replied, 'A horde has begun to gather at the north edge of the city.' He pointed, though Sicarius knew exactly where he meant. 'They've never attacked so boldly and in such large numbers before,' Scarfel went on, pulling on the reins to bring his beast to heel. 'A few of the scouts report some kind of wooden obelisk. That it's whipping the bone-swine into a frenzy.'

'Your lord,' said Daceus shrewdly, 'does he take the field to the north end of the city? Is that why he's not with you?'

'Baron Athelnar seldom takes to the field,' said Scarfel, his face carefully impassive. 'As castellan, it's my duty to lead the army.'

'Then lead us,' said Sicarius, gesturing to his warriors. 'We have four ready swords.'

A few of the Farrodum warriors looked nervous at this proclamation, but Scarfel smiled as he turned his steed about to face northwards. 'You honour us, Sicarius.' He arched his neck over his shoulder so he could face Sicarius as he talked. 'Why is it then that I reckon you've commanded armies far larger and more impressive than this one?'

'It doesn't matter how large or impressive,' Sicarius replied, 'only that it fights and fights well. We have a code, we knights of Macragge. It exemplifies who we are and what matters to us the most as warriors. Courage and honour.'

Scarfel nodded, trying out the words. 'Courage and honour. I like that,' he said, his steed turning in a circle before facing northwards again. 'We will fight. We must. Our very existence depends upon it. I only hope that you are as tough as you look.'

'Oh,' said Daceus, a feral glint in his eye, 'you don't need to worry about that. There's a saying in our country about knights of Macragge. It's a little long and overblown as sayings often are, but one thing about it holds true. If you ever manage to kill one of us, you had best make sure we are dead.'

CHAPTER NINE

THE OBELISK

Pillium threw himself at the ork. Debris still rained from the hole in the roof as he tackled it around the neck and it fell, driven by his momentum, crashing through the shattered door arch and down the stairs beyond. Pillium went with it, hanging on through every collision against the steps, every bruising crash against the walls. The beast roared, spraying hot and rancid spittle against his face, but Pillium clung on.

They landed hard, stone cracking audibly beneath them, the ork on its back, Pillium on top with his hand around its thickly corded neck. It fought back, swiping at his shoulder guard and ripping it off completely. The ceramite rang like a tolling bell as it hit the ground. Pillium got his other hand over the ork's face, digging in under its upper jaw with his fingers. It champed at him, its sharp teeth gnawing at the metal of his gauntlet, but he managed to grab the lower jaw with his other hand. Then he pulled.

Tongue lolling, throat warbling in half-choked rage, the ork raked at Pillium's side, tearing open the shrapnel wound and making a mess of his meshweave. Though durable, it wasn't crafted to repel blades or bullets and came apart against the onslaught. Blood instantly dampened his legs and abdomen but Pillium held on, slowly prising apart the ork's jaws until they broke. The beast screamed, a porcine shriek that had Pillium clamping his own jaw shut, such was its intensity. But he kept going. When the lower jaw came apart, wrenched off in his bloody hand, he seized the upper jaw and rammed the ork's head against the ground over and over until it was nothing but gory pulp.

He sagged then, flat against the ork's body as the last of its air wheezed from its lungs like a deflating bladder. He heard the medicus from above, her voice getting closer as she descended the stairs. Belatedly, he realised the outer door to the infirmary had been ripped open. The street yawned from it. The night looked blacker than he thought it would, like a funerary veil had been drawn across it and he was looking through its gauzy material. Two figures loped through that blackness, patches of hard oil shimmering with sweat. One dropped something. It landed wetly and Pillium realised it was a part-chewed human arm.

He struggled to his feet, his hot blood turning cold – or perhaps that was just him. He had no weapon. His bones were cracked in several places and he was bleeding from wounds to his back and sides. He could feel his transhuman physiology working to repair him but even Martian genetic science had its limits.

'I just need a moment...' he rasped to the orks.

The beasts snarled to one another in some crude approximation of language. They looked hungry through the funerary veil, a deeper darkness brought on by Pillium's injuries.

If he died now, Cwen died, and Reda and Gerrant too. He

barely knew the armsmen and had only just met the medicus but he could not allow that. If he did, he would have failed them, he would have failed his Chapter. So he forced himself to stand straight and look his killers in their piggish, red eyes.

'Courage and honour...' he whispered bitterly, knowing his end would be an ignominious one but hoping it would give the mortals enough time to slip away. He'd had such hopes of glory.

It had begun to rain, slow at first but growing to a fierce downpour. Ork skin glistened in the weak light.

Rivulets of water ran down Pillium's face, washing off some of the blood. It gathered in pinkish puddles at his feet. He felt it dampen his beard and it plinked loudly off the sheath of his armour, a drumbeat to match his twin hearts. He did not need a weapon. *He* was the weapon.

'Come, then!' he roared, summoning up his strength, the furnace of his defiance burning hot. 'Come and face a knight of Macragge!'

And they did.

The first ork had dropped to all fours, and had kicked into a loping stride when an armoured blur struck it in the side and smashed it onto its back. The second came up short, confronted by a warrior in blue war-plate, a shining sword in his hand.

Vorolanus drew a second blade, a combat knife which he held in a reverse grip as the ork charged. He turned as it lunged, dipping his shoulder so the beast flew right past him. It slid, scrabbling uncertainly and wondering how half of its entrails had unfurled behind it. A deep slit in the ork's belly provided the answer, and it looked down dumbly at the savage wound, Vorolanus' gladius slick with its vitae. It stumbled forwards, still intent on the warrior's murder before it collapsed, entangled in its own steaming offal. Pillium stomped on its neck to end it.

The first ork had recovered, grunting as it shook off its disorientation.

Vorolanus flung his knife. A silver flash lit the dark as a hilt appeared in the ork's skull, the blade already buried all the way. The ork rocked on its heels, nerveless fingers scratching dumbly at the hilt before it crashed back and stayed dead.

'Well met, Vorolanus,' said Pillium, and smelled copper in his icy breath. He had one hand against the door frame holding himself up.

'You look in need of an Apothecary, brother.'

'I am mending. Besides, I already have one,' he said, as the medicus appeared behind him with Reda. 'Is that the last of them?'

Vorolanus had walked over to the dead ork, and retrieved his knife with a savage pull. 'A horde gathers at the northern edge of the city,' he said, wiping the blade clean on his cloak. 'Sicarius goes to meet it.' He looked up at Pillium. 'Can you fight?'

Pillium laughed loudly, ignoring Vorolanus' evident confusion at his reaction.

'Hand me a sword and we'll see.' He let go of the door frame and found he could stand unaided.

'I don't have a sword, brother,' said Vorolanus, but pulled forth a spear that had been strapped to his back and tossed it over. 'I do have this.'

Pillium caught the haft one-handed.

'This will do,' he said, appraising the weapon approvingly.

Cwen stepped forwards. 'He cannot fight,' she told Vorolanus. 'He needs rest so he can heal.'

'I have rested too long already,' Pillium told her, though

not unkindly. 'I thank you, medicus. But I need you to bind these wounds one last time so that I can do my duty.'

Cwen looked about to protest but relented in the end, giving Pillium a shallow nod. He turned to tramp back up the stairs.

'Where are you going?' asked Cwen.

'To retrieve my armour from where you left it, medicus.'

The northward wall had collapsed into rubble and a horde of greenskins swarmed through the breach, bellowing and hooting. They dragged a massive carved totem with them, the *obelisk* as Scarfel's scout had dubbed it. Hewn from wood, it crudely depicted the faces of the brutish ork gods, one atop the other, each huge and leering. It tottered, ungainly but upright, rolled along on six ramshackle stone wheels that churned furrows of earth into the ground wherever it went.

An ork, its skin painted in gaudy colours, a plume of ragged feathers sprouting from a wooden crown upon its head and the stone torcs around its thick arms, stood at the summit of the totem. It carried a gnarled staff of wood in one clawed hand, the skulls of birds and vermin rattling against the haft as it shook with the ork's frenzied capering. It teetered on the totem's edge several times but never fell, always swinging back as if held by some invisible thread.

Eight burly orks, their skin even blacker than the others, heaved the totem forwards on thick ropes, and surrounding them was the horde itself.

'Orruk! Orruk! Orruk!' they bellowed, as the rain hammered down and lightning split the sky.

Standing on a parapet that overlooked the courtyard leading to the north wall, Daceus gauged around a hundred orks, but more were scrambling over the rubble all the time.

'We have to stop them here,' he said to Sicarius and the

others, 'or they'll overrun the city. Digging them out then will be painful and arduous.'

Scarfel's warriors had backed off, allowing the orks at their head to roam unchecked through the outer district. It had been abandoned already, the people moving further into the city and away from the horde as what was left of their army came to meet it.

Three towers looked out upon the square and archers garrisoned each one, but held their quarrels for now. And three gates led from the square, wide enough for ten men abreast to pass. Two had been sealed by portcullises and then braced to further reinforce them. A small guard protected each one, twelve men with spears and crossbows stationed behind the barrier. The third gate lay open, and it was here the remnants of the force that had been engaging the horde retreated to.

Sicarius looked down upon it now, standing right above it. The orks had stopped to celebrate their victory and eat the spoils of that triumph. Arrow shafts silenced the injured, a last mercy before the orks fell upon them with hungry tooth and claw. Somewhere in the distance a drum began to beat, a slow and dolorous rhythm that wove a thread of despair through Scarfel's men.

'That gate is all that stands between the city and the horde?'

Scarfel, a diminutive figure next to the knights of Macragge on the wall, nodded. 'There are no other ways in. No tunnels or postern gates. This is it.'

'That *sport*,' offered Vandius, his lip curling in distaste, 'will not occupy them for long.'

'Agreed,' said Sicarius, and turned to Scarfel. 'I have a plan, if you would hear it?'

'Of course. I am eager to learn how battles are won in the south.'

Sicarius raised a wry smile, and Daceus caught his stray glance.

'Orks, bone-swine, they are eager for the fight,' said Sicarius. 'So we give it to them. Have your men raise a clamour, have them beat hafts and hilts against shields. Draw them in and then stop them. The narrow aperture of the gate will keep them penned in, and Fennion,' he gestured to Iulus, who gave Scarfel a casual salute, 'will stand with you to galvanise your courage.'

'I see,' said Scarfel. His jaw twitched, signalling his mild consternation at the remark about courage. 'And what will you do?'

Daceus answered, unable to keep the eagerness from his voice. 'We shall enter the fray, my friend. There,' he pointed to the obelisk, 'is the object of our wrath. Break it and we break the will of the horde. Orks are cowards at heart.' He smiled grimly. 'And they do not like the taste of Macragge steel.'

'Are we in agreement, Scarfel?' asked Sicarius once Daceus was done posturing. 'We have fought these bone-swine many times before. This is how we will beat them back and save your city.'

Scarfel regarded the orks as rain pounded and drumbeats bruised the air. There were signs they had almost finished their revelling, a restiveness that bordered on frenzy.

'You are either brave or mad to want to run into that,' he admitted. 'Truly, I hope you do not die, Sicarius. I have found I rather like you and your kin, and think perhaps I should like to visit the south one day.'

Sicarius laughed, and there was a certain reckless abandon to his mood. 'You would be an honoured guest, Scarfel. Let's be at it, shall we? These orks won't kill themselves.'

CHAPTER TEN

THE HORDE

The path to the obelisk had been bloody. As they neared the crudely carved edifice, its malign power increased. Daceus felt it in the heavy heat of the air, a quickening of breath and a sharp migraine pain at the back of his skull.

Close to the obelisk, the faces in the wood had begun to change and turned angry. Green smoke exuded from the grain, thin and wispy at first but quickly churning into a dense fog that swallowed everything for several feet around it.

Daceus and his brethren fought in this fog. A beast came screaming, a crude stone axe still gummed with human blood raised aloft. He swept below the cut, ramming his gladius up into the ork's chin, pushing it all the way and out of the crown of its skull. Daceus yanked the blade loose with a jerk of his arm as a second beast roared for his blood, careening madly through the green mist. He cut off its weapon, a broad flint dagger, at the wrist before slashing open its throat. Hot, rancid blood painted his armour and face. Daceus embraced it as warpaint, emitting a bellow of his own. He killed a third ork, then a fourth, slashing and cutting freely now, laughing with every blow as the drums throbbed against his temples and he began to hear voices on the air. A deep, bestial refrain, the voice uttered words that had no meaning but drove deep into his primordial heart. Primitive urges bubbled to the fore, geysering up through Daceus' throat until they came out in an animalistic roar.

The fog grew thicker, choking. He spluttered, finding it hard to see, to even breathe through the heady miasma and the red-rimmed fury of his own rage. He took a blow to the shoulder. A second to his side. He had become reckless, swinging with neanderthal abandon. An ork fell nearby and the arterial spray struck his eye, blinding him. It stung like fire and Daceus cried out in pain, trying desperately to see through all the red. Something struck the side of his head and he fell, down to a knee. A blade, possibly a spear, stabbed down into the joint at his neck, but he twisted before his attacker could push it all the way through and impale him. The shaft shattered as Daceus moved, cracking apart and into splinters. He wiped at his eye, and managed to clear some of the blood. The scent of the greenskins loomed close, and intense enough to make him gag. On his knees, he looked up and the obelisk looked back, the ork gods peering down hungrily, mocking him for his weakness. The feathered shaman that rode the summit danced and cavorted and capered, hammering out a berserk tattoo against the wood with his staff. He had grown huge in Daceus' eye, a colossus that eclipsed one of the Primaris Marines threefold. Bones rattled; green lightning began to gather above the battlefield, turning into a massive thunderhead. Even the rain stank of ork.

Daceus tried to rise as a savage punch spun his head and a

veil of darkness descended. He shook it off, parrying the next blow, but he still couldn't get to his feet. He fought on one knee, fending off one ork and then the next, stone spears and flint daggers breaking off against his armour. A few bit deep.

'Sicarius!' Daceus roared. 'Sicarius!'

He had almost lost all sense of geography, hemmed in by the greenskins and surrounded by the obelisk's unnatural fog. He cried out to his only true north.

A brilliant flash, azure lightning on a winter's day, cut through the fog, drawing it apart like curtains. It peeled away to admit the Suzerain, his sword unleashing flares of bright magnesium fire wherever it struck. He seemed untouched by the fog or the barbaric drumming, as deadly and focused as an ice storm.

Sicarius wasn't alone. Vandius stood at his right shoulder, his own sword art carefully looping and cutting around his captain's, two masters at their work in perfect synchronicity. The orks fell back from this onslaught, clutching the stumps of severed limbs or crumpling down headless to be broken underfoot. They reeled from the attack, stampeding towards the gates as a merciful gap in the throng of bodies began to form. Those that reached the portcullised gates found only an impasse or the stinging cuts of thrust spears and loosed arrows. Most piled towards the middle gate and the line of desperate warriors that held it, Fennion exhorting them to fight on and make the orks pay for every inch they took.

Daceus gasped, sucking in a relieved breath, punch-drunk but able to rise. Sicarius reached out a steadying hand, taking advantage of the momentary respite to get one of his Lions back onto his feet.

'Blood of Guilliman...' breathed Daceus. 'I saw only... only rage. It felt unfettered. Primal.'

'Courage and honour, Retius.' Sicarius' teeth clenched. 'We all feel it.'

Repelled at the gates, the orks swilled back into the courtyard, their numbers intensifying again.

'The obelisk must fall,' Sicarius shouted, the drumbeat growing ever louder and merging with the orkish voices like thunder on the wind.

'Go!' cried Vandius, cutting down three orks in as many strokes of his sword. 'Go and destroy it.'

Daceus urged Sicarius on. The obelisk was close, and the horde around it had thinned as they had run for the gates. 'Cato, only you can do this. I'll stay with Vandius.'

Sicarius clasped the other warrior's forearm and then went to his business. He hacked down a greenskin in his path, then two more, leaving a glittering trail of pure light in his wake. Above, crossbow quarrels hailed down relentlessly, a greenskin finally succumbing to half a dozen shafts. Sicarius rushed through the bolt storm, not so much as grazing his armour, finishing any ork injured by the archers. Then it slowed and finally stopped as quivers emptied, and all eyes went to the heavens as the green storm reached its crescendo. Two faces manifested in the clouds, large enough to fill the entire sky. Men screamed. Some fled, abandoning their weapons as the sight rendered them insane.

A lightning blast speared from the thunderous dark above, spat from the mouths of the gods. It came unerringly for Sicarius, an arcing green fork sent to obliterate.

Vedaeh watched the battle from the wall, cowering behind one of the merlons as the thunder rolled overhead.

It was reaching its zenith, clouds coiling like serpentine tails or tongues, and the storm would soon vent its wrath.

She thought she saw faces in the emerald-tinged darkness, two leering, bestial gods. The orks saw it too, or at least they turned and bellowed at the unquiet heavens, roaring fury and exultation.

Then the lightning fell, a jagged bolt like a cast spear but as thick as an ancient oak.

It struck Sicarius, who had raised his sword, crying out the name of his primarch.

'Guilliman!'

His voice shook the courtyard, pure as a clarion cry, as a dazzling flare of green then white light erupted from the Tempest Blade as the lightning fork struck it.

Vedaeh's eyes streamed with tears and she clung to the merlon for fear of falling.

The orks shrieked, agony rolling through their ranks like a wave as they recoiled and covered their eyes against the brilliant light. Even the feathered shaman stumbled, almost slipping from his perch, a fledgling fearful of tottering out of its nest.

The light faded and Sicarius stood unscathed, a coruscating bolt of lightning running down his sword, the blade absorbing it like a piece of frozen fire. Then he ran, charging for the obelisk. He cut down the first of the bearers, and the rope went slack in its dead hand. The second he killed saw the obelisk teeter, leaning so hard that the shaman had to cling on, its claws digging urgent furrows in the wood.

Sicarius used it. He sped for the obelisk, slaying every greenskin sent against him until he was running up the thing like a ramp.

Daceus and Vandius had followed him, and now Pillium and Vorolanus emerged through the fog too, having descended into the melee, slaughtering greenskins like cattle and tearing into the other rope bearers. The gates had all but been forgotten in the greenskins' urgency to stop the Ultramarines. Vedaeh knew it was too late for that. She looked on breathlessly as the obelisk lurched dangerously, the wooden axles of its wheels snapping as it began to topple over. Two giant orks strained to hold on to it, their shaman clinging to it like a drunken spider.

Sicarius paused for a few seconds to adjust his footing, and the wood writhed beneath him as if filled with some kind of restive anima. Every step took him closer, until the shaman was before him.

A defiant roar tore from the beast's throat but Sicarius saw the fear in its narrow porcine eyes. They were white, a gift or deformity from its brutish gods. It did not matter. Death had found it anyway.

'We. Are. Macragge!' Sicarius shouted back.

It hissed, spitting some brutish invective that he brushed aside with a sweep of his sword that cleaved the ork's head from its shoulders.

The shaman fell, loose-limbed, feathers fluttering and coming away from their false pinions. The orks wailed and at last the final two rope bearers let their burden slip. The shaman struck the ground hard and a moment later was crushed by the felled obelisk.

Sicarius rode it down, leaping off at the last moment to land in a crouch, his sword tip held downwards and to the ground.

'Guilliman…' he breathed, gratified to see his brothers alive and coming to his side.

The orks fled, boiling out of the city like wasps deserting the hive. They dragged their injured with them, chased by the raucous cheers of Farrodum's warriors. The men bellowed as the skies began to clear and a palpable sense of relief took hold. Some cried. They hugged one another as their fear slowly drained away, and laughed and jeered at their enemies.

Only the knights of Macragge did not celebrate. They stood like towering armoured islands amidst the wash of humanity, watching as the orks departed. Not a warrior amongst them so much as raised a sword. They were silent as sentinels.

'What is it?' asked Scarfel, coming up by Sicarius' side. He had a shallow cut to his forehead and his sword was badly notched, but he looked ebullient. 'We won, didn't we?'

Sicarius shared a glance with his brothers and spoke aloud what they were all thinking.

'We did. But the orks will return. They always do. And next time they will bring their entire tribe.'

CHAPTER ELEVEN

THE HALL OF TRIUMPHS

It was called the hall of triumphs. As far as Daceus could tell, it was on account of the various threadbare tapestries and faded banners depicting the battles of Farrodum and its greatly diminished army. Whoever the artist had been, he or she had a gift for the fatalistic. Every piece described a desperate last stand or a glorious charge into the bone-swine hordes. Several depicted the baron himself or what might possibly have been his father; it was difficult to ascertain genealogy based on a crudely rendered painting on cloth. In contrast to the beleaguered army, the baron or barons were triumphant, often drawn with a foot on the head of an enemy, with sword aloft, or at the head of a glittering warhost, armour shimmering in the painted sun.

It smacked of vainglory and delusion, if the current state of affairs was any measure.

The entire company of the knights of Macragge had been gathered for an audience with the baron, who had yet to occupy the empty golden throne sitting at the summit of a raised stone dais at the back of the room. Here, too, was the largest and most expansive tapestry, a huge curtain of cloth that had painted upon it an effigy of the baron as a towering, deific figure who blessed his diminutive subjects with an outstretched hand. In this rendering, he had the raiment of a priest-king, a staff and not a sword in his hand.

'I do not think I am going to approve of the potentate of this land...' muttered Daceus, earning a look of agreement from his captain.

Vedaeh had been invited to the gathering too, at Sicarius' request, and she stood at the head of the Ultramarines, hands clasped over her stomach as she waited patiently. She was surrounded by warriors in chipped blue ceramite, their long cloaks brushed and cleaned but still carrying the scars of recent battle like their wearers. Pillium stood a head taller than the others and occupied the rearguard of their formation. Daceus stood to the left and one step behind Sicarius; Vandius to the right. Fennion and Vorolanus stood behind them and so the six were arranged.

They, too, were surrounded. Daceus had counted thirty armoured warriors standing silently in alcoves to either side of the hall, which was long and in an obvious state of disrepair. Braziers had been lit, and cast their trembling glow upon dark stone and even darker wood. A ragged pelt, stitched and dyed crimson, ran half the length of the hall and ended at the foot of the dais.

At the dais itself stood Scarfel, his armour polished though still dented, his helmet under one arm and his hand resting easily on the pommel of his sheathed sword. Daceus liked the old campaigner and admired him for his courage. Much about Scarfel reminded him of himself, and a bond had naturally formed. Behind Scarfel, and to the left of the throne loomed the largest man of Farrodum Daceus had seen yet. Wearing a cuirass of black plate over a hauberk of chain-mail and thick, heavy boots, he came close to the size of an Adeptus Astartes initiate. Considering the man had no visi-ble physical enhancements, it was impressive. He carried a sword to match, a double-handed and broad-bladed weapon that he held downwards, both hands on the pommel. His helm was closed, wide cheek-plates and a slitted visor offering little in the way of the man's actual face under all the metal.

'We should recommend this one to the sons of Dorn,' Van-dius had remarked under his breath, earning a gruff laugh from Daceus that Vedaeh had silenced with a glare as they made entry to the hall and the giant black-armoured war-rior had been revealed. He had little time for the chronicler and thought her influence on the Suzerain deleterious. Cato had his own mind, Daceus had no doubt about that, but the way she insisted the Ultramarines kowtow to the natives sat poorly. Yes, they needed to find the power source and then have Haephestus determine a way to get it back to the *Emperor's Will* – assuming the Techmarine was still out in the wilds somewhere – but they were warriors, not diplo-mats. The mantle fell uncomfortably on Daceus' shoulders, and he railed against its burden and how it blunted their efficacy. Still, he had to concede, it would not serve them at this point to make enemies of their hosts. Particularly in the current situation. Daceus had also noticed archers amongst the guards, though these made a practice of hiding in the vaults above the hall. A deep parapet extruded, largely closed off from view, but he had seen the watchful eyes regarding them through the narrow embrasures as the Ultramarines had taken up position in front of the throne.

And there they waited, patiently, quietly and unmoving until their host arrived.

'I have never heard of this land, this *Macragge*,' said the baron, resting languidly on his throne. He looked young, Sicarius thought, and wore crimson robes with a gold trim that caught the firelight. An ostentatious crown nestled on his brow, amongst thick dark hair that fell almost to his shoulders, though he had no beard to speak of. The sword he wore at his hip looked finely made and scarcely used. He turned to who Sicarius assumed was the vizier, standing below him on the lower step of the dais. 'Have you heard of it, Nehebkau?'

The vizier shook his head, though there was an element of tedious theatre to it, as if it were a conversation played out many times already and repeated here for the strangers' benefit. The vizier was a fat-faced man dressed in long, lustrous jade robes, with a compass-like amulet hung around his bulging neck. He had cultivated a sharp beard that extruded in a point like a dagger from his flabby chin, the rest of his scalp contained beneath a tan leather skullcap. The minor slope of his shoulder, the slightly hunchbacked shape to his bearing suggested an old leg injury that made Sicarius wonder if the vizier had seen more battles than his liege lord. He appeared unassuming but curious, the look of a keen scholar about him, and he held a simple bronze staff with a sapphire fixed to the end.

The baron looked Sicarius up and down like a man inspecting a thoroughbred horse. There was fear there too, though.

'Are you from the south then?'

'We are, my lord,' Sicarius replied, and felt Daceus stiffen in anger at the use of the word. They should not be bowing and scraping to these men. They should have declared their presence and the needs of their company, but, diminished as they were, that way held no guarantee of success and would only have led to death. And there was something else, something Sicarius had felt but not yet been able to identify. Sicarius would commend Daceus on his resolve later, though he was more concerned about Vedaeh, who looked tense enough that she would shatter at any moment. 'And we thank you for taking us into your fine city of Farrodum.'

Vandius bowed his head at that, to better hide the grim smile on his face.

The baron wafted away the flattery like an odour he didn't care to experience.

'A debt is owed to you and your kind...' he said, and leaned over to whisper into the vizier's ear. Sicarius caught every word as clearly as if he had spoken them aloud.

Was it the castellan's notion to bring them here stinking and dressed like beggar knights?

His jaw tensed, but he thought of poor Vedaeh and kept his composure. He gave the shallowest shake of the head to Daceus, who mouthed *Our kind?!* It was fortunate he had not heard the rest of what the baron had said.

'Our castellan, Scarfel, has vouched for you and spoken warmly of your valour.' He glanced at Scarfel, who sketched a short, simple bow. 'He tells us of how you turned the tide against our aggressors. He also states that you claim the beasts will return, and that you might yet rid us of their plague?'

'I would recommend hunting them down and slaying them,' said Sicarius, his eye straying to the vizier, who gave nothing of his thoughts away. 'They have suffered a defeat but they will lick their wounds, gather a larger force and return. We should attack them in their lair before that happens. Your castellan mentioned a gorge?'

'Yes, the gorge,' replied the baron, almost dismissive. 'We took warriors to the gorge, an army of them.' He gestured around the room. Sicarius noticed Scarfel's expression darken at the memory. 'This is what remains. Most did not return. We would be foolish to attack again. No, we must refortify the city walls and hold the bone-swine off until they tire of battering impotently at stone and wander off.'

'With respect,' began Daceus as he stepped forwards, though he actually meant the opposite. The hulk in the black warplate stirred, but an amused glance and a wag of the finger from the baron put his dog to heel again. 'Orks do not just wander off. Now they know you are–'

'Orks?' asked the baron, interrupting and momentarily perplexed until his frown smoothed to a smile, 'Ah, you mean the bone-swine, yes? Carry on, carry on.'

Daceus gritted his teeth, prompting a surreptitious calming gesture from Sicarius that thankfully went unseen by the baron, though he thought he caught the slightest reaction from the vizier.

'They do not wander off,' Daceus concluded firmly. 'They know you are here and will not be satisfied or deterred until they have breached your walls and killed or eaten everyone within. Orks do four things really well,' said Daceus, counting them off on his gauntleted fingers. 'Eat, fight, shit and make a mess. Those last two are usually connected. I would wish none of them upon your city.'

'All very well, but what are we to do?' asked the baron. 'Or are you hard of hearing as well as half-blind, southerner?'

'Daceus is one of my sword brethren,' Sicarius quickly interceded before words were spoken or deeds done that could not be unsaid or undone, 'and speaks the truth. You cannot defeat the orks alone, but you are not alone.' Sicarius opened his arms in an expansive gesture indicating his warriors. 'Allow us to fight them on your behalf.'

The baron's eyes narrowed, the prospect of ridding himself of the orks evidently intriguing, presumably as well as the fact that he had an aversion to all four of the evils Daceus had mentioned. Sicarius found he did not like the conspiratorial look there.

'What do you propose?'

Sicarius called fowards Vorolanus, who came to stand beside him.

'Scipio is our finest scout. He and Vandius,' he nodded to the Lion, who remained as impassive as a statue throughout the exchange, 'will venture to the gorge and gauge the strength of the enemy, their numbers and disposition. From this, I will devise a strategy to destroy them. All of them.'

'Bold,' remarked the baron, stifling a yawn – but it was feigned. He was more interested and desperate for the knights' help than he let on. 'You could do that,' he asked, 'kill them all?'

Sicarius nodded slowly. 'We only need a guide to take us to the gorge.'

At this, Scarfel stepped up. 'I would gladly do it, my liege,' he told the baron, but with a comradely look to Sicarius.

The baron frowned, as if bored, then shrugged as if it were a matter of little import. 'Very well. See it done, castellan. Take these knights to the gorge and have them make their plans. What then for the rest of your... *men*?' he said, a sneer still clinging to his face despite attempts to conceal it.

'We fortify the city, help rebuild the walls,' said Sicarius, a fiery glint in his eye that saw the baron shrink a little in his pampered arrogance. 'We make ready for war as we have always done.'

The baron nodded, slowly at first but then with greater vigour, as if suddenly warming to everything that had been discussed. He turned to his vizier, who continued to look studious and unaffected.

'These men from the south, Nehebkau, do they have the means to accomplish all of this?'

The vizier watched them keenly, his deeply sunken eyes unblinking as they met Sicarius'.

'Yes, my liege, I believe they do.'

CHAPTER TWELVE

SAVIOURS

An awestruck populace watched as the knights of Macragge slowly marched back through the muddy streets of Farrodum. They peered from doorways or in the gaps between shuttered windows, dirty-faced and thin. Many gathered together, unwilling to step out of their hovels alone as the giants strode amongst them. Some of the impoverished citizens laid leaves or bunches of wild flowers in the path of their new saviours. A few even sang, the lilting melodies a soft refrain to the dolorous tolling of bells mourning for the dead and celebrating victory.

A girl in a tattered shift, barefoot and shivering in the cold, raced up to Scipio, the tender stem of a leaf in her tiny hands. The procession of warriors carried on as Scipio slowed and knelt down before the girl with his hand outstretched.

'You are a brave one,' he said softly as she placed the leaf in his gigantic palm.

She smiled, not speaking but with bright eyes full of fear and wonder, before her mother called her back.

Scipio arose, tucking the leaf into his belt, and regarded the mortals.

'Temple of Hera, such suffering...' said Iulus, having lagged behind with Scipio. The others had slowed too and were not far ahead.

The Ultramarines had left the hall of triumphs behind, along with the baron's keep, where he still hid behind fortified walls, and were on their way back to the abandoned feast hall where they had been barracked when the people of Farrodum had emerged in a throng.

'I see hope in their eyes, Iulus. They believe we can save them from the orks.'

'And can't we?'

'Yes, it's our duty, but I do not think that is the only threat that besets these people.'

They resumed walking, but picked up the pace to try to catch the rest of their brothers. Pillium, now at the back, moved hesitantly, his injuries still not properly healed.

'Something about this place...' Scipio continued as they walked, cloak trailing in the dirt. 'It feels familiar.'

'Suffering looks the same across worlds and star systems, brother.'

'It's not that. The banners in that hall... Did anything seem awry to you, Iulus?'

Iulus made a face as he considered the question. 'I think that potentate seemed awry, and I believe Veteran Daceus would very much like to tell him so at the point of his sword.'

Scipio chuckled at that. 'He would be at the front of a long line, I think.'

'What of the banners then?' he asked. They had almost caught up with Pillium. Vandius walked beside him, but the two warriors did not speak.

'They were aged,' said Scipio, 'but almost uniformly, as if to precisely the same degree. And the shape of the city, its walls and structures, does it not remind you of an Imperial colony template?'

'I cannot say I have spent much time analysing Imperial repopulation, but if you say so. Have you spoken to Sicarius?'

Scipio glanced ahead at the front of the group where Daceus and the captain were conversing. Ahead of them was the warrior, Scarfel, whom Scipio and Vandius would accompany to the gorge.

'And say what? It's a feeling. A scout's instinct.'

'Perhaps it was a colony once. I read Haephestus' report.'

'You read?' said Scipio with a glint in his eye.

Iulus gave him a scathing look. 'It was on the retinal feed as we broke from the void. He postulates that a catastrophic environmental upheaval may have set the world back, technologically speaking. The materials change as the generations die off and knowledge is lost, but the templates remain.'

'And yet there are no records?'

Iulus gestured to Vedaeh, who walked in Sicarius' shadow.

'I expect the chronicler will seek them out, if there are any to be found. Any records may have been lost too. What can be done about it, though? We're warriors, Scipio, not inquisitors.'

'It does not remove our ability to question.'

Iulus shrugged, indicating the conversation was over, or at least his meaningful contributions to it.

Scipio decided to change the subject. 'How is the arm? I see you're keeping it close to your body.'

Iulus grimaced. 'Stiff. It barely functions. I'll need Haephestus to look at it when we get back to the ship.' He paused then said, 'That's why, of course.'

Scipio frowned. 'Why what?'

'Why it's you and Vandius that are going to the gorge.' He made a fierce effort to raise the stricken bionic limb a few inches. He did so, lifting a few fingers too. 'That's about the extent of it,' he said. 'I'll remain here and see to the defences while you chase across the wilderness with Vandius in the rain and the mud.' He grinned, showing slab-like teeth. 'You know... scout work.'

'They should put you in the wall breach,' Scipio replied. 'A redoubtable cliff. You have the face for it, brother.'

The two veterans laughed, but their levity was short-lived.

'Be careful, Scipio,' said Iulus as they left the scattered crowds of Farrodum behind and moved into a more sparsely populated area of the city. 'I think you're right. I think there is more danger here than we realise.'

'And you too, Iulus. I have comrades around me, battle-brothers I trust with my life, but I think you are my last true friend in this company we serve.'

They said nothing further. Scarfel had stopped as they reached a stable house, his mount tethered and waiting for him under its sloped roof. The party slowed, pausing to exchange a few words and lock forearms in the way of warriors, before leaving Scipio and Vandius behind as the rest moved on.

The baron watched from his tower, the looming presence of his henchman behind him and the vizier to his right, lurking in the shadows.

'I do not trust these men,' said Athelnar, a worried look on his face that he kept to himself. 'Did you smell them? They reek! Beast sweat and blood. And the way they speak...' His expression turned to disgust. 'They use our language but they are not of our kind. And that one at the back of their ranks. Enormous. What kind of men could they possibly be? No... they are *other*.'

'They did take up arms in our defence,' offered the vizier gently.

'They sought to ingratiate, Nehebkau,' snapped the baron, hand tightening on the pommel of his ceremonial sword, sweating and fidgeting with the impotence of not being able to do anything with his anger. It only rose further as he saw the people flocked around them, throwing flowers and tokens of appreciation. 'What do they want here?' he demanded. 'They claim to be our saviours and yet they are as ragged as peasants. Only their size and strength is impressive.'

'They are unusual, my lord,' agreed the vizier, 'but their potency in battle should not be underestimated. A move against them would... be unwise.'

'You think they plan to supplant me? That captain. He and his men looked at my hall with avaricious eyes, only staying their hands from their blades because of the arrows and spears aimed at their foreign throats! I do not like this imposition, Nehebkau. I want to be rid of it.'

'And what of the bone-swine? If these strangers can do as they say...'

'We need them for now. But after?'

'What do you propose, my lord?'

Athelnar braced his hands against the lip of the window, daring to step forwards only when the knights had almost slipped from view.

'We cannot fight them as they are, but the bone-swine might cull their numbers, make them weak enough for us to overcome. Before that though, I want to know who they are.' He smiled, pleased with his own scheming. 'Haukberd...'

he said, and the plate-armoured hulk behind him shifted his stance. 'Take a few men, follow the trail the strangers took to Farrodum and find out where they actually came from. If they are honest men, the trail will lead to their ship. This land, this *Macragge*,' Athelnar's expression soured further. 'I have never heard of it. I think these men are liars, and I would know the truth.'

Haukberd nodded, the armour around his trunk-like neck rattling. It kept rattling as he stomped out of the room.

CHAPTER THIRTEEN

THE GORGE

Scarfel rode at a canter and Scipio had no difficulty keeping up. Vandius lagged a step or two behind him, but appeared none the worse for wear. He had merely elected to take the rearguard, his sword strapped across his back and the tightly wound cloth of the company banner tied at his belt. Even in unpowered armour, the Ultramarines could travel distances at speed. They ran as Scarfel rode, two outriders on foot, ranging through the rugged terrain of Agun.

'Tell me, Scarfel,' Scipio ventured, and pointed to the eastern horizon, 'what is that spire in the distance?'

He gestured to the strange landmark they had seen upon first making planetfall, still drenched in a distant fog though the pale sun had burned away some of the mist. It was incredibly tall, and as sharp as a dagger, but little else by way of detail presented itself.

Scarfel followed his arm, squinting with old eyes at the spire. For a moment he looked confused, as if struggling for a memory he possessed but which was just out of his reach. After a few seconds, his face went blank and he shrugged in the saddle.

'No one knows. It is too far from the city and with the bone-swine, no party would ever return from such a journey.' He seemed content to leave it at that, pressing on ahead, but Scipio looked across to Vandius, whose expression suggested he did not believe the old campaigner. The spire did not look that far away.

It had felt like a lie, but not one Scarfel knew he was telling.

'The gorge is close,' he said, as if sensing the sudden disquiet amongst his companions. 'A few miles northwards and we'll be at the edge of it.'

They followed a rough trail, though the spoor of the ork lay everywhere, in the way the earth had been churned, or the heaps of dung, or the carcasses of prey beasts left to spoil.

'How long have you been fighting the orks, Scarfel?'

'For as long as I can remember.' His answer came swiftly, though he stopped short again as if not knowing how to explain further.

'Have they always been a plague upon Farrodum? What about the other cities?'

'I know of no other cities,' Scarfel replied.

'Have you ever seen or heard of another civilisation on Agun?'

He looked ahead, his eyes vague but then sharpening again. 'Only Farrodum. I have heard of lands to the south. The vizier is from there and now there's Macragge, of course. But we have always fought the bone-swine, or the orks as you call them. I have known this land my entire life. I raised my sons here, loved my wife here. It is all I've ever known.' He turned in the saddle to glance at Scipio, who almost came up to his mounted height. 'Have you a wife, a family?' he asked. 'Or you, Vandius?'

The Lion grunted in reply.

'Our brotherhood is our family, Scarfel,' said Scipio, a little more forthcoming than his battle-brother.

Scarfel look confused. 'No wife, no bond of any sort?'

'Our blood is our bond. We are devoted to a higher cause.'

'You are monks then?'

'Of a sort, I suppose.'

'It is an ascetic life?'

'It could be described like that.'

Scarfel paused. He looked melancholic for a moment. 'Sounds lonely.'

'A life pledged in service is never lonely.'

'Are we close?' asked Vandius, apparently eager to end the questioning. It was the first time he had said anything in several hours.

Scarfel blinked, as if emerging from a momentary stupor. 'Not far,' he said.

They reached the edge of the gorge before nightfall as the sun bled across the horizon in veins of ochre and red. It had almost dimmed to an ember as Scarfel led Scipio and Vandius through the narrow path he had once taken.

From amongst thick scrub and scattered boulders, Scipio looked down into the gorge. It was deep, its high sides made up of several overlapping ridges, but also narrow like a canyon. He took in every detail, every slip of rock that fell inwards of its own accord, the overlapping plateaus on either side. To know the battlefield was just as important as understanding the enemy. Master both and victory became much easier.

Rather than enter directly through its mouth, they had

taken the highlands that rose up either side of the gorge and descended into it. Better for remaining hidden, Scarfel had said. He had good reason to be cautious. Orks gathered in tribal groups along the snaking basin of the gorge, its craggy flanks extruding inwards to break up their numbers. But they had numbers. A great many. Scipio took careful note here too. Seeing the horde like this, he realised they had engaged but a fraction of it at the city wall.

'How many, do you think?' asked Vandius, crouched by his side.

'Hundreds,' Scipio answered grimly. 'At least five or six times what we fought in the city.'

The orks had lit fires all along the lower ridge line. Some burned in craters along the basin too. A greasy black pall fed into the sky, smothering it and filling the air with the stench of human fat. They brawled and laughed and ate. The gorge was littered with a profusion of yellowed bones. Skulls turned in the breeze, clicking hollowly as they spun and collided on strings of sinew. More dung lay here too, though some of it had been combined with what appeared to be blood to make a daubing of the two-headed ork god. It was massive, stretching almost to the gorge's summit, and old. Gangs of greenskins toiled to refresh the 'paint', grunting and snorting with their crude labours.

'Where is it?' murmured Vandius.

Scarfel had fallen into an agitated silence, and though he kept himself back from the edge of the small ridge where the knights had taken position he still could not look away.

Vandius thumbed over his shoulder. 'He will be of no further use to us.'

Scipio spared the old campaigner a pitying glance, but he was lost to memory as the old fears returned. 'He got us this far. That's all we need.' His eyes narrowed. The orks were fifty feet or so below them. 'There...' Scipio nodded.

A savage grin crept across Vandius' features. 'Ah, yes... you big ugly bastard.'

A hulking brute of an ork had just emerged from a shallow cave in the gorge wall. Much, much larger than the others and with a gut that spilled over elephantine legs, this was obviously the chieftain. It had lost an eye, perhaps fighting a rival or during the battles against Farrodum's now-depleted army, and clenched a huge bone club the size of Scipio's arm. It wore pelts too, and had a furred cloak slung over its broad, sloping shoulders. The skull of some large predator beast served as a crown, but the lower section was missing. One of the horns had broken off halfway as well, but the other curved in a yellowed crescent.

In its other hand, it clutched the dead shaman's staff. It must have been retrieved by the fleeing greenskins when they realised the crushed corpse wasn't going anywhere. The beast raised the staff, brandishing it at the sky and gesticulating to the horde that had begun to coalesce. The orks beat their chests, bellowing and pulling on their tusks.

'He is aggravating them,' said Scipio.

'*He*?'

'He looks male to me.'

The orks roared louder at the chieftain's ranting, his deep guttural voice carrying loudly through the narrow gorge until every greenskin looked to him. He beat his chest as he shook the staff, gesturing to his brutish kin before smashing the bone club over and over against the ground.

'He wants vengeance,' said Scipio. 'For the obelisk, for the shaman.'

'What's this now?' Vandius pointed to a gaggle of Farrodum

slaves that had just appeared from another cave. Bound hand and foot, they were yanked into the light. Bloodied and beaten, they looked in a poor way. A few wailed plaintively, but only succeeded in stirring up anger and derision in their captors. Others bore it stoically with the resignation of men headed for the gallows.

'Old men and boys... Guilliman's mercy, when did they take them?' breathed Scipio, and turned to meet Scarfel's gaze. 'You do not need to see this.'

'Yes, I do,' said Scarfel.

'They're headed deeper in,' said Vandius as the orks began to move in a great horde, a green river flowing into the gorge. He edged around the ridge line for a better look, spurring the others to do the same.

They went carefully and quietly, but as the spies crept that little bit closer they saw what the orks intended. And they saw a second obelisk, except this one was not hewn from wood.

'Blood of the primarch,' hissed Vandius. 'Is that it?'

Scipio nodded. He was not trained as a Techmarine, but he recognised a generator when he saw one. This one looked old, *extremely* old, and jutted from the earth like a huge metallic monolith. It, like the gorge wall, had been daubed in tributes to the ork gods. It wore two faces and the greenskins had covered it in glyph graffiti. There was no mistaking what it was, though. The thick cabling, the densely housed power plant. This was the energy source that Haephestus had seen via the ship's augur. It stood as high as the facsimile totem the orks had brought to the city. And they worshipped it as if it were the manifestation of their two-headed god.

'Another bone-swine monument,' said Scarfel, not understanding.

Scipio didn't answer. He was watching as the prisoners

were led to the base of the generator and then lashed to it with rope.

Vandius smoothly drew his sword and made to move down the side of the ridge. He only stopped when Scipio gripped his arm.

'They are about to torture those men,' he said.

'And we have to let them,' Scipio replied. 'Unless you can kill that many greenskins?'

Vandius looked as if he were considering whether he could when he relented and sheathed his weapon.

Scipio gripped Scarfel's shoulder. 'We can do nothing for your comrades now, only avenge them later.'

There were tears in the old campaigner's eyes but he nodded.

As if sensing the end and the futility of fighting against it, the prisoners had stopped wailing. They looked on with dead eyes, numb to their fate but accepting of it anyway.

The chieftain raised his club and the horde felt silent. It was this, the demonstration of absolute dominance, that disturbed Scipio more than what happened next. With a blow that echoed through the gorge, the chieftain struck the obelisk. It tolled metallically, like a bell. Like a death knell. The resonance washed over the horde but still they kept their silence, the piggish eyes enrapt. He struck again, releasing a second tolling that overlapped the first like a heart pushing out its final beats before it arrested. A third blow and the generator hummed to life, as energy uncoiled across its surface. The men screamed as the energy touched them, setting their bodies afire and burning their bonds to ash so that their blackened skeletons slid to the ground in a crumpled heap and broke apart.

The ork chieftain threw back his head, roaring his exultation to the gods. The horde roared too, a clamour so deafening and so primal that Scipio gritted his teeth.

'We will avenge them,' he said.

'How can you kill that many?' asked Scarfel, wiping a thin trail of blood from his nose.

Scipio's gaze took in the high sides of the gorge. 'I think I know of a way.' He turned to Vandius and told him of his plan.

It took almost another hour before they were finished, Scarfel keeping watch the entire time as the greenskins hooted and fought and ate.

When the Adeptus Astartes were done they slipped back into the night, leaving the orks to their revels.

CHAPTER FOURTEEN

DEFENCES

It had grown dark over Farrodum and light slowly flared into being across the city from dozens of braziers. It bled in long trails, and the aroma of woodsmoke and burning coal lay thick on the air. Wreaths of flowers and wicker effigies of the knights had been left in the streets. For one night at least, the people would sleep soundly in their beds.

'They honour you,' said Vedaeh, joining Sicarius where he stood upon a wall overlooking a small square. The feast hall was below, though empty of its guests.

'I see as much fear in their eyes as reverence,' said Sicarius. 'And blood in the streets.' Though sluiced by endless buckets of water, the dark stains remained along with the other detritus of battle, the pieces of a broken arrow haft, the cheekplate of a helmet, a shattered sword missing its hilt.

He saw something else, though he would not confide in Vedaeh what that thing was. Sicarius felt his jaw harden just at the sight of it.

'You think you have let these people down like those aboard the *Emperor's Will*?' Vedaeh laughed. 'Quite the feat, Cato, given you have only just arrived. You can't win every battle.'

'We did win, and still we lost.'

'You are melancholic this evening.'

'I am eager to be away from this place. Did you find anything?' he asked, choosing not to be baited. She wanted him to talk, to gain some insight. He felt no guilt for the befallen people of Farrodum, only a desire to return to the *Emperor's Will* and get back to the crusade.

'There are no scholars here, to speak of. No historians either. I found no evidence of an archive, nor books of any merit. It is almost as if they are without history. But then again, Farrodum is hardly open to me. The city is not large but it is a warren.'

Vedaeh had spent the last few hours touring the defences with Fennion. He had his duty, and she hers.

'How do you think they can speak Low Gothic?' Sicarius asked.

'I had been wondering that,' Vedaeh confessed. 'Perhaps they are an old colony, somehow regressed to a more primitive culture.'

'That could be true. I'll think on it.' He turned to her. 'You look tired. You should rest.'

'And what about you, Cato? Won't you also rest?'

'Daceus will be here soon enough to relieve my watch. I heard there was a problem with your companions?' he said, shifting the dialogue back to Vedaeh.

She grew sombre. 'Something happened to Vanko, Corporal Gerrant. It was during the attack. He was injured. Lieutenant Reda is keeping an eye on him.'

'They are close, the armsmen?'

'I believe they are.'

Sicarius looked back out into the city, at the flickering flames and the shadows they drew. He saw Daceus tromping up the stairs, his gait heavy in his armour.

'Whatever you see out in the dark,' said Vedaeh as she took her leave. 'You will have to confront it sooner or later.'

She passed Daceus on the stairs, who grunted in reply before he came to Sicarius' side.

'Iulus is still tightening our defences,' he said by way of report. 'I left Pillium with the medicus. He is a stubborn bastard, that one.'

'He believes Helicos is punishing him.'

'Isn't he?'

'Pillium is punishing himself.'

'Why do you think Helicos did it, sent one of the Primaris Marines?'

'Why do you think he did it?'

'To remind us they are there. To have representation on the mission. You are still his commanding officer, he would want to show willing.'

Sicarius had come to the same conclusion and nodded. 'How are Pillium's injuries?' he asked.

'Severe, though he is made for severe. He was being held together by meshweave and ceramite. For now he sleeps.'

'Does he need a watch placing upon him?'

'The medicus has not left his side, it would seem. I doubt he would appreciate a guard.'

Sicarius rapped his armoured fingers against one of the stone merlons. 'We are spread thinly, and not exactly in optimum condition either.'

'You're worried?'

'About threats we can and cannot see, yes I am.'

'Perhaps we should fetch Haephestus,' suggested Daceus. 'He could assist with the fortification efforts.'

'No. He has more important duties. The city will have to make do with us. In any case, how would we explain his presence? Did you feel all that fear in the hall of triumphs?'

'The baron?' Daceus scowled. 'I could almost smell it on him. I noticed he has kept a cadre of warriors at his side, though the rest of the army is made up of boys and old men. He spends his days being afraid. I do not trust him, Sicarius.'

'Nor I, but I won't leave these people to be slaughtered by greenskins. If he tries to betray us, we will deal with that. For now, we stay vigilant.'

Daceus arched an eyebrow. 'You really *are* worried. What threat are these primitives to us?'

'A blade is a blade, and when it's a hundred blades or a hundred arrows… No, I'm not concerned about that. We could take the city if we wished, and I think the baron knows it deep down or else he would have done something already.'

'If I might be plain, why don't we?'

Sicarius turned to him. 'Are you serious, Retius?'

'I mean only to impose military order. We have subjugated cities before.'

'In the Imperium's name, and in service of a greater goal. This is not the same.'

'Conceded, but at some point we may have no other choice. Once the orks are dead and the threat removed, what do you think will happen then?'

'I promised Vedaeh we would not harm these people, either directly or indirectly.'

'And what of those aboard the *Emperor's Will*, servants of the Imperium who we are sworn to protect?'

'I can't fail one people to rescue another, Retius. I won't. Guilliman made us warriors but he also gifted us with the intelligence and foresight needed for diplomacy. We follow that path, at least until it reaches an end. Then we'll have no choice.' His eyes went back to the darkness and the sense of looming threat he felt, either real or imagined. 'Then we'll go to the sword.'

Reda had left the feast hall with food and blankets. She bundled up what she could, tucking it beneath her arm, and hurried through the streets. She kept her head low and her hood up. The victory against the greenskins had given the Ultramarines as well as those in their charge a certain leeway, but these were still strange lands and she felt the air of tension in every ceramite-armoured body. They were preparing, all of them. She didn't need to be a part of their unknowable brotherhood to realise that. But she had greater concerns. No one else knew about what had really happened with Vanko. She had begged the medicus to keep this confidence and Cwen had agreed, but only if Reda allowed Vanko to be taken somewhere safe whilst his injuries could be assessed.

She approached the old keep now. It was not so far from the infirmary and acted as an armoury but also a gaol for Farrodum's wayward citizens. A gate admitted her, the watchman barely interested in her presence as he waved her on. From there she took a short walkway to a corridor. It looked deserted and there were precious few weapons left in the armoury. The odd spear or sword glimpsed through barred apertures. The soldiers were always armed, and fear followed them like an invisible fog, dulling their senses and good judgement. She hadn't seen the green thunderhead that had manifested in the sky during the battle, but she had been told about it. Several men had been driven mad by the sight of it and left gibbering. They too, like Vanko, were being held here for their own safety and that of the wider populous. As Reda moved inside the cloistered halls, it was not unlike stepping into an asylum for the damned and the insane. Desperate moaning emanated from every corner, sobs echoed through the dark. There were those who scratched at the doors, not to escape – each cell was locked behind stout wood and iron bolts – but out of some maddened repetitive instinct.

She reached Vanko's cell. Little light penetrated the gloomy confines of the keep and the torches were kept low so as not to agitate the inhabitants. Vanko sat on a hard-looking cot, his back to her. The bars of the door's viewing slit dissected him in three strips of wan light. It was dark, but she could tell he was gently rocking and murmuring. He had some cuts to the back of his neck, the side of his face, and his arm was bandaged, but he looked in better condition than she expected. But it wasn't his physical injuries that worried Reda.

'Vanko…' she began, crouching down to slide the food and other items under a hatch at the bottom of the door.

When she returned to the viewing slit, he had stirred and was facing her.

'How do you feel?' she asked.

'Better, I think.' He sounded tired, unfocused.

'You look better. Healed. I've brought you some food. More blankets in case you are cold.'

'Thank you, Arna,' he said.

As he was stooping to retrieve them, Reda said, 'Vanko. Let me see you up-close.'

He stopped what he was doing and like a servitor ordered to task straightened up, took a step forwards and looked back at her through the bars.

'Holy Throne, Vanko…' Her voice was barely a whisper at this point. He looked gaunt to the point of cadaverous in the light, the combined effects of fatigue, malnutrition and psychological trauma. He needed proper medicines, nutrients.

He frowned. 'You are crying, Arna.'

'Only a little,' she said, wiping away an errant tear.

'Are those tears for me?'

'I think you know that they are.'

He smiled, and for a fleeting moment reminded her of the man she knew. And loved. War had been hard on them both, but they had lived and found a way to express a feeling not born out of anger or fear or retribution, but something far rarer in such a benighted age. She wished then that they were back aboard the *Emperor's Will*. She knew the ship, its bones and blood. Fighting insurgents in full gear, boarding shield and all, was preferable to this. Something of herself had been lost since they had come to this place. Her sense of purpose and position. On the ship, she had wielded authority. Not the authority of the Adeptus Astartes, but some, and it was hers. Now she only had Vanko, and was powerless to do anything about his condition or her situation. Silently, she cursed Vedaeh for ever forcing them to come here. None of that really mattered now though. All that mattered was Vanko. But she had to know.

'Why did you do it, Vanko?'

He looked away, and his face in profile appeared even more skeletally thin. Shrapnel wounds from the explosions were also glaringly apparent.

'I don't know,' he confessed. 'It was…' he struggled to find the right words to describe it, 'it was as if I were no longer truly in my body but something else had taken over.' He scrubbed agitatedly at his hair. 'It's difficult to explain. It was still me, but I needed to show you what was inside.'

'Inside?'

'Inside me. Inside you.' His voice had softened to a whisper, and he started weeping.

'Throne, Vanko...' She felt the blade of his anguish slide deep into her own chest. 'You could have killed yourself. You could have killed me.'

'I know, I know...'

'Where did you even get the grenade from?'

'They have a cache,' said Vanko, drying off his tears as some composure returned. 'The Adeptus Astartes.'

'Holy Emperor, I thought we'd run out of munitions.'

'Apparently not.'

Reda looked away for a moment, but quickly snapped out of these new thoughts. She couldn't worry about this now. Vanko needed her full attention.

'Did you see something?' she asked, looking at him again. 'In Barthus' chamber? Back in the infirmary you said "the eye demands". You meant the eye of the warp, didn't you?'

'Truthfully, I don't know what I meant,' he replied, his eyes downcast.

'Look at me, Vanko, damn it!'

He did, turning to Reda, who was trembling with anger and half-understood grief.

'What did you see?' she asked, more quietly. Almost pleading.

Vanko opened his mouth to utter something but stopped. Eventually he said, 'I don't know. I *glimpsed...* something.' He brightened then, just for a moment, 'But I haven't seen anything since the infirmary or felt an urge to do anything violent. You have to believe me, Arna.'

'I believe you,' she said, hoping that was actually true.

Reda poked her fingers through the bars for Vanko to take. His touch was cold, but she held on to his hand as if she were dangling over an abyss and it was the only means of hanging on. She wondered if that actually was not so far from the truth, when she abruptly let him go and edged back from the slit.

He frowned again, hurt. 'What is it?'

'It's… it's nothing,' she said. 'It's nothing. I can't stay, that's all. Just a fleeting visit. I have other things I need to do,' she lied. 'For Vedaeh, you understand. I'll come back later.'

Vanko nodded dully and backed away. He didn't take the food or blankets Reda had left, and she didn't wait to see if he would. As he had leaned forwards to grasp her outstretched fingers, she had happened to glance over his shoulder and see the back wall of his cell. He had drawn on it using some chip of coal or loose stone he'd found. He had drawn an eye, a blazing warp eye, over and over and over again.

CHAPTER FIFTEEN

ABOMINATION

The loss of power to the war-plate had been egregious. Haephestus still had no answer for it. He had postulated a theory that whatever phenomenon had depleted the generators and almost critically disabled the ship would abate once they had broken warp, but something of the machine ague had remained like a dam with an undetected leak.

Although unpowered, each suit of armour would still yield protection to its wearer – its materials were both durable and resistant to most martial and elemental conditions – but the increased strength, servo-enhanced manoeuvrability and all automated systems would cease to function. Combat efficacy would significantly diminish. Mag-locks would also disengage, meaning weapons would need to be holstered or strapped to make carrying them outside of battle feasible. Bearing such a mass would have been impossible or at least highly debilitating to any unaugmented baseline human, but the Adeptus Astartes had the genetic advancements to overcome such issues. To them, it would be like wearing a heavy suit of armour.

Whatever the cause, the armour generators could not be restored until the starship lying in high anchor in the void was restored also, or until they managed to dock at some Imperial station with the means to refit and repair Adeptus Astartes armaments, but that scenario had an extremely low probability. With so many of the other tech-priests and adepts slain during the numerous attacks, it had been all Haephestus could do to maintain the strike cruiser's basic systems. Reinvigorating the entire ship, relighting its dormant engines and restoring both void shields and weapons would require power. A lot of it. The augurs had detected an enormous energy spike, its exact origin point unknown but evidently dormant given the medieval state of the world and ready to be reawakened. His brothers had only to find it and secure it, and then Haephestus would devise a way to realise it.

The crash at least had been unrelated to the warp siphoning, and many of the other gunships aboard the *Emperor's Will* were still functional, if in short supply, but this too presented its own series of questions. Haephestus had managed to attribute the cause of the engine failure to a dampening field, projected over the majority of the planet and undetectable via conventional augur or sensorium. Unlike the warp siphon, whose effects were slow, continuous and pervasive, the dampening field had simply triggered a brief but violent loss of power as the gunship had passed through it. Why the field had been deployed and by whom remained a mystery. It was potent. Vox was non-responsive and even his own, enhanced sensors had become increasingly unreliable and reduced to such extreme short range as to be almost worthless.

The Techmarine considered these factors as he hunched over a bench in the gunship's hold, the low light picking out the edges of tools and mechanical components. There were small chain-cutters, drills, a hand flamer. Unlike the power armour, his tools at least were functional and he had managed to repair the damage sustained during the crash. The gunship would fly, though fuel reserves were near redline, but it was grounded on Sicarius' orders. Out here, they were isolated, and hopefully unnoticed. Farther inland... well, they did not want to terrify the natives with a steel dragon descending from the skies.

In the hold, which now served as a workshop, Haephestus engaged in the other task Sicarius had given him before the party had set off in search of civilisation. After almost three days, he had considered venturing out into the wild himself, but someone needed to remain with the ship.

Using parts from the gunship's vox and antenna array, and boosted by what little dregs of power remained in his battle-brothers' disengaged armour generators, he had rigged up a transmitter beacon. It broadcast codes in Ultramarian battle-cant to the *Emperor's Will* requesting reinforcement and warning of the dampening field. With the gunship lacking enough fuel to reach high orbit, they would need additional means of egress.

As of yet, no signal had been received, and Haephestus was attempting different vox frequencies and readjusting the circuitry to improve the gain in order to override the field, but generating sufficient amplification was proving difficult.

'Omnissiah...' he began, uttering a few canticles of function in the hope of appeasing whatever malady was afflicting the transmitter's machine-spirit. It was to no avail, and he had been about to strip the device back to its components, engaging his still-functioning mechadendrites to try a different configuration, when he heard the intruders.

Haukberd knew he was the strongest warrior in all of Farrodum. At least, he had been until the strangers had arrived. He had not met knights before, not like these, and he wondered briefly as his party stalked through the wild lands whether he might have some southern blood in his veins.

A shrill whistle from up ahead caught his attention. One of the rangers had found something. His hand was raised, just visible through the thick mist. Haukberd grunted at the footmen with him, urging them to follow as he slogged through the rough hills to where the ranger waited.

It had taken a little time to find their trail – the lands around Farrodum were vast and largely looked the same – but once the rangers had it the rest was easy enough. They trod heavily, these knights, and their boot impressions were not only distinctive but also left a deep crater that rain or churned earth could not hide. The closer they came to whatever lay at the end of the trail, the more eager Haukberd found he was to meet it. He wanted to match his strength against one of these southern knights. It chafed that he had never fought in the war against the bone-swine. Always at the baron's side, his dutiful henchman, just as Athelnar's father had decreed on his deathbed. Thinking back now, he became momentarily frustrated. His memories of those earlier days felt vague and gossamer thin. He remembered them only in pieces, and incomplete ones at that. He had begun to wonder why that was when a slab-sided wall emerged through the mist.

'Is it a keep of some sort?' asked one of the rangers.

Haukberd shook his head, not knowing. He decided to

draw his sword regardless and the massive blade slid from its scabbard with a whisper of metal against leather.

It was colossal, the keep, and wrought impossibly from iron or some metal. Painted blue, though chipped to grey in places, it matched the knights' armour. The shape of it confounded him, squat and angular as it was. Two flat pieces extruded from a long, rectangular middle and reminded Haukberd of avian wings. And there were other protrusions, cast in a darker metal, obscured by mist. These he could not fathom, but he thought they had the look of weapons and this stirred a measure of greed within him.

'Whatever it is,' he said, his voice deep and gravel-coarse, 'I want to find out what's inside and kill it if we have to.'

A few of the other soldiers turned to him at that remark, their faces pale.

'Make ready...' he growled, uncaring of their fear as he hefted his blade in a two-handed grip.

A profusion of spears and swords were raised and pointed at the keep. The rangers drew bows, hastily nocking arrows.

Haukberd gestured to three swordsmen closest to the front.

'Scare up the quarry,' he said.

Alone for so long out in the wilds, he had slipped into a partial catalepsean meditation to rest his body and clarify his thought process. His reactions were slower than optimal. That fact, married to the loss of power in his war-plate, meant he was at something of a disadvantage when the warriors came across the threshold of the ship.

Three scruffy men in padded jerkins and rough leather armour confronted him. His bionic eye, though slower than usual, caught the slight trembling of their drawn swords. It whirred noisily as the focusing rings shifted, accumulating data.

'What is it?' breathed one of the men.

'A golem of iron and flesh...' rasped another.

'He has the evil eye,' uttered the third.

Haephestus raised his arms in a surrendering gesture and started to move towards the men.

'It's attacking!' shouted the first man, prompting another to leap forwards and lash out with his sword.

The blade broke against the Techmarine's vambrace, shattering into pieces that rattled loudly as they hit the deck of the hold.

'Impervious...' the ignorant man uttered, glaring disbelievingly at the ragged hilt of his weapon.

'Stop this,' said Haephestus, his voice cold and metallic. He did not want to hurt these men but he would if they gave him no other choice. 'What is your name? I am Haephestus and I mean you no–' He was advancing slowly towards the man with the broken sword when the second man lunged in with his own weapon.

The blade skidded off the edge of Haephestus' breastplate, stripping back a line of red paint before it slid a few inches into the softseal of his armpit and bit. He growled, shocked at the pain, though it was minor. His distress encouraged a renewed attack from all three at once, the first having drawn a long dagger from his belt. Blades rang against his armour, repelled by ceramite and adamantium, fury and fear driving every blow.

'You were warned...' said Haephestus, hearts thumping as his body switched into a battle-heightened state, and went on the offensive.

He backhanded the second man, the one who had cut him through the softseal, and the warrior flew back against the wall, struck his head and lay still. The one with the dagger Haephestus pushed hard, the flat of his hand against the man's solar plexus, and sent him sprawling down the hold's open ramp and back outside. He parried a desperate swipe from the last assailant and smashed his shoulder with a counterblow to disable him. The man screamed, sword falling through his nerveless fingers, and scurried back outside.

Haephestus followed him into the mist-shrouded light and found a host of warriors waiting.

Haukberd's eyes widened as he saw the beast. Half-metal, half-man, it was unlike anything he had ever before encountered.

It stood as tall as the other knights, but was clad with intricate red metal plates covered in strange toothed sigils. Metal ropes of intestine or something even fouler hung from its belt and though its knife-like talons slid back into its gauntleted hands, Haukberd immediately recognised it as a threat.

'What are you?' he growled, nodding to his remaining men to surround it. The red paladin, for this is how Haukberd thought of it, let them do it, edging forwards into their killing circle.

'I am a man like you.'

Its voice did not sound like a man's. It was hollow, cold. Haukberd had dreamed of such voices, of the dead things that haunted the wilds. He had never spoken of it to anyone, but the memory of it chilled him now.

'You may have met my brothers,' the red paladin tapped his armour with a dull resonant *tunk*. 'They wear blue livery and with this same icon.' He pointed at the inverse horseshoe Haukberd had seen on the southerners' armour.

'From the land of Macragge,' he thought aloud.

The red paladin mistook it for a question.

'They are my lands too. I mean you no harm,' it said.

As he met its pupilless red gaze, Haukberd knew what he had to do.

'Loose...' he commanded.

The whip and snap of sinew presaged a volley of iron-tipped arrows as the four archers let fly, only to see their missiles snap against the red paladin's armour.

'Its face and eye!' snapped Haukberd, urging the sword and spearmen to close the circle so the beast could not escape.

A second arrow volley followed smartly on the heels of the first. One quarrel smacked against an armoured gorget, a second and third hit the metal side of the beast's face and bounced away but the fourth cut the red paladin's cheek and managed to draw a line of crimson.

'It bleeds!' gasped a spearman.

'Kill it, kill it!' said another.

Haukberd roared and they rushed the red paladin together.

The first row of spears broke against his armour, like twigs hitting a metal shield. He dashed the men wielding the spears too, using his bulk and mass to overwhelm them. Disarmed, terrified, the men scattered into the mist as he looked on.

A sword screeched against his back, hacked down two-handed. Haephestus turned, about to smash the warrior aside when an arrow struck his neck. He wrenched it out, releasing a thin gout of blood, but it was enough of a distraction for the larger warrior with the sword to strike a second blow. Pain flared around his knee joint, the sword blade finding the softseal at the back of his leg. A flung spear ricocheted off his plastron, its tip dangerously close to his eye as it skidded off the metal. The large warrior had retreated, sending three sword-armed lackeys in his stead. He was large for a baseline human, heavily armoured in lacquered black war-plate and evidently the leader.

Another slew of arrows crashed and broke against his

armour. He was practically invulnerable to their primitive weapons, except for his face and the softseals between the joints in his armour.

He counted nine men left, four of those fighting at range with crude but effective bows. He had to resort to his cog-axe, which, although no longer powered, was still a formidable weapon.

'I have no desire to kill you,' he said, seizing and hurling a spearman into two of the archers. The leg wound was bleeding through where the meshweave had broken. He felt it welling up around his greave.

The last two archers fled as he charged at them, the pounding of his heavy footfalls enough to finally break their fragile courage. As he turned to engage the last of them, he felt something crash into him from behind. The swordsman he had poleaxed in the hold clung to his back with a fearsome strength, heaving at the gorget around Haephestus' neck.

He half turned, reaching behind his back to grasp the man's scruff when sharp, agonising pain exploded down his left side.

'You are no man...'

The leader had rammed his sword into the softseal between the upper arm greave and breastplate.

'...abomination!'

Haephestus swept down with his arm, snapping off the blade before it could be pushed any deeper. Then he smacked the flat of his gauntleted hand against the warrior's breastplate, denting it and sending him sprawling backwards. He rolled three or four times, end over end, until he stopped and did not rise.

Haephestus clawed for the figure on his back, surprised at the man's strength. He got a grip of his shoulder and tore the wretch loose, hurling him off, but like an arachnid the man jumped to his feet and threw himself at the Techmarine.

The cog-axe extended in Haephestus' grip, its killing arc cutting the manic swordsman in half across the midriff and halting his bizarre rampage. The two severed halves collapsed in a tangle of limbs and spilled innards. It was too much for the three ragged spearmen who were left. They threw down their weapons and ran, heaving the black-armoured leader to his feet. He fled too when he saw the steaming remains. Haephestus didn't pursue and let his assailants vanish like apparitions into the mist. A grimace seized his face. He needed to extract the sword blade still lodged in his body and stitch the wound. The gunship carried a rudimentary medi-kit. Either it would suffice or he'd use the acetylene torch from his tool array to cauterise.

He briefly regarded the upper and lower parts of the corpse lying on the ground.

He needed to get word to Sicarius. He needed to breach the dampening field. But this had to come first. The enhanced strength, the apparent resurrection. They were gaps in his understanding. Such things were dangerous. He considered they may have underestimated the threat presented by this world and its primitive inhabitants.

'More questions...' Haephestus muttered, taking the upper half of the body by the arms, dragging it back up the ramp and into the ship. The ramp slammed shut behind him.

CHAPTER SIXTEEN

WE MARCH

They returned a few hours before dawn.

Vedaeh was standing in an empty watchtower that over-looked the recently repaired northern wall. Hands clasped in front of her, she gazed out into the darkness of the wild. Three figures approached the town in the distance, visible for a fleeting few seconds as they crested a high ridge before becoming lost in the mist-flooded valleys. A white veil lay heavy across the land, like a belt of low cloud refusing to rise or dissipate. The rugged geography of Agun undulated beneath. The low hills drowned in the mist, grey islands mostly subsumed by a white ocean, but the larger tors pro-truded, their lower flanks clung to by ghostly tendrils as if something were trying to drag itself up from the abyss below.

It was peaceful, she reflected. The Imperium had so little natural wilderness left and that which did still exist was either toxic wasteland, rad-desert or the blighted plains of an overtaxed agri world. Mankind had left its mark on every scrap of earth and had saturated it with industry or left it desolated by war. The only lands and worlds that remained untamed now were, of course, inimicable to human life. Which made Agun only more anomalous.

'A miracle that we ever lasted this long...' she said to herself.

'Who's lasted?' asked Reda, blowing on her cupped hands to warm them.

She'd joined Vedaeh half an hour ago and the two of them had shared a companionable silence. She was worried about Gerrant, Vedaeh could tell from the tight set of her lips and the faraway look in her eyes. That drive, that certainty Vedaeh had seen on the *Emperor's Will*, it wavered in the face of Reda's new reality.

Labourers toiled below, making good the stone they had laid and the reinforcing braces they had placed according to Sergeant Fennion's instructions. A guard patrolled the rampart, though it was threadbare on account of the fact that Farrodum had few soldiers left who could still carry a spear or sword.

The war against the orks had bled them almost dry.

'Mankind,' Vedaeh answered at length. She pulled the furs around her shoulders tighter. A harsh wind was blowing, and it wailed and whipped around the tower's summit. It was cold up here, but it had a stunning view of most of the city and the surrounding lands.

'Something ails this place,' said Reda, pulling her cloak around her body so it didn't blow open again.

Vedaeh framed a sad smile. 'I was only just thinking how beautiful it was. Stark, but beautiful.'

'It's in the air, Vedaeh,' Reda replied. She sniffed, taking in a long draught. 'Can't you smell that?'

The stench had begun to emanate in the wake of the battle against the greenskins, possibly a pungent reminder of their spore. All the corpses, both human and ork, had been taken from the city and burned, but the evidence of the dead had a tendency to linger.

'I would say it's death, but that would be overly poetic. And, yes, the city reeks, and not just literally. But out there is beautiful. So rare and untouched.'

'I had never seen sky before I came to this place. Not really, not without a thick layer of pollutants hiding the sun.'

'And what do you make of it?'

'It's wide, grey and cold. But at least it's clean.'

'You should bring Vanko up here. The air, stench notwithstanding, might do him some good.'

'Perhaps,' replied Reda, and let the word hang for a while. 'I don't know what's wrong with him,' she admitted at last.

'I had heard there was an explosion,' said Vedaeh, though she suspected much more than that.

'A scratch, nothing more, especially to a man like Vanko. He is… troubled. Ever since Barthus' sanctum, something's been off about him.'

'Off?'

Reda met her questioning gaze. 'Like he's a different person.'

Vedaeh became very serious very quickly. 'What are you saying to me, Arna? Do I need to fetch Captain Sicarius?'

'Throne, no,' Reda answered quickly. 'I just… I just need time with him, that's all.'

Vedaeh's mood softened again. 'This journey has put a great strain upon all of us.'

Something had broken in Gerrant, and it had left its mark on Reda too.

'I think he saw something.'

'Saw?'

'In the eye, Barthus' eye. Everyone else who looked in that eye is either dead, or went insane and then died.'

'I can see why you'd be concerned,' said Vedaeh. 'What was he doing with the grenade?'

'You know about that?'

'I know explosions don't manifest out of thin air. It was either that or the medicus needs to exercise better discipline with how she stores her combustible elements.'

'I don't know why he had it, or when he took it, but he used it trying to kill the ork battering its way in.'

Vedaeh nodded. Mentally troubled or not, Vanko Gerrant was a military man with a military heritage. She couldn't quite believe he would have been so careless with handheld munitions as to injure himself and almost kill the other two people in the room with him.

'I can speak to him, if you want?' Vedaeh suggested gently. 'I have some experience ministering to troubled minds. Perhaps I can help him. Help you both.'

Reda seemed to consider that.

'Let me talk to him first. See if he'll agree to it.'

'You think he won't? Why is that?'

Reda was about to answer when the blaring of horns sounded across the city, signalling the return of the scouts.

'Scipio and Vandius are back,' she muttered, briefly forgetting Reda.

From her excellent vantage in the tower, Vedaeh could see the main gates where three figures waited to be reunited with their brothers. They stood in a row, a few feet between each of them, Sicarius in the middle with Daceus and Fennion left and right of him. Their ragged cloaks stirred lightly in the breeze but did little to hide the battle scarring on their armour. They might not be from this place, this time, but they had the look of well-seasoned medieval knights.

She feared for them then, these three though soon-to-be five who would march out and face the horde. They would do it because honour and duty demanded it. They had made their oaths, kneeling in darkness, a sword hilt pressed to their foreheads, not only to the people of Farrodum but to each other. A Space Marine would rather die than break his vow. The wilderness would succumb again, Vedaeh knew, drowned in blood and churned underfoot. No place was ever sacrosanct. Peace would surrender itself to war, and so the wheel turned ever onwards. She trembled, wiping an errant tear that had run unchecked, chilling her skin as it dried into a salty tract.

Across the courtyard, she saw the baron watching from a high parapet. He hadn't seen Vedaeh, or she was beneath his concern, but he watched the Ultramarines closely. His advisor, the vizier, stood behind him, content to be in the noble's shadow. Unlike the baron, who wore a thick furred cloak to ward off the cold, the vizier had only a thin robe but gave no outward sign of discomfort. He had several layers of fat, however, which likely offered some insulation. Several townsfolk had gathered to see the knights off – or see them arrive, depending on whose point of view you had. They carried garlands of wild flowers and held close their children, who looked on with awe at the warriors. None of the usual terror or religious fervour pervaded here. The reaction of the crowd was as if to cheer on the champions about to risk their lives to rid the common folk of tyranny and fear.

'For they shall know no fear,' said Vedaeh, repeating the old aphorism and thinking on how in less 'enlightened' times it would be easy to consider them as heroes, and not the scarcely human demigods she knew. To see a Space Marine meant death. As an Imperial citizen, you should never wish for it. Seldom were they truly liberators. They were bred to kill and they did it ferociously well.

Sicarius had stepped forwards to meet Vorolanus and Vandius. He greeted them warmly. The old castellan, Scarfel, nearly fell off his horse, and Vedaeh briefly considered he must have ridden hard and all night to return so quickly. The two Adeptus Astartes barely looked fatigued at all. They exchanged a few words, Sicarius then turning to Scarfel, a reassuring hand upon his shoulder. He was sending the castellan back. The gesture was heartening but it was really a facsimile of compassion. It also meant one thing – the knights of Macragge would fight the orks alone.

They didn't linger, Scarfel's sentimentality wasted on them as he watched them depart into the mist, and then, like the low hills, they were suddenly gone.

'Do you think they'll come back?' asked Reda.

'I have never known a fight that the Adeptus Astartes cannot win.'

'With bolters and chainswords, perhaps. With powered warplate and gunships. They have swords and lumpen armour.'

'They are also sons of Guilliman, and that's ingrained.'

'Five against Throne knows how many.'

'My point still stands. They'll die before letting even one greenskin live.'

'And if that happens?'

Vedaeh regarded the baron. He was no longer looking north, and instead had turned his attention southwards.

She couldn't see what had caught his interest, not at first. Then a handful of mounted figures emerged through the white fog, at their head the baron's henchman. The grim cast to the warrior's face, the way he rode hard across the rugged landscape, bothered Vedaeh. He looked scared.

'I didn't know scouts had been despatched southwards,' said Reda, following Vedaeh's eye to the returning hunting party.

'Nor did I,' Vedaeh replied.

Reda frowned, narrowing her eyes at the chronicler. 'Are you worried?'

'I am. You should get Vanko. Now, Arna.'

She was already running by the time Vedaeh had turned around.

CHAPTER SEVENTEEN

CATACOMBS

A sense of disconnected urgency drove Reda as she ran through the city streets. She knew something was wrong, just not exactly what. It reminded her of a soldier's instinct for danger. Anyone who had served in the Navy or Militarum for any length of time had it, that self-certain belief that something was about to go extremely and irrevocably badly. That it was Vanko she ran towards only made it worse, because it wasn't just her own safety that was potentially at stake but his too.

The crowds were still making their way back to their homes after seeing their champions off, and Reda had to pick her way through their dawdling masses. Every few bodies she would catch a glimpse of a man in an old military uniform, his face obscured as ever. This only heightened her concern and made her run harder. She wanted to shut her eyes to him, to not remember. She wanted to believe he wasn't always a harbinger of something awful and she hoped his presence now didn't presage the unthinkable.

She reached the old keep after what felt like an hour but was actually much less than half that. The same watchmen let her through, the same empty halls presented themselves. She only slowed when she reached the cells, taking a firm grip of her maul as she heard the gaol's occupants. It was worse than before. They banged their heads against the doors and rattled the bars of the viewing slits like caged beasts driven mad by confinement. That might not be far from the truth. But it was the sounds that disturbed her the most. Before, she'd heard weeping and moaning; now they screamed until they were hoarse, one word repeating over and over.

Eye! Eye! Eye! Eye!

Reda was halfway down the cells when she saw where Vanko should be. His door was open. She ran to it, pulling the maul from the hoop of leather on her belt but confronted only shadows as she burst into the small room. The door was undamaged. He'd either picked the lock or been released.

At her feet, the food she had brought had spoiled and the blankets were untouched.

'Throne of Terra...' the words caught in her throat as she saw the warp eye repeated across every inch of wall and floor, dizzying in its multiplicity.

She edged out of the room, stifling tears as she hurried back into the shadowy halls, reaching down within herself for that cold core that had kept her alive for so many years in the hazardous depths of an Imperial starship. She hardened herself again to grief, and pushed down selfish desire, smothering it with duty. And she cursed Barthus for ever sharing his madness, and then she cursed herself for ever letting Vanko become a part of it.

She had been about to take a left fork that would bring her to a stairway and back into the outer halls of the keep, determined to find Vanko and not sure how he could have slipped past her, when she saw something farther down the corridor in the opposite direction. He was standing right at the very end. The man with the old military uniform, his face obscured by shadow.

'Father...'

She had never known him, not really; only what she had been told. She had lied to Vedaeh, though. She knew how he had died. A missive had been sent to her, when she was still a low-level Naval rating aboard a minor starship. Vutich Reda had died during the Urid campaign, a relatively minor action that had seen an understrength Militarum force engage and eventually destroy a xenos cult uprising on the system's primary world, Karbak. He had been killed in battle during one of the last major combat actions of the campaign. His death had earned him posthumous decoration, the Medallion Crimson, an award traditionally given to soldiers for continuing to perform their duties in spite of horrific injury. Reda didn't know if that was actually true, but the missive did disclose that Vutich Reda had been burned egregiously. She could not imagine what that was like, though she sometimes awoke to the feeling of her skin being eaten away by acid or fire. Her father then had become an enigma, a literal faceless man whom she dared not confront for fear of what it might reveal. Better to be ignorant, to try to manage her fear.

Now she had to run towards it.

The apparition had gone by the time she reached where it had been standing. She let out a long breath, ashamed at the relief she felt, and she faced what appeared to be a dead end. Except it wasn't. A cold, foul-smelling breeze whistled through the brick. Reda put her face towards it, trying to trace its source. A column of bricks jutted out ever so slightly from the rest, ruining the flush finish. It could have been mistaken for a simple deformity. In the darkness, it would have been missed completely if you weren't looking for it. Reda realised what it actually was.

Another door.

She got her fingers around the protruding edge and pulled hard. It didn't yield much but gave up enough of a gap that she could feed her maul into it and use it to lever the door the rest of the way. Darkness lurked beyond, though with the faint promise of light, little more than a pale smudge of white beckoning her.

'What do you want me to see?' she asked the dark, though she wasn't sure if she addressed her father or Vanko or both.

A short platform led to a stairwell. With little choice, she descended, and about halfway down heard voices. She quickened her pace, but slowed again as she came to the end of the steps.

They had led Reda into a subterranean catacomb, a procession of crumbling arches like rib bones disappearing into further darkness. Low-burning torches had been lit, held up by wall sconces. The flames flickered inwards like mercurial fingers of light, beckoning her.

He was there too, standing in the shadows, his face obscured as always. Reda wanted to scream at him, to tell him to leave her alone, but he wanted her to find something. The voices grew louder too. They sounded agitated. As she went further into the catacombs, she realised they must stretch under most of the city, a subterranean realm forgotten by all except those whose voices she heard.

Closer now, she saw shadows, dark and elongated against the ground. The stench, the one she had remarked to Vedaeh about up in the tower, had grown stronger too. It must be coming from down here. Subconsciously she gripped the maul a little tighter. She went slowly, never taking her eyes off the shadow. The voices were muffled, distorted by the strange acoustics of the catacombs, but she thought she recognised one of them.

'Vanko...' she whispered.

'Here.'

Reda nearly broke open his skull, her heart pounding as she turned on Vanko, who had been waiting in the dark for her.

He was crouched down, which is why she had missed him, eyes dead ahead, fixed on the shadows too.

'What are you doing down here, Vanko?' she whispered. 'What in the hells of the warp did you write on the walls?'

He had the look of an addict who was trying to straighten out.

'I know, I'm sorry.'

'The eye demands?' Reda snapped, her voice a loud rasp.

'I'm sorry,' Vanko said again. 'I saw something, I did. A glimpse. I think I understand it now. The eye, it helped me see.'

'You're not making sense, Vanko. If Sicarius or any of the Adeptus Astartes hear you talking like this, there'll be nothing I can do to stop them from executing you.'

'I know, I know. I think it was the future. That's what Barthus gave me. I had to open the door, lead you here. You had to see it too.'

'See what?' she hissed, her anger boiling over. The other voices stopped.

Vanko gestured to the shadows as they began to move.

The medicus stepped into the light cast by the braziers.

'What are you doing here?' asked Cwen.

Reda had heard two voices in the catacombs – the owner

of the one she recognised was standing in front of her, and now she knew the other one wasn't Vanko.

'Looking for him. Who are you hiding?'

Cwen looked downcast. She quietly turned and Reda followed her, Vanko just behind.

It was a man. Slumped against a dirty wall, sitting on a bed of straw. There were blankets, mostly threadbare. He looked ragged, thin, although judging by the scraps at his bare feet Cwen had been trying to keep him fed. He also wore a chain through an iron ring fixed to his ankle. He took one look at Reda and said, 'You're not from here.' His voice was reed thin and husky from the wretched air, which stank like a combination of trenchrot and groxshit.

Cwen went to him, padding softly against the cold floor. Their eyes met and she touched her palm to his cheek. She rested her forehead against his and the two of them briefly closed their eyes, sharing a moment of peace. After a few seconds, the man gave Cwen's shoulder a light squeeze and she stepped back, her fingers slow to leave his face, lingering like the last kiss of leaves on an autumnal branch, reluctant to depart.

Chains rattled as the man got to his feet, a tepid sort of fever seeming to seize him all of a sudden now that Cwen had withdrawn her presence.

'You're not from here,' he repeated, louder this time. 'You're not even from this world. This place, everything you've seen is a lie. It's all a damn lie,' he said, turning to Cwen and jabbing an angry finger at Reda. 'She knows the truth. Deep down, she knows. They both do.'

'You see now why I had to hide him away,' said Cwen, as she looked from the man back to Reda. 'This madness... He wasn't always like this.'

'Your husband, I presume. The one you said died in the war.'

'I'm sorry about that too. It's easier, safer if I say that he's dead.'

Reda scowled. 'Meanwhile, he lives in this pit.'

Cwen gave her a firm look. 'It's that or death.'

Deciding on the bold approach, Reda took a step towards the man.

'What do you mean, "the truth"?' she asked. 'What "truth"?'

'I told you he's mad,' said Cwen. 'Fanciful tales of flying ships and empires in the stars.'

Reda and Gerrant exchanged a glance.

He didn't look mad, she thought. He looked scared and even a little relieved.

She took another step until they were almost face-to-face.

'What. Truth?' she repeated, slowly and firmly. 'What do you know?'

'He doesn't know–' Cwen began but was interrupted.

'That you're from the Imperium,' he said, then gestured to Cwen, 'and so are we.'

CHAPTER EIGHTEEN

FLENSED BONE

It had taken several gruelling minutes to pull the broken blade from his body. Haephestus did not consider himself an Apothecary and he doubted Venatio would approve of his crude methods but they had proven effective. The hold, now sealed, still reeked of burnt flesh. He had opted for cauterisation over sutures. The pain had been considerable but he, like his brothers, had been made for such discomforts. It was as commonplace as breathing for one of his kind.

His other task was considerably more delicate, taking hours, and here he had exercised a surgeon's care. The upper half of the dead body he had cut in two lay on the bench, the tools swept away to make room for it. Phosphor lamps had been clamped to guide rails immediately above the remains, and lit the grim scene with brilliant light. Haephestus leaned over the corpse, determined to uncover its secrets. He found the skull had suffered a deep fracture that had partially collapsed the left temple. This, Haephestus reflected as he considered the flensed bone, still red from where he had peeled back the face, was curious.

It meant two things. Firstly that his initial attack against the native had been stronger than he had intended. Regulating impact and potential damage was difficult for an Adeptus Astartes when his intent was to subdue, not kill. So often, the calculation need not be made. In this instance, the blow that had seen the swordsman collide with the hold's interior wall had been significant. This led to the second thing. The injury that the man had sustained to his left temple would almost certainly have killed him. In the face of these facts, a startling question presented itself.

'How did you return from your mortis state?'

He had witnessed greenskins fight on long past the point where they should be dead, often absent limbs or even, in some rare cases, heads. Cybernetic organisms such as combat-servitors or Mechanicus skitarii could maintain some fighting efficacy after suffering injuries that should rightly have killed them, but this man, to every available piece of evidence, was mortal. He supposedly possessed none of the greenskins' resilience, nor the endurance of the part-man part-machine. And yet here they were.

Not only had motor function returned and a limited, albeit feral, cognition, the man had also manifested significantly increased strength. Certain adrenal conditions could explain the latter, but only to a degree. Further analysis was needed.

The scalpel blades attached to Haephestus' exposed mecha-dendrites twitched. They slid back into their sheaths as a diamond-edged saw started up. The teeth went from a gentle burring to a falsetto whine as they bit into ruddy skull bone. With a surgeon's exactness, Haephestus slowly cut a perfectly rectangular hatch in the crown of the skull, which he then removed to expose the cranial vault.

The matter inside looked ordinary enough. No sign of abnormal swelling or mechanised inputs of any kind. He further intensified the light, combining the improved illumination with the scrutinising magnification of his bionic eye. Only then, between the irregular folds of the cerebral cortex, was he able to see what he could only describe as minuscule boreholes that appeared to tunnel down into the thalamus, hypothalamus, hippocampus and amygdala. Cutting through the cerebellum with a fresh scalpel blade revealed tiny bore tracts. He went deeper, severing an entire cross section of the brainpan. He was about to dissect further when something stirred in the dead meat and burrowed upwards into the light.

'Omnissiah…' he gasped.

It was insectile, metallic, its leaf-shaped carapace glazed in oily pink. And it moved. Fast. He pinned it to the bone as it scuttled across the skull, apparently seeking fresh matter to infest. The tiny carapace cracked against the scalpel, briefly revealing the minuscule workings of a machine before it dissolved in a crackling flare of light.

It wasn't alone. The emergence of one led to a swarm of the creatures, flowing like mercury from the cavities in the brain. Haephestus reached for his tools, his fingers closing around the grip of a hand flamer.

He knew what this was. What its presence meant.

He burned everything, every scrap of flesh, hair and cloth until there was nothing left but ash. He had to warn the others and be damned what the natives made of the Thunderhawk. The ones he had fought earlier had left a trail that he could track with the ship's instruments. He gambled on it leading him to Sicarius.

Sitting in the cockpit again, Haephestus murmured the rites of function, imploring the gunship's machine-spirit to ignition. A low whirr sounded through the airframe, growing to a drone as the turbofans started up. A boost of thrust let out a roar and the ship began to vibrate, eager to be aloft once more.

'Fly swift…' said Haephestus, easing the throttle and lurching into the sky.

An old enemy had returned, one they had buried years ago.

CHAPTER NINETEEN

AGAINST THE HORDE

Thunder rolled through the gorge, overlapping and magnifying, channelled by its narrow sides. It was the beat of colossal drums and six hundred bestial voices bellowing as one. The orks roared their challenge to the sky and saw it answered in streaks of incandescent lightning. The entire heavens were in ferment, the clouds churning and boiling like a turbulent ocean. The dawning sun was swallowed by it. Ghoulish faces leered in the shadowy depths of cumulus and cumulonimbus. They roared too, the echoes of their words unintelligible, but it was the belligerent speech of gods.

A moment of silence fell at the raised hand of the chieftain. He let the sky rage and listened to the bestial deities as the flashes above cast his scarred features into cold relief. It is said the ork has two faces, one for each of its gods: one bellicose and warlike, the other cunning and deadly. Here, the orks embraced the first, eyes gleaming like blood-red rubies, eager with the promise of violence.

Five warriors stood at the mouth of the gorge watching the ritual play out. It was narrow enough that they could fill the gap with their single rank. Cliffs rose up either side, impassable and too sheer to climb. The warriors had to face them here, where the violence of the horde could be funnelled into this single, deadly choke point.

No one spoke at first. Vorolanus and Vandius had described what they had found and Sicarius and the others had listened. Their objectives had converged; a twist of fate or the simple arithmetic of probability? It didn't matter. The orks were here, and so too was the power source that would get them back to the crusade. Kill the enemy, claim the prize. How often did it come to this? Except here they were outnumbered by more than a hundred to one. The Ultramarines were amongst the finest and bravest warriors in the galaxy, but even they had limits. So they simply watched and waited, swords drawn and low by their sides. The orks needed to come to them for the plan to succeed.

Sicarius decided to give them some encouragement. He raised the Tempest Blade and rapped the hilt against his chest.

'Ah ugh!'

No sense in wasting words on these animals. They respected only brawn and aggression. Let them have it, then.

'Ah ugh!'

It was a drop of noise in a roiling, cacophonous sea.

'Ah ugh!'

Louder this time. The blow against his chest resonated like a chime.

'Ah ugh!'

Daceus joined him, and then Vandius.

'Ah ugh!'

Then Vorolanus and Fennion.

The rhythm pealed faster and louder, as urgent as a heartbeat, as belligerent as a war drum. The orks at the back of the horde, the ones closest to the warriors, turned first. They snarled and pulled at their tusks. They squealed and spat porcine curses at the interlopers. They bellowed and beat their chests. One jabbed a finger, grasping at another greenskin to get its attention. It died with an axe head buried in its skull, the one it had interrupted slathered in the dead ork's blood. The sudden rush of violence drew more greenskins as if they scented it on the breeze, potent as any drug. Some foamed at the mouth, others died coughing up slugs of crackling green phlegm. A minor skirmish broke through the mob and twenty or thirty orks lay maimed or butchered by the end of it. This was but a prelude.

'Hot hands and ready swords...' murmured Daceus.

'War calls...' said Sicarius.

'We answer,' Vandius replied.

Sicarius raised his sword in mimicry of the distant chieftain who bellowed atop his rocky dais. The war chant stopped. Discordant grunting rushed to fill the silence, thickening air already fouled by ork stink. The sky vented its wrath and a bone club lifted to the heavens caught a flash of light. When it fell, the stampede began.

The orks exploded through the gorge in an unruly mob, clawing and biting at each other to be first. Several were crushed against the walls or smashed against the jutting crags of narrow canyons. The blood only seemed to invigorate them further. Sixty feet separated them from the line of Ultramarines.

Then fifty.

Then forty.

Sicarius cast off his cloak, prompting the others to do the same.

Then thirty.

He charged. He *leapt*. Then he set about the enemy with the fury of a storm unleashed. He barrelled into one, impaling it through the chest and riding its corpse to the ground. A flash of storm-wrack adamantium and a head slipped free of its shoulders. A lunge disembowelled another, a savage kick to sweep it from his murderous path before he hacked right to split an ork's head in two and then left to cleave through shoulder to hip.

Daceus was closest on his heels, and lightning flashes lit the gloom with every blow, casting gruesome shadows. He pierced an ork through the eye, before pulling out the blade to parry a clumsy axe swipe. He hacked down, severing the wielder's wrist before Vandius stepped in to cut off the beast's leg. It squealed before Vandius stabbed down in a two-handed grip.

Vorolanus and Fennion fought together. The latter fought one-handed, his right arm a petrified metal limb curled in to his body. Fennion jabbed a gladius through an ork's neck. It was a pugilist's blow, fast, efficient and designed to inflict the maximum damage for the least effort. The beast was still clutching ineffectually at the wound and spewing blood as Vorolanus thrust a blade through its heart and ended it.

They moved quickly, the Ultramarines. It was ugly but it got the job done.

After less than two minutes they stood alone again. Twenty-three dead orks lay around them.

The first of the orks to reach the gorge mouth had been cut down like swine. It was a culling, plain and simple. A second ragged throng followed the first and met the same fate.

This time the Ultramarines stood their ground, fighting with discipline and restraint, inspired by their captain. Greenskin corpses began to amass and it was over again in short order.

Daceus wiped his red blade on one of the bodies.

'Dregs,' he said, scowling at the stench, disdainful of the orks' reckless abandon.

'Just the opening skirmish,' Sicarius replied. 'The overeager and the foolish. We've bloodied them. Now let's see what strength they really have.'

A second gap had formed between Ultramarines and greenskins as the horde was brought to heel by a band of larger, veteran orks. These beasts wore scraps of bone armour, their faces daubed with crude bloody markings. The horde started to coalesce and the chieftain joined them, descending from his rocky plinth to shove his way through the masses.

As the orks began to stomp towards them, Sicarius exchanged a look with Vorolanus.

The sergeant eyed the ridge line on both sides of the gorge.

'Not yet,' he said. 'Closer.'

Sicarius nodded.

'What now then?' asked Daceus. They were slowly retreating back to the very mouth of the gorge.

'We stand here at the mouth of the defile and let none pass.' He nodded to Vandius, who pulled out the spear that had been strapped to his back. He rammed the haft into the earth then untied the bundle bound to his belt. The Second Company's banner unfurled, its fringed edges catching on the wind and snapping. He tied it off quickly, the movements deft but reverent. Then he grasped the spear, snatching it from the ground with a rapid swipe of his arm, and held the great banner aloft.

'Guardians of the Temple!' he bellowed, vying with the

lightning and the booming voices of greenskin gods, and brought his sword up to his face in a sharp salute.

As one, the other Ultramarines matched him.

CHAPTER TWENTY

TWO FACES

'Who are you?' Reda demanded.

The man in chains who claimed he knew of the Imperium lowered his eyes.

'My name's Yabor. I'm a colonist.' He seemed to calm down now he was able to share what he knew with someone who might actually believe him.

'As I said,' Cwen whispered sadly, a furtive look at the man she said was her husband, 'madness. I had to chain him down here, keep him hidden. If the vizier ever found out...'

Reda glared at her as if she'd just stabbed at a nerve. Her own soldier's instincts were suddenly firing off a warning. 'What's the vizier got to do with any of this?'

'He advised the baron to use this place to imprison any-one ever stricken by the *malady*.'

Now Reda turned on her.

'Please,' said the man, raising his eyes, 'she didn't know. None of them know. They had no choice.'

'What's the *malady*?' she asked Cwen, who looked from Reda to her husband and back again. She seemed confused, afraid.

'There have been people, citizens that would say or do things. Insane things.'

'What things?'

'About the Emperor, the Throne,' said the man. 'The Imperium.'

Cwen snapped. 'Stop it! Stop saying these things.'

'It's true,' said Reda.

Cwen turned. 'What? You have the malady too.'

Reda seized her by the arms, forcing a grimace onto Cwen's face. She struggled initially, but Reda gripped her firmly and held her angry gaze.

'It's true,' she repeated. 'The Imperium, the Emperor, the sky ships – it's all real. There is no land called Macragge. It's a world, one of several in a galactic realm called Ultramar. We did not travel here across the wilds or over the ocean. We came in a ship, a *star*ship. We call it the void, a great dark sea of stars. I don't expect you to take this in straight away, but I think I am starting to understand. You've been manipulated, Cwen. I don't know how, or why, but ever since we've arrived something has been off about this place. You have a single city, and no knowledge of any others. You have a ruler but no social structure to speak off. You are fighting a war that none of you really remembers starting and you have no damn history. Nothing. No archive, no library. And our language,' said Reda. 'It's the same.'

'But you're from the south…' said Cwen, clinging desperately to anything that made sense, but Reda could see through the fear, through the abject confusion, that deep down she knew. 'We could speak the same tongue.'

'Except I'm not. None of us are. The language you're

speaking is called *Gothic*, and it's the universal tongue of the Imperium, an effort at linguistic hegemony.'

'I can't... I don't. This is not...' She squirmed loose, backing away until her husband held her. She fought him at first, but then settled into his gentle embrace. He murmured something into her ear, something reassuring. She wept then, but stopped fighting it.

'This was, still is, a colony,' the man who had identified himself as Yabor said to Reda. 'Not a large one. We were meant to be agri-farmers, but something changed.'

'Changed how?' asked Vanko.

Yabor frowned, his face pained. 'I don't exactly know. My memory... there are gaps. I only know that this isn't real. We aren't blacksmiths or farriers or masons. We are colonists and servants of the God-Emperor of Mankind, but something has been done to us.'

'You were afraid they'd kill him to silence him,' Reda said to Cwen.

'Reda...' Vanko's voice interrupted the interrogation. Reda turned sharply, about to snap at him when she saw the look on his face. 'You smell that? That foulness on the air?' he said.

He was right, the stench had worsened. She'd almost forgotten about it what with Yabor's bizarre confession, but now her attention had been drawn to it again she realised it had grown so much more potent. She also heard scratching, as of clawed feet treading lightly across the ground, trying not to be heard.

'It's the greenskins,' she realised. 'They must have infiltrated the city, got in somehow and hid out down here until... Oh no.'

'What is it?' asked Cwen, pulling from Yabor's arms, still reeling but coping.

'Sicarius and the others. They're gone, left for the gorge.' She looked down at the chains. 'We have to get these off.'

'We can't release him,' Cwen said.

'You still don't get it, do you? None of this is real. It's a falsehood, all of it. But what is real are those orks. They're here, medicus. In *this* catacomb. How far do these tunnels run?'

Cwen blinked but didn't reply.

'How far?' Reda demanded.

'Throughout the city, I think. Most have been closed off.'

'Most?'

'Some are still intact.'

'Then they're coming. The orks are coming. That thrice-damned stench is them. Their odour. He's dead if we don't get him loose. Now, step the hell back,' she said to Yabor, who shuffled against the wall.

'They're getting close, Arna,' Gerrant warned.

'I know, Vanko, but I'm not leaving him.'

Reda struck the chain, a solid blow with the maul that bent the lock but didn't break it. She swung again. The scratching sounds coming from deeper in the catacombs were getting louder. After three heavy hits, she broke the lock. With Reda's help, Yabor slid the length of chain through the metal loop on his ankle. 'Do you have any weapons? A lasgun?'

'You can use one?'

'I'm trained as a colonial fusilier, so yes.'

'No lasguns.' She showed him the maul. 'This is all we've got.'

Yabor gave the solitary weapon a rueful look. 'Then we need to get moving. I'll take her,' he said with a tender glance at Cwen.

'What's happening?' she asked in a quiet voice. 'I don't... None of this makes any sense...'

Yabor gently touched her face. 'The bone-swine are coming, my love. And we have to go.'

Cwen nodded and that was that.

Reda only realised she was staring, longing for the same kind of understanding between her and Vanko, when Yabor said, 'We need to move now.'

They ran, Reda leading them out as Cwen and Gerrant helped Yabor, whose stiff legs had atrophied during his incarceration.

Behind them, the orks were closing. They must have realised they had been discovered, for they threw off all caution now and an echoing chorus of squealing, grunting voices chased Reda and the others through the darkness.

Reda only slowed as she passed the cells where the other madmen were still screaming.

Yabor was breathing hard, his body not used to the physical exertion, but he looked eager to be away from the old keep.

'They're not far off,' he said. 'We can't save these men.'

'We have to try,' said Reda. 'Maybe we can–'

'They are safer behind those cell doors than we are in the open,' said Gerrant. 'You saved one, Arna. Let that be enough or we're all dead.'

The orks had reached the stairs; she could hear them bellowing and hooting to each other, their heavy feet slapping loudly against the steps.

'Throne forgive us...' Reda whispered, and ran on.

She cast a glance over her shoulder just as the orks burst into the corridor. A host of red eyes glared back. They looked hungry.

A light rain was falling and cast a grey pall across the sky as they staggered out of the old keep. It felt cool against her skin after the heat of the catacombs. Reda dragged in a lungful of air. She bellowed a warning but the streets were near deserted, no soldiers in sight.

'Where the hell is everyone?'

Shutters were closed, doors locked. They were alone and backing away across a muddy square when the first ork emerged, blinking and snorting, into the drab dawn.

It was alone for now, and at first looked lost but excited, a raider who had just made landfall and was eager for the pillaging to come. It clapped its porcine eyes on Reda, who swung her maul in readiness, and pushed out a roar.

It looked rangier than the other greenskins, its leathery flesh crosshatched with numerous scars. A stone axe hung lazily in its grip. Reda noted the edge was notched with blood, and suddenly she understood why the other greenskins had yet to appear.

Vanko came to her side, a borrowed sword in hand.

'We die together,' he said.

Pain, anguish, anger, hope, they all warred for supremacy in Reda's heart. She nodded, 'Together…' and ran at the greenskin.

It swung at her, the notched axe cutting the air overhead as Reda ducked and cracked her maul against its leg. Vanko hacked into the ork's side but the blow did nothing. The beast lashed out with a claw, ripping Vanko's old armour to shreds. Four red lines blossomed against his ragged shirt. He staggered and almost fell.

Taking advantage of the brief distraction, Reda hit the ork as hard as she could across the back. She felt something yield to her blow and crack. The ork squealed, turning savagely, saliva flying and a curse spitting from its mouth. Reda didn't see the kick. It was fast and caught her so unawares that she sprawled back across the mud, tumbling like a drunken clown, the maul flying from her grasp.

She saw light, sparks of magnesium flashing at the corners of her eyes, and tasted blood. Someone had set fire to her ribs. Either that or everything was burning. Lurching onto her front, she regarded the blurred silhouette of the hulking figure lumbering towards her. It took its time, still sniffing and lapping at the air like an animal. It *was* an animal, acting on instinct, on its desire to kill and eat. She tried to look past it, to see Vanko. To let that be the last thing she saw, but he was gone, lost to the darkness crowding at the edge of her sight, so she closed her eyes and tried to picture him instead.

The other orks had emerged from the low keep, spilling out in the daylight, eager for killing. She could hear them even over the heavy breathing of the one that was going to murder her, a cacophony of bestial grunting. And she could smell them, the sourness of stale sweat, the overpowering reek of dung.

Strong fingers grabbed a clump of her hair, so roughly they cut her scalp, and yanked hard. She thought of Vanko, gladdened by what they shared however brief it turned out to be.

I'm sorry, my love.

Its hot breath dampened her cheek, so foul it made her eyes water. Reda gave a shout, a last scream of the promised vengeance she hoped would come in her wake, the final act of her defiance.

'We are Macragge!'

Heart thumping, lungs heaving, skin tingling, bracing for the last pain she would ever feel. So afraid, so very, very afraid, at the thought of that thing tearing into her, that Vanko would see her spilled out red and ragged into the dirt.

The fingers tightened, then their grip eased and something splashed against her face and hair. The hand fell loose, it actually just *fell*, limpid and dead. Reda opened her eyes and saw the ork's hand shorn clear of its wrist, twitching in its final nerve spasms like a dead spider. Its owner twitched too, the spear lodged in its heart making it difficult for it to do much of anything else.

A shove and the beast toppled backwards, the stump of its missing hand still fountaining crimson, its blank eyes rolling back in its head.

'Get behind me.' Pillium's gruff voice possessed an irresistible command that Reda had no choice but to heed. Groaning with the pain, fear slowly bleeding away to reveal the well of hope she had kept deep at the base of her emotions, hope becoming relief and then fear again as she saw the horde they faced alone, Reda crawled backwards. Her hand found Vanko's and she held it, so tight she thought she would stop the flow of blood.

Cwen and Yabor had gone, fled into the night.

Good for them. Someone should live through this.

There was nothing left to do but watch. And pray.

He stood before them, spear held across his body, a bloody sword in his other hand. Only his legs were armoured, the rest of his body half-covered by a layer of dark mesh and wrapped in bloodstained bandages. He placed a boot on the neck of the ork he had just gutted, his spear still slick with its vital fluids. It writhed, dying.

'This is your fate,' he told them.

CHAPTER TWENTY-ONE

REMOVE THE HEAD

The orks were coming. Their footfalls thumped loudly against the earth, shaking smaller rocks loose from either side of the gorge. From a lope, their momentum gathered and then they were running, hurtling towards the Ultramarines.

Daceus cried out. 'Sicarius!'

He called again and again, and the others joined him with only the captain staying silent.

'Sicarius!'

'Sicarius!'

The greenskins clamoured for the defile, shoving and pushing each other to be first to reach the enemy. As they came to within twenty feet, boiling into the narrow neck of the gorge like a tidal swell of heat and green flesh, Vorolanus and Vandius stepped back. They unclipped grenades from their belts, Vandius having planted the banner anew, and hurled them into the high reaches of the gorge.

A chain of explosions ripped into the shadows, throwing

off light and fire. The orks stumbled and slowed almost to a halt, suddenly afraid, cowering at the voice of destruction that was louder than their gods. Then there came a crack, a deep sundering of the earth, as huge chunks of stone and clods of earth rained down on them.

The orks panicked. Some ran for the mouth of the gorge, slamming other greenskins bloodily into the rock face, and died to Ultramarian swords. Those that tried to scurry backwards became entangled with the ones behind them and got no further. The larger orks roared at the avalanche, defying its fury, but were crushed all the same. It was deafening, and huge plumes of dust rose skywards, obscuring the horde behind a cascade of rock and mud.

A handful of orks emerged from the pall of dust choking and near-blind, some missing limbs or terribly maimed. Daceus and Vorolanus despatched them as they staggered within reach of their blades. Hundreds had been killed or incapacitated by the rockfall but many had survived, caked in filth and badly bleeding. The chieftain stood amongst them, on the other side of a hillock of rocks and greenskin corpses.

'Take the high ground!' shouted Sicarius and led the others up the side of the mound.

They reached the summit just as the orks had begun to scramble up the foot of the hillock on the other side.

'Hold this vantage for as long as we can,' said Sicarius as the others joined him.

The orks hit them in a dense slab of hard muscle and aggression. Daceus kicked an ork back down the mound, taking several other greenskins barrelling in its wake. He felt an impact across his arm and shoulder as he parried a heavy blow, throwing out a punch with his free hand to distract another ork before slitting its throat. He hacked into the meaty shoulder of a third, taking a stab to his side with a stone knife before he wrenched out his blade and slammed it down onto the ork's skull. Bone snapped, cracking like an eggshell with red gory yoke. Shoving the beast aside with his shoulder, he met two more and was almost pitched off his feet. He held his ground, barely. One of the greenskins had a hand around his face, claws trying to dig furrows in his cheek, his forearm lodged in its champing mouth. The second ork died to the gladius lodged in its gut. As Daceus fended off the first greenskin, he began to saw his blade free from the other. It was like cutting boiled leather, thick, messy and noisome. The gladius came free in a welter of blood and bone slivers. Daceus sheathed it in the right ear of the ork trying to chew off his arm and tear up his face. The claws dragged free as it died, and he stifled a cry of pain as a deep cut opened up his left cheek. Blood soiled his face. He tasted it in his mouth like old copper pipes. An elbow strike dazed another greenskin, its head snapping back before Daceus thrust his blade through its neck and kicked off the body to see it tumble back.

It was frenzied, his movements swift and economic as he drew on every ounce of his training and experience. He cut and slashed and cleaved until his armour had more red than blue. Dozens of minor chips, dents and gouges marred it further, but as of yet none had penetrated. After almost twenty-three minutes, he was tiring. To fight constantly without respite, no mortal could achieve such a feat. Against an enemy as physically intimidating as feral greenskins, it went beyond taxing. Daceus felt his muscles burn, his every sinew straining, his secondary heart pumping like an engine, fuelling every blow.

He estimated he had overcome nearly twenty greenskins, almost one every minute, and dealing not merely wounds but actual deathblows. The stink of it, the death and the blood, the sweat of bodies and excrement. It made him want to vomit.

The banner was torn, ripped by an axe or an ork claw; Daceus hadn't seen it happen, so he didn't know. Vandius still held the spear haft, letting the greenskins come to him, letting them enter a savage rending arc. He cut fingers, hacked off hands and feet. A few he killed but he could not commit fully with the banner and so he wounded instead.

Vorolanus and Fennion stood to one side of the banner, shoulders almost together, and striking out with twinned blades. Fennion sliced off an ork's ear, Vorolanus gutted it. He opened up a torso, Fennion speared it through its open mouth. They worked methodically, and as a unit.

All of this Daceus perceived in a heartbeat.

If the others were dogged and unyielding, Sicarius was a brutal artisan. His sword leapt across the ork ranks, whip cracks of lightning following its arcing, deadly path. He cut through bone armour and flesh, he severed the hafts of spears and crude shields as if they were parchment. He killed with every stroke, a ruthless, deadly force. Some warriors might have allowed the battle lust to overtake them but not Sicarius. He jabbed and turned, he thrust and decapitated with cold lethality. If he had to step out to administer a kill, he stepped back in, always maintaining coherency, always holding the line. He led by example, an almost peerless standard of military discipline and strategic invention, and his men loved him for it. They would gladly lay down their lives for Cato Sicarius, who showed no weakness, only resolve and a fierce determination to win.

To fight like this, with armour as heavy as lead and only bare blades, it took a toll.

Together, they could hold the defile. As a chain with all of its links connected, they were inviolable. Until the moment that they were not.

The mound of sundered earth and broken bodies made for poor footing. Orks slipped constantly on their dead or snagged ankles to jutting pieces of rock. They often died for it. When Vorolanus slipped, he almost pitched forwards, staggering into the savage bodies of his enemies. An axe blow cleaved into the place between his neck and his shoulder guard. It drew a thick arc of blood in the air as the blade was withdrawn, which is how Daceus knew it had gone deep. A spear thrust bit into his forearm and Vorolanus dropped his sword. He fought with his fists, but a tattooed beast of a greenskin was about to smash open his skull with a massive stone hammer when Fennion stepped in. He barged into the beast, leading with his useless shoulder, using it as a battering ram. It teetered, suddenly unbalanced by the ferocity of the attack and fell back, Fennion going with it.

He was quickly on his feet, lashing out with his gladius to open up an ork's neck. He stabbed another through the chest, just as Vorolanus was stooping to retrieve his own blade. But Fennion had stepped out of the aegis of his fellow battle-brothers and was briefly surrounded.

Daceus called to Sicarius, and the captain turned mid-deathblow and saw the danger. As Sicarius cut his way to Fennion, Daceus stepped into the breach he had left but still saw what happened next.

Fennion had been turning to face his next assailant when the spear impaled him. It ran right through his lower back and out of his upper chest, spitting him like a boar. He writhed in agony, coughing up blood before crying out. His gauntleted fingers just about clung on to his sword.

Vorolanus cried out too, hacking down four orks before he could get to the spear-wielder. 'Iulus!'

He cut this one apart as well, but by then a stone axe was embedded in Fennion's stomach and blood leaked from half a dozen stab wounds. Vorolanus wrapped an arm around his stricken brother and hauled him backwards, Fennion's legs kicking weakly as they dragged through the dirt.

Seeing weakness, the orks scrambled to make the kill but Sicarius was already amongst them. They recoiled from his lightning blade, too afraid to face him.

'Lions!' he roared, cutting a red swathe through the orks. 'With me!'

He drove like a lance into the greenskins, no longer on the defensive but taking the fight to them. Daceus went with him. So did Vandius, who had planted the banner and drawn a second blade in his off-hand.

Unprepared for the sudden attack, the orks were cowed at first but then rallied, emboldened by violence. Their numbers had been severely culled but Daceus counted at least thirty or so left and these were amongst the largest, the ones with bone armour and painted in tattoos. They had metal weapons too, crudely wrought from pieces of salvage. Daceus turned a rough cleaver aside, the pig-iron rasping sparks as the blades collided. The blow jolted his shoulder, but he got the better of the exchange as he forced the ork's arm wide and stabbed up into its gullet. The gladius punched through the crown of the ork's skull but it kept on fighting. Daceus left the red-rimed weapon embedded, drawing a shorter combat blade from the back of his belt as the ork flailed at him. He went under its reach, getting in close and stabbing it repeatedly in the torso. As it collapsed like a felled tree, Daceus took a firm grip of his sword and let the ork's momentum tear it loose.

He no longer had sight of Sicarius, the captain lost to the gloom and surrounded by orks, who sought to bring him down through sheer weight of numbers.

Vandius was just ahead of Daceus. His arms were like pistons, his speed of motion belying the fact of his cumbersome war-plate. He cut down two orks with two quick diagonal slashes of his sword, opening up a path to the chieftain. Vandius charged at him.

The beast met him with pure aggression, bulling through the ranks of the other greenskins like a train. It laughed as Vandius lashed out, catching the sword in its open hand. Dark blood ran vigorously down the blade, the contempt in the beast's eyes reflected in the red mirror sheen.

The bone club struck Vandius across the chest and hurled him back. He staggered, a deep crack down his plastron, the gladius wrenched from his grip and thrown aside, but he came at the ork again. The beast roared, revelling in the fight, but stopped laughing when Vandius' flung combat blade protruded from its neck. It gurgled, only just catching up to what had happened.

Vandius was still moving, but was now unarmed. He'd beat the chieftain to death if he had to.

'Vandius!' It was Vorolanus, stained with Fennion's blood, returning to the battle. He drew a sword from his back and tossed it to the banner bearer, who caught the hilt in one hand. Using a dead ork to get a foot up, Vandius leapt at the chieftain wielding Praxor Manorian's old sword...

The beast raised an arm to defend himself, still choking on the knife sticking out of his neck. The sword cleaved through the arm, severing it just below the elbow. The blade scraped against the chieftain's armour, tearing through but snagging in the ork's thick hide. Blood gushing from his arm stump, the chieftain lunged with the bone club. It punched through the crack in Vandius' breastplate and came out through his back.

The banner bearer hung in mid-air, legs dangling limply and clawing at the bone club impaling him. The beast gave a hefty swing to shake Vandius loose and he hit the side of the gorge hard. He tried to rise, his teeth pinked with blood. Praxor's old blade clattered to the ground, chiming like a funeral bell. He got up on one elbow, and struggled to reach for it.

Daceus was pinned, three against one, and could barely fend his opponents off. He saw Vorolanus in his peripheral vision, a gladius in his hand. He could find no sign of Sicarius and feared he might have been overwhelmed in the press of bodies.

Chuckling, seemingly ignorant or uncaring of his grievous injuries, the chieftain sidled up to Vandius' crumpled form and pushed the bone club up under his chin. He wanted to look into the warrior's eyes before he killed him. In a perverse way, the ork was showing him respect.

The chieftain snorted, deciding Vandius was not so impressive, and let his chin drop so he could raise the club for a killing blow. The weapon didn't get higher than his shoulder. It stopped abruptly, the chieftain momentarily dumbstruck as the tip of a crackling sword poked out of his chest. He looked at it as if it were an apparition, a figment of his crude imagination. The blade thrust out further and then moved rapidly with the cutting inexorability of a disruption field, carving open the chieftain from hip to shoulder. The beast turned, stumbling on its swollen legs, and stared in impotent fury at Sicarius as its two halves parted, venting a slew of gory innards onto the ground.

It was over. The last of the orks fled or were killed by the Adeptus Astartes as they ran. Above, the storm broke, and the first wan shafts of the sun pierced through.

After he was finished chasing down greenskins, Daceus returned to stand before the captain, and met his gaze.

'Remove the head...' he rasped, reprising something Sicarius had said years ago.

Sicarius arched his brow then gestured to Vorolanus. 'See to Vandius.'

Incredibly, the chieftain still lived. He was holding his guts with one arm and breathing rapidly as Daceus and Sicarius stood over him. A deep, ugly sound issued from his throat, shaking the beast's body.

'Is it... laughing at us?'

An uneasy feeling entered Daceus' gut as he followed the line of the ork's feverish gaze. A large piece of ork graffiti had survived the rockslide. It took up a large part of the gorge wall, daubed in blood and foul greenskin spore. It depicted the two-headed ork god.

'Two faces,' said Sicarius. He looked down at the chieftain again, at the half-helm he wore, the jaw piece missing. 'One bellicose and warlike...'

Daceus turned to his captain, as a stark realisation came to light. 'The other cunning and deadly.'

Sicarius sheathed his sword. 'Damn it. There are two of them.'

'Where to, then?'

'Where else? Back to Farrodum. They lured us here and the rest waited for us to be gone.' He looked at the power source, jutting from the floor of the gorge, too heavy for them to carry, but not for a gunship. 'We need Haephestus.'

'So, do we go back? To the city, I mean?' Daceus pointed

at the power source. 'That's it, isn't it? That's what we need to restore the ship.'

'That's what we need,' Sicarius replied.

'What is it? A generator? Capacitor? Can we even use it?'

'All good questions, Retius, that we shall need our Tech-marine to answer. This is what Haephestus discovered on the augurs, I am sure of it.'

'So we can't leave it.'

'We can't. But we must,' said Sicarius. He called out to Vorolanus, 'Scipio…'

'Vandius lives, but barely,' he called back. 'Fennion too.'

'Can you walk, Iulus?' asked Sicarius, as the other sergeant shambled into view and sat down heavily next to where Voro-lanus had slumped Vandius against the gorge wall.

'I'll only slow you down. I can scarcely stand. I'll stay with Vandius,' he said. 'Someone should watch him.'

Sicarius nodded, hiding his dismay at the condition of his warriors, but Daceus knew him well enough to guess what he was feeling.

'I won't abandon the mortals. We three must go,' he decided.

'Back to Farrodum? That's half a day's march at least. Even for us.'

'Then we have to make all haste, Daceus.'

'Or perhaps not…' Scipio was pointing to the horizon, where a black angular shape flew towards them.

Daceus narrowed his eye. 'Is that…?'

As the shape grew closer, it was possible to make out swooping wings, prow and a battered fuselage.

'Glory to Guilliman,' uttered Sicarius.

Haephestus had found them.

CHAPTER TWENTY-TWO

THIS IS YOUR FATE

The orks had gathered in a mob outside the old keep. Their fear of the off-worlder made them hunker together, despite the fact they outnumbered him more than twenty to one. Silence had fallen, barring the quiet drumming of rain. It gathered in pools and slowly turned the mud into a quagmire. Pillium's body and close-shaven scalp glistened, his many scars even more pronounced. He took in the high walls on three sides, the old keep in front of him. He had been here before. Perhaps he had never really left. The arena beckoned again.

The eyes of the mob regarded him, measuring, deciding, but Pillium ignored them. He wasn't here to entertain. He was here to prove his worthiness. He hefted the spear – an uncommon weapon for a Space Marine, but he liked the feel and the balance of it.

'This is your fate,' he repeated, crushing the ork's neck beneath his boot and ceasing its writhing.

A greenskin muscled to the front of the mob, the lower

jawbone of some primordial beast strapped to its jutting chin. The tips of its canines reached up to be almost level with the ork's narrow eyes. And then the strangest thing happened. The beast smiled. It grunted twice in its crude language and the mob divided into two flanks, with Jawbone charging up the middle. They were trying to outflank him.

Despite the protests of his wounded body, Pillium moved quickly. He went left, refusing to be caught in the crude pincer movement. He stabbed the first ork through the neck, a punch-dagger blow with the sword. In, out. A slash carved up the face of another, a spear thrust disembowelled a third and then Pillium was moving again, surging through the throng of greenskins, trusting to shock and awe to get them off balance. He struck with all the intensity and suddenness of an artillery barrage and was only scarcely less devastating.

He parried a loose blow against the haft of his spear, turning defence to attack as he spun the polearm around, forcing the orks back before spearing the one who had tried to strike him. One thrust. The leaf-bladed spear severed the spine and came back out again with a gut-grinding twist. A short back step saw another axe slash wild, Pillium hacking off the unfortunate greenskin's head while it was overbalanced.

He revelled in it, the cold calculus of battle, the split-second measuring of effort and strength and speed. His accountancy of war was effortless, pure. But twenty against one was never a balanced fight, and the equation was bound to run foul at some point.

The first cut raked his arm, deep enough that Pillium felt it. His sword wavered, just a fraction, but it was enough to let in the second blow. This one bit his torso, the gash leaking all the way down to his fingers. He lost the sword, the grip sliding from his wet hand.

Three, four, five more cuts. None fatal, all debilitating in their own cumulative way. Pillium felt his reactions slowing, he felt the dulling of senses that comes from blood loss and pain and old injuries reopened. He barged a pair of green-skins, bracing them against the spear haft, ramming it up under their brutish chins and pushing hard. They reeled, the orks, scampering against his strength, and sprawled onto their backs. Pillium could not capitalise. He had to turn to fend off a jab aimed at his neck. It skidded against his hasty defence, ripping up his other shoulder instead.

He killed his attacker, a swift punch to its throat, hard enough to crush the larynx. It was still choking to death when he brought the spear up into the guts of another ork, pushing the weapon deep enough that he could drive the greenskin into its kin. They hacked at it, hacked it apart, the improvised meat shield reduced to flesh scraps and bones dangling on strips of sinew.

Pillium wrenched out his spear but wasn't fast enough. More cuts, every one edging him closer to death. His body was a shredded mess, his face not much better. One eye was half closed from a bludgeon's gnarled head. Sparks flashed in his vision.

There were six orks left.

He cast the spear, a throw so hard and savage he felt his shoulder pinch with the effort. Two orks were impaled, trans-fixed to a wooden post holding up a slatted stable roof. He stopped the swipe of a club, grasped the attacker's wrist and broke its arm across his knee. It was still squealing when he sent a brutal blow into another ork's midriff. Bones shattered. It collapsed. He broke the squealing ork's neck to shut it up. This indulgence cost him. Two spears struck him in the back. A crude sword stabbed his torso. Red poured down over everything, thinning with the rain, pooling at his feet in a bloody tract of churned mud. He wrenched out one spear, took another stab for his trouble and broke the second spear off at the haft. The flint tip was still embedded.

Two remained.

He crushed the skull of one with his bare hands, like breaking an eggshell between slowly clenching fingers. That left the leader.

Jawbone had the sword, whereas Pillium remained unarmed. He could scarcely see, clawed fingers of darkness pulling at his vision. But it was scared. He could smell its fear sweat and feel its trepidation. Despite the cleansing rain, the mudhole stank of offal and death.

One eye left, the other closed over, Pillium spat out a gobbet of blood and flesh.

'They're all dead,' he told the last greenskin.

Jawbone hesitated, confidence sluicing away like the blood and filth underfoot. It stumbled back but got no further as an arrow pinned its foot to the ground and it let out a porcine squeal of agony.

A crowd had gathered, archers and a ragged group of footsoldiers standing on the rampart overlooking the muddy square. Pillium had no idea how long they had been watching. His sense of time and place was fraying. Water trickled down their faces as they looked on coldly. No cheers or cajoling, just impassive stares beneath the brims of iron helmets. The bowman who had shot the ork held his weapon steady, rain droplets running down the catgut string, a quarrel notched ready to loose.

'Kill it, then…' said the baron, Athelnar. He lurked amongst his soldiers, the rain drumming against the thick hood of his cloak. 'End it, sir knight.' His black-armoured henchman stood beside him, paler than Pillium remembered, fresh wounds visible on his hard face.

It was the way he said it. Athelnar's contempt had become something else, something more dangerous. Fear. The air reeked of it. Pillium blinked out the rain from his good eye, shaking his head and hoping some sense would return. His world clarified just long enough to see Jawbone tear the arrow loose and fly at him. Pillium turned the blade aimed for his gut aside, seizing the ork's wrist and pulling it around and in front of him at just the perfect moment. Arrows turned its back into a pincushion, feathered hafts sprouting like ears of corn. They had been meant for him.

He was an Astartes, an Ultramarine Primaris. He was also unarmed, without his armour and losing too much blood. At least ten archers could draw a bead on him, and the foot-soldiers carried spears. Able-bodied, he could have leapt the rampart and killed these men with his bare hands. It would have been over in seconds. But he was dying and bled from over a hundred cuts.

'Let them go,' he breathed, surprised at the weariness in his voice.

The two armsmen had huddled together, she cradling him in her arms. He was bleeding over her but very much alive.

Pillium lowered the greenskin corpse.

'Let them go,' he said again, and saw Vedaeh in the crowd. The chronicler looked ill, her face gaunt and waxy, and he realised it was anguish. Grief. For him.

Athelnar hesitated. He saw the henchman say something, a muttered request through clenched and angry teeth. The baron gave the deftest of nods. The archers lowered their bows, though their arrows remained nocked.

Pillium waited. He felt a soft hand grasp two of his fingers, like a child to an adult, and saw Reda. She had tears in her eyes, either that or it was the rain, but she mouthed her thanks with the slightest parting of her lips. He met her gaze and her hand fell away, as she and Gerrant hobbled out of the square and beyond the wall.

His eyes followed them until they were gone. He spared one last glance for Vedaeh before fixing his gaze on the baron.

'For Ultramar,' said Pillium. 'For Guilliman.'

The arrows were loosed.

CHAPTER TWENTY-THREE

THE NARROW SPIRE

Sicarius stood in the Thunderhawk's cockpit alongside Haephestus. He had just joined him from the hold, having left Vandius and Fennion with the others.

'They are in need of an Apothecary,' he said, sitting down in the gunner's seat.

'I regret that I was not alongside you at the gorge, captain.'

Sicarius had told Haephestus everything that had happened since they had parted ways a few days ago, of Farrodum, the orks and the battle at the gorge, the grim evidence of which lay bleeding all over the floor of the near-empty hold.

'You were missed, Brother-Techmarine.'

He stared out of the cracked glacis at the patches of wild land peeking through gaps in the fog. As his eyes went to the horizon, he saw the narrow spire growing closer.

'We are not headed for Farrodum?'

'We cannot, captain. Not yet.'

'Those people are very likely at the mercy of the orks, Haephestus.'

'If you order me to change course, I will obey, but ever since we crash-landed I have been attempting to track the source of the dampening field.'

'Is this what prompted you to leave the wilds?' Sicarius had seen the scorched parts of the hold where the Techmarine had immolated something. He also saw the bloodstains and the dents in the inner fuselage.

'They found me,' he said. 'I suspect they followed your trail back to the ship, and here I was.'

Sicarius cursed under his breath, angry with himself that he had not considered the natives might try to backtrack his route.

'I had to kill one of them. My life was in mortal danger. But I found something.'

'Athelnar,' said Sicarius ruefully.

'Captain?'

'The baron of Farrodum. He has betrayed us.'

'Fear is a pernicious motivator.'

The gunship rattled, its engine shuddering for a few seconds until Haephestus had managed to correct the fault. 'Fuel is low,' he explained, 'and engine functionality is suboptimal but it will keep us aloft.'

'It's miraculous that you got the ship airborne at all.'

'It was in a debilitated state,' Haephestus conceded.

'And what did you find?' asked Sicarius, resuming the earlier conversation as the spire grew ever closer.

'The one I killed did not stay deceased.'

'He survived somehow?'

'No, he was certainly dead.'

'How is that possible?'

'I asked myself the same question. I cut open his body to examine it. Please do not ever mention this to Venatio, for the autopsy was crude but yielded information.'

'On my honour, Haephestus. What did you find?'

'An organism of sorts, a construct to be more precise. Several in fact, burrowed deep inside the subject's brain. Behavioural manipulation. It had familiar hallmarks in terms of function and design. Something is deeply wrong here.'

'I find myself in agreement, Haephestus.'

'And to answer your initial question,' the Techmarine went on, 'no, discovering the origin point of the dampening field was not why I left the wild.'

Through the glacis, the spire came close enough that details were possible to discern. Sicarius even recognised elements of the iconography. It was ancient. Alien.

'You have only just traced it to a source,' he guessed.

'Indeed, captain.'

'This is it,' he said, and meant the spire. It was narrow like an antenna. 'It's necron...' He remembered the apparition he had seen when he had been aboard the *Emperor's Will* and again in the wilds outside Farrodum. An old enemy. He cast his mind back to the skeletal legions emerging from under the ice. Soulless machine hordes, the necrons were older than the Imperium, and they had very nearly killed him.

'They are here on Agun, captain.'

Sicarius clenched his fist and smiled bitterly. Damnos simply would not let him go. 'You've found them?'

'Not as such. There were the constructs I discovered in the dead man. But while perfecting the beacon and attempting to overcome the dampening field, I unearthed a familiar carrier signal. Xenos. I am certain of it.'

Sicarius looked ahead to where the spire now loomed.

Lightning arcs crackled across its glossy surface, too small to be a threat or seen from far away, but evidence of function. They could not return to Farrodum. Not yet.

'What ordnance do we still have aboard this vessel, Techmarine?'

'Two Hellstrike missiles.'

'How long until we reach optimum firing range?'

Haephestus paused to check the ship's internal chrono. 'Imminently, captain.'

Sicarius eyed the crackling spire and saw the gunship reflected in its obsidian flanks. A lightning bolt spat from the surface, arcing lazily like a mass coronal ejection.

Haephestus banked hard, the engine screaming in protest, fuel gauges ticking into the red zone. The crackling energy scorched the wing tip, setting it aflame. Fire warnings blared throughout the ship.

'That was... unexpected.'

The lightning reached out again, tendrils like questing fingers coming for the gunship. A whip-crack of energy lashed in the ship's wake as Haephestus put it into a steep dive and Sicarius clung on.

'If you know how to recite the canticles of function,' the Techmarine said, teeth gritted as he fought to bring the gunship back level again, 'then now would be the ideal time.'

'Bring us back around,' snarled Sicarius, their evasive manoeuvres having thrown off the attack run.

The lightning arc whipped out again, grinding like a hot blade as it raked the ship's dorsal aspect. Haephestus went under it and to the side, strafing wide as he attempted to slingshot around for a better angle of approach. Sirens continued to wail and several alert runes lit on the ship's control console.

'I will require all of my attention to fly the ship, captain.'

Sicarius nodded, and engaged the targeting mechanism for the Hellstrikes. A reticule appeared across the glacis, crazed by the damaged armourglass but still functional. As the ship continued to bank and swerve, Sicarius carefully aligned the targeting array.

'I assume I am looking for a weak point?'

'Affirmative, captain.' Haephestus heaved at the flight-stick, every turn and sudden change of direction an immense effort. Outside, the lightning storm intensified. 'A point of minimal armour density.'

The reticule turned green as it passed over a narrow part of the spire, releasing a data-stream across the glacis that Sicarius ignored.

'I have a target,' he said.

The cockpit shook, buffeted by the lightning storm that was trying to rip them from the skies.

'I will keep the ship as steady as I can, captain.'

The reticule shifted, thrown briefly out of alignment as the ship banked to avoid an arcing green bolt.

'Bring her back, Haephestus,' said Sicarius, bellowing over the engine roar. Every one of the gunship's systems was screaming now.

The door to the cockpit slid open and Daceus stumbled through.

'What's happening?' He saw the spike of obsidian through the prow-facing armourglass. 'Guilliman's mercy, is that…?'

'Hold on, Retius…' said Sicarius.

The ship came back around again as Haephestus corrected course, wings groaning with the effort. A turbo-fan blew out, smoke, fire and aerial debris suddenly thrown against the glacis, obscuring Sicarius' view.

He fired, the first Hellstrike dropping from its cradle before its rockets kicked in and it was searing towards the spire on flaming contrails.

It impacted in seconds, the detonation audible inside the ship, which shook with explosive reverberation.

The view through the glacis cleared, but the spire was still standing. It was damaged but evidently still functional.

'You missed,' Daceus remarked.

Sicarius swore under his breath. 'You are welcome to try in my stead, brother-sergeant.'

'Turning around for a second run,' said Haephestus, ending any further debate.

The lightning chased them, seemingly determined to bring the ship down.

Haephestus flew through it.

'Hold on,' he said, banking steeply, seesawing left then right as a backwash of energy buffeted the ship.

Sicarius aimed the reticule again, fighting with the abrasive movements of the ship, his view marred by the trailing corposant of the lightning arcs. The targeting array turned green then red, flickering wildly. The margin for error was narrow.

'Bring us in closer,' said Sicarius.

Haephestus didn't answer, but the rangefinder on the glacis steadily decreased.

A flash of light coursed overhead, scything off the dorsal-mounted antenna.

'We are losing pieces of the ship,' said Daceus, clinging on to the door frame.

Sicarius ignored him. 'Closer...'

The reticule briefly alighted on the designated target zone. Sicarius fired.

'Missile away.'

It arced, a savage, fiery parabola that struck the narrow point of the spire and blasted it apart. The detonation blew right through, spitting debris out of the other side. The spire lurched and split, lightning coursing over shattering obsidian, slivers shearing off and fragmenting like shards of broken glass. Secondary explosions erupted down its long shaft, and a chain of incendiary flares saw the entire structure immolate from within.

'It's done,' said Haephestus. 'The dampening field is down.'

'Then let us hope our brothers are listening.'

Daceus let go of the door frame. He was staring out of the glacis at the still-burning spire. 'That was necron, wasn't it?'

Sicarius nodded, already on his feet, and headed back for the hold.

Haephestus had turned the ship, easing it away from the destruction and pushing the engines as much as he dared to get them clear.

'Tell me something,' said Daceus and laid a hand on Sicarius' breastplate as the rattling of the airframe slowly began to subside. 'Where are they? We saw that spire days ago. We should be swarming with those bastards by now. The undead bloody legions.'

Sicarius gave him a dark look and Daceus released him. 'None of this is as expected, Retius. Farrodum, the people, even Agun itself.'

'There is deceit here,' Daceus agreed.

'And we will root it out,' Sicarius replied, 'but we cannot leave the city undefended.' He left out the part about how Haephestus had been attacked. 'We have to go back and hope we are not too late.'

CHAPTER TWENTY-FOUR

NOT MEN

Vedaeh wept. She wanted to scream but she needed to see this, to remember it, so that if she lived then others would know what had happened. Pillium's story would live on.

He staggered, spitting blood as he wrenched arrows from his body or broke the shafts in half. He fell to one knee but through a supreme effort righted himself again to face his murderer.

The henchman had descended the ramparts, and emerged from an archway that led out onto the muddy square.

'Your kind...' he said, and Vedaeh heard the fear and the shame in his voice above the rain, and she wondered what had happened to him out in the wilds. 'Your kind are not men. I have seen your true faces. You are monsters.' A broad-bladed sword slid out of the scabbard on his back. It was a savage weapon and he had to hold it in two hands.

'They saved your city!' cried Vedaeh, unable to keep her peace any longer. 'You're right,' she said, hoping her words might stir some mote of gratitude for what the Ultramarines had done. 'They are not men. They are more than that. More than you. They saved you.'

The baron gave her a curt glance. 'Shut her up.'

Vedaeh felt rough hands grab her wrists, and dropped her cane. She struggled at first but knew it was pointless. She looked out onto the ramparts for Scarfel or any of his men, feeling sure he would at least see sense, but he was not there. Only the baron's cronies stood in audience, and a handful of shocked onlookers drawn to the spectacle but too afraid to say anything. In the crowd, a woman was weeping.

The henchman paused at the sound, his will seeming to falter.

The baron made sure it did not. 'Haukberd, do your duty.'

He looked back at his liege lord, just once, then nodded. 'You die now...' he told Pillium, and charged at him.

The first cut carved a savage line down the Ultramarine's left flank, Haukberd stepping away from his opponent's desperate lunge. A second blow slashed open Pillium's leg and put him down on one knee again. He could barely hold himself upright.

His eyes found Vedaeh's.

'Courage and honour...' he whispered, the words all too plain on his ashen lips, a moment before Haukberd ran him through.

Fighting had broken out across the far rampart, but it seemed remote as everyone's attention was fixated on the square.

Haukberd pushed the sword as deep as it would go, drawing a gasp from Pillium as the blade exited through his back. He murmured something, grinning savagely, but his face changed abruptly when the broken arrowhead tore out his throat. Dumbfounded, he let go of his sword, backing off uncertainly before falling onto his backside in the mud and then collapsing, his hands still patting ineffectually at his throat until they were still.

Pillium dropped the arrowhead in the dirt, and raised up his chin to meet his end.

Stunned silence ringed the square until the baron, his face a portrait of abject shock, screamed at his archers.

'Finish it!'

'Stop this,' declared Scarfel, a cohort of warriors in tow.

Upon seeing the castellan, the archers hesitated.

'Don't listen to him! I am your baron. Do it!'

'No,' Scarfel said softly, 'you won't.' He had brought his own archers. He had Reda and Gerrant too. Both were armed. 'It's over, Athelnar.'

The baron looked to his men, a mere handful still loyal in the face of the sudden coup. Scarfel had men coming up both of the flanking ramparts. More people were gathering at the edges of the square and had started to jeer and shout at their liege lord.

Looking left and right, then to the grey-faced corpse of his protector, slowly drowning in the mud, Athelnar ran. His warriors locked their shields to cover his escape but relented as soon as they realised how badly outnumbered they had become.

A few of the footmen made to follow, but Scarfel called them back.

'He won't get far. There's nowhere for him to go.'

Vedaeh shrugged off her aggressor, who looked shocked at her sudden strength as she pushed him back. She then retrieved her fallen cane and rushed down the steps, through the archway and into the square. She hurried to Pillium, skirts trailing in the mud, and caught up to him just as he fell onto his side. He was too heavy to hold up, so she wiped the blood and dirt from his face instead.

He lived, barely, but would not last long.

She looked back at the crowd, at Reda and Gerrant, at Scarfel, who had taken charge of the ramparts and the army.

'Where is he?' she said.

Scarfel gave her a confused look.

'The vizier, where is he?'

There was no time to answer. A roar approached on the wind, the throaty burn of engines and the dull throb of turbofans. They all heard it and looked skywards.

Vedaeh knew what it was.

The Ultramarines had returned.

They had betrayed him. He should have known. Their petty minds, their petty insignificant lives. Easily bent to whichever wind currently blows strongest.

Athelnar cursed himself for not seeing the castellan's ambition.

'I am protecting us...' he said aloud, hurrying through the secret undercroft of the city, headed for his keep and the treasure vaults. There were men who were still loyal, those he paid in coin. He would need to be quick, though. Find a wagon, good horses. He would need another protector too, for even the thought of sullying his ceremonial sword in combat sent a sick feeling rushing through his gut.

He paused in the darkness, the flaming brand held by one of the guards who had accompanied him from the square flickering patiently just ahead.

'Sire...' a second guard began, this one stationed behind him.

Athelnar waved off the guard's concern, annoyed at his own weakness.

It was all crumbling, at least it was for now.

'I will find a way back,' said Athelnar, hurrying through the catacombs now. No one had seen fit to follow. Few even knew of the tunnels under the city. He had more men waiting at the keep. His own warriors, the ones he kept around him and with full purses to ensure they stayed that way. A small army. He had already planned it out. He would flee, taking the men with him. The knights of Macragge had been exposed as monsters. They would doubtless take what they wanted and then leave. All Athelnar needed to do was wait for that to happen and then return. Scarfel would have to die, of course, but the people would fall in line. He was sure of that.

'Yes… I can have it all back,' he muttered, a smile easing its way across his face as they emerged into a larger chamber and were confronted by a mob of bone-swine.

'Defend your baron!' he said, quavering at the sight of the creatures stirring in the darkness. They blinked at the light, their eyes hungry, and sniffed at dank air suddenly pickled by sweat and fear.

The two guards came forwards uncertainly to protect their liege lord, swords drawn and shields up. Bellowing, the bone-swine lumbered at the men.

Athelnar looked away, too afraid to see death coming for him. He thought about going back, running down the corridor, but that path was closed to him now. Perhaps he could slip past, if his guards kept the bone-swine occupied for long enough. He had been about to push one of the guards into the onrushing beasts when an intensely bright flash of light briefly filled the corridor and he clenched his eyes shut. When he opened them again, the steaming husks of bone-swine flesh littered the ground, blasted apart. All dead.

'Gods...' breathed Athelnar, relieved and afraid at the same time. Then he saw who was standing before them in the catacombs, a faintly glowing staff in his right hand. His expression went from fear and wonder to confusion and annoyance. 'You!' he said, shoving the guards aside now the danger had passed. 'You wretched coward. Where have you been? It's a rebellion.'

Nehebkau met the baron's angry gaze.

'It is,' said the vizier, and raised his staff as the light around it began to build anew. 'But that is no longer your concern.'

The guards died, burned to ash in what seemed like a heart-beat. Time slowed and felt heavy for the baron, like someone had stitched metal coins into his robes. He tried to draw his sword, an unfamiliar sensation, but it was as if it weighed the same as an anvil.

'What...?'

Even his words were sluggish, stretched like soft leather, barely discernible.

The vizier held a device in his hands, an amulet that looked very much like a compass.

'I am not a vizier – not yours, at least,' said Nehebkau.

The baron's face contorted slowly with abject terror as he forced out the word, 'Sorcerer...'

'Chronomancer,' Nehebkau corrected. 'See...' He gestured to the baron's fingers as they wizened, the skin thinning and stretching and ageing impossibly in moments. 'I am a shaper of time. Let me show you whom I serve.'

Apparitions bled into the baron's mind, of skeletal legions rendered in metal, of crescent-shaped sky ships and arachnoid monstrosities, of a one-eyed vizier, deathless, indomitable, the curse of living metal and an ancient empire that meant to reconquer the stars. It was impossible but as his mind and body collapsed, wrenched across time itself, the baron knew it was all true.

He tried to scream as that cyclopean eye stared back at him, but as he opened his mouth all that emerged was dust.

CHAPTER TWENTY-FIVE

MONSTERS

The dragon descended on steel wings, its nostrils gusting with smoke and fire. It was loud, so loud that Cwen had to clasp her ears, but as afraid as she was she could not take her eyes away from the magnificent creature as it landed in the muddy square. Roofs shuddered, the ground trembled underfoot and the rain went whirling in every direction. Its claws dug furrows in the earth, as sharp as swords and just as long. A roar emanated from deep in its belly, vibrating the air and turning it hot with the furnace warmth of its breath.

Never in her born days had Cwen beheld such a spectacle. Even Yabor, who professed he came from a different age, an age of wonders and the stars within man's grasp, gazed up at the dragon with awe.

Then as the roar died away, and the air grew still and the ground ceased shaking, Cwen saw something she did not expect. A hatch opened in the dragon's flank, a battered metal scale that gleamed blue in the light, and out stepped the knights of Macragge to the fear and wonder of all who saw them.

She held Yabor's hand, grasping it tightly as myth gave way to truth and she started to believe that what he had said might be real. Some of the citizens fled, overwhelmed at the sight, fear welling up until it threatened to drown them. Cwen was amongst those who stayed, more curious than afraid as she stared through the gaps in the crowds. She had run when she was told, but had come back upon seeing Reda return to the square with the castellan and his warriors behind her.

'I have to go,' she said, provoking a curious look from her husband, who then understood and released her hand. 'I have to try to help.'

Cwen slowly edged through the crowds until she was past the closely packed bodies and confronted by the dragon. It radiated heat and its wings were rigid, not leathery or scaly or attached to clawed pinions. Bulky weapons hung beneath them, for what else could they be, as black and hard as soot-stained anvils. It was no dragon, but actually a ship, a metal ship that sailed the sky as readily as a galleon would sail the ocean. Not that she had seen either before.

Pillium was lying on the ground in the dragon's shadow, collapsed in a pool of his own blood. She hesitated as one of the knights regarded her, his face as grave as winter ice. He and another warrior had formed an honour guard, their backs to Pillium and their blades drawn. They were scarred and battle-worn but still emanated a sense of threat and power. Reda was talking with one of them. He had an eye-patch, and Cwen recognised him as the lord's seneschal, though she couldn't remember his name.

'She's asking them not to kill us,' Yabor whispered softly in her ear.

She hadn't realised he had followed her and Cwen almost jumped when she heard his voice.

'Would they?' she asked, suddenly afraid again.

'They take honour extremely seriously, and have been betrayed.'

'But they are good men. They saved us.'

'They are not men, not as we would understand them. What they must have seen and endured to reach Agun, I cannot imagine.'

'I spoke to him,' said Cwen. 'He did not seem so different.' She shrugged off Yabor's hand, recognising in him the same dread that kept everyone else at bay, and took a tentative step forwards. The knights of Macragge were not the glorious heroes they had been after saving Farrodum from the bone-swine, they had become foreign and frightening. Other.

Cwen vowed she would not succumb to such small-minded terror.

'Please,' she called out to one of the knights. 'I am the medicus.'

Cwen saw beyond the knight to where his lord knelt down in the dirt, clasping Pillium's hand in a warrior's grip. He was whispering something. It looked like a prayer or perhaps an oath of vengeance.

'He is beyond healing,' the knight told her coldly, and Cwen shrank back into the crowd and the awe and the majesty of it all dimmed. There were no dragons here, but there were monsters. Not the monsters who had come up from the ground and attacked the city, but the ones who had turned their weapons on an injured man and who had watched and done nothing as he was wounded near to death. The monsters fear created.

Cwen stopped herself. She pushed to the front of the crowd again.

'You have injured. Let me help.' She stood her ground, even when the knight began to approach.

It was then that the lord looked up and gestured for her to be allowed through. She nodded as she did so, careful not to meet their gaze for too long in case they considered that a challenge. The smell on them... Sweat and heat, but something else, a chemical odour that stung her nose. It was heady and she found herself trembling.

As Cwen approached the lord of the knights, Pillium gave her a side glance and nodded.

Standing on the outside of the exchange, Reda had the good sense to stay out of it.

'I am Sicarius,' said the lord knight, and she could tell he was measuring her, her worth, her sincerity, in a glance. 'Pillium is dying. There is nothing you can do for him,' he told her flatly, though she thought she heard suppressed anger in his voice. 'But I have others who need a physician...' He gestured to the ship's open hatch, where one of the knights sat slumped, his left arm cradled close to his chest, his eyes deep wells of pain. Rents and splits in his armour suggested savage wounds. He turned to look at Cwen, his face as stern as the granite cliff but as grey as stone too.

'I will do everything I can,' said Cwen, surprised at her tears. Perhaps they were for Pillium? He looked ahead, as if seeing some mythic afterlife – or perhaps it was simply the darkness encroaching – and he was pale as chalk. It seemed appalling in its way, that a warrior such as that, so indomitable, so beyond mortal frailty, could be killed at all.

'Do not weep for him,' Sicarius told her. 'He died with honour. None of us here can ever ask for more than that.'

He called to one of his men and she was ushered away to the ship. Her last sight was of Pillium, uttering his last words.

His hand shook until Sicarius clasped it. Pillium had been strong, but now his grip was weak and infirm. Injuries that would have killed a lesser man a hundred times over ravaged his pale body. Not even Venatio could have saved him.

'I know...' he breathed, so quietly that Sicarius had to lean in to hear him. 'I know...' he repeated, his last breaths shallow, sighing rasps. 'I thought I was being punished. But Helicos sent me with you to prove to myself... that I was worthy... of this.'

He reached out and touched the white sigil emblazoned on the captain's armour. Then his arm drooped and fell.

Sicarius bowed his head.

'Cato...' Vedaeh had just emerged through the throng of onlookers. She stood a little way back out of respect.

'Are you going to tell me he fought with honour?'

'You already know he did,' she said. 'The baron is dead. Scarfel and his men just found him and two of his guards. The guards were burned, Cato, as if by an energy weapon. But the baron... his body was little more than dust, as if it had aged centuries in seconds. And the vizier is missing.'

Sicarius looked up not at Vedaeh, but at Daceus.

Daceus kept his voice low. 'It's them.'

'You asked why we weren't swarming with necrons,' said Sicarius. 'They *can't swarm*. They are dormant.'

'The necrons are here?' Vedaeh only sounded a little surprised.

'They have always been here, Vedaeh,' Sicarius replied. 'And they need the same thing we do.'

'The power source,' said Daceus. 'Guilliman's blood... and we handed it to them when we slaughtered the greenskins.'

'Not them, *him*,' said Vedaeh. 'The vizier. Nehebkau.'

Sicarius got to his feet. He turned to Vedaeh. 'Fennion is staying. He can barely walk, let alone fight. His presence should be enough to keep you safe.'

'I'm not worried about that. We can trust Scarfel and I have Reda and Gerrant.'

'Regardless. Watch him. Watch *them*.' He nodded to the crowds, who had begun to disperse. 'Vandius is near death, and I cannot–'

She rested her hand on his arm. 'I will keep vigil over them, Cato. You have to stop him.'

Sicarius held her gaze for a few moments, then he turned and headed for the ship. He had no doubt where Neheb-kau was headed.

CHAPTER TWENTY-SIX

THIS FALSE FLESH

Nehebkau faced the mouth of the gorge.

Corpses littered the ground. A few of the orks had survived, but the vizier despatched any who stirred close by as he walked calmly through the carnage.

The device was ahead. He could detect it. It was crude but it would serve. He would make it serve. To wake them. To save them.

A wall of rubble from where one side of the gorge had collapsed impeded his path. From within his robes, he brandished a small amulet. A half-turn of the compass-like device and the rubble fragmented as the rigours of rapidly accelerated entropy transformed it into dust. Without the lych-spire to augment its power, this was about all he could accomplish. Nehebkau passed through the cloud, unblinking, not breathing. He did not even feel the abrasion of gritty particulate against his exposed skin. Like everything on Agun, his form was a simulacra, an idea of flesh. In truth, he longed for it, as so many of his kind did. Not so much that his mind had broken, like some of his less fortunate kin, but enough that wearing this false flesh was a form of torture for him. He bore it. It had been convenient in its way.

The *homo sapiens* had accepted him as a stranger from a far-off land, a native of their world. It had fit with the narrative Nehebkau had provided. Reduce any society to a more primitive state and they will more readily believe what is fed to them by a more advanced mind. First creating and then maintaining this illusion had required a combination of hyper-advanced chronomantic manipulation on a vast scale and subtle mental alteration. The natives had to *believe* their culture was a primitive one.

The orkoid had presented a problem. Native to the world, they, like the Imperial colonisers, had been reduced to a feral state but had mistaken the device for some monument to their deities. They had congregated around it to worship in great numbers, far greater than Nehebkau could overcome alone. He had no army as such, not one that would be effective against such feral brutes. Here, his plan had momentarily stalled. When reduced to their baser states, technologically speaking, the *homo sapiens* had a distinct disadvantage against the orks. As their numbers dwindled and the orks' increased, the humans became prey and spent their military strength, such as it was, in a few short months. Extinction had been imminent, and Nehebkau had been considering how he might present himself as some form of prophet to the orks when a ship had fallen from the sky and everything had changed.

At first, he had observed the newcomers, as he had done in the beginning when the colonists had first arrived. They had brought ships in abundance, so many that they darkened the sun. The air grew clogged with their fumes, and as the humans disgorged they hurried back and forth like diligent ants. Larger vessels brought structures, walls and the shells of domiciles, prefabricated and then machined together. It was noisy and ugly. Towering drilling rigs were erected, along with processors and silos. The ships departed, leaving the colonists to their fate. They had weapons, soldiers, workers. A nascent society had begun to coalesce.

Its deterioration was slow. Machines they had relied upon ceased to function, their smaller parts rusted and beyond repair. Their signalling equipment broke down, strangely dysfunctional to the point where they simply stopped using it. No help would reach them. Metals started to corrode, weapons stopped working. It was around this time that the orkoid happened upon the settlement. Skirmishes at first, fended off with enough force. But the orks came back with greater numbers. Larger battles took place. By now several years had passed, and the humans had taken to quarrying stone and forging swords. They had horses already and bred more. A societal shift had begun, brought about by a sudden and inexplicable regression of materials and crucial scientific knowledge.

The further the humans regressed, the stronger the orks became. The balance tipped.

All of this Nehebkau observed as he manipulated time itself. The world had already been a long-forgotten backwater. It was harsh and unforgiving, a wild place that would give way to the rise of his people. Except they would not rise. Could not. Something had gone wrong. Nehebkau had realised it the instant of waking. They had slept too long. Only a jolt of considerable raw power could end the aeons-sleep.

And so Nehebkau's path had led him to this moment.

None of what came before mattered now. He had reached the device, an atomic fusion core. A swarm of lesser constructs, canoptek scarabs, had already colonised it at Nehebkau's unspoken imperative, stripping back the outer casing and spinning glistening mono-filament wires that would carry the energy reserve and redistribute it to the revivification node buried half a mile beneath the surface.

A jolt of considerable raw power.

Scurrying down the flanks of the device, the scarabs reached the earth and began to burrow, dragging the wires with them like arachnids pulling on gossamer threads.

A sound rippled the air, far off but closing. They were coming. Nehebkau looked off into the distance at the fallen lych-spire and lamented its destruction. The chronomantic effects would slowly unravel. It would not matter. It was too late to prevent what came next. He had worked too hard to see it fail. His was a lesser dynasty, but he would see it rise again. The sleepers would wake.

CHAPTER TWENTY-SEVEN

THE SLEEPER WAKES

The gunship's airframe creaked ominously against the wind as it whistled through bent sheaths of ablative armour and dozens of fissures in the hull. They were running on fumes too, and a starved rattle emanated from the barren fuel tanks.

Up front, in the cockpit, Haephestus tried to keep them airborne. Sicarius sat with Daceus and Vorolanus in the forward hold, heads bowed, making their silent oaths. The ship's missiles were spent and the ammunition for the heavy bolters was long gone. No grenades remained either. Sicarius had his Tempest Blade and they each carried a gladius and combat knife. It felt woefully inadequate for what they might face below.

'Brothers...' Sicarius' voice stirred the others from their silent meditations.

Daceus and Vorolanus looked up.

'He is injured,' said Sicarius, 'and he's alone.'

'For now,' said Daceus.

'For now. Without the vizier, whatever sleeps beneath the earth cannot be woken. We kill him and it's over, but it must be done quickly. I believe in the martial supremacy of our Chapter but we will not prevail against an army.'

'And how do we kill him, captain?' asked Vorolanus. He'd had a dark expression on his face ever since the battle at the gorge and Fennion's injury. Sicarius knew that look. He felt responsible. 'The necrons have a tendency not to stay dead.'

'I think he's more vulnerable than he wants us to believe. He needs that power core but it's about more than waking the tomb.'

'He can't self-repair,' said Daceus.

Sicarius nodded. 'One blow will end it, but we'll need to get in close.'

Haephestus' voice interrupted, emanating from up front. 'Approaching the gorge,' he said, loud enough to be heard over the protesting engines. The door was open and they could see the rugged highlands through the prow's cracked armourglass.

Sicarius made his way to the cockpit, steadying himself with the overhead handrails. The gorge was as they had left it. Ork dead lay strewn all about, a few still clawing through the blood and debris, tenaciously refusing to expire. The gunship banked gently as the power eased off and they dipped.

'Take us in,' said Sicarius, staring at the rough flanks of the canyon as they flew past. Dust and grit whirled in the gunship's wake, tiny vortices spilling outwards as if clearing a path. It led all the way to the power core.

It had been altered from when they had first seen it. Parts of the casing had been stripped away as if corroded by acid, and from these points taut threads of crystalline wire had been fed into the earth. A host of diminutive beetle-like creatures scurried over the surface of the power core, repairing, rerouting and carrying the crystalline thread.

'It's already begun,' said Sicarius. 'Haephestus, get us down now.'

Through the swirling dust, a robed figure emerged. He limped, leaning on his staff, and stopped partway down the gorge with the power core in the distance behind him. A glint of light caught the edge of the staff, a spark that presaged a blaze.

Sicarius turned and yelled into the hold. 'Brace!'

Haephestus hauled on the control stick but the ship was sluggish and nearly out of fuel. The glacis filled with light, as bright and hot as magnesium. A beam sheared through the cockpit, cutting through the metal hull. It separated the prow and most of the hold, slicing off a wing and sending both into a tumbling downward spiral.

Sicarius roared, grasping the overhead rail as his feet left the deck. Wind scythed through the remnants of the ship, cutting like ice shards and filling his ears with its howling. He gave a glance to his brothers as the hold spun away from him and was lost from view. Haephestus pulled at the control stick but any agency he once possessed had disappeared with the rear section of the ship.

They struck the ground hard, the prow taking most of the impact and crumpling as it ploughed into the earth. The armourglass shattered, rupturing explosively. Haephestus disappeared, crushed by the violently capitulating nose cone as it first flattened then caved and swallowed him behind a tide of twisted metal.

Pain bludgeoned Sicarius' back as he hit the ceiling. The deck hit him like a clenched fist, smashing his body before he was yanked up again and slammed into the wall. He spun, trying to grab hold of something, trying to see. He needed an anchor. He saw light then felt shattered armourglass rip at his skin and cloak as he was thrown right out of the ship. For a few seconds he felt weightless, cool air whipping his face, and then he came down hard, his body caroming wildly like a ricochet before he slewed to a halt.

Hot agony seared every nerve and his mouth was filled with the taste of hot copper. He couldn't rest. Not yet. He hurt, which meant he was still alive. Groggy, breathing hard, Sicarius lurched to his feet. He still had his sword, and thanked Guilliman for that as he drew it from the scabbard. There was blood on his face, and the pain knifing down his left side felt like burning promethium. He staggered, sighting the vizier just ahead. The ship was wrecked and Haephestus either trapped or dead, but he couldn't do anything about that right now.

His vision clearing, he saw the hold lying in front of him and could only conclude that when the ship had been shorn in half it had spun, momentum flinging the disparate parts in opposite directions. The hold looked battered, dented but otherwise intact. The rear hatch flew out, kicked off its broken hinges. Daceus and Vorolanus stumbled out. Raggedly, they drew their swords as Nehebkau stepped before them. His bulk was imposing. Sicarius was running.

Nehebkau raised his staff.

Thunder pealed through the gorge, sound and pressure collapsing into each other, so loud and violent that Sicarius staggered. The air immediately thickened and felt heavy as a sense of extreme inertia imposed itself upon him. The drifting dust caught shafts of murky light, turning, colliding and whirling in concentric harmony, so slowly that Sicarius could perceive every grain. Sound deadened, so dense that every languid heartbeat tolled like an artillery shell.

The light around the staff faded, not the eye-searing white magnesium that had cleaved the ship in apart, but a cooling blue radiance that stilled the air. Daceus and Vorolanus laboured in its afterglow, moving only fractionally so that they appeared almost statuesque. Only their eyes gave away the lie, full of silent urging and desperation.

The stillness broke. The clamour of the gorge returned as sudden as a gunshot, but Daceus and Vorolanus were still ensnared and Sicarius realised they must have borne the brunt of whatever weapon had been used against them. He saw Nehebkau, just a few feet before him, and leapt, blade surging with the storm, sweeping out his arm for a killing stroke.

Nehebkau turned aside a moment before the blade would strike and Sicarius found his sword buried in the ground and not the vizier's skull. He pulled it loose, whipping the blade around for another blow when something flickered in his peripheral vision and he heard a solitary *click*.

Darkness engulfed him, so suddenly he lost all sense of place and time. He drifted, like a ship without a sail on strange tides. For the briefest moment he was falling. Then he blinked and the earth beneath him grew solid again, but he was surrounded by a grey mist.

'Face me!' he bellowed, but his voice was flat and echoless. He dragged furrows in the mist with his armoured fingers that slowly filled again, like resin seeping back into a mould. This was not the gorge, but a sense of familiarity stole over him nonetheless.

He smelled refineries, oil, and felt the heat of smelting metals.

Something loomed in the fog. A hulking shape imposed itself upon his grey, featureless world. An axe blade carved the mist like jelly, revealing more grey behind it and the massive figure of an ork.

Sicarius parried the axe. A second, brutal blow sent him reeling and forced him onto the back foot. The ork attacked swiftly, savagely, and gave him no chance to gather his bearings. Half-blinded by the mist, mind reeling, Sicarius fought by instinct. He lashed out, severing the ork's wrist. It squealed, before he impaled it on the Tempest Blade. Only then, as it bled onto the ground, its porcine eyes meeting his, did Sicarius truly see it.

'Zanzag...'

The ork warlord had died at Black Reach years ago. It had died by his hand. He looked up and beheld a hive city, Ghospora, ablaze, smoke curling into the air as distant figures fought across every level.

A figure ran through the fog, glimpsed in his peripheral vision and Sicarius followed it, anticipating another attack. It wasn't an enemy. It was an old comrade, Numitor. He turned to Sicarius, urging him onwards.

'With me, brother-sergeant!'

The grey bled back over Ghospora Hive but revealed a different scene in its wake, a sprawling battlefield of gunships and troops hurtling through the air on spits of flame. Assault Marines fighting the T'au Empire. This was Damocles. Before Black Reach. But the vista felt wrong, hazy, like watching through the smeared glass at the bottom of a bottle. Sicarius tried to follow, triggering his own jump pack just as he had back then, but the grey swept back in like a tide and swallowed him.

Ice rimed his fingers and his own breath ghosted from his mouth in steamy plumes. Promethium gave the air an actinic scent, and as he breathed it in Sicarius felt a chill enter his body that had nothing to do with the cold. The grey became sleet, then snow, then an ice blizzard.

Sicarius staggered through it, shielding his face until he saw two emerald eyes piercing the storm ahead. Old wounds flared anew, forcing a grimace to his lips as he faced the creature that had once nearly killed him on Damnos.

The Undying.

The necron towered over Sicarius, a metallic overlord wielding a shimmering war scythe in its cold, skeletal hands. The energy blade crackled as it vaporised the ice, the necron's rictus grin promising death as it raised the weapon...

Sicarius brought up his sword to counter but the blades never met.

The Undying had gone, taken by the mist, and in its place a raging elemental storm. Damnos again, but later, over twenty years later. The unleashed fury of the C'tan shard roiled overhead, the sliver of a star god. Sicarius felt himself reach for the vortex grenade just as he had done before, mimicking the moment, hurling the device...

The grey mist swept in again, smothering the C'tan and hurling Sicarius through a river of broken history.

Holding aloft the banner at Ghospora Hive... Fighting side by side with Numitor... The cold ice of Damnos as he lay dying... Leading his warriors on Bael, their helmets marked with red... Alone and injured on a dying world as the tyranids closed in...

On and on it went like a fractured mirror, each shard a different piece of history, each piece fragmenting again into further shards. Dozens of kaleidoscopic moments, rising and collapsing in an endless procession of disjointed memories. Some of it he didn't even recognise, and wondered if it was some genetic recollection reawakened from one of his forebears.

He felt himself slipping, as though sand was giving way beneath his feet, falling deeper and deeper. He tried to focus, to remember where and *when* he was. Agun. *The Emperor's Will*. Gaius and Elianu, Pillium, the names of the dead went on. They could not die for nothing. He tightened his grip around the Tempest Blade's haft, searching the darkness, ignoring the slivers of time, and found it. An emerald gaze that pierced the gloom, watching him from his chamber, from the lifter, through the mists of Agun. The two eyes became one blazing orb.

Nehebkau.

Sicarius lunged and as the sword pierced flesh, pierced metal, the darkness lifted.

Nehebkau was on fire, lit by the Tempest Blade's disruption field. Like old parchment put to a flame, the skin and cloth and false trappings burned to nothing and revealed what was beneath.

A cyclopean creature unfolded from the false flesh, much taller, much thinner. The obesity of the vizier had been cleverly crafted to hide something inhuman, a necron cryptek, a skeleton of living metal. He looked old, shawled in a patina of rust, his gilded finery having long since lost its lustre.

'The sleepers must wake...' he rasped in a cold, metallic voice.

'He already has,' snarled Sicarius, and rammed the Tempest Blade deep into the necron's mechanised innards. Then he pulled the sword upwards, tearing through cables and mechanisms until he had ripped it through the cryptek's shoulder.

Nehebkau fell back in a heap of sparking, fluid-spitting machine parts, not quite able to comprehend what had happened to him. He dropped his staff and the amulet, releasing Daceus and Vorolanus, who sagged gratefully to their haunches.

'I only want…' said Nehebkau, 'to save my people.'

Sicarius looked down on the necron without mercy. 'So do I,' he said, splitting Nehebkau's head in half.

Exchanging a weary look with his brothers, he nodded.

'It is done,' he said, looking up at the roar of engines and the ships descending through Agun's pale sky.

CHAPTER TWENTY-EIGHT

IN THE DEPTHS

Haephestus had found a crack that led into the earth, wide enough for him to pass through. He did not venture into the dark beneath Agun alone; he had a squad of Primaris Marines with him, who panned the shadows warily with their stab-lamps.

The tomb was here. Much smaller, at least by the accounts he had read, than the one on Damnos, but its presence had meant the Ultramarines could not yet leave the planet. They had to be sure.

It had taken almost two weeks to arrange an expedition, the rest of the time having been spent on installing the atomic core in the ship's enginarium. Mercy of the Omnissiah, it had restored the vessel to something resembling operational capacity. It also meant the Techmarine was wearing fully powered war-plate and not the lumpen and inert suit he had been forced to endure previously. It made the delve into the tomb easier. He still limped, his left knee shattered and crushed in the wreckage of the gunship. A makeshift brace served for now and allowed slow but steady perambulation, but it would require a bionic replacement. That would have to wait.

'Brother-captain...' declared one of the Primaris Marines.

Sicarius eased his way towards him, Daceus at his heel.

The Primaris Marine stepped to one side, gesturing to a large angular doorway with his bolt rifle. 'I think we have found it.'

The rest of the subterranean caverns were mainly earth and the occasional dusty, obsidian node emblazoned with an alien glyph. Way markers, Haephestus assumed.

Sicarius turned to the Techmarine. 'Confirmation?'

He read the glyph structure around the edge of the portal and looked through to the vaulted chamber beyond. It went deep, widening the lower it got. He saw cradles, or more like open caskets. Humanoid forms hung from them, limp and apparently inert.

'More light...' said Haephestus.

A bank of phosphor lamps engaged with a heavy *shunk* of a thrown lever and the vault lit up pellucidly.

The necrons were here but they were rusted and broken down by the rigours of age or some metallic contagion; it was impossible to determine. The upper cradles carried nondescript skeletal warriors, stained by corrosion, partly eaten through. Some were missing limbs, others the entire lower halves of their bodies, perhaps piled up like a lair of bones in the nadir of the vault far, far below. A scarab creature scuttled languidly out of the shadows. Many of the others had fallen from their perches and languished on their backs, legs twitching or some not moving at all like arachnids in their death throes. Daceus impaled the creature on his sword to end its aimless wanderings.

Haephestus led them farther into a chamber recently occupied.

'The cryptek's quarters,' he said, noting the dead scarabs and arcane paraphernalia. 'Touch none of it,' he warned, though the majority of Nehebkau's trappings appeared to be non-functional or discombobulated. Several severed necron skulls stood on a rack. Suffering from the same decomposition as the others, the heads were made distinctive by synthetic flesh draped across their morbid features.

'I've seen necrons try to disguise themselves in human skin before,' said Daceus, 'but nothing like this. Those were mad, depraved creatures. Whereas this…'

'Is calculated,' uttered Sicarius, 'and iterative. Nehebkau wore an effective mask.' He looked out of the chamber at the ranks of caskets spreading out below. 'How many do you think are in here, Haephestus?'

'At least a thousand. The royal court will occupy the deepest part of the tomb.'

'Find out how deep it goes. Take every servitor we have left aboard the *Emperor's Will* if you need them. Search every alcove. Every inch. I want you to be sure.'

'Of course, captain. Sure of what?'

'That they're dead. And when that's done… bury it. The Mechanicus can do what they like with it once we're back to the crusade.'

Satisfied, Sicarius left and took Daceus with him.

Haephestus regarded the tomb. He was going to need all of those servitors.

Scipio knelt in silent meditation. Praxor's old sword lay in front of him. He resolved that he would need to stop thinking of it in that way. He was armoured, and privately revelled in the strength afforded by his restored war-plate.

Another warrior came to kneel beside him, bowing his head as he mouthed his silent oaths just as Scipio did. His arm had been fixed. Scipio heard the dulcet whirring of the servos as the warrior adjusted his position, and smelled the freshly applied oil.

They had lived, and would go on. Another battlefield beckoned as it always did.

His observances complete, he opened his eyes and uttered two simple words.

'For Praxor.'

'For Praxor,' Iulus echoed him.

It had been several weeks, edging into months, and Reda knew the Ultramarines would be eager to return to the crusade. She had not yet gone back to the ship. Instead, she hiked through the wilds of Agun, a few miles from Farrodum. The city was still visible to the east, swathed in mist, as was the way on this world. It was already changing. Materials had been brought from the *Emperor's Will*, what little could be spared but enough perhaps to restart the colony as was originally intended. The people had begun to revert back to what and who they had been before. It was a frontier settlement though, surviving and not thriving. It might be decades before the Imperium ever returned, if it ever did at all.

Perhaps that would not be so terrible. Agun was a wild land, but untamed and fresh with possibility. It had dangers. The orks, though all but decimated, would likely return, and much of the landscape remained uncharted. She tried not to think about what might lie *below* the earth, but had heard the explosions sealing the tomb. The Ultramarines would not leave if they weren't sure. At least that's what she told herself.

Vanko walked ahead of her, the sun on his skin and the

harsh wind rasping around his body. He kept his cloak tight but embraced the elements, turning his face skywards as a light rain began to fall. He seemed better, if still a little distant. There were nightmares. She had them too, but Reda dared to hope the worst of that was behind them.

'Vanko,' she called to him, just as he had crested a rugged tor.

He turned back and smiled, beckoning her.

'Not so terrible,' Reda said to herself and went to join him.

Sicarius faced the sun, the last of the gunships waiting behind him. His armour had been restored. Even his cloak fluttered proudly in the wind, restitched by the Chapter artisans.

Above in the upper atmosphere, the *Emperor's Will* waited too. It had waited long enough.

'To perish unremarked, to die an ordinary death. To be forgotten,' said Vedaeh, standing by his side. They were alone on the near-empty landing field and just outside the city gates. 'They were your words.'

'I remember them,' said Sicarius.

'Your greatest fear, if one such as you can really feel fear.'

'We can feel it, just differently to you.'

'It's not my fear,' Vedaeh told him. 'It's my wish. I have lived an extraordinary life, Cato. I have fought alongside gods, after all.'

'We are not gods.'

'Try telling that to the people in that city when your flying ships came out of the sky on tongues of fire several months ago.'

'They have adapted well. The colony is restored.' He turned to her and his stern face, the one she often found so unreadable but at times possessed of surprising empathy, softened. 'You want to stay and be a part of it.'

'I do, if you will allow it.'

Sicarius looked off into the distance and then his eyes went skywards to the heavens, to the unseen void of stars that called to him.

'You are not bound to me or the *Emperor's Will*, not any more. There are many ways to serve the Imperium, Vedaeh.'

'Yes, Cato, there are.'

'And the others, the armsmen of your retinue, you wish for them to stay too?'

'They have expressed a desire to. I would be glad of their company.'

Sicarius gave a signal. It was so barely perceptible that Vedaeh almost missed it. The gunship's engines started to engage. Their growing backwash bent the stalks of long grass forwards and kicked up grit and dirt in the process.

'You have honoured me, Vedaeh,' he said, as he started to walk to the gunship's open ramp.

She wept freely now, unashamed, humbled.

'It has been the greatest part of my life serving you, my lord.'

'Serve them now. They will need it. The Imperium will come. We may yet meet again.'

'I doubt it, my lord.'

'No,' Sicarius uttered sadly. 'You're probably right.'

Vedaeh watched him go the rest of the way and climb aboard the ship. He stood upon the ramp, facing her as it took off, and did not go inside until the vessel was almost out of sight.

EPILOGUE

'Of Captain Sicarius, I will say only this – none have borne battle more nobly or with greater prowess. I will mourn my brother when I know he is lost. Until then, I will hold out hope that he may some day return to us. If any can do such a thing, it will be him. And when he does return, then think of the tales he will have to tell us.'

— Marneus Calgar, upon hearing of the disappearance of the *Emperor's Will*

The warrior hurried through the cloisters of the ship, heedless of the serfs who scurried from his path, his armoured footfalls beating a rapid staccato against the metal deck. Giving a crisp salute to the sentry, the gilded gates to his lord's chambers parted and he entered swiftly.

One of the Victrix Guard stepped into his path, brandishing an ornate sword, a finely wrought shield with the crest of Ultramar emblazoned upon it thrust in front of him. The eyes behind the retinal lenses of the guard's gold-winged helmet were unwavering.

'Let him through...' uttered a deep, gritty voice.

The Victrix Guard lowered sword and shield at once, and stepped aside.

'Captain Agemman,' said Marneus Calgar, leaning forwards on his throne, his great gauntlets clutching the arms with barely repressed strength. The Chapter Master of the Ultramarines radiated dominance and power. He was resplendent in his artificer armour and one of the greatest warriors and commanders of Ultramar. One did not intrude upon his chambers lightly.

'I assume you have urgent news,' he said.

'I do, my lord,' Agemman replied, the Regent of Ultramar and a vaunted hero in his own right. He bowed on one knee, showing the proper deference before rising and standing straight as a mast.

'It must be a matter of some import if you are here bringing it to me yourself.'

Agemman removed his helm. His hair and face were plastered with sweat and his many scars deepened in the chamber's brazier light but he was, nonetheless, ebullient.

Calgar's eyes narrowed, as his patience thinned. 'Out with it, then. What brings you here to disturb my meditations?'

Agemman smiled proudly, his chest filling with purpose and belief.

'He has returned,' he told Calgar.

Calgar's eyes widened and he shook his head in joyful disbelief. He laughed loudly and the sound carried throughout the room.

'I never met an Ultramarine harder to kill than him. Thank Guilliman. Sicarius has returned.'

ABOUT THE AUTHOR

Nick Kyme is the author of the Horus Heresy novels *Old Earth*, *Deathfire*, *Vulkan Lives* and *Sons of the Forge*, the novellas *Promethean Sun* and *Scorched Earth*, and the audio dramas *Red-Marked*, *Censure* and *Nightfane*. His novella *Feat of Iron* was a *New York Times* bestseller in the Horus Heresy collection, *The Primarchs*. Nick is well known for his popular Salamanders novels, including *Rebirth*, the Sicarius novels *Damnos* and *Knights of Macragge*, and numerous short stories. He has also written fiction set in the world of Warhammer, most notably the Warhammer Chronicles novel *The Great Betrayal* and the Age of Sigmar story 'Borne by the Storm', included in the novel *War Storm*. More recently he has scripted the Age of Sigmar audio drama *The Imprecations of Daemons*. He lives and works in Nottingham.

FIST OF THE IMPERIUM
by Andy Clark

Sent to avenge the deaths of his brothers and purge a dangerous cult, Imperial Fists Primaris Librarian Aster Lydorran finds a foe beyond imagining on Ghyre. Lydorran must use all his strength, will and psychic might to defeat his hidden enemies and avert catastrophe.